USA TODAY bestselling and RITA® Award–nominated author **Caitlin Crews** loves writing romance. She teaches her favourite romance novels in creative writing classes at places like UCLA Extension's prestigious Writers' Programme, where she finally gets to utilise the MA and PhD in English Literature she received from the University of York in England. She currently lives in the Pacific Northwest, with her very own hero and too many pets. Visit her at caitlincrews.com.

Canadian **Dani Collins** knew in high school that she wanted to write romance for a living. Twenty-five years later, after marrying her high school sweetheart, having two kids with him, working at several generic office jobs and submitting countless manuscripts, she got The Call. Her first Mills & Boon novel won the Reviewers' Choice Award for Best First in Series from *RT Book Reviews*. She now works in her own office, writing romance.

CHOSEN FOR HIS DESERT THRONE

CAITLIN CREWS

WHAT THE GREEK'S WIFE NEEDS

DANI COLLINS

MILLS & BOON

First Published in Great Britain 2020
by Mills & Boon, an imprint of HarperCollins*Publishers*
1 London Bridge Street, London, SE1 9GF

Chosen for His Desert Throne © 2020 Caitlin Crews

What the Greek's Wife Needs © 2020 Dani Collins

ISBN: 978-0-263-28226-9

MIX
Paper from
responsible sources
FSC C007454

This book is produced from independently certified FSC™ paper
to ensure responsible forest management.
For more information visit www.harpercollins.co.uk/green.

Printed and bound in Spain
by CPI, Barcelona

CHOSEN FOR HIS DESERT THRONE

CAITLIN CREWS

For Eileen, of course.

CHAPTER ONE

SHEIKH TAREK BIN ALZALAM had accomplished a remarkable amount in his first year as undisputed ruler of his small, mighty country.

He had accomplished more than he'd lost.

This was not only his opinion, he thought as he greeted the one-year anniversary of his father's death. It was fact, law, and would become legend.

He stood at the window of the royal bedchamber, gazing out on the ancient, prosperous walled capital city that was now his own. The city—and the desert beyond—that he had fought so hard for.

That he would always fight for, he asserted to himself as the newly risen desert sun bathed his naked body in its light, playing over the scars he bore from this past year of unrest. The scars he would always wear as they faded from red wounds to white badges of honor—the physical manifestation of what he was willing to do for his people.

His father's death had been sad, if not unexpected after his long illness, twelve months ago. Tarek was his eldest son and had been groomed since birth to step into power. He had grieved the loss of his father as a good son should, but he had been ready to take his rightful place at the head of the kingdom.

But his brother Rafiq had let his ambition get the best of him. Tarek hadn't seen the danger until it was too late—and it was his younger brother's bloody attempt to grab power no matter the cost that had required Tarek to begin his reign as more warrior than King. In the tradition of those who had carved this kingdom from the mighty desert centuries ago, one rebellion after another.

Or so he told himself. Because his was not the only brother in the history of this kingdom who had turned treacherous. There was something about being close to the throne yet never destined to rule that drove some men mad.

As King, he could almost understand it.

As a brother, he would never understand it—but he rarely allowed himself to think of that darkness. That betrayal.

Because nothing could come of it, save pain.

His mother had always told him that love was for the weak. Tarek would not make that mistake again. Ever. His blind love for Rafiq had nearly cost him the kingdom.

And his life.

But now his brother's misguided and petty revolution was over. Tarek's rule was both established and accepted across the land—celebrated, even—and he chose to think of the past year's turmoil as more good than bad.

Some rulers never had the opportunity to prove to their people who they were.

Tarek, by contrast, had introduced himself to his subjects. With distinction.

He had shown them his judgment and his mercy in

one, for he had not cut down his younger brother when he could have. And when he knew full well—little as he wished to know such things—that had Rafiq accomplished his dirty little coup he would have hung Tarek's body from the highest minaret in the capital city and let it rot.

Tarek could have reacted with all the passion and anguish that had howled within him, but he preferred to play a longer game. He was a king, not a child.

He had made Rafiq's trial swift and public. He'd wanted the whole of the kingdom to watch and tally up for themselves his once beloved brother's many crimes against Tarek—and more important, against them. He had not taken out his feelings of betrayal on his brother, though that, too, would have been seen as a perfectly reasonable response to the kind of treachery Rafiq had attempted.

His brother had tried to kill him, yet lived.

Rafiq had been remanded to a jail cell, not the executioners block.

"Behold my mercy," Tarek had said to him on the day of his sentencing. There in the highest court of the land, staring at his younger brother but seeing the traitor. Or trying to see nothing but the traitor his younger brother had become. *"I do not require your blood, brother. Only your penance."*

The papers had run with it. A Bright and New Day Has Dawned in the Kingdom! they'd cried, and now, standing in the cleansing, pure heat of the desert's newest sun, Tarek finally felt as if he, too, was bright straight through.

Now the dust was settled. His brother's mess had been well and truly handled, cleaned away, and countered. It was time to set down sword and war machine alike and turn his thoughts toward more domestic matters.

And while you're at it, think no more of what has been lost, he ordered himself.

He sighed a bit as he turned from the embrace of the sun. He did not need to look at all the portraits on his walls, particularly in the various salons that made up his royal apartments. Kings stretching back to medieval times, warlords and tyrants, beloved rulers and local saints alike. What all those men had in common with Tarek, aside from their blood, was that their domestic matters had dynastic implications.

If Tarek had no issue and his brother's co-conspirators rose again, and this time managed to succeed in an assassination attempt, Rafiq could call himself the rightful King of Alzalam. Many would agree.

It was time to marry.

Like it or not.

After his usual morning routine, Tarek made his way through the halls of the palace. The royal seat of Alzalam's royal family was a sixteenth-century showpiece that generations of his ancestors had tended to, lavishing more love upon the timeless elegance of the place than they ever had upon their wives or children.

"The palace is a symbol of what can be," his wise father had told him long ago. *"It is aspirational. You must never forget that at best, the King should be, too."*

Tarek was not as transported by architecture as some of his blood had been in the past but he, too, took pride in the great palace that spoke not only of Alzalam's military might, but the artistic passion of its people. Like many countries in the region, packed tight on the Arabian Peninsula, his people were a mix of desert tribesmen and canny oil profiteers. His people craved their old ways even as they embraced the new, and Tarek understood that his role was to be the bridge between the two.

His father had prepared him. And before his death, the old King had arranged a sensible marriage for his son and heir that would allow Tarek to best lead the people into a future that would have to connect desert and oil, past and present.

Tarek tried and failed to pull to his mind details of his bride-to-be as he crossed the legendary central courtyard, a soothing oasis in the middle of the palace, and headed toward his offices. Where he daily left behind the fairy-tale King and was instead the London School of Economics educated CEO of this country. He could not have said which role he valued more, but he could admit, as the courtyard performed its usual magic in him, that he was pleased he could finally set aside the other role that had claimed the bulk of his attention this last year. That of warlord and general.

Everything was finally as he wished it. There had been no unrest in the kingdom since his brother had surrendered. And with him locked away at last, the kingdom could once again enjoy its prosperity. No war, no civil unrest, no reason at all not to start concentrating on making his own heirs. The more the better.

He inclined his head as he passed members of his staff, all of whom either stood at attention or bowed low at the sight of him. But he smiled at his senior aide as he entered his office suite, because Ahmed had not only proved his loyalty to the crown repeatedly in the last year—he had made it more than clear that he supported Tarek personally, too.

"Good morning, Sire," Ahmed said, executing a low bow. "The kingdom wakes peaceful today. All is well."

"I'm happy to hear it." Tarek paused as he accepted the stack of messages his aide handed him. "Ahmed, I think the time has come."

"The time, Sire?"

Tarek nodded, the decision made. "Invite my betrothed's father to wait attendance upon me this afternoon. I'm ready to make the settlements."

"As you wish, Sire," Ahmed murmured, bowing his way out of the room.

Tarek could have sworn his typically unflappable aide looked…apprehensive. He couldn't think why.

Again, Tarek tried to recall the girl in question. He knew he had known them once—if only briefly. His father had presented him with a number of choices and he had a vague memory of a certain turn of cheek—then again, perhaps that had been one of his mistresses. His father had died not long after, Rafiq had attempted his coup, and Tarek had not allowed himself the distraction of women in a long while.

It was a measure of how calm things were that he allowed it now.

Tarek tossed the stack of messages onto the imposing desk that had taken up the better part of one side of the royal office for as long as he could remember. He crossed instead to the wall of glass before him, sweeping windows and arched doors that led out to what was known as the King's Overlook. It was an ancient balcony that allowed him to look down over his beloved fortress of a city yet again. These stones raised up from sand that his family had always protected and ever would.

He nodded, pleased.

For he would raise sons here. He would hold each one aloft, here where his father had held him, and show them what mattered. The people, the walls. The desert sun and the insistent sands. He would teach them to be good men, better rulers, excellent businessmen, and great warriors.

He would teach them, first and foremost, how to be brothers who would protect each other—not rise up against each other.

If he had to produce thirty sons himself to make certain the kingdom remained peaceful, he would do it.

"So I vow," he said then, out loud, to the watching, waiting desert. To the kingdom at his feet that he served more than he ruled, and ever would. "So it shall be."

But later that day he stared at the man who was meant to become his father-in-law before him without comprehension.

"Say that again," he suggested, sitting behind his desk as if the chair was its own throne. No doubt with an expression on his face to match his lack of comprehension. "I cannot believe I heard you correctly."

This was no servant who stood across from him. Mahmoud Al Jazeer was one of the richest men in the kingdom, from an ancient line that had once held royal aspirations. Tarek's own father had considered the man a close, personal friend.

It was very unlikely that the man had ever bent a knee to anyone, but here, today, he wrung his hands. And folded himself in half, assuming a servile position that would have been astounding—even amusing—in any other circumstances.

Had not what Mahmoud just told his King been impossible.

On every level.

"I cannot explain this turn of events, Sire," the older man said, his voice perilously close to a wail—also astonishing. "I am humiliated. My family will bear the black mark of this shame forever. But I cannot pretend it has not happened."

Tarek sat back in his chair, studying Mahmoud. And letting the insult of what the other man had confessed sit there between them, unadorned.

"What you are telling me is that you have no control over your own family," he said with a soft menace. "No ability to keep the promises you made yourself. You are proclaiming aloud that your word is worthless. Is that what you are telling your King?"

The other man looked ill. "Nabeeha has always been a headstrong girl. I must confess that I spoiled her all her life, as her mother has long been the favorite of all my wives. My sons warned me of this danger, but I did not listen. The fault is mine."

"The betrothal was agreed upon," Tarek reminded him. "Vows were made and witnessed while my father yet lived."

He remembered the signing of all those documents, here in this very room. His father, already weak, had been thrilled that his son's future was settled. Mahmoud had been delighted that he would take a place of even greater prominence in the kingdom. But it had taken Ahmed's presentation of the dossier the palace kept on the woman who was to be his Queen to refresh his recollection of the girl in question, who had not been present that day, as it was not her signature that mattered.

Perhaps that had been an oversight.

"I would have her keep those vows," Mahmoud said

hurriedly. "She was only meant to get an education. A little bit of polish, the better to acquit herself on your arm, Sire. That was the only reason I agreed to let her go overseas. It was all in service to your greater glory."

"Those are pretty words, but they are only words. Meanwhile, my betrothed is…what? At large in North America? Never to be heard from again?"

"I am humiliated by her actions," Mahmoud cried, and this time, it was definitely a wail. And well he should wail, Tarek thought. For his daughter's defection was not only an embarrassment—it would cost his family dear. "But she has asked for asylum in Canada. And worse, received it."

"This gets better and better." Tarek shook his head, and even laughed, though the sound seemed to hit the other man like a bullet. "On what grounds does the pampered daughter of an international businessman, fiancée of a king, seek asylum?"

"I cannot possibly understand the workings of the Western governments," the man hedged. "Can anyone?"

Tarek's mouth curved. It was not a smile. "You do understand that I betrothed myself to your daughter as a favor to my father. An acknowledgment of the friendship he shared with you. But you and I? We do not share this same bond. And if your daughter does not respect it…"

He shrugged. The other man quailed and shook.

"Sire, I beg of you…"

"If your daughter does not wish to marry her King, I will not force her." Tarek kept his gaze on his father's friend, and did not attempt to soften his tone. "I will find a girl with gratitude for the honor being done her, Mahmoud. Your daughter is welcome to enjoy her asylum as she sees fit."

Despite the increased wailing that occurred then, Tarek dismissed the older man before he was tempted to indulge his own sense of insult further.

"*You must take the part of the kingdom*," his father had always cautioned him. "*Your own feelings cannot matter when the country hangs in the balance.*"

He reminded himself of that as he looked at the photograph before him of the blandly smiling girl, a stranger to him, who had so disliked the notion of marrying him that she had thrown herself on the mercy of a foreign government. What was he to make of that?

Then, with a single barked command, he summoned Ahmed before him.

"Why have I not been made aware that the woman who was to become my bride has sought, and apparently received, political asylum in a foreign country?"

Ahmed did not dissemble. It was one reason Tarek trusted him. "It was a developing situation we hoped to solve, Sire. Preferably before you knew of it."

"Am I such an ineffectual monarch that I am to be kept in the dark about my own kingdom?" Tarek asked, his voice quiet.

Lethal.

"We hoped to resolve the situation," Ahmed said calmly. No wailing. No shaking. "There was no wish to deceive and, if you do not mind my saying so, you had matters of far greater importance weighing upon you this last year. What was a tantrum of a spoiled girl next to an attempted coup?"

Tarek could see the truth in that. His sense of insult faded. "And can you explain to me, as her father could not, why it is that the girl would be granted political asylum in the first place? She was allowed to leave the kingdom to pursue her studies. Supported entirely by me and my government. She would face no reprisals of any kind were she to return. How does she qualify?"

Ahmed straightened, which was not a good sign. "I believe that there are some factions in the West who feel that you have...violated certain laws."

Tarek arched a brow. "I make the laws and therefore, by definition, cannot violate them."

"Not your laws, Sire." Ahmed bowed slightly, another warning. "There are allegations of human rights abuses."

"Against me?" Tarek was genuinely surprised. "They must mean my brother, surely."

He did try not to speak his brother's name. Not thinking it was more difficult.

"No, the complaint is against you. Your government, not his attempt at one."

"I had the option for capital punishment," Tarek argued. "I chose instead to demonstrate benevolence. Was this not clear?"

"It does not concern your brother or his treatment." Ahmed met Tarek's gaze, and held it. "It is about the doctors."

He might as well have said, *the unicorns*.

Tarek blinked. "I beg your pardon?"

"The doctors, Sire. They were picked up eight months ago after an illegal border crossing in the north."

"What sort of doctors?" But even as Tarek asked, a vague memory reasserted itself. "Wait. I remember now. It is that aid organization, isn't it? Traveling doctors, moving about from one war zone to another."

"They are viewed as heroes."

Tarek sighed. "Release these heroes, then. Why is this an issue?"

"The male doctors were released once you reclaimed your throne," Ahmed said without inflection, another one of his strengths. "As were all the political prisoners, according to your orders at the time. But there was one female doctor in the group. And because she was a Western woman, and because there are no facilities for female prisoners in the capital city, she was placed in the dungeon."

Tarek found himself sitting forward. "The dungeon. *My* dungeon? Here in the palace?"

"Yes, sire." Ahmed inclined his head. "And as you are aware, I am sure, prisoners cannot be released from the palace dungeons except by your personal decree."

Tarek slowly climbed to his feet, his blood pumping through him as if he found himself in another battle. Much like the ones he had fought in his own halls on that bloody night Rafiq and his men had come. The ones he wore still on his body and always would.

"Ahmed." The lash of his voice would have felled a lesser man, but Ahmed stood tall. "Am I to understand that after the lengths I went to, to show the world that I am a merciful and just ruler of this kingdom…this whole time, there has been not merely a Western woman locked beneath my feet, but a *doctor*? A do-gooder who roams the planet, healing others as she goes?"

Ahmed nodded. "I am afraid so."

"I might as well have locked up a saint. No wonder an otherwise pointless girl, who should have considered herself lucky to be chosen as my bride, has instead thrown herself on the tender mercies of the Canadians. I am tempted to do the same."

"It was an oversight, Sire. Nothing more. There was so much upheaval. And then the trial. And then, I think, it was assumed that you were pleased to keep things as they were."

The worst part was that Tarek could blame no one but himself, much as he might have liked to. This was his kingdom. His palace, his prisoners. He might not have ordered the woman jailed, but he hadn't asked after the status of any state prisoners, had he?

He would not make that mistake again. He could feel the scars on his body, throbbing as if they were new. This was on him.

Tarek did not waste any more time talking. He set off through the palace again, grimly this time. He by-passed graceful halls of marble and delicate, filigreed details enhancing each and every archway. He crossed the main courtyard and then the smaller, more private one. This one a pageant of flowers, the next symphony of fountains.

He marched through to the oldest part of the palace, the medieval keep. And the ancient dungeons that had been built beneath it by men long dead and gone.

The guards standing at the huge main door did double takes that would have been comical had Tarek been in a lighter mood. They leaped aside, flinging open the iron doors, and Tarek strode within. He was aware that not only Ahmed, but a parade of staff scurried behind him, as if clinging to the hem of his robes that towed them all along with the force of his displeasure.

He had played in these dungeons as a child, though it had been expressly forbidden by his various tutors. But there had never been any actual prisoners here in his lifetime. The dungeons were a threat, nothing more. The bogeyman the adults in his life had trotted out to convince a headstrong child to behave.

Tarek expected to find them dark and grim, like something out of an old movie.

But it turned out there were lights. An upgrade from torches set in the thick walls, but it was still a place of grim stone and despair. His temper pounded through him as he walked ancient halls he hadn't visited since he was a child. He tried to look at this from all angles, determined to figure out a way to play this public relations disaster to his advantage.

Before he worried about that, however, he would have to tend to the prisoner herself. See her pampered, cared for, made well again. And he had no idea what he would find.

It occurred to him to wonder, for the first time, what it was his guards did in his name.

"Where is she?" he growled at the man in uniform who rushed to bow before him, clearly the head of this dungeon guard he hadn't known he possessed.

"She is in the Queen's Cell," the man replied.

The Queen's Cell. So named for the treacherous wife of an ancient king who had been too prominent to execute. The King she had betrayed had built her a cell of her very own down here in these cold, dark stones. Tarek's memory of it was the same stone walls and iron bars as any other cell, but fitted with a great many tightly barred windows, too.

So she could look out and mourn the world she would never be a part of again.

This was where he—for it was his responsibility and no matter that he hadn't known—had locked away a Western *doctor,* God help him.

But Tarek had been fighting more dangerous battles for a year. He did not waste time girding his loins. He dove in. He rounded the last corner and marched himself up to the mouth of the cell.

And then stopped dead.

Because the human misery he had been expecting… wasn't on display.

The cell was no longer bare and imposing, the way it was in Tarek's memory. There was a rug on the floor. Books on shelves that newly-lined the walls. And the bed—a cot in place of a pallet on the stone floor—was piled high with linens. Perhaps not the finest linens he'd ever beheld, but clearly there with an eye toward comfort.

And curled up on the bed—neither in chains nor in a broken heap on the floor—was a woman.

She wore a long tunic and pants, a typical outfit for a local woman, and the garments did not look ragged or torn. They were loose, but clean. Her dark hair was long and fell about her shoulders, but it too looked perfectly clean and even brushed. She was lean, but not the sort of skinny that would indicate she'd been in any way malnourished. And try as he might, Tarek could not see a single bruise or injury.

He assessed the whole of her, twice, then found her eyes.

They were dark and clever. A bit astonished, he thought, but the longer she stared back at him, the less he was tempted to imagine it was the awe he usually inspired. And the longer he gazed at her, the more he noticed more things about her than simply the welfare of her body.

Like the fact she was young. Much younger than he'd imagined, he realized. He'd expected to find an older woman who suited the image of a *doctor* in his head.

Gray-haired, lined cheeks… But this doctor not only showed no obvious signs of mistreatment, she was…

Pretty.

"You look important," the woman said, shocking Tarek by using his native tongue.

"I expected you to speak English," he replied, in the same language, though Ahmed had only said she was Western, not English speaking. She could have been French. German. Spanish.

"We can do that," she replied. And she was still lounging there on the bed, whatever book she'd been reading still open before her as if he was an annoyance, nothing more. It took Tarek a moment, once he got past the insolent tone, to realize she'd switched languages. And was American. "You don't really look like a prison guard. Too shiny."

Tarek knew that his staff had filed in behind him at the shocked sounds they all made. He lifted a finger, and there was silence.

And he watched as the woman tracked that, smirked, and then raised her gaze to his again. As if they were equals.

"Important *and* you have a magic finger," she said.

Tarek was not accustomed to insolence. From anyone—and certainly not from women, who spent the better part of any time in his presence attempting to curry his favor, by whatever means available to them.

He waited, but this woman only gazed back at him, expectantly.

As if he was here to wait upon her.

He reminded himself, grudgingly, that he was. That he had not fought a war, against his own brother, so that the world could sit back and judge him harshly.

At least not for things he had not done deliberately.

"I am Tarek bin Alzalam," he informed her, as behind him, all the men bowed their heads in appropriate deference. The woman did not. He continued, then. "I am the ruler of this kingdom."

The doctor blinked, but if that was deference, it was insufficient. And gone in a flash. "You're the Sheikh?"

"I am."

She sat up then, pushing her hair back from her face, though she did not rise fully from her bed. Nor fall to her knees before him, her mouth alive with songs of praise.

In point of fact, she smirked again. And her eyes flashed.

"I've been waiting to meet you for eight long months," she said, the slap of her voice so disrespectful it made Tarek's eyes widen.

Around him, his men made audible noises of dismay.

Once again, he quieted them. Once again, she tracked the movement of his finger and looked upon him with insolence.

"And so you have," Tarek gritted out.

There was still no sign of deference. No hint that she might wish to plead for her freedom.

"I'm Dr. Anya Turner, emergency medicine." Again, her dark eyes flashed. "I'm a doctor. I help people. While you're nothing but a tiny little man who thinks his dungeon and his armed guards make him something other than a pig."

CHAPTER TWO

ANYA HAD EXPECTED this moment to be sweet and satis-fying, if it ever came, but it went off better than she'd imagined.

And she'd done very little else *but* imagine it.

For months.

The Sheikh of Alzalam himself stood before her. The man who every guard she'd encountered had spoken of in terms of such overwrought awe and glory that they'd made it a certainty that Anya would have loathed him on sight.

Even if she wasn't incarcerated in his personal prison.

She didn't much care for arrogant men at the best of times, which this obviously was not. Between her own father and every male doctor she'd ever met—not to mention the surgeons, who could teach arrogance to kings like this one and would not need an invitation to do so—Anya was full up on condescending males. An eight-month holiday in the company of these prison guards had not helped any.

And the way the Sheikh stared back at her, as if *dumbstruck* that she wasn't even now weeping at his feet, did not exactly inspire her to change her mind about the male ego.

The stunned silence went on.

Anya found herself sitting a little straighter, a little taller, as if that would protect her if the Sheikh had finally turned up only to go medieval on her. It occurred to her that, perhaps, she should have tried to get herself out of the dungeon before shooting off her mouth.

A lesson she never seemed to learn, did she?

After all these months, she'd figured she already knew how bad things could get here. She'd decided that sharing her unbridled feelings couldn't make things *worse*. What was worse than finding herself locked away in a literal dungeon in a country she wasn't even supposed to be in—separated from her colleagues who were very possibly dead and being kept alive for reasons no one had seen fit to share with her?

But as she stared back at the tall, ferocious, and obviously powerful man on the other side of her cell door, she was terribly afraid he might have a few answers to that question she wouldn't like.

Anya held her breath, but he didn't move. He only stared her down, inviting her to do the same.

There was a wall of other men behind him, staring at her in shock and disapproval, but *he* looked like he was attempting to crawl inside her head.

Anya didn't know what was wrong with her that she wanted to let him. Just because staring at him made her feel alive again. Just because it was different.

It had been *eight months*. Some two hundred and forty days, give or take. At first she'd intended to scratch each day into the walls, because wasn't that what people did? But she'd quickly discovered that someone—quite a few someones, or so she hoped, given the number of slash marks she'd found—had beaten her to it. She'd found that depressing. So depressing that she'd covered up the marks once the guards started permitting her furniture.

She had already cycled through fear. Despair. Over and over again, in those early days, until the panic faded.

Because that was the funny thing about time. It had a flattening effect. The human body couldn't maintain adrenaline that long. Sooner or later, routine took over. And with routine, a tacit acceptance.

She'd become friendly with her guards, though never *too* friendly. She'd learned the language, because that meant she was less in the dark. They'd made her comfortable, and over time, it became more and more clear that they had no intention of hurting her. Or no immediate plans to try, anyway.

Anya would have said she didn't have much fear left. She would have meant it.

Though the longer she stared at the man before her, stern and forbidding and focused intently on her, the more it reintroduced itself to the back of her neck. Then began tracing its way down her spine.

Maybe that's not entirely fear, something inside her suggested.

But she dismissed that. Because it was crazy.

And she had no intention of losing her mind in here, no matter how tempting it was. No matter how much she thought she might like a little touch of oblivion to make the time pass.

Okay, yes, she told herself impatiently. *He is remarkably attractive for a pig.*

Though *attractive* was an understatement.

He was dressed all in white, and in a contrast to the variously colored robes all the men wore around him, his fit him more closely. And more, were edged in gold.

She probably should have known from that alone that he was the man in charge.

Sheikh. Ruler. King. Whatever they called him, he looked like the love child of the desert sun and some sort of bird of prey. A falcon, maybe, cast in bronze and inhabiting the big, brawny body of an extraordinarily fit man.

She was holding her breath again, but it was different. It was—

Stop it, Anya ordered herself.

This was no time to pay attention to something as altogether pointless as how physically fit the man was. So what if he had wide shoulders and narrow hips, all of it made of muscle. So what if he made gilt-edged robes look better than three-piece suits.

What mattered was that he'd thrown her into his dungeon and, as far she could tell, had thrown away the key, too. Anya had done a lot of dumb things in her lifetime—from allowing her father to bully her into medical school to focusing on emergency medicine because he'd told she was unsuited for it, to accepting the job that had brought her here, mostly to escape the job she'd left behind in Houston—but surely sudden-onset Stockholm syndrome would catapult her straight past dumb into unpardonably stupid.

She was sure she saw temper glitter in his dark, dark eyes. She would have sworn that same temper made that muscle in his jaw flex.

She *did not* feel an echo of those things inside. She refused to feel a thing.

"Please accept my humblest apologies," he said, and now that she wasn't gearing up to tell him what she thought of him, there was no escaping the richness of his voice. He spoke English with a British intonation, and she told herself it was adrenaline that raced through her, then. She'd forgotten what it felt like, that was all. "There has been great unrest in the kingdom. It is unfortunate that your presence here was not made known to me until now."

That was not at all what Anya had been expecting.

It felt a lot as if she'd flung herself against the walls—something she had, in fact, done repeatedly in the early days—only to find instead of the expected stone and pitiless bars, there was nothing but paper. She suddenly felt as if she was teetering on the edge of a sharp, steep cliff, arms pinwheeling as she fought to find her balance.

Something knotted up in her solar plexus.

It was a familiar knot, to her dismay. That same knot had been her constant companion and her greatest enemy over the last few years. It had grown bigger and thornier as she'd grown increasingly less capable of managing her own stress.

When here she'd been all of five minutes ago, feeling something like self-congratulatory that no matter what else was happening—or not happening, as was the case with whiling away a life behind bars—she was no longer one panic attack away from the embarrassing end of her medical career.

Thinking of her medical career made that knot swell. She rubbed at it, then wished she hadn't, because the Sheikh's dark gaze dropped to her hand. A lot like he thought she was touching herself *for* him.

Which made that prickle of sensation tracing its way down her spine seem to bloom. Into something Anya couldn't quite convince herself was fear.

"Are you apologizing for putting me in your dungeon or for *forgetting* you put me in your dungeon?" she asked, a little more forcefully than she'd intended. But she lifted her chin, straightened her shoulders, and went with it. "And regardless of which it is, do you really think eight months of imprisonment is something an apology can fix?"

He shifted slightly, barely inclining his head at the man beside him, who Anya knew was in charge of these dungeons. As the round little toad had pompously informed her of that fact, repeatedly. And she watched, astonished, as the keys were produced immediately, her cell was unlocked, and then the door flung wide.

The Sheikh inclined his head again. This time at her.

"I can only apologize again for your ordeal," he said in that low voice of his that made her far too aware of how powerful he was. Because it *hummed* in her. "I invite you to leave this prison behind and become, instead, my honored guest."

Anya didn't move. Not even a muscle. She eyed the obvious predator before her as if, should she breathe too loudly, he might attack in all that ivory and gold. "Is there a difference?"

The man before her did not shout. She could see temper and arrogance in his gaze, but he did not give in to them. Though there were men all around him, many of them scowling at her as if she was nothing short of appalling, he did not do the same.

Instead, he held her gaze, and she could not have said what it was about him that made something in her quiver. Why she felt, suddenly, as if she could tip forward off of that cliff, fall and fall and fall, and never reach the depths of his dark eyes.

Then, clearly to the astonishment and bewilderment

of the phalanx of men around him, Sheikh Tarek bin Alzalam held out his hand.

"Come," he said again, an intense urging. "You will be safe. You have my word."

And later, Anya would have no idea why that worked. Why she should take the word of a strange man whose fault it was, whether he'd known it or not, that she'd been locked away for eight long months.

Maybe it was as simple as the fact that he was beautiful. Not the way the men back home were sometimes, mousse in their hair and their T-shirt sleeves rolled *just so*. But in the same stark and overwhelming way the city outside these windows was, a gold stone fortress that was, nonetheless, impossibly beautiful. Desert sunrises and sunsets. The achingly beautiful blue sky. The songs that hung over the city sometimes, bringing her to tears.

He was harsh and stern and still, the only word that echoed inside her wasn't *pig*. It was *beautiful*.

Anya didn't have it in her to resist.

Not after nearly three seasons of cold stone and iron bars.

Before she could think better of it—or talk herself out of it—she rose. She crossed the floor of her cell as if his gaze was a tractor beam and she was unable to fight it. As if she was his to command.

Almost without meaning to, she slipped her hand into his.

Heat punched into her as his fingers closed over hers. Anya was surprised to find them hard and faintly rough, as if this man—this King—regularly performed some kind of actual labor that left calluses there.

Snips of overheard conversations between guards

echoed inside her, then. Tales of a king who had risen from his bed and held off the enemy with his own two hands and an ancient sword, like something out of a myth.

Surely not, Anya thought.

She saw a flicker of something in his dark eyes, then. That same heat that should have embarrassed her, yes, but something else, too.

Maybe it was surprise that there was this *storm* between them, as if a simple touch could change the weather.

Indoors.

You have been locked up too long, Anya snapped at herself.

He did something with his head that was not a bow of any kind, but made her think of a deep, formal bow all the same.

Then, still gripping her hand and holding it out before him—like something out of an old storybook, wholly heedless of the way sensation lashed at her like rain—the King led her out of the dungeon.

And despite herself—despite every furious story she'd told herself over the past months, every scenario she'd imagined and reimagined in her head—as they emerged from the steep stone steps into what was clearly the main part of the palace, Anya was charmed.

She told herself it was as simple as moving from darkness into light. Anyone would be dazzled, she assured herself, after so many months below ground. Especially when she'd been brought here that terrifying night they'd been captured, hustled through lines of scary men with weapons, certain that the fact she'd been separated from her colleagues meant only terrible things.

Today Anya still had no idea what she was walking into, but at least it was pretty.

More than pretty. Everything seemed to be made of marble or mosaic, inlaid with gold and precious stones or carved into glorious patterns. It was all gleaming white or the sparkling blue water of the fountains. There were splashes of color, exultant flowers, and the impossibly blue sky there above her in wide-open courtyards, like a gift.

She found herself tipping back her face to let the sun move over it, even though she knew that gave too much away. That it made her much too vulnerable.

But if he was only taking her from one cell to another, she intended to enjoy it.

Anya had learned the language, but still, she didn't understand what Tarek muttered to a specific man who strode directly behind him. The rest of the men fell away. There were more impossibly graceful halls, statues and art that made a deep, old longing inside her swell into being, and then this blade of a king led her into a room so dizzy with light that she found herself blinking as she looked around.

The light bounced off all the surfaces, gleaming so hard it almost hurt, but Anya loved it. Even when her eyes teared up, she loved it.

Tarek dropped her hand, then beckoned for her to take a seat in one of the low couches she belatedly realized formed a circle in the center of the room. But how could she notice the brightly patterned cushions and seats when the walls were encrusted in jewels and the room opened up on to a long, white terrace? She thought she saw the hint of a pool. And off to one side, more chairs, low tables, and lush green trees for shade.

"This is your suite and your salon," he told her. "I'm going to ask you some questions, and then I will leave you to reacclimate. You will be provided with whatever you need. Clothes to choose from, a bath with whatever accessories you require, and, of course, access to your loved ones using whatever medium you wish. My servants are even now assembling outside this room, ready to wait on you hand and foot. In the meantime, as I cannot imagine that the food in the dungeon speaks well of Alzalam and because I am afraid I must ask you these questions, I've taken the liberty of requesting a small tea service."

"A tea service," Anya repeated, and had to choke back the urge to burst out laughing. She coughed. "That is... the most insane and yet perfect thing you could possibly have said. *A tea service.*"

She suspected she was hysterical. Or about to be, because she was clearly in shock and attempting to process it, when that was likely impossible. She was out of her cell, and that was what mattered. More, she did not think that Tarek had chosen this room bursting with light and open to the great outdoors by accident.

Yet somehow, she thought that after all of this, she might not survive if she broke apart like that. Here, now, when it seemed she might actually have made it through.

She would never forgive herself if she fell apart now.

When he was sitting opposite her, all his ivory and gold seeming a part of the light that she was suddenly bathed in. As if he was another jeweled thing, precious and impossible.

If she cried now, she would die.

And as if to taunt her, that knotted horror in her solar plexus pulled tight.

"You do not have to eat, of course," he said with a kind of matter-of-fact gentleness that made the knot ache and, lower, something deep in her belly begin to melt. "Nor am I suggesting that a few pastries can make up for what was done to you. Consider it the first of many gifts I intend to bestow upon you, as an apology for what has happened to you here."

Anya didn't really know how she was expected to respond to that. Because the fact was, she was still here and she couldn't quite believe what was happening. She shifted in her plush, soft seat and dug her fingernails into her thigh, hard. It hurt, but she didn't wake up to find herself in her cell. She'd had so many of those dreams at first, and still had them now and again. They were all so heartbreakingly realistic and every time, the shock of waking to find herself still stuck in that cell felt like the kind of blow she couldn't get up from.

Slowly, she released her painful grip on her own thigh and assessed her situation.

She hadn't been tossed on a truck headed for the border, or shot in the back of the head, or sent back to the States so she could throw herself off the plane to kiss the ground—not that she thought an airport floor would inspire her to do any such thing.

If this was truly freedom, or the start of it, she was still a long way off from having to sort through what remained of the life she'd left behind.

That was not a happy thought.

When the door swung open again, servants streamed inside bearing platters and pushing a cart. Her stomach rumbled at the sight. Plate after plate of delicacies were delivered to the low table between her and the King. Nuts and dates, the promised pastries, meats and spreads, breads and cheeses. Cakes and yogurts and what she thought was a take on baklava, drenched in a rich honey she could smell from where she sat. Bowls filled with savory dishes she couldn't identify, all of which looked beautiful and smelled even better. Pitchers of water, sparking and still. Tea in one silver carafe and in another, rich, dark coffee.

Anya might not trust her own happiness, or what was happening around her, but she could eat her fill for the first time in months, and for the moment that felt like the same thing. Because there were flavors again, as bright as the sun that careened around this room. Flavors and textures, each one a revelation, like colors on her tongue.

She glutted herself, happily, and didn't care if it made her sick.

While across from her, the Sheikh lounged in his seat and drank only coffee. Black.

Anya told herself there was no reason she should take that as some kind of warning.

When her belly was deliciously full, she sat back and took a very deep breath. And for the first time in a long while, Anya was aware of herself as a woman again. Not a prisoner. Not a doctor.

A woman, that was all, who had just engaged in the deeply sensual act of enjoying her food.

Perhaps it was because Tarek was so harshly, inarguably, a man. Here in the dizzy brightness and jeweled quiet of this room, there was no doubt in her mind that he was a king. Mythic or otherwise, and everything that entailed. It was the way he sat there, waiting for her—yet not precisely waiting. Because she could feel the power in him. It was unmistakable.

He filled the room, hotter than the sunshine that

poured in from outside. Richer than the coffee and more intense than the sugar and butter, tartness and spice on her tongue.

And his gaze only seemed darker the longer he studied her.

Waiting her out, she understood then. Because he was in control, not her. Yet in a different way than her guards had been in control below, or the cell itself had contained her. Tarek did not need to place her behind bars.

Not when he could look at her and make her wonder why she couldn't stay right where she was, forever, if that would please him—

Get a grip, Anya, she ordered herself.

She'd thought him beautiful in the dungeons, but here, he was worse. Much worse. There was no getting away from the stark sensuality of his features, with that face like a hawk's that she wouldn't have been surprised to find stamped on old coins.

Anya felt distinctly grubby by comparison. She was suddenly entirely too aware that she had not had access to decent products in a long, long time. Her hair felt like straw. Her prison-issue clothes had suited her fine in the cell she'd eventually made, if not cozy, livable. But the gray drabness of the clothes she'd lived in for so long felt like an affront now. Here where this man watched her with an expression that, no matter what pretty words he spouted, did not strike her as remotely apologetic.

"You said you had questions for me," she said, when it became clear to her that he was perfectly willing to sit there in silence. Watching her eat.

Making her feel as caged as if he held her between his hands.

It only made her feel more like a bedraggled piece

of trash someone had flung onto his pristine marble floors. That, in turn, made her think of her long, quiet, painful childhood in her father's house. Her succession of stepmothers, each younger and prettier than the last.

Anya had never been a pretty girl. Not like her stepmothers. She'd never wanted to do the kind of work they did to remain so. And her father had always frowned and asked her why she would lower herself to worries about her appearance when she was supposedly intelligent, like him, thereby making certain Anya and the stepmother *du jour* were little better than enemies.

And sometimes a whole lot worse than that.

That didn't mean she wasn't aware of the ways she could use her appearance as a springboard toward confidence, upon occasion, when she wasn't feeling it internally. She didn't need a gown, or whatever it was the ladies wore in a place like this. But she wouldn't have minded a shower and some conditioner.

Still, he'd said he had his questions and Anya didn't know what would happen if she refused. Would it be straight back into the dungeon with her?

"Tell me how you came to be in my country," he invited her, though she felt the truth of that invitation impress itself against her spine as the order it was. "In the middle of a minor revolution."

"Minor?"

The Sheikh did something with his chin that she might have called a shrug, had he been a lesser man. "Loss of life was minimal. My brother anticipated a quiet coup and was surprised when that was not what he got. He lives on in prison, an emblem to all of his own bad decisions and my mercy. Despite his best efforts, the country did not descend into chaos."

Anya didn't have a brother, but doubted she would sound so remote about a coup attempt if she did. "I guess you must not have been out there in the thick of it."

His lips thinned. "You are mistaken."

Anya blinked at that, and found herself clearing her throat. Unnecessarily. And more because of that storm in her than anything in her throat. A storm that wound around and around, then shifted into more of that melting that should have horrified her.

She told herself it was shock. This was all shock. Her whole body kept *reacting* to this man and she didn't like it, but it wasn't him.

You're not yourself, she told herself, but it didn't feel like an excuse.

It felt a lot more like permission.

But Anya had trained in emergency medicine. Then had trained more by flinging herself into the deep end, in and out of some of the worst places on the planet and usually with very little in the way of backup.

She could handle tea with a king, surely.

There were fewer bodily fluids, for one thing.

"Crossing into Alzalam was accidental," she told him. She'd gone over it a thousand times. Then a thousand more. "We were working in one of the refugee camps over the border. You know that civil war has been going on for a generation."

"Yes," the man across from her said quietly. "And it has ever been a horror."

As if he felt that horror deeply. Personally.

Her heart jolted, then thudded loudly.

"I'm surprised you think so," she said without thinking, and watched a royal eyebrow arch high on his ferociously stark brow. "That you are even aware of the scope of that kind of disaster from…" She glanced around. "Here."

"Because I am no different from a tyrant who rules by fear." His voice was soft, but she did not mistake the threat in it. "We are all the same, we desert men in our ancient kingdoms."

Her heart and that knot in her chest pulsed in concert, and she thought she might be shaking. God, she hoped she wasn't *shaking*, showing her weaknesses, letting him see how easily he intimidated her.

"To be fair," she managed to say, "my experience of desert kings has pretty much been nothing but death, disease, and dungeons. Not to discount the pastries, of course."

She was holding her breath again. His gaze was so dark, so merciless, that she was sure that if she dared look away—if she dared look down—she would find he'd made her into some of that filigree that lined his archways. An insubstantial lace, even if carved from bone.

And then, to her astonishment, the most dangerous man she'd ever met, who could lock her up for the rest of her life with a wave of one finger—or worse—

Smiled.

CHAPTER THREE

TAREK HAD NEVER before considered food erotic. It was fuel. It was sometimes a necessary evil. It could, upon occasion, be a form of communion.

But watching the doctor eat with abandon, as if every bite she put in her mouth was a new, sensual delight, was a revelation. She had him hard and ready. Intensely focused on her and the unbridled passion she displayed as if she was performing her joy for him alone.

He could not recall ever experiencing anything quite like it.

And certainly not because of a captive still in her prison attire.

Still, Tarek smiled at her as if none of this was happening. He reminded himself—perhaps a bit sternly—that honey attracted more bees than vinegar. And that even a king could allow himself to act sweet if it suited him. It helped that his plan of how to handle the world's reaction to her incarceration began to take form in his head.

But she did not look particularly pleased to receive a smile from him. On the contrary, she looked… poleaxed.

"Perhaps this is not the time to ask you these questions," he said after a moment, when she only stared back at him. Her passionate eating on pause.

Tarek tried to let consideration and concern shine forth from within him, and it wasn't entirely an act for her benefit. He liked to think he was a compassionate man. Had he not proved it this dark year? He was certainly the most compassionate King the country had ever seen.

Surely the life he'd led had given him ample opportunity to practice.

Anya straightened her shoulders, a slight, deliberate jerk that he'd watched her do several times now. As if she was snapping herself to attention. And when she did, her brown eyes sharpened on him and he wondered, idly enough, if this was the doctor in her. That focus. That intensity.

That, too, made his sex heavy.

Later, Tarek promised himself, he would take a moment to ask himself why, exactly, he found himself attracted to a prisoner only recently released from his dungeon. Surely that spoke to issues within himself he ought to resolve. Especially if he truly thought himself compassionate in some way.

"I'm happy to answer questions now," she said, with a certain bluntness that made Tarek blink.

He wondered if it was simply that she was a Western woman, doctor or no. They were different from the women of his kingdom; he knew that already. Anya Turner was forthright, even so recently liberated from her prison cell. She appeared to have no trouble whatever meeting his gaze and more, holding it. The women of his country played far different games. They were masters of the soft sigh, the submissively lowered eyes, all to hide their warrior hearts and ambitions—usually to become his Queen and rule the kingdom in their own ways.

Not so this doctor, who had clearly never heard the word *submissive* in her life.

It was an adjustment, certainly.

"I had no idea you were being held here," Tarek told her. He lifted his mobile as if she could read the documents Ahmed had sent him while she ate. "But I have read your file."

"Would anything have been different if you had known?" she asked, and it wasn't precisely an interruption. He had paused.

Still. That, too, was different.

He reminded himself, with a touch of acid, that this was the woman who had cheerfully called him a pig while still behind bars. Unaware that he had come to liberate her, not punish her further.

Perhaps *blunt* and *forthright* did not quite cover it.

"I cannot alter the past, much as I would like to," he said. He studied her, and the easy way she held his gaze. As if she was the one measuring him, instead of the other way round. "Do you know why you were imprisoned in the first place?"

She let out a sharp little laugh of disbelief. Not a noise others generally made in his presence. "Do you?"

Again, he indicated his mobile. He did not react to the disrespectful tone. Much. "I know what was written in your file when you were taken into custody."

Another deeply impolite sound, not quite a laugh, that he congratulated himself on ignoring. "I believe the pretext for our arrest was an illegal border crossing. The fact that we were administering humanitarian aid and were in no way dissidents fomenting rebellion or revolution did not impress your police force. Mostly there was a lot of shouting. And guns."

"That was an upsetting period here," he agreed. "There was an attempt at a coup, as I mentioned. Dissidents tried to take the palace and there were a few, targeted uprisings around the country."

If he had only listened to his mother, he might have armored himself against the unforgivable affection that had allowed him to minimize his brother's behavior over the years. He'd convinced himself Rafiq's bad behavior was not a pattern. And even if it was, that it wasn't serious.

"*A man who will be King cannot allow love to make him a danger to his country,*" his mother had warned him. "*What a man loves is his business. What a king loves can never be anything but a weapon used against him.*"

Tarek had never imagined that weapon would be a literal one. Or that he would wish, deeply and surpassingly, that he had listened more closely to his mother when he'd had the chance.

There was something about the sharp focus Anya trained on him, complete with a faint frown between her brows, that he liked a lot more than he should. When he knew he would consider it nothing short of an impertinence in anyone else. And would likely react badly.

But even this doctor's *focus* felt like passion to him.

"A coup? In the palace?" She waited for his nod. "You mean they came for you. Here."

"They did." He did not precisely smile. "More accurately, they tried."

Rafiq had tried. Personally. A bitter wound that Tarek doubted would ever truly heal.

Still, he had the strangest urge to show her his scars. An urge he repressed. But he found himself watching the way her expression changed, and telling himself there was a kind of respect there.

"You're lucky you have so many guards to protect you, then."

He opted not to analyze why that statement bothered him so much.

"I am," Tarek agreed, his voice cooler than it should have been, because it shouldn't have mattered to him what this woman thought—of him or the kingdom or anything else. "Though they were little help when my brother and his men tried to take me after what was meant to be a quiet family meal commemorating the two-month anniversary of our father's death."

He did not like the memory. He resented that he was forced to revisit it.

Yet Anya's expression didn't change and Tarek could feel her…paying closer attention, somehow. With the same ferocity she'd used while demolishing a plate of pastries earlier.

Why did that make him want her so desperately?

But even as he asked himself the question, he knew the answer. He could imagine, all too well, that fierce, intent focus of hers on his body. On what they could do together.

He wrestled himself under control and wasn't happy at how difficult it proved. "It was a confusing time. I regret that there were far more imprisonments than there should have been, and, indeed, your colleagues were released as soon as order was restored. But due to the vagaries of several archaic customs, you were not. I could explain why, but what matters is that the responsibility is mine."

She broke her intense scrutiny of him then, glancing away while her throat moved. "They were released? How long ago?"

"As I said, when order was restored to the kingdom."

She looked back at him, her eyes narrow. "Thank you. But is that a week ago? Seven months ago? Twenty-four hours after they were taken in?"

"I do not think they were incarcerated for very long." That was no more and no less than the truth, as far as he knew it. He should not have felt that strange sense that he'd betrayed her, somehow. By telling her? Or by allowing it to happen in the first place—not that he'd known? Tarek felt the uncharacteristic shift about in his seat like a recalcitrant child. He restrained it. "No more than two months, I am given to understand."

Across from him, Anya sat very still in her gray, faded tunic, that hair of hers tumbling all around her. She shook her head, faintly, as if she was trying to shake off a cloud. Or perhaps confusion. "I was forgotten about?"

Tarek held her gaze, surprised to discover he did not want to. He reminded himself that this was the foremost duty of any king, like it or not. Accountability.

It didn't matter that he hadn't known she existed, much less that she and her colleagues had been caught up in the troubles here. Just as it didn't matter that he hadn't known until this very afternoon that she had been languishing in his very own dungeon. He was responsible all the same.

He might as well have slammed shut the iron door and turned the key himself.

Tarek inclined his head. "I'm afraid so."

She nodded, blinking a bit. Then she cleared her throat. "Thank you for your honesty."

And for a moment, there was quiet. She did not reach for more food from the platters before her. She did not hold him in the intensity of her brown gaze, shot through with gold in the hectic light that filled this salon.

For a moment there was only the faint catch of her breath, hardly a sound at all. The sound of birds calling to each other outside. The lap of the fountain out on her terrace.

And the improbable beat of his own pulse, hard and heavy in his temples. His chest. His sex.

Tarek could not have said if it was longing…or shame.

He had so little experience with either.

"You should know that your presence here has created something of an international crisis," he said when he could take the pressing noise of the silence between them no longer. "Something else I'm embarrassed to say I was unaware of until today."

She smirked. "It's created a crisis for me, certainly. An unwanted and forced eight-month vacation from my life."

"I want to be clear about this," Tarek said. "Were you harmed in any way?"

"Define harm," she shot back. "I expected to be beaten. Abused."

"If this happened, you need only tell me and the perpetrators will be brought to justice. Harsh justice to suit their crimes. I swear this to you, here and now."

"None of those things happened," Anya said, but her voice was thicker than it had been before. "And maybe your plan is to throw me right back into that cell today, so let me assure you that it's an effective punishment. That cell is deceptively roomy, isn't it? It's still a cell, cut off from the world."

He leaned forward, searching her face. "But you were not harmed?"

Her lips pressed into a line. "How do you measure the harm of being captured, shouted at in a language you don't speak, separated from the rest of your colleagues, and then thrown into a cold stone cell? Then kept there for months, never knowing if today might be the day the real terror might begin? Or you might be trotted out for an execution? I don't know how to measure that. Do you?"

Tarek studied her closely. Looking for scars, perhaps. Or some hint of emotional fragility or tears, because that, he would understand. But instead, this woman looked at him as if she was also a warrior. As if she too had fought, in her own way.

He felt his own scars, hacked into his flesh in this very same palace, throbbing as if they were new.

"It is all unfortunate," he said quietly. "There are many ways to fight in a war, are there not? And so many of them are not what we would have chosen, had we been offered a choice."

"I'm a doctor," she replied, matching his tone. Her dark eyes tight on his. "When I go to war, it's to heal. Never to fight."

"We all fight, Doctor. With whatever tools we are given. Whether you choose to admit that or do not is between you and whatever it is you pray to."

And for another long, impossibly fraught moment, they only stared at each other. Here where the desert sun made the walls shimmer and dance. A fitting antidote to the dungeon, he thought. Abundant, unavoidable sunshine made into a thousand different colors, until the sheer volume of it all made breath itself feel new.

But as the silence wore on, he found the glare she

leveled on him with those sharp, clever eyes of hers far more intriguing.

Another thing he did not plan to look at too closely.

"Do you have more questions?" she asked. Eventually. "I find the longer I'm out of that cell, the harder it is not to want to scrub myself clean of the experience. Assuming, that is, that this isn't all a great ruse."

Tarek understood, then, how easy it would be if this was the trick she thought it was. His brother, for example, would have thought nothing of fabricating some explanation for keeping this woman locked up—a law she'd broken that no one could prove she hadn't—and then tossing her back down in the dungeon to rot. His treatment of his own staff had been the despair of the palace. Rafiq would not have cared about international opinion. If things grew tense, he would have closed the American embassy, shut the Alzalam borders, and continued to do as he pleased.

But Tarek was not his grasping, morally vacant younger brother. His vision of the kingdom did not involve petty tyrannies, no matter the inconvenience to him, personally.

"I am not the kind of man who plays games," he told her, which should have gone without saying. He accepted that she was unlikely to know this about him. "Ruses of any kind do not impress me nor appeal to me. You will not be returning to that cell, or any other cell in my kingdom."

"Because you say so?"

"Because I am the King and so decree it."

"That sounds impressive." She did not sound impressed.

He shoved that aside. "But should you choose to reach

out to the outside world, I would have you recognize that the moment I knew of your imprisonment, you were released."

She blinked again. Tarek wondered if he was watching her *think*. And sure enough, her gaze sharpened even further in the next moment. "Wait. My imprisonment is your crisis? Not my *presence*. But the actual fact that I've been locked away for eight months."

There were so many things he could have said to that. He entertained them all, then dismissed them, one by one.

"Yes."

Anya's lips quirked. "What level of crisis are we talking about here?"

"I have not had time to study it in any detail, I am afraid. As I was more focused on removing you from the dungeon as quickly as possible."

"Your mercy knows no bounds, I'm sure."

These were extraordinary circumstances and she was the victim in this, so Tarek ignored the insolent tone. Though it caused him physical pain to do so.

Or perhaps you only wish for an excuse to touch her, something insidious and too warm within him whispered.

"My understanding is that your imprisonment is considered a humanitarian crisis in many Western countries. And as our papers have only recently begun discussing the outside world again, after this long year of unrest, it has gone on far longer than it should have."

Anya nodded. "And I'm not a thoughtless tourist smuggling in drugs in a stranger's teddy bear, am I? That can't look good for you."

Tarek unclenched his jaw. "As a token of my embarrassment and a gesture of goodwill, I will throw a dinner this very night. We will invite your ambassador. You can assure him, in your own words, that you are safe and well."

That little smirk of hers deepened. "And what if I'm neither safe nor well?"

Tarek wanted to argue. She had eaten, she was sparring with him—*him*—and a glance at her cell had told him that she had not been suffering unduly while in custody. There were far greater ills. As a doctor, she should know that.

But he thought better of saying such things. What did he know about Americans? Perhaps the harm she'd spoken of was real enough. She could not possibly have been raised as hardy as the local women. Equal to sandstorms and blazing heat alike, all while keeping themselves looking soft and yielding.

It was only kind to make allowances for her upbringing.

"Then you may tell the ambassador of your suffering," he said instead of what he wanted to say. Magnanimously, he thought. "You may tell him whatever you wish."

"You will have to forgive me," Anya said, sounding almost careful. It was a marked contrast to how she'd spoken to him before, with such familiarity. "But I can't quite wrap my head around this. I expect to be seized again at any moment and dragged back to the dungeon. I certainly can't quite believe that the King of Alzalam is perfectly happy to give me carte blanche to tell any story I like to an ambassador. Or to anyone else."

Tarek made his decision then and there. The plan that was forming in his head was outrageous. Absurd on too many levels to count. But the more it settled in him, the more he liked it.

It was simple, really. Elegant.

And while bracing honesty was not something he had ever imagined would factor into his usual relationships with women, such as his betrothal, this woman was different. If she wasn't, she would not have ended up in his dungeon. She would certainly not have been here, telling him to his face that she doubted what he said to her. His word, which was law.

He ought to have been outraged. Instead, he accepted that he had to treat his doctor…differently.

It wouldn't be the first time in this long and difficult year that he'd had to change strategy on the fly. To set aside old plans and come up with new ones, then implement them immediately. Tarek liked to think he'd developed a talent for it.

The kingdom was ancient. Yet the King could not be similarly made of stone, or he would be the first to crumble. His father had taught him that, his mother had tried to warn him, but Tarek had lived it.

"Of course I wish that I could control what it is you might say about your time here," he told her, and watched the shock of that hit her, making her fall back in her seat. "I have no wish to be thought a monster, and I would love nothing more than to present your emancipation… carefully and in a way that brings, if not honor to the kingdom, no greater shame. But that is not up to me."

If Tarek was not mistaken, that dazed light in her eyes meant he had succeeded in being…disarming. Imagine that.

He continued in the same vein. "I will leave it up to you. You have no reason to trust me, so I will not ask such a thing of you. I would request only this. That if asked, you make it known that the very moment I learned that you were here, I freed you myself."

That dazed light faded, replaced by something far sharper.

"You want me to be your press release," she said softly.

"I would love you to be my press release." He even laughed, and as he did, it occurred to him that he wasn't faking this. "If there exists any possibility that you will sing wide the glory of the kingdom, I would be delighted."

Her head tilted slightly to one side, and Tarek still wasn't used to her direct gaze. To the way she unapologetically *considered* him, right where he could see her do it. "I can't speak to any possibilities or press releases, I'm afraid. I haven't taken a proper shower in eight months. Much less soaked myself in a good, long bath. Or used moisturizer. Or any of a thousand other everyday things that now seem luxurious to me."

"I understand, of course." Tarek smiled, again astonished to discover it was not a forced smile. He did not think of honey or vinegar, bees or business. Only what he could do to make her look at him without suspicion. "You must do what you feel is right."

He should not have taken pleasure in the way she looked at him, as if he wasn't quite what she expected. Surely he should not have introduced *pleasure* into this in the first place, no matter how tempting she was when she ate so recklessly, so heedlessly.

Tarek could not help but wonder how else she might approach her appetites. How else she might choose to sate them.

That is enough for now, he snapped at himself.

He stood, inclining his head to her in what he doubted she would realize was more of an apology than anything he might have said. Or would say.

"I will leave you to your luxuries, Doctor," he said. He nodded toward the door. "As I mentioned before, my staff waits outside to attend to you, should you wish it. This suite has both indoor and outdoor spaces, so you need not feel confined. Should you have need of me, personally, I will make myself available to you. You need only ask."

Her eyes darted around the room as if she was looking for a way out. Or for a lie. "Um. Yes. Thank you."

And Tarek left her then, aware as he strode from the room that he was battling the most unusual sensation.

Not fury at the circumstances.

Not distaste at what fate had thrown before him on this day, just as he'd imagined he was over the worst of this complicated year and ready to settle into a brighter future.

Not the usual bitterness that surged in him when he thought of his brother's betrayal.

But the exceptionally unusual feeling that, even though all she was doing was fencing words with him—with an insolence Tarek would have permitted from no other—he would have preferred to stay.

CHAPTER FOUR

THE BATHROOM ALONE was at least three times the size of her cell, and Anya intended to enjoy every inch of it.

She spent a long while in the vast shower, with its numerous jets and showerheads, offering her every possible water experience imaginable. She conditioned her hair three separate times. She slathered herself in all the shower creams and gels and soaps available. When she was done, having scrubbed every inch of her body to get the dungeon off, she drew a bath in a freestanding tub. She filled it with salts that felt like silk against her skin and she sat in the water for a long while, letting emotion work itself through her in waves. She stared out the windows, sank down deeper into the embrace of the water, and let whatever was inside her work its way through her while she breathed.

And pretended it was the steam on her cheeks, nothing more.

After her bath, she wrapped herself in one of the exultantly thick robes that hung on the wall, and sat at the vanity piled high with every hair implement she'd ever dreamed of. And a great many more she'd never seen before. Then she thought of absolutely nothing while she blew out her hair, then put in a few well-placed curls, until the woman who looked back at her from the mirror was actually...her again.

"Me," she whispered out loud.

Her chest felt so tight it hurt to breathe, but she made herself do it anyway—long and deep—trying to keep that knotted thing below her breastbone at bay.

Anya got up then, snuggling deeper into the lush embrace of the robe. Now that she was so clean she was pickled, she let herself explore. She enjoyed her bare feet against the cool stone floors, or sunk deep into the thick rugs. She wandered the halls, going in and out of each of the bright rooms, then out onto the wide terrace so she could stand beneath the sky.

She hadn't invited any staff inside, because that felt too much like more guards. Instead, she wandered around all on her own, as thrilled with the fact she was alone as anything else. All alone. No one was watching her. No one was listening to her. It amazed her how much she'd missed the simple freedom of walking through a room unobserved.

Through all the rooms. A media center with screens of all descriptions. There was that brightly colored room she'd sat in with Tarek, and three other salons, one for every mood or hint of weather. She had her own little courtyard, filled with flowers, plants, and a fountain that spilled into a pretty pool. There was a fully outfitted gym, two different office spaces, each with a different view, and a small library.

There was also a selection of bedchambers. Anya went into each, testing the softness of the mattresses and sitting in the chairs or lounging on the chaises, because she could. And because it made her feel like Goldilocks.

But she knew the moment she entered the master suite. There was the foyer of mosaic. The art on the walls.

In the bedchamber itself, she found a glorious, four-poster bed that could sleep ten, which made her feel emotional all over again.

And laid out on top of the brightly colored bed linens, a rugged-looking canvas bag that she stared at as if it was a ghost.

Because it was. The last time Anya had seen it, the police had taken it from her.

Suddenly trembling, she moved to the end of the bed, staring at her bag as if she thought it might…explode. Or she might. And then, making strange noises as if her body couldn't decide if she was breathing or sobbing, she pulled her bag toward her. Beneath it she found the jeans, T-shirt, and overtunic she'd been wearing that night. The scarf she'd had wrapped around her head. And inside the bag, her personal medical kit, her passport, and her mobile.

Charged, she saw when she switched it on. Anya stayed frozen where she was, staring at the phone in her hand and the now unfamiliar weight of it. Her voice mailbox was full. There were thousands of emails waiting. Notifications from apps she'd all but forgotten about.

The outside world in a tiny little box in her palm. And after all this time—all the days and nights she'd made long and complicated lists of all the people she would contact first, all the calls she would make, all the messages she would send—what she did was drop the mobile back down onto the bed.

And then back away as if it was a snake.

Her heart began to race. Nausea bloomed, then worked

its way through her. Her breath picked up, and then the panic slammed straight into her.

It didn't matter what she told herself. It never had mattered. Anya sank down onto her knees and then, when that wasn't sufficiently low enough, collapsed onto her belly. And as it had so many times before, the panic took control.

"You are not dying," she chanted at herself. "It only feels like it."

Her heart pounded so hard, so loud, it seemed impossible to her that she wasn't having a major cardiac event. She ordered herself to stop hyperventilating, because the doctor in her knew that made it worse, but that didn't work. It never worked.

Anya cried then, soundless, shaking sobs. Because it felt like she was dying, and she couldn't bear it—not when she'd only just escaped that dungeon.

But she knew that there was no fighting these panic attacks when they came. That was the horror of them. There was only surrendering, and she had never been any good at that.

It felt like an eternity. Eventually, she managed to breathe better, slowing each breath and using her nose more than her mouth. Slowly, her heart beat less frantically.

Slowly, slowly, the clench of nausea dissipated.

But she still had to crawl across the floor on her hands and knees. Back into the bathroom, where she had to lie for a while on the cold marble floor. Just to make sure that *this time* it really wasn't the sudden onset of a horrible influenza.

As she lay there, staring balefully at the literally palatial toilet before her, it occurred to her that in all the months she'd been imprisoned, she'd never once had one of these attacks. If asked, Anya would have said that her whole life had taken place on a level of intense stress and fear. Especially before she'd begun to learn the language, and had been forced to exist in a swirl of uncomprehending terror.

Stress, fear, and terror, sure. But she hadn't had one of these vicious little panic attacks, had she?

And in fact, it was only when she thought about the world contained on her mobile—and the inevitable messages she would find from her father—that her heart kicked at her again. And another queasy jolt hit her straight in the belly. She could feel her shoulders seem to tie themselves into dramatic shapes above her head, and apparently, it was here on the bathroom floor of a grand palace in Alzalam that Anya might just have to face the fact that it wasn't her eight-month imprisonment that really stressed her out.

It was the life she'd put on hold while stuck in that cell.

"That's ridiculous," she muttered at herself as she pulled herself up and onto her feet, feeling brittle and significantly older than she had before.

When she staggered back out of the bathroom, she didn't head for her bag again. Or her mobile, God forbid. She went instead through the far archway and found herself in an expansive dressing room, stocked full of clothing, just as the forbidding and beautiful Tarek had promised.

Anya told herself that she was erring on the side of caution. But she suspected it was more that she didn't want to be alone any longer, stuck with nothing but her panic, too many voice mail messages she didn't want to listen to, and the horror of her inbox.

Whatever it was, she went out and called in the servants.

"I am to have dinner with the Sheikh and the American ambassador," she told the two women who waited for her, both of them smiling as if they'd waited their entire lives for this opportunity.

"Yes, madam," one of them said. "Such an honor."

Anya had not considered it an honor. Should she have? When Tarek had made it clear that it was likely damage control? Maybe she really did need to sit down with her mobile, get online, and read the story of what had happened to her as told by people she'd never met. But the thought of picking up that phone again made something cold roll down her spine.

She smiled back at the women. "I'm hoping you can help me. I've never attended a formal dinner in your country and I have been...indisposed for so long."

"Don't you worry, madam," said the other woman, smiling even brighter. "We will make you shine."

And that was what they did.

They spared no detail. They buffed Anya's fingernails and her toenails, then added polish. They clucked disapprovingly over her brows, and then, as far she could tell, removed every errant piece of hair from her entire body. There was a salt scrub, because they did not feel that her long shower, or deep soak in the bath, was up to par.

Nor were they impressed with her hair, and when they were finished restyling it, she could see why. Anya looked luminous. Soft, pampered, and something like happy.

They had rimmed her eyes with dark mascara. They'd

slicked a soft gloss over her lips. And when she looked in the set of full-length mirrors in the dressing room, she found herself resplendent in a bright tunic and matching trousers, flowing and lovely. Topped off with a long scarf with a pretty, jeweled edge that complemented the outfit and made her seem like someone else. The kind of woman who dined with ambassadors and kings, maybe.

"Thank you," she said to the women when they were done. "You've worked miracles here tonight."

Anya found herself smiling when they led her out of her rooms, then through the halls of the palace.

Night was falling outside, but the palace was still filled with light. She could see the last of the sun creep away a bit more every time they walked across a courtyard. And when they reached the grand central courtyard—that she vaguely remembered studying on the plane out of Houston a lifetime ago, because she'd known she was heading into the region—she paused for a moment as the night took over the sky.

Because she wasn't in the cell. There was nothing between her and the stars, save the palace walls that stood, then, at a distance. As if they understood, the women seemed content to wait while she stood there, her head tipped back and the half-wild notion that if she jumped, she would float straight off into the galaxy.

But she didn't. And when she came back to earth, the servants led her into a smaller room off the courtyard that was filled with Americans.

"His Excellency wishes you to speak with your countrymen for long as you desire," the woman closest to her said, not in English. "Only when you are satisfied will the formal dinner begin."

"Thank you," Anya said quietly.

"You learned the language?" asked one of the men who waited for her, slick and polished in his suit and shiny shoes, with a sharp smile to match. "Smart move, Dr. Turner."

Anya heard the door close behind her, and surely she should have felt…something different, now. Some sense of triumph, or victory. Instead, she felt almost as if she was back in one of the hospitals she'd worked in before she'd come abroad, forced to contend with competitive doctors and high-stakes medical issues alike.

There were too many men in suits in the room and somehow, what she wanted was a different man. One in ivory and gold, with a predator's sharp gaze, and the quiet, inarguable presence of heavy stone.

"Was it smart?" she asked, smiling faintly because she thought she should. "Or survival?"

"It's an honor to meet you, Dr. Turner," said the most polished of the men, his face creased with wisdom and his smile encouraging. "I'm Ambassador Pomeroy, and I have to tell you, I can't wait to take you home."

Home. That word echoed around inside of her. And as the circle of men tightened around her, all of them making soothing noises and asking about her state of mind and general welfare, she told herself it was joy.

Because it had to be joy.

But it wasn't until she walked into the dining room that had been prepared for them—another triumph of mosaic and marble, beautifully lit and welcoming—that she breathed easy again.

Because Tarek waited there, lounging with seeming carelessness at the head of a long table. His gaze was hooded and dark, a clear indication of the power he was choosing not to wield, so obvious to Anya that it made her feel hollowed out with a kind of shiver. He was wearing a different set of robes that should have made him look silly compared to the pack of American diplomats in their business suits. But didn't.

At all.

"Welcome," the King said, his voice a ruthless scrape across the pretty room. "I thank you for joining me in this celebration of—" and Anya could have sworn that he looked only at her, then "—resilience and grace."

"Hear, hear," cried the men, a bit too brightly for strangers.

And despite how she'd feasted earlier, and how sure she'd been that she couldn't eat another bite, she found when she was seated at Tarek's right hand that she was starving. So while the men engaged in the sort of elegantly poisonous dinner conversation that she supposed was the hallmark of international diplomacy, or perhaps of tedious dinner parties, Anya indulged herself. Again.

It was only when she was quietly marveling at the tenderness of the chicken she was eating—simmered to tearjerking tenderness on a bed of fragrant rice and doused in a thick, spicy sauce with so many *flavors*—that Anya realized that the Sheikh was not paying any attention to the arch wordplay of the ambassador and his aides.

Instead, Tarek was focused on her.

"The food in the dungeon wasn't terrible," she told him, realizing only as she smiled at him that she was… not embarrassed, exactly. But something in her heated up and stayed hot at the notion he was watching her again. "Just, you know. Bland."

"That is unpardonable."

Was she imagining the heat in his gaze? The faint trace of humor in that dark voice of his?

"How did you find your ambassador?" he asked, doing something with his chin that brought one of the waiting servants over to place more delicacies in front of her. "Appropriately outraged on your behalf, I trust?"

"Are you asking if I issued that press release?" she heard herself ask, in a tone she was terribly afraid was more flirtatious than not.

Good lord. Maybe when she'd had that panic attack, she'd hit her head on the stone floor. That was the only explanation. She dropped her gaze to her plate.

But she could still feel Tarek beside her. The burn of his attention all over her.

"I have a far more interesting question to ask you than what you did or did not tell a career diplomat," he said, all quiet force and the dark beneath. Like the night sky she'd wanted to float away in, ripe with stars. "Who will tell his own tales to suit himself, let me assure you."

Anya's heart was picking up speed again, but this time, without all the other telltale signs that she was descending into a panic attack. Because she wasn't.

She recognized the heat. And what felt an awful lot like need, curling inside her, like flame.

It had been there from the moment she'd first seen him. And now, buffed and plucked and polished to please, she understood that it had been for him as much as for her. She'd felt pretty in her mirror.

But when Tarek looked at her, she felt alive.

It was crazy. Maybe *she* was crazy. At the very least, she needed to leave this country and sort out what had happened to her—and how she felt about it—far, far away from the very dungeon where she'd been held all this time. This was likely nothing more than PTSD.

But tell that to the softest part of her, that melted as she sat there.

"You appear to be filled with questions," she said. Less flirtatiously, to her credit.

"I have spent a long year as a man of action, primarily," he said, and she made a note to look up the coup he'd mentioned. And what he'd done to combat it when his brother had been involved. "But I have always found that intellectual rigor is the true measure of a person. For without it, what separates us from the beasts?"

Anya forgot the plates piled high before her. "Some would say a soul."

"What would you say?"

She was dimly aware that they were not alone. That the ambassador and his aides were still at the same table, sharing the same meal. But she couldn't have said where they were seated. Or what they were talking about. Or even what any of them looked like.

It was as if there was only Tarek.

"I think that when everything is taken from you, what's left is the soul," she said quietly. "And it is up to you if that sustains you or scares you, I suppose."

There was a different, considering light in his gaze then. "What did you find, then?"

Something in her trembled, though she knew it wasn't fear. But it was as if some kind of foreboding kept her from answering him, all the same. Instead, she made herself smile to break the sudden tension between them. She reminded herself that they were not alone in this room, no matter how it felt.

And that he might have told her that he intended to be honest, but that didn't make it true. He was a very powerful, very canny king who had proved that he was more than capable of holding on to his throne, the ambassador had told her earlier.

"*He is not to be underestimated*," the man had said.

Anya spread open her hands, shrugging. "Here I am. I suppose that means that I found a way to sustain myself, whatever it took."

Tarek lifted the glass before him, sitting back in his chair. He looked every inch the monarch. Currently indulgent, but with that severity lurking beneath.

She should certainly not have found him remotely compelling.

She told herself that of course she didn't.

Yet as the dinner wore on, she admitted privately that something about this man seemed to be lodged beneath her skin. She might have told herself it was simply because he was the first truly, inarguably beautiful man she'd seen since her ordeal had begun. But a glance around the table put paid to that idea.

Because the ambassador's men were all perfectly attractive. She could see that…but she didn't *feel* it. Her body didn't care at all about these bland men with their overly wide smiles and targeted geniality.

But the brooding, dangerous Sheikh who could have them all executed with one of those tiny flicks of his finger made her pulse pound.

Anya made a mental note to seek out psychiatric help the moment she returned to American soil.

"We're prepared to take you to the embassy tonight," the ambassador said at the end of the meal. "You must be anxious to leave the palace behind."

His smile was slick and aimed directly at Tarek.

Tarek looked faintly bored, as if these discussions

were beneath him. "Dr. Turner is, of course, welcome to do as she pleases."

Anya thought that what would have pleased Dr. Turner the most would have been to remain full and happy again, without the unmistakable tension that filled the room. Especially because she doubted very much that any of the diplomats particularly cared about her feelings in this. She was a figure. A cause.

She was tired of being something other than a woman.

"I thought I made this clear before dinner," she said, as if she was concerned that the ambassador had gotten the wrong end of the stick when she knew very well he hadn't. "I'm not being *held* here. Not anymore."

Though it took everything she had in her not to look at Tarek when she said that, to see if that was actually true.

"I know it suits you to think of me as your pet barbarian," Tarek said to the ambassador, in a voice of silk and peril. "But I am nothing so interesting as a monster, I am afraid. Some things are regrettable mistakes, nothing more."

"Then there should be no trouble removing Dr. Turner from your custody," Ambassador Pomeroy replied with a toothy smile. "The American people would breathe a little easier, knowing she was safe at last."

"That is entirely up to Dr. Turner," Tarek replied. "As I have said."

Anya thought of her mobile, still on her bed back in her suite. She thought of the life that waited for her, in that phone and back in the States. Of the time she'd spent in Houston. Of her father.

Mostly she thought of Tarek, the heat in his dark gaze, and the question he had yet to ask her.

Because she knew he hadn't forgotten. Neither had she.

She picked up the linen napkin in her lap and dabbed gently at the corner of her mouth. "I would love to put the American people at ease. And I appreciate your assistance, Ambassador." She smiled, as punctuation. Or performance, maybe. It was hard to tell with so much molten heat making her ache. "But I spent eight months locked beneath this palace. I'm going to spend at least one night sleeping like a princess before I go. It's literally the very least this palace can do for me."

There were protestations. Some dire mutterings from the ambassador and far louder commentary from his aides. Still, eventually, they left her to the fate she was almost certain she already regretted choosing.

Yet Anya didn't open up her mouth and change that fate, even though she knew she could. And almost certainly should.

When the palace staff retreated after the Americans had left, she found herself once again alone in a room with this obviously ruthless man who really should not have fascinated her the way he did.

Especially when he took a long, simmering sort of look at her, setting fire to the quiet between them.

"I take it your rooms are to your liking, then," Tarek said, almost idly. "And though I am glad of it, surely you must be in a great hurry to resume your life. To see your family, your friends. To pick up where you left off eight months ago."

Anya felt that knot in her chest tighten a painful inch or two. "The funny thing about spending so long locked away is how little some things seem to matter, in the end. My friends are scattered all over the globe. I miss them, but we're used to not seeing each other. And my life had become nomadic. I haven't truly *lived* in a place since I left my last hospital job in Houston."

He was watching her almost too closely. "And your family?"

"It's only my father and his wife." She could feel herself getting tighter, everywhere, and was horrified at the idea she might collapse into panic here. With him. "We aren't close."

Anya didn't want to talk to him about accommodations or her lonely little life. Not now they were alone. Not now he seemed looser as he sat there. Lazier, almost, though she did not for one second mistake that leashed power in him for anything else. She could feel it as if it was a third presence in the room.

She could feel it inside her, turning her to flame.

Anya frowned at him. "Is that the question you wanted to ask me?"

He laughed at that, as if it was funny, when she felt so sure that it was crucial that he ask her his question. That it was *fate*.

But he was laughing. And Anya took the opportunity to ask herself what she was doing here. Why wasn't she on her way to the American embassy right now? And if she really wanted to sleep in that glorious bed—which she truly did, after a prison cot—why wasn't she up in that suite right now, continuing to pamper herself?

Why was she sitting here next to Tarek, imprisoning herself by choice, as if he was cupping her between his palms?

Worse still, she had the distinct sensation that he knew it.

"It is more a proposition than a question," he told her.

And Anya did not need to let that word kick around

inside her, leaving trails of dangerous sparks behind. But she didn't do a thing to stop it. "Do you often proposition your former captives?"

"Not quite like this, Doctor." He didn't smile then, though she thought his eyes gleamed. And she felt the molten heat of it, the wild flame. She thought she saw stars again, but it was only Tarek, gazing back at her. "I want you to marry me."

CHAPTER FIVE

"*MARRY* YOU?" HIS suspicious doctor echoed.

Notably not in tones of awe and gratitude, which Tarek would have expected as his due from any other woman not currently seeking asylum in the Canadian provinces.

But then, that somehow felt to Tarek like confirmation that this woman was the correct choice for this complicated moment in Alzalam's history. And for him, because she was…different. A challenge, when women had always been an afterthought at best for him.

"It is an easy solution to a thorny problem." He watched, fascinated, as a hint of color asserted itself on her fine cheeks. "I assume you acquainted yourself with the media coverage of your case before dinner."

Her color deepened. "I did not."

He lifted his brows. "Did you not? I find that surprising."

She moved her shoulders, but it was less a straightening, or even a shrug. It was more…discomfort, he thought. And he found he liked the idea that she was not immune to him, to this. That he was not the only one wrestling with entirely too much sensation.

"I haven't had access to the internet for a long time," she said after a moment. "It seemed almost too much, really. I'm sure that will pass and I'll find myself addicted to scrolling aimlessly again. Isn't everyone?"

Tarek did not allow himself the weakness of addiction. But he did not say this here, now. He liked, perhaps too much, that she had not raced off to look herself up. That the stories others told about her—and about him— had not been her first priority.

That she was in no hurry to resume her old life could only support his proposition, surely.

He should not have let that notion work in him like heat. "I assume your ambassador and his men shared with you that you have become something of a cause célèbre."

Anya didn't meet his gaze. And though he hadn't known her long at all, it was clear that looking away was not usual for this woman. She was all about her directness. She was forthright and pointed. A scalpel, not a soft veil.

That, too, was its own heat inside him.

"I don't exactly know how to process the notion that anyone knows who I am," she said after a moment. "I know some people enjoy being talked about like that, but I'm not one of them."

"Allow me to recap," Tarek offered, sitting back in his chair so he would not indulge himself and touch her. Though he marveled at how much he wished to do so. "Because I did spend the evening catching up on the sad tale of the American doctor we so cruelly imprisoned here while handling a small, inconsequential revolution. After she illegally crossed our border."

Her gaze snapped to his then, and Tarek wondered why it was he preferred her temper when he would not have tolerated it from anyone else.

"Careful," she said softly. "The mocking tone doesn't help your case."

"Forgive me. It is only that looking at you, it is hard to imagine that you suffered at all." She looked too ripe. She glowed. She was… *You must remain calm*, he ordered himself, when he could not recall the last time he was not calm. Supernaturally calm, his brother had once claimed. It was only now that Tarek understood that had been a warning he should have heeded. "I know, of course, that is not the case."

"You're always welcome to lock yourself away for eight months and see how you enjoy the experience." Her smile was sharp. "I wonder how you'd look at the end of it."

He felt his lips curve despite himself. "Touché. Consider me adequately chastened."

Her smiled lost its sharpness. "You were telling me my story."

"Indeed. The fact is, while there was certainly interest in all the doctors disappearing that night, when the male doctors were returned but you were not, it created…consternation."

She looked amused. "Consternation?"

"Concern," he amended. "The news reports have been increasingly more frantic as time has gone on."

"I'm surprised the ambassador didn't insist upon seeing me sooner, then." Her gaze darkened. "Or at all."

"There is no possibility that the ambassador could have visited you before now," Tarek assured her, not pleased with that sudden darkness. Not pleased at all. "At the best of times, the palace does not comment on internal matters and therefore, never confirmed nor denied that you were held here. And during the troubles, the palace was locked down completely. There was no access. Regrettably, what that meant was that as far as the world knew, you went into the same prison as your colleagues, then disappeared."

She toyed with the gleaming edge of her scarf. "That does sound dramatic."

"Had I been less preoccupied with putting down a coup and suffering through the very public trial of my own brother for high treason, I would have paid more attention to international headlines myself."

"I am moved, truly, by this non-apology."

Again, he found himself moved to smile when surely he should rage. "Alas, my focus was on putting my kingdom back together. That brings us to today and your immediate release once I learned of your incarceration."

"And your solution to this tale of the world's cruel mischaracterization of your perseverance is…marriage?" Anya laughed, and even though Tarek knew the laugh was directed at him, he found himself…entertained. Or not furious, anyway, which amounted to the same thing. "Maybe you can explain to me why the King of Alzalam, who surely could marry anyone, would want to marry a woman he quite literally lifted out of a cell."

"It is practical," he told her, though the heat in him was surely nothing of the kind. "You could not have suffered any great abuses here, could you, if you end up marrying me. Your experience will be seen as romantic."

"A romantic imprisonment." Her tone was dubious. "I don't think that's a thing."

Tarek only smiled. "Is it not?"

She flushed again, and he felt that too distinctly. Like her hands on him.

He took pity on her. "Western audiences live for romantic love. They insert it into the most unlikely scenarios. You must know this is so. How many stalkers do you suppose are heralded as romantic heroes? I can think of dozens and I am no particular aficionado of your Western stories, no matter the media."

"I think you underestimate the difference between fiction and reality," she replied, no longer looking or sounding the least bit flustered. "And hard as it might be for you to imagine, the average Western woman is perfectly capable of judging the difference between the two."

"But is the average Western journalist capable of the same?" Tarek shrugged. "I do not think so."

Anya nodded slowly, as if taking it all on board. "This is all a bit out of left field, but I understand where you're coming from. It even makes a kind of sense. But what can you imagine is in it for me?"

The answer should have been self-evident, but Tarek could not allow himself to dwell on the day's indignities. "That is where it comes in handy that I am the King."

"I see that more as a detracting factor, to be honest, given my people gave up on kings in the seventeen hundreds."

"Ah, yes, the lure of independence. So attractive." He waved a hand. "But this is not practical, Anya. You can find independence anywhere. Meanwhile, I am a very powerful, very wealthy man. A sheikh and a king who can, if I desire, make my wishes into law. Tell me what you want and I will make it so. Anything at all."

"For all you know I'm going to ask for a spaceship."

"Then one shall be built for you." He bit back his smile. "Is that what you want? I assumed it would be more along the lines of wishing to practice medicine here in the capital city, even once you become Queen."

But to his surprise, she paled at that.

He didn't know quite how to feel about it when she blew out a breath, then met his gaze once more as if she hadn't had that extreme reaction. "You say that as if a female doctor is as fantastical as a spaceship."

But Tarek found he liked her spiky voice better than watching her pale before him.

"Alzalam is not in the Stone Age, Doctor," he murmured. "No matter what foreign publications may imagine. We have a great many female doctors. But what we do not have, and never have had, are queens who work. Perhaps that is an oversight."

Anya huffed out another breath, as if she couldn't comprehend that. "I have to tell you, of all the endings I imagined to my time in prison, talk of queens did not enter into it."

She was too pretty, he thought. And getting more so by the moment, to his mind. Because he liked her bold. He liked how little she seemed in awe of him. He could not deny that he also liked the hint of vulnerability he saw now.

Did he want to give her a throne or did he simply want to take her to bed?

Tarek found he couldn't answer the question. Normally, that would have been all the convincing he needed that he was headed down the wrong path. He had never let a woman turn his head and he would have sworn on Alzalam itself that he never would.

But then, when it came to his doctor, there were practical considerations that outweighed everything else. Trade implications, for example, and potential sanctions.

He could weather those, as his ancestors had upon occasion, but if there was no need to put himself in bed with only those economies who did not fear the taint of a regime considered monstrous, why would he condemn his country to such a struggle?

That he found himself longing to taste her was a problem when his country was at stake. Tarek tried to focus. "You have yet to tell me what it is you want most, Anya."

Had he said her name aloud before? He couldn't recall it. But it sizzled there, on his tongue. It felt far more intimate than it should. And in case he was tempted to imagine that it was only he who felt these things, he saw her eyes widen—her pupils dilating—as she sat there within reach.

But he did not use his hands. Not yet.

"I'm going to tell you something I've never told anyone before," Anya said, her voice softer than he had ever heard it. She leaned forward, the flowing scarf she wore making even the way she breathed look like a dance. She propped her elbows on the table and smiled at him over the top of the fingers she linked together. "I don't know why. Maybe it's because you're a stranger. A stranger who asked me to marry him after locking me up. If I can't tell you my secrets, who can I tell?"

"Tell me your secrets, Anya," he found himself saying, when he shouldn't. When he ought to have known better. "And I will show you my scars."

He was fascinated by watching her *think*. He watched her blink, then her head tilted slightly to one side as her gaze moved all over him. "Are your scars secret?"

"Naturally." Tarek kept his tone careless when he felt anything but. "Who wishes to see that their King is little more than a mortal man, frail and easily wounded?"

It seemed to take her longer than usual to swallow. "But surely the point of a king is that he is a man first."

"A king is only a man when he fails," Tarek bit out. He gazed at her until he saw, once more, that telltale heat stain her cheeks. "But first you must tell me your secrets. That is the bargain."

"My father is a doctor," she said, and he had the notion the words tumbled from her, as if she'd loosed a dam of some kind and could no more control them than if they'd been a rush of water. "Not only a doctor, mind you. He's one of the foremost neurosurgeons in the country. Possibly the world. He would tell you that he is *the* foremost neurosurgeon, full stop. Even now, years past what others consider their prime, his hands are like steel. He's deeply proud of that."

"Is this secret you plan to tell me actually his secret? I will confess I find myself less interested in the deep, dark secrets of a man I have never met."

Anya sighed. "Surgeons are a very particular type of doctor. A very particular type of person, really. They don't think that they're God. They know it."

"My father was a king, Anya. I am familiar with the type."

Her smile flashed, an unexpected gift. "And look at you, not only happy to be your father's heir but apparently prepared to fight off a revolution so you can assume your throne after him, as planned."

It was tempting to thunder at her about duty and blood, but Tarek did not. He thought instead of what it was she was implying with her words. None of it having to do with him.

He chose to simply sit and watch her. To wait.

"There was never any question that I would become a

doctor as well," Anya said, her voice something like careful. "To be honest, I don't know if I would have been permitted to imagine a different path for myself. My mother died when I was small and I wish I could remember what my father was like with her, but I don't. After she was gone I had a succession of stepmothers, each younger and more beautiful than the last. My father liked to praise their beauty while making a point of letting me know that the only thing he was interested in from me was my intellect. It never occurred to me to rebel. Or even to question. It was what he wanted that mattered. But then, for a long time, I wanted it as well. I wanted to show him that I could be smart like him, not merely a pretty plaything, easily ignored, like the stepmothers he replaced so easily. I wanted to make certain I was *special*."

Tarek waited still, his gaze on her and the storm in her eyes.

"But when it came time to pick my specialty in medical school," she said quietly, "I failed him."

"I do not understand." Tarek lifted a brow. "You are a doctor, are you not?"

"My father likes to refer to emergency medicine as fast food," Anya said. She shook her head. "Where's the art? Where's the glory? It's all triage, addicts, and Band-Aids slapped over broken limbs while bureaucrats count beds. That's a quote."

"But you knew his opinion and you did it anyway."

Anya smiled again, though it was a sad curve that didn't quite reach her eyes. "That was my form of rebellion. My father accused me of being afraid of the responsibility a surgeon must assume. He's not wrong."

Tarek was baffled. "Surely handling emergencies requires you to save lives. Potentially more lives than a brain surgeon, if we are to count volume alone."

"Sometimes he would sneer that it was ego. Mine. That I was afraid to enter into the same arena as him because he was so clearly superior to me. And that might have had something to do with my choices, I can't deny it. But mostly, I didn't want to compete with him." She took a breath. "It took a long while for me to recognize that it wasn't that I didn't want to be a surgeon. It's that really, I never wanted to be a doctor."

Tarek noticed her fingers were trembling, as if she'd just confessed to treason. He supposed, by her metric, she had.

"I couldn't tell him this," she continued, her voice shaking along with her fingers. "I couldn't tell anybody this. After all those years of study. All that work. All that knowledge stuck in my head forever. People are *called* to be doctors—isn't that what everyone wants to believe? You're supposed to want to help others, always. Even if it means sacrificing yourself." She paused to take another shaky breath. "My father is unpleasant in a great many ways, but day in and day out, he saves lives no one else can. How could I tell him that having already failed to live up to his example, I was actually, deep down, not even a shell of a decent person because I didn't want to anymore?"

Tarek waited, but he no longer felt the least bit lazy. Or even indulgent. He was coiled too tight, because he could see the turmoil in Anya's gaze. All over her face. And she was gripping her hands together, so tight that he could see her knuckles turn white.

"I couldn't tell him any of that," she said, answering herself. "I simply quit. I walked out of my job and refused to go back. I signed up for the charity the next day, ensuring that I couldn't have gone back even if I'd wanted to. And I don't know why I didn't tell him everything then, because believe me, Dr. Preston Turner was not on board with me heading off to what he called *sleep-away camp for doctors*."

"I am fascinated by this man," Tarek drawled, sounding dangerous to his own ears. "It's not as if you joined the circus, is it?"

"He knew that I was putting myself at risk," Anya said softly. "He thought I was doing it because I was too foolish to see the potential consequences of my decision. By which he didn't mean an eight-month stint in a dungeon. He assumed I would get killed."

Tarek thought of his own father, and the expectations he had placed on his heir. "He does not have much faith in you."

Anya smiled again, edgily. "The responsibility of bearing his name comes with a requirement to help others. And surely the best way to do that is in controlled circumstances, like a surgical theater. Emergency rooms can be rowdy enough. But to risk myself in the middle of other people's wars? He disdained these choices."

"Surely the risk makes the help you give that much more critical."

"I would love to sit here, agree with you, and puff myself up with self-righteousness." Anya's gaze was direct again, then. And this time it made his chest feel tight. "But it wasn't as if I felt some glorious calling to immerse myself in dangerous places, all to help people who needed it. I know the difference, because every single one of my colleagues felt that call. But not me."

"Then why?" Tarek asked, though he had the distinct impression he did not wish to know the answer. The twist of her lips told him so. "Why did you do it?"

Anya let out a faint sort of laugh, and looked away. She loosened her grip on her own fingers. "You have no idea what it's like. The pressure. The endless stress. The expectation that no matter what's happening in your own life, or to you physically, you will always operate with the total recall of everything you learned in medical school, be able to apply it, and never make a mistake. It's a high-wire act and there is no soft landing. It's day in, day out, brutal and grueling and all-consuming. And that's just the emergency room."

"As it happens," Tarek said quietly, "I might have some idea."

Her gaze slid back to him. "All that gets worse in a war zone. You have to do all of the same things faster and more accurately, with or without any support staff. All while knowing that any moment you could be caught up in the crossfire."

"You say you were not called to do these things, but you did them," Tarek pointed out. "Maybe the call you were looking for does not feel the way you imagine it will."

He knew that well enough. Because it was one thing to spend a life preparing for duty, honoring the call from his own blood and history. And it was something else to stand beside the body of a man who had been both his King and his father, and know that no matter how he might wish to grieve, he had instead to step into his new role. At once.

Then to do it.

Even in the face of his own brother's betrayal.

"I didn't have a death wish, necessarily," Anya told him, as if she was confessing her sins to him. "But I took risks the others didn't because deep down? I wanted something to happen to me."

He felt everything in him sharpen. "You mean you wished to be hurt?"

"Just enough." She looked haunted, hectic. He could see how she was breathing, hard and deep, making her whole chest heave. "Just so I wouldn't have to do it anymore."

"Courage is not the absence of fear, Anya," Tarek said, his gaze on hers, something hot and hard inside his chest. "It is not somehow rising above self-pity, wild imaginings, or bitter fantasies that you might be struck down into oblivion so you need not handle what is before you. I'm afraid courage is simply doing what you must, no matter how you happen to feel about it."

She sat back in her chair, her eyes much too bright. "Thank you," she whispered. "But I know exactly how much of a coward I am. Because I also know that there was a part of me that actually enjoyed eight months of rest. When no one could possibly expect me to pick up a stethoscope or try to make them feel better. I got to rest for the first time since I entered a premed program at Cornell."

Tarek was riveted, despite himself. When surely, he ought to wrest control of this conversation. Of her. Instead, his blood was a roar within him. And he could not seem to make himself look away.

"So, yes," Anya said softly. "I will marry you. But I have two conditions."

"Conditions," he repeated, provoked that easily. He

made a show of blinking, as if he had never heard the word. "It is almost as if I am any man at all. Not the King of Alzalam. Upon whom no conditions have ever been applied."

"If you want a press release, there are conditions."

Tarek tamped down the sudden surge of his temper, telling himself that this was good. If she'd leaped into this, heedless and foolish, surely it would have been proof that she would be a terrible queen. He could not have that.

"Very well then," he said, through gritted teeth. "Tell me what it is you want. I promised I would give it to you."

"First," Anya said, searching his face, "promise me that I will never have to be a doctor."

"Done. And the second condition?"

He was fascinated to watch her cheeks heat up again. "Well," she said, her voice stilted. "It's a bit more...indelicate."

"Was there delicacy in these discussions?" His voice was sardonic. "I must have missed it."

"I want a night," she blurted out. "With you. To see whether or not..."

And Tarek did not plan to ever admit, even to himself, what it cost him to simply...wait.

When everything inside him was too hot, too intent. Too hungry.

Anya cleared her throat. "To see whether or not this is real chemistry. Or if it's because you were the first man I interacted with outside that cell. I...need to know the difference."

A good man might have pointed out that it seemed

likely this was all yet another attempt at self-immolation on her part.

But then, Tarek had no problem being her fire.

"Come," he said, reaching out his hand as he had at the mouth of the prison cell, his gaze hot enough to burn. "Let us find out."

CHAPTER SIX

A WISE WOMAN would have questioned her own sanity, Anya thought. Or certainly her motives.

Wise or foolish, Anya hadn't stopped trembling for some time. Deep inside, where every part of her that shook was connected to the heat that seemed to blaze between her and Tarek, and that aching, slick fire between her legs.

She told herself that what mattered was that it all made sense in her own head.

He wanted a queen. A press release and the performance that would go with it.

And she wanted a different life. With the clarity she'd gotten in the dungeon, Anya knew she could never go back. Not to who she'd been, destroying herself with stress, locking herself away when the panic hit, terrified that she was moments away from being found out for the fraud she truly was. She couldn't keep moving from one way of administering medicine to another, until she started hoping that mortar fire might take her out and save her from her inability to walk away from the life she'd spent so long—too long—building.

Maybe if she was the Queen of a faraway country she

could do more good than she'd ever managed as a doctor riddled with her own guilt and shame.

And somehow, all of that seemed tied together with Tarek himself. Not the King, but the man.

Too beautiful. Too intense.

And unless she was mistaken, feeling all the same fire that she was.

Anya didn't want to be mistaken. But she also wanted to feel *alive*.

She didn't need a primer on all the ways it could go badly for her to marry this man on a whim. All the ways it could turn out to be a far worse prison than the one she'd just left.

She wanted one night. One night, just the two of them, to see.

"No kings, no queens," she said, looking up at him as he rose to stand there before her, his hand extended. "Just a woman and a man, until dawn."

"Come," he said again, with all that power and confidence. Heat and promise.

Anya took her time getting to her feet, not sure her legs would hold her up. But they did. And as she had hours ago, she reached over and slid her hand into his.

Once more, the heat punched through her. She pulled in a swift breath, but that only made it worse. His hand was too hard. His grip was too sure.

And the way he watched her, those dark eyes fixed on her, made her quiver.

She expected him to bear her off again, marching her through the palace with the same courtly formality he'd shown earlier.

Instead, Tarek pulled her closer to him.

With an offhanded display of strength that had her

sprawling against the hard wall of his chest, and gasping a bit while she did it.

Because it had been one thing to say she wanted this. And something else to be so close to another person.

To him.

Her pulse skyrocketed as she gazed up at him. If it was possible, Tarek was even more beautiful up close. Even more compelling. He smoothed his hands over her head, sliding that scarf out of his way.

And she watched, transfixed, as he pulled a long, glossy strand of her hair between two fingers. Looking down at it, very seriously, as if it held the mysteries of the universe.

Then he shifted that look to her.

"Tarek—" she began.

His hard mouth curved. "I like my name in your mouth. But I have other priorities."

Then he bent his head and put that stern mouth of his on hers.

Everything inside of Anya, all that fire and need, exploded.

Tarek gripped her head, he angled his jaw, and then he swept her away.

His kiss was a hard claiming. He possessed her, challenged her and dared her. Anya surged forward, pressing her palms harder against the glory that was his hard chest as if she could disappear into all his heat.

And she kissed him back, pouring everything she had into it. Into him.

Again and again.

He made a low, gloriously male sound, then tore his mouth from hers.

"No," Anya breathed, heedless and needy. "Don't stop."

He laughed. Deep, dark, rich. It rolled through her, setting her alight all over again.

Anya felt swollen and desperate straight through, and he was still laughing.

"Order me around, Doctor," he suggested, his voice moving inside her as if it was a part of her. As if it was the sun, even now, in the dark of night. "Tell me what to do and see how that works for you."

But before she could try, mostly to see what he would do, Tarek bent slightly to sweep her into his arms.

Anya knew that none of this made sense. That she should have left with the American ambassador when she'd had the chance. That she certainly shouldn't have exposed herself to this man, telling him secrets she'd never breathed to another living soul.

Yet she had.

What was another vulnerability to add to the list? Maybe she was lucky she hadn't become a psychiatrist. She doubted she would enjoy knowing the inner workings of her own mind. Not when there was a king gazing down at her, his expression stern and possessive, sending a spiral of delight all the way through her.

Maybe, finally, it was time to stop thinking altogether. And to let herself feel instead.

Because she already knew what it was like to sit frozen in the dark. Literally.

Tonight, Anya intended to shine. And live. And feel everything—every last drop of sensation she was capable of feeling. Every touch, every sigh, every searing bit of flame she could hoard and call her own.

It took her a moment to realize that Tarek was moving. His powerful body was all around her, those arms of his holding her aloft as if she weighed little more than a notion. The granite wall of his chest. The tempting hollow at the base of his throat. His scent, a faint hint of smoke and what she assumed gold might smell like, warmed through and made male.

She assumed he would carry her off to his bed, wherever that was in this sprawling place, but instead he headed out through the grand, windowed doors that led outside. Anya caught a glimpse of the lights of the old city, gleaming soft against the desert night. Then he was setting her down, and it took her a moment to get her bearings, to find herself out on one of the palace's many balconies.

This one was made for comfort. He placed her on one of many low, bright couches, ringed all around with torches, and a canopy far above. There was a thick rug tossed across the ground at her feet and lanterns scattered across the table, making her think of long-ago stories she'd read as a child.

Tarek stood before her, gazing down at her as if she was the spoils of the war he'd fought, and he intended to fully immerse himself in the plunder.

Her entire body reacted to that thought as if she'd been doused in kerosene. She was too hot. She had too many clothes on. She was *burning alive*.

Looking at him was like a panic attack, except inside out. Anya's heart pounded. She could feel herself grow far too warm. And she felt a little dizzy, a little unsure.

But what was laced through all of that wasn't fear.

There was only him.

And how deeply, how wantonly and impossibly, she wanted him.

As she watched, Tarek began to remove those robes of his, casting them aside in a flutter of ivory and gold. He kept going until he stood before her, magnificently naked.

And when he made no move toward her, she felt a moment's confusion—

But then, as her gaze moved over his body, roped with muscle and impossibly powerful, she found the red, raised scars. One crossed the flat slab of his left pectoral muscle. Another cut deep across his torso, all along one half of the V that marked where his ridged wonder of an abdomen gave way to all the relentless masculinity beneath. Those were the biggest, most shocking scars—but there were more. Smaller ones, crisscrossing here and there.

Anya realized she was holding her breath.

And she thought he realized it too, because with no more than a simmering look, he turned so she could see the ones on his back.

"Your scars," she whispered.

"They came in the night like the cowards they were," Tarek told her, slowly turning back to face her. "But let me assure you, their wounds were far greater than mine."

"Wounds are wounds," Anya said. And she wondered what lay beneath his. What it must have felt like for him, with his own brother involved in the plot against him. "And the marks we carry on our skin is the least of it, I think."

"Perhaps." He inclined his head in that way of his. So arrogant, every inch of him the absolute ruler he was, that she didn't know whether to scream or launch herself at him. "But what matters is that I won."

Anya had spent hours with this man by now. And had

thought only of herself. Rightly so, maybe, given what had happened to her.

But she thought of his words from earlier. *Tell me your secrets, and I will show you my scars.* She thought of the fact that he hid them in the first place.

That he clearly had no intention of discussing his *feelings*, God forbid.

And it occurred to her, in a flash that felt a lot like need, that though he stood before her, the very picture of male arrogance, what he was showing her was vulnerability.

This was how this man, this King who had fought off his enemies and protected his throne and his people with his own hands, showed anything like vulnerability.

Anya understood, then. If she showed him softness, it would insult him. If she cried for the insult done to his beautiful body, she would do nothing but court his temper.

Tarek was not a soft man. And he did not require her tears.

So she responded the only way she could.

She flowed forward, moving from the edge of the cushion where she sat to her knees before him. She tipped her head back to look up at him, catching the harshness of his gaze. Matching it with her own.

Bracing her hands on either side of his hips, Anya took the hard, proud length of him deep into her mouth.

He tasted like rain. A hint of salt, that driving heat, and beneath it, something fresh and bright and male.

She had never tasted anything so good in her life.

Anya sucked him in as far as she could, then wrapped her hand around the base of him to make up for what she couldn't fit in her mouth.

And then, using her mouth and her hands together and his hard length like steel, she taught herself what it was to live again.

His hands fisted in her hair. Anya thrilled at the twin pulls *this close* to pain that arrowed straight to where she ached the most. Sensations stormed through her as she took him deep, then played with the thick, wide head, using her tongue. And then suction. And anything else that felt good.

He groaned, and that sent bolt after bolt of that wildfire sensation streaking through her body to lodge itself in her soft heat, where it pulsed.

Tarek was muttering, dirty words in several languages, and Anya loved that, too.

She wanted all of him. She wanted, desperately, for him to flood her mouth so she could swallow him whole. So she could take some part of him—of this—inside her and hold on to it, forever.

And this time, she was the one who groaned when he pulled her away from him. It took her a few jagged breaths to recognize that the man who looked down at her then was not the King. Not the indulgent monarch.

He looked like a man.

A man at the end of his rope. And he was somehow more beautiful for that wildness.

Tarek hauled her up to her feet.

"You will be the death of me," he growled at her.

"But a good death," Anya replied, though her mouth felt like his, because he was all she could taste. "Isn't that the point?"

"I have no intention of dying," Tarek told her fiercely. His hands were busy, and she felt too limp, too ravaged by lust and need, to do anything but stand there as he stripped her of her tunic, her trousers, her silky underthings. "Certainly not before I had tasted every inch of you, *habibti*."

And when he bore her down to the soft cushions behind her, they were both gloriously undressed at last.

Anya felt as if she'd been waiting a lifetime for this. For him.

At first it was almost like a fight, as they each wrestled to taste more. To consume each other whole.

She kissed his scars, one after the next, until he flipped her over and set about his own tasting. Each breast. Her nipples. The trail he made himself down the length of her abdomen, until he could take a long, deep drink from between her legs.

But even though she bucked against him, on the edge of shattering, he only laughed. That dark, rich sound that seemed to pulse in her. Then he nipped at the inside of her thigh.

"Not so fast, *habibti*," he said, climbing back up her body. "I wish to watch you come apart. So deep inside you that neither one of us can breathe. So there can be no mistake that no matter what else happens in the course of my reign, no matter what we find in this practical arrangement of ours, we will always have this."

And before she could react to that, he twisted his hips and drove himself, hard and huge, deep inside of her.

Anya simply…snapped.

She arched up, shattering all around him with that single stroke that was almost too much. Almost too deep.

She rocked herself against him, over and over, as the storm of it took her apart, shaking her again and again until she forgot who she was.

And as she came back, she was gradually aware that

Tarek waited, smoke and gold and dark eyes trained on her face, as if he was drinking in every last moment.

He was still so hard. Still so deep inside her she could feel him when she breathed. He braced himself above her, that beautiful predator's gaze trained on her. And the sight of all that barely contained ferocity above her while he was planted within her made the heat inside her flare all over again.

"This is not a hallucination brought on by a prison cell," he told her, his voice no more than a growl.

"No," she agreed, breathlessly. She wrapped her legs around him because she knew, somehow, that she needed to hold on tight. "This is who we are."

And Tarek smiled at her, though it was a fierce thing, all teeth and sensual promise.

Only then did he begin to move.

It was like coming home.

He wasn't gentle. She wasn't sweet. It was a clashing of bodies, pleasure so intense it made her scream.

Tarek pounded into her, his mouth against her neck. They flipped over once and she found herself astride him. She braced herself against his chest as she worked her hips to get *more*, to ride that line between pleasure and pain when it was all part of the same glory.

To make them one, to make them *this*.

Then they flipped again and he was on his knees, lifting her so he could wrap his arms around her hips and let her arch back as she wished. She did, lifting her breasts to his mouth for him to feast upon while he worked her against him, over and over.

Until she couldn't tell if he pounded into her or she surged against him. It was all one.

Finally, Tarek gathered her beneath him again. He

reached down between them while still he surged into her, that same furious pace, and pinched the place where she needed him most.

Hard enough to make her scream.

And while she screamed for him, explode.

Anya sobbed as he kept pounding into her, again and again, aware that she felt like she was flying. Like she was finally free.

She felt him empty himself inside her with a shout as they both catapulted straight into the eye of the storm they'd made.

And shook together, until it was done.

For a long while, Anya knew very little.

Slowly, she became aware of herself again, but barely. And only when Tarek shifted, pulling out of the clutch of her body, but moving only far enough to stretch out beside her. He shifted her to his chest and she breathed there while the night air washed over her body, cooling her down slowly.

Anya thought she really ought to spend some time analyzing what had just happened. If it was possible to analyze…all that. She should consider what to do now. Now that she knew. Now that there was no going back from that knowing.

But that felt far too ambitious.

Instead, she rested her cheek against his chest. She could feel the ridge of his scar and beneath it, the thunder of his heart. It felt a lot like poetry. She watched the torches set at intervals around them dance and flicker. From where they lay, stretched out on the wide sofa, she could see the tallest spires of the city in the distance. Rising up above them as if they were keeping watch while the desert breeze played lazily with the canopy far above.

Anya was wrecked. Undone.

And she had never felt so alive, so fully herself, in all her days.

"Well?" came Tarek's voice, from above and beneath her at once.

He sounded different, she thought, as she shifted so she could look at him. And though he gazed at her with all his usual arrogance, there was an indulgent quirk to his fine, sensual lips.

She hungered for him, all over again, her body heating anew.

It should have scared her, these postprison appetites. But she knew that what charged through her was nothing so simple as fear.

Fear left her sprawled out on bathroom floors, gasping for her breath. It didn't make her feel sunlight in a desert night, or as if she'd discovered wings she'd never known were there. Fear reduced her into nothing but a set of symptoms she couldn't think through. It created nothing, taught her nothing, and never left her anything like sated.

Anya had never considered it before, but fear was simple.

What stormed in her because of Tarek, *with* Tarek, was complicated. Possibly insane, yes. But there were too many layers in it for her to count. Too many contradictions and connections. Scar tissue and the stars above, and that delirious heat, too.

"And if I say that I have never been so disappointed?" she asked, though she couldn't keep herself from smiling.

His smile did not change his face, it made him more of what he was. *Like a hawk*, she thought, as she had from the first. He made her shiver with a single look.

But he also held her there, tight against his body, as if he would never let go.

"Then I will call you a liar," he said, dark and sure. "Which is no way to begin a marriage, I think."

He waited, that fierce gaze of his on her. Stark and certain. And yet Anya knew that all she needed to do was roll away from him. Thank him, perhaps, and he would let her go.

She could be back in the States before she knew it. Back to whatever her life was going to look like, on the other side of this. And by *this* she wasn't sure she meant the dungeon so much as the fact she'd finally admitted all those dark, secret things in her heart. She had finally said them out loud.

How could she go back from that?

"Be my Queen, Anya," Tarek urged her, his voice a dark, royal command. She could feel it in every part of her, particularly when he shifted so he could bend over her once more, bringing his mouth almost close enough to hers. Almost. "Marry me."

He was holding her tight, yet she felt set free.

Whatever else happened, surely that was what mattered.

"I take it you want a real marriage," she said as if the idea was distasteful to her, when it was nothing of the kind. "Not one of those 'for show' ones royals supposedly have. For the people and the press releases and what have you."

And this time, she could feel his smile against her mouth. "I will insist."

"All right then," Anya muttered, trying to sound grumpy when she was smiling too. "I suppose I'll marry you, Tarek."

From captive to Queen, in the course of one evening. It made her dizzy.

Then he did, when he took her mouth in a kiss so possessive she almost thought it might leave a bruise.

Anya wished it would.

And she told herself, as she melted against him all over again, that Tarek might be a king. That the King might have his practical reasons for this most bizarre of marriages. That the man who had fought his own family and wore their marks on his skin might have all kinds of reasons for the things he did, and he might not have told her half of them.

But that she was the one claiming him, even so.

CHAPTER SEVEN

LIFE IN THE DUNGEON was slow. One day crawled by, then the next, on and into eternity, every one of them the same. The world outside the windows turned. Changed. Seasons came and went, but the dungeon stayed the same.

But after Anya agreed to marry Tarek, everything sped up.

"First," said Ahmed, the King's dignified, intimidating aide and personal assistant in one, a few days after she and Tarek had come to terms, "I believe there is the issue of press releases to local and international outlets alike."

"Oh," Anya said after a moment, staring back at the man. "You mean real ones."

"Indeed, madam. They would otherwise be somewhat ineffective, would they not?"

She was seated in the King's vast office, trying to look appropriately queenly. Trying also not to second-guess herself and the choices she'd made. But she'd snuck a look at Tarek then. "We wouldn't want that."

And she'd taken it as a personal victory when the stern, uncompromising King of Alzalam, sitting like a forbidding statue behind his appropriately commanding desk, had visibly bit back a smile.

If Anya was fully honest she didn't really want to face the outside world. Every time she thought of her overly full mobile, she shuddered. But she also knew that as much as she might have liked to do absolutely nothing but lose herself in the passion she had never felt before in her life, that slick and sweet glory only Tarek seemed to provide, that wasn't the bargain they'd made.

She was going to have to face the real world sooner or later, she reasoned. That might as well be under the aegis of the palace, so they could control the message. And help shelter her from the response.

"Timing is an issue," Tarek said after a moment, no trace of laughter in his voice. "We would not wish to suggest that there was any romance conducted while you were more or less in chains."

"A king romancing a captive can really only occur within a certain window," Anya agreed merrily. "Lest we all forget ourselves and start fretting about upsetting power dynamics."

"No one who has met you, Doctor," Tarek murmured then, "would have the slightest doubt where the power lay."

And though Ahmed looked at her as if that was meant to be an insult, Anya knew it wasn't.

Because when they weren't discussing media campaigns, wedding arrangements, or thorny issues of which family members to invite—what with her father being her father, and a number of Tarek's relatives being in jail for attempting to kill him—they were exploring that fire that only seemed to blaze hotter between them.

Tarek, it turned out, hid a sensualist of the highest order beneath his stern exterior.

"You are always hungry," he mused one night as Anya

happily polished off yet another feast. They'd taken to eating in one of the private rooms in her apartments, the two of them sitting cross-legged on the floor where it was far easier to reach for each other when a different sort of hunger took control.

She paused in the act of pressing her linen napkin to her lips, waiting for a comment like that to turn dark. For Tarek to make her feel bad the way her father always had, with snide little remarks like knives.

But instead, he smiled. "I take pleasure in sating each and every one of your hunger pangs."

And he made good on that at once, tugging the napkin from her fingers and laying her out flat before him on the scattered pillows. He drew the hem of the long, lustrous skirt she wore up the length of her legs. Then he lifted her hips and settled his mouth at her core, licking his way into her molten heat.

Only when he had her bucking against him, shattering and sobbing out his name, did Tarek sit back again. Then sedately returned to his dinner, merely lifting an arrogant brow when she cursed him weakly, lying there amongst the pillows in complete disarray.

"I do not wait for my dessert," he told her, as if he was discussing matters of state. "If I wish to indulge myself, I do so immediately."

"As you wish, Your Majesty," she panted.

It took Anya a full week to face up to the reality of what awaited her on her mobile, much less the repeated requests for appointments with the American embassy. Not to mention the press releases—more a press junket, Ahmed informed her solemnly—that she'd promised Tarek.

A week to face her new reality and another week to

decide that she was well enough prepared to handle it. Or if not prepared, not likely to suffer irreparable harm when subjecting herself to reporters and their intrusive questions.

She did the biggest interviews first, sitting in a room of the palace that seemed like an anachronism. It was tucked away next to an ancient courtyard that a small plaque announced had existed in one form or another even before the palace had been fully built. Truly medieval, yet it invited any who entered to breathe deep and forget about the passage of time.

But inside the media room, it was very clear what century Anya was in. It was all monitors and lights, cameras and green screens. The palace's senior press secretary ushered her through the roster of engagements, where all Anya had to do was tell her story.

And more critically, her reasons for remaining in Alzalam now she'd been freed.

"It's hard to imagine what would keep you there," said one anchorwoman. She wrinkled her brow as if in concern—or tried. "Surely most people in your position would try to get home as quickly as possible."

"I don't know that many people in my position," Anya replied. She reminded herself to smile, because if she didn't, people asked why she was *so mad.* "Captured, held, then released into a royal palace. Maybe I think that having spent so much time in the kingdom, it might be nice to explore it a little."

And then, on the heels of a morning filled with interviews from all over the world, she marched herself back to her rooms, dug her phone out of her bag, and forced herself to deal with all of her messages and voice mails.

It took hours. But when she was done, she felt both

more emotional than she'd anticipated, and less panicky. A good number of the voice mail messages were from an array of journalists, some of whom she'd already spoken to. A few friends had called over the past eight months, claiming they only wanted to hear her voice and letting her know they'd been thinking of her during her ordeal. She took a surprising amount of pleasure in discovering that a bulk of her email was, as always, online catalogs she couldn't remember shopping from in the first place.

It made her feel as if, no matter what, life went on.

Better still, Anya felt somewhat better about the fact she still hadn't called her father, because he had neither written nor called her. Not once in all the time she'd been held in the dungeon. And, of course, not before that either, because he hadn't approved of her wasting her time in an aid organization when she could do something of much greater status and import.

Maybe it told her something about herself—or him—that she felt a bit triumphant when she finally dialed the number of the house she'd grown up in. She knew the number by heart, still, even though the house and the number attached to it hadn't been hers in a long while. Since long before she'd left it, in fact.

She stood in her elegant suite, looking out the window as yet another desert sky stretched out before her. Impossibly blue to the horizon and beyond. Looking out at so much sky, so much sand, made her feel as if she was just as expansive. As if, should she gather up enough courage, she might run through these windows, out to her terrace, and launch herself straight into the wind. Then fly.

It made her heart ache in a good way.

Anya had never felt that way in the excruciatingly tidy

Victorian house on a Seattle hill where her father still lived. More care had been put into the gardens than her feelings. She had grown up guilty. Because she barely recalled her own mother. Because she was forever disturbing her father. Because she didn't usually like the women he married and presented to her as so much furniture. Because they mostly didn't care for her, either—and as the window between her age and the current stepmother's age narrowed, she felt even guiltier at how relieved she was to stop pretending.

She had left for college and had never returned for more than a brief visit over the holidays. She would have said that she barely remembered the place that her father's cleaners kept so pristine that it was sometimes hard to believe people actually lived there. Even when she'd been one of them.

But she could see it all too clearly, now.

As if all this time away forced her to look at it face on, at last. Not the house itself, but the fact it had never been a home.

The dungeon beneath this palace, hewn of cold, hard stone, had been cozier. Happier, even. She had catapulted herself out of her father's house as quickly as she could. The urgency to get it behind her—the kind of urgency the anchorwoman thought Anya should feel about Alzalam—had guided her every move after she'd graduated high school. But it wasn't as if she'd ever made herself a home elsewhere.

She'd been moving from place to place ever since, concentrating on school, then her job, then how much she hated her job. She'd never settled anywhere, she'd only endured wherever she'd found herself.

Until the dungeon had settled on her.

First she'd despaired, as anyone would. Then she'd tried to make someone tell her how long she could expect to be left there. But after the despair and the bargaining, there was only time.

When she'd told Tarek that prison had been a kind of holiday, she'd meant it. Now she had the unsettling realization that it had also felt a whole lot more like a home than any other place she'd ever lived. No expectations. No demands.

Just time.

What was Anya supposed to do with that?

"Oh," came the breathy voice of her latest stepmother when she picked up the phone. For a moment, Anya couldn't remember her name. Or more precisely, she remembered a name, but wasn't sure it was the right one. It had been eight months, after all. "Anya. My goodness. You've been all over the news."

Charisma, Anya thought then, recognizing her voice. That was this stepmother's name. It was, of course, a deeply ironic name for a creature with all the natural charisma of a signpost. But Charisma was young. Anya's exact age, if she was remembering right, which said all kinds of things about Dr. Preston Turner that Anya preferred not to think about too closely.

Charisma was not smart, according to Anya's father. He liked to say this in Charisma's hearing, and she always proved his hypothesis to his satisfaction by giggling as if that was an endearment. Charisma was blonde in that silky way that seemed to require endless flipping of the straw-colored mass of it over one shoulder, then the other. Her hobbies involved numerous appointments at beauty salons and sitting by the pool in a microscopic bikini.

Charisma also managed to make it sound as if Anya had gone on the news in a deliberate attempt to provoke her father. As if she was indulging in attention-seeking behavior by telling her story.

Anya didn't have the heart to tell this woman that she'd given up on attempting to get Preston Turner's attention a long time ago. Or that she should do the same.

"I would prefer not to be on the news," Anya said, proud of how steady she kept her voice. With a hint of self-deprecation, even. "But apparently you become a person of interest when you're snatched up in a foreign country, thrown into prison, and then disappear for eight months. I don't see the appeal myself."

Charisma made a breathy, sighing sort of sound. "Your father's at the hospital," she said. "Do you want me to tell him that you called? He's very upset."

"He's been worried about me?" Anya asked, in complete disbelief.

"There have been a lot of questions," Charisma hedged. "And you know how your father is. When he's at the country club he really doesn't like to be approached or recognized. So."

"So," Anya echoed. She did not point out that the entire purpose of her father's snooty country club was to be recognized. What would be the point? "What I think you're telling me, Charisma, is that my imprisonment was an inconvenience."

"It was just all those questions," her stepmother said airily. "He would have appreciated it if you'd given him a little warning, maybe."

Anya's good intentions deserted her. "Funnily enough, they didn't offer me the opportunity to make a lot of phone calls," she said, and her voice was not even.

It was inarguably sharp. "I was thrown in a dungeon. And then kept there, without any contact with the outside world, for the better part of the year."

"Well, I'm not going to tell him *that*." Charisma laughed. "You know how he gets. You can tell him that if you want."

"I'll go ahead and do that," Anya said, already furious at herself for showing emotion. When she knew Charisma would report it back to her father and it would only give him more ammunition to disdain her. "The next time he calls."

Which would be never.

After she ended the call she stayed where she was, standing still in the bright glare of the desert sun, trying to make sense of all the competing feelings that stormed around inside her.

She could feel that sharp pain in her chest, that knotted thing pulling tight again. Anya rubbed at it with the heel of her hand, then wheeled around, heading toward that bright, happy room Tarek had showed her that first day. She liked how dizzy the light made her, still. She liked that if it became too much, she could go out and dunk herself in that infinity pool. It soothed her to float there, folding her arms over the lip of it while she gazed out across the city to the desert, always waiting beyond.

Before now, Anya had always considered herself an ocean sort of person. She'd always love the sea, its immensity and pull. She'd grown up in a city surrounded by water, and had imagined she would always live where she could see it, or access it, because it was what she knew. But she hadn't.

And something about the desert stirred her, deep inside. It was like the ocean inside out. It was a reminder, always, that no matter what was happening to her, something far greater and more powerful than petty human concerns stood just there. Watching. Waiting. And perfectly capable of wiping it all away.

She supposed other people might not find that comforting.

But then, when had Anya ever been like other people? If she was anything like other people, she might have remained a doctor in the emergency room of her busy hospital in Houston, Texas. She might have felt called to medicine like so many of her fellow doctors. Or even called to money and prestige, like her father.

Instead, she found as the days passed that becoming a queen gave her far more opportunities to truly help people. Without having to run triage, check vitals, or desperately operate a crash cart.

Even thinking about those things made her blood pressure rise.

She sat down with her own aides, who showed up one day at Tarek's order. They discussed different sorts of charity work. Initiatives Anya could undertake. Both the traditional province of Alzalam queens, and new ideas about the sorts of things she, as the most untraditional Queen in the kingdom's long history, could attempt.

A month after Tarek had appeared at the door of her cell, they announced their engagement.

But they did it in the traditional Alzalam fashion.

Meaning, the announcement was made and the nation launched itself into a week-long celebration that would culminate in the wedding itself.

"Your people do not waste any time," Anya said, standing out on a balcony Tarek had told her was built for precisely this purpose. The King and his chosen bride together, waving at the cheering crowd gathered below. "What's the rush? Are you afraid the bride will change her mind?"

"Historically yes." He shot her a narrow look, laced with that amusement she had come to crave. Because she knew it was only hers. "Many brides were kidnapped from an enemy tribe, and it was always best not to leave too much time between taking her and claiming her, in case the warriors from her tribe came to collect her."

"Romantic," Anya murmured. "Practically to Western levels, really."

She was rewarded for that with the bark of his laughter.

And she was starting to get used to how deeply she craved such things. His touch. His laughter. *Him.*

Not that she dared say such things to Tarek.

It wouldn't do to throw too much emotion into their very practical arrangement. She knew that. And no matter that she found it harder and harder to pretend her feelings weren't involved.

Anya sobbed out his name regularly, but kept her feelings to herself.

Just as she decided it was best not to tell this man of stone that sometimes, her own panic dropped her to the floor. Because that might not only involve emotions— Tarek's response to such a weakness might spark an attack.

She had spent hours in fittings over the past month, as packs of the kingdom's finest seamstresses descended upon her, determined to make sure that everything she wore—whether traditional or Western, depending on which day of the wedding week it was—reflected the glory of the King.

"And accents your own beauty of course, my lady," the head seamstress had murmured at one point, after there had been quite a lot of carrying on about Tarek and the honor due him from the women assembled in the room.

With more than a few speculative looks thrown her way, not all of them as friendly as they could have been.

But she understood.

"Of course," Anya had replied. "But I must only be an accent. It is the King who must shine."

That had changed the mood in the room. Considerably.

And it was not until later that Anya—who would once have ripped off heads if anyone had suggested she was an *accent* to a man—realized that somehow...she meant that.

The realization hit her like a blow as she stood in her glorious shower, and when her heart kicked in, she froze. She expected the panic to rush at her, to take her to the shower floor. She expected to sit there, naked and wet and miserable, until it finished with her.

But the panic didn't come.

No nausea, no hyperventilating, no worries that she might aspirate her own saliva and choke while unable to help herself.

The hot water rained down upon her. Anya pressed the heel of her hand into that tightness in her solar plexus, hard.

But still, though she could feel that she was *agitated*, there was no panic.

"Because I chose this," she whispered out loud. "I chose him."

It was hardly a thread of sound, her voice. She could barely hear herself over the sound of the water.

But it rang in her, loud and true, and kept ringing long after she left the shower and dried herself off.

The night they announced their engagement, Tarek did not eat dinner with her the way he'd been doing, too caught up was he in matters of state. Anya ate alone, enjoying her solitude now that it was not enforced. She read a book. She caught up with her far-flung friends, many of whom could not make it to this remote kingdom on such short notice, no matter how they wished they could. She let herself...be part of the world again.

After she ate, she sat outside. She found she couldn't get enough of the desert evenings. The sunsets were spectacular, a riot of colors that never failed to make her catch her breath. And even in the dark, she could feel the desert itself, stretching on and on in all directions, almost as if it called to her. She wrapped herself up in a blanket when she grew cold and stayed tucked up under the heaters, watching the magical old city bloom as the lights came on. Her aides had taken her on a guided tour of the narrow streets, the ancient buildings stacked high, and the more she saw of it, the more she loved it.

A mystery around every corner. History in every step. And wherever she turned, the people who smiled at her and called out their support of Tarek. Making her foolish heart swell every time she heard it.

They were not the only ones who adored him.

She didn't think she fell asleep, but one moment she was gazing out at the city and the next, he was there. As if she'd conjured him from the spires and lights that spread out behind him.

Anya smiled, then studied that face of his, sensual and harsh at once. "What's the matter?"

She was learning how to read him now, this man

she would marry in seven days. He was always fierce. He was always, without question, the King. But there were different levels of ferocity in him, and tonight it seemed…darker.

Something inside her curled up tight in a kind of warning. The knot inside her grew three sizes.

But she kept her gaze on Tarek, and ignored them both.

"Nothing is the matter," he told her, standing there at the foot of the chaise where she was curled up. In a voice that was little more than a growl. "Save my own weakness."

"You have a weakness?" Anya asked lightly. "Quick, tell me what it is, so I might exploit it."

Tarek didn't laugh at that. His hard mouth did not betray the faintest curve. Anya ordered herself not to panic, or note that it felt too much like loss.

Or worse, ask herself how she could feel the things she felt after so little time.

"I spent the night in tense negotiations," Tarek said, staring down at her as if he couldn't quite make sense of her. Or as if Anya had *done something* to him. "It is the kind of diplomacy that I abhor. Snide remarks masquerading as communication. All employed by men who would never last a moment on any kind of real battlefield. Still, these things are part of what I am called to do. As such, they deserve my full attention."

"I'm sure you give everything your full attention."

As it happened, Anya had become something like obsessed with the force of Tarek's full attention. With the sorts of things he could do with all that *focus*. Her body shivered into readiness at once, her nipples forming hard peaks, her belly tightening, and the soft, yearning place where she wanted him most like fire.

The ways she hungered for this man never ceased to surprise her. But the way he looked at her now did. As if she'd betrayed him in some way.

"The only thing I could think about was you," he told her, his voice a rough scrape against the dark.

It was not a declaration of feelings. It was an accusation.

An outrage.

For a moment, Anya froze, feeling as if he'd kicked her. That terrible knot grew teeth. But in the next moment, she breathed out. And again, as she had the night he showed her his scars, Anya understood that this was not something she could laugh away. She couldn't show him her first reaction. Once again, it was not softness or emotion he needed.

Maybe, something in her whispered, *all that medical training was not to keep your cool in an emergency room. Maybe it was so you could stare down a king no matter his mood, and be what he needs. Whether or not he knows how to ask for it.*

Not because she was losing herself in him, as one article she'd read about herself tonight had suggested. But because he wasn't simply a man, who a woman might argue with about domestic arrangements or respect or any number of things.

His people needed him to rule above all else. They had told her so themselves, out in the winding streets of this age-old city. And if she wanted to marry him, to be his Queen as well as his woman, she needed to support the King first.

Only once the ruler was handled could she tend to the man.

Because she was the only one who got both.

"You're welcome," Anya said, neither gently nor particularly apologetically.

He blinked at that, a slow show of arrogant disbelief that made her pulse pick up. "I beg your pardon?"

She didn't quite shrug. "Tedious negotiations with terrible people, you say? How lucky you must feel to know that I'll be waiting for you at the end of it." Anya nodded regally toward the foot of her chaise. "And you are even more lucky that I find myself in the mood for a king."

"Are you suggesting that it is possible that you might ever *not* be in the mood for your King?" Tarek was gazing down at her as if thunderstruck. Far better than the look that had been in his eyes before, by any reckoning. "An impossibility, surely. Or treason. You may take your pick."

"I am the Queen of this land," she told him grandly, and only just kept herself from waving an imaginary scepter in the air between them.

Tarek's dark eyes gleamed with the fire she knew best. "Not yet, Anya. Not quite yet."

"I will be the Queen in a week, and you are trying my patience." She sniffed haughtily. "Daring to come before me and speak to me of petty concerns when you could be pleasuring me, even now."

She was sure she could see him waver there. He looked torn between the sort of erotic outrage she was going for or more of whatever temper had brought him here, too much like a storm cloud for her liking.

Anya held her breath. She waited. And she could see

exactly when that hunger that never seemed to wane between them won.

"You may not like the way I worship you, my Queen," Tarek told her then, his voice deep, suggestive, and a kind of dark threat that made her shiver, happily. "But I will."

Then he fell upon her. Both of them ravenous, both of them wild.

And when he held her before him, on her hands and knees so he could take her as he liked, Anya gloried in it, in him. The impossible iron length of him was a wildfire inside her. A gorgeous catastrophe of sensation and need. She was bared entirely to his gaze and to the desert sky, vulnerable and invulnerable at once, while he surged deep inside of her and made her scream.

It was quickly becoming her favorite melody.

A song she wanted to sing out, heedless and loud, for the rest of her days.

But Tarek wasn't done. And as he pounded them both sweet again, until they were *them* again, Anya gave herself over to the only form of wedding vow she thought she'd ever need.

Again and again and again.

CHAPTER EIGHT

THE WEDDING GUESTS began to pour in the day after their announcement.

From near and far they came. Tarek welcomed in men who had fought with him, relatives and business allies, foreign heads of state and an inevitable selection of celebrities. He pretended he did not know which of his guests had spoken against him over the course of the last year and which had given him nothing but their quiet support.

But he knew. And they knew. And there was a power in the invitation to his would-be enemies, to permit them to witness how wrong they'd been about him up close. It was the logical extension of the press junket he and Anya had undertaken and Tarek could not pretend he didn't enjoy it.

There was a grand party that night to kick off the traditional week of celebrations. It was also the first opportunity for Anya to prove to the international crowd that she was not under duress. And for the people of Alzalam, that she was worthy of the role she was to assume at the end of the week.

"No pressure, then," she'd said earlier in the flippant manner only she dared employ in his presence.

Tarek had found he had to have her, in a slick rush of need, even if it meant that her aides would have to reapply all the beauty enhancements—to his mind, wholly unnecessary—that they'd used on her to prepare her for the evening.

"You will be a natural."

"Because you say so?" She had been slumped in a delicious sort of ruin where he'd left her, bonelessly draped over an ottoman in her bedchamber.

"Yes, because I say so," he'd replied. "Am I not the King?"

Anya had smiled at him, the way he liked best. Dreamy and sweet. Private.

The Anya who appeared in public never looked that soft. That was for him alone.

And as he stood in the middle of the grand party in one of the palace's ballrooms that night, Tarek found himself thinking about that smile more than he should.

Just as he thought about her more than he should, when he knew better.

Because while it turned out that the former prisoner he was marrying for purely practical reasons was remarkably good at distracting him from the things he brooded about, that didn't change the truth of them.

Like the fact he was obsessed with this woman.

Tarek knew better than that. The history of his kingdom was filled with examples of why romantic obsession was a scourge. Nothing but a curse. Many of his ancestors had been endlessly derailed by theatrics in the harem. Favorite wives seemed to lead inevitably to catastrophes—witness his former betrothed and the shame she had brought to her family. Tarek had always vowed he would never succumb to such pettiness.

He had already paid dearly for the affection he'd held for his younger brother. He could not afford a far worse blindness. He would never forgive himself.

"*Imagine my surprise*," Anya had said at dinner one day after she'd finally got a comprehensive tour of the Royal Palace. "*I thought the dungeon was the scariest place in this building. But you actually have a harem.*"

Tarek had been feeling expansive and relaxed. He had eaten, then spread his woman out on the table. He had eaten his dessert from her skin—sweets from the sweet—before burying himself inside her to the hilt. Then they'd gone out to the tiled tub on her balcony and sunk into the hot water. He had smiled at Anya's wide eyes and scandalized tone.

"*I was raised in the harem*," he told her. "*My mother was only the first of my father's many wives.*"

And he was not a nice man, and nothing like a good one, because he had greatly enjoyed Anya's look of horror.

"*The only words we've discussed were wife and queen*," she'd said then. Her shoulders had straightened with a sharp jerk, enough to make the water slosh around them. "*Wife was never plural. And neither was queen.*"

"*I enjoyed my childhood*," Tarek had told her, reaching over to pull her to him, settling her before him, her back to his front. "*My brother and I were doted upon and when our half siblings arrived, they were, too. We all grew up together. We had maternal attention from all sides, and therefore felt that any attention we received from our father was a gift.*"

He had not wanted to think about those years. When he and Rafiq had been so close. When it would have seemed laughable to him that anything could ever change that.

Even now, he sometimes forgot what had happened and thought to call his brother. Only to remember it all over again, with a sickening sort of lurch.

Anya's shoulders were no longer braced for an attack. She'd softened against him, and he liked that better.

"It's so hard to imagine that he could grow up and... do what he did," she said quietly.

Tarek tensed, and hated that she could feel it. *"When it comes to my brother, I do not imagine anything but his prison sentence."*

And his voice was so forbidding he could actually watch her respond to it. Her shoulders had risen all over again. Her breath went shallow.

He told himself he did not, could not mind it. His brother had no place here. Childhood memories were one thing, but he would have no...*imagining.*

"I think you would love the harem," he had continued after a moment. He'd tried to sound relaxed again, looking over her head toward the city before them. The sky above, the lights below. And Anya between. It made something in him...settle. *"It would certainly be one way to make friends in the kingdom."*

He'd wondered if she would nurse her upset. If she would act as if he'd bruised her—

But this was Anya.

All she did was twist around to glare at him as if his brother had never been mentioned.

"That, right there, is why I have no intention of filling my harem with all the wives I can support, though I certainly could. It is not worth all the fighting. The jealousy, the petty attacks, the attempts at power grabs."

He'd shaken his head, thinking of those years. Thinking of his father's wives, not Rafiq. "*My father always acted as if he was unaware of such things, but I've never seen greater personal viciousness than I did then. It was never directed at me, but that didn't mean I didn't see it.*"

"*Thank you for this lesson on the historical use of harems here,*" Anya had said darkly. "*I have no desire to be in one, thank you. I would rather become a neurosurgeon.*"

"*The same accuracy and skill is needed to rise to power within one, I assure you.*" He'd laughed. It had been a shade more hollow a laugh than it might have been otherwise, but it had still been a laugh. "*I might assemble one for the sheer pleasure of forcing your hand. I suspect you would rule with an iron fist.*"

She had sniffed. She had not mentioned his brother again. "*You can try.*"

Tarek had a different way of trying. He'd pulled her astride him, pushing his way inside her again. Then he'd watched as she wriggled to accommodate him. It was his favorite show and no matter how many times he watched, it never grew old. Her indrawn breath, especially when she was already faintly swollen from before. The way she bit down on her lower lip. Her marvelous hips and how they moved against his as she adjusted to his length, his girth. The way she rocked slightly until it felt good.

And all the while she softened around him, drenching him with her fire.

Until there were no memories left to haunt him.

Until there was only Anya.

There was no way around it, he thought now, only

half attending to the deeply boring world leaders standing around him. He was obsessed.

And he couldn't be any such thing. He was the King.

The country was the only obsession he allowed himself. The only memories he permitted. How else could he have fought off Rafiq? How else would he rule?

Against his will, he found Anya in the crowd. He didn't know what he wanted. To assure himself he was not obsessed or to feed that obsession? But whatever dark thoughts he might have had in either direction, when he located her he was instantly struck by the way she was holding herself.

Anya was wearing a glorious gown in a Western style for this first celebration of the week. It was a sweeping number that left her collarbone bare, a perfect place for the jewels he'd placed there himself when he'd finished wringing them both dry earlier. The rest of the dress was a glorious fall to the floor in a deep aubergine shade that made her glow. Her glossy hair was swept up so the whole world might see the elegance of her neck, the delicate sweep of her jaw, and all of that was nothing next to the sophistication she seemed to carry in her bones.

She looked like a queen. His Queen.

But she was staring at the woman before her in a manner Tarek recognized all too well. Her shoulders were tight and her chin was tilted up at a belligerent angle that Tarek knew was a tell. It was outward evidence of her ferocity.

It should not have been happening at a party in her honor.

And certainly not in the presence of so many cameras. Though that particular consideration was an afterthought—another indication that Tarek was not in his right mind where this woman was concerned. Surely, with the international press present at this party, his only thoughts should have been on their joint performance instead of her feelings.

You are a king, he reminded himself icily. *Perhaps act like one.*

He excused himself and crossed to her, moving swiftly through the great hall. The crowd of guests parted before him as he moved, and he did not waste his time nodding greetings or allowing anyone to catch his eye. He bore down upon his betrothed.

And Anya alone did not instinctively move out of his way. She stayed where she was, only glancing his way— with a frown—when he appeared beside her.

"I do not care for the look on your face, *habibti*," Tarek told her. In his language, because the froth of a blonde woman before her and the older man beside her who looked as if he smelled something rank were clearly American.

Anya's gaze softened. Her frown smoothed out, and Tarek thought he saw something like relief there. He took his time shifting to gaze directly at the people who dared upset her. Here in the royal palace, right beneath his nose.

"Your Excellency," Anya murmured in formal greeting. She smiled at the couple. "Dad, Charisma, I would like to introduce you to Tarek bin Alzalam, the King of this country and my fiancé." Then she looked at him again. "Tarek, this is my father, Dr. Preston Turner, and his wife, Charisma Turner."

"Ah, yes." Tarek neither smiled nor offered his hand, as was his right as sovereign. That it also made the man before him *tut* in outrage was merely a bonus. "The doctor, yes?"

It was possible he made *doctor* sound a great deal like *snake*.

But then, Anya's father did not look sufficiently honored to find himself in the presence of a king. Nor particularly pleased to reunite with his only child after such a long separation—that had included said child's incarceration. Tarek did not expect or want an emotional display, certainly, but surely there should have been something other than the haughty expression on the older man's face.

"I was telling my daughter that I was forced to reschedule several surgeries," the man said, as if relaying an outrage. "In order to fly across the world at a moment's notice."

Then he waited, as if he expected Tarek to react to that.

And Tarek did. He gazed down at the man the way he imagined he might look at an insect, should it dare to begin buzzing at him. Right before he squashed it.

Beside him, Anya made a soft sound that he thought was a suppressed laugh.

"My father is referring to his schedule at the hospital," she said quickly. "He is…distressed that he had to alter it to come here for these celebrations. I explained to him that he could have come in later in the week, of course."

"You may not care what people think of you, Anya," her father said, making no apparent attempt to curtail the snide lash in his words. "But I'm afraid I do. However inconvenient it might be, I can hardly pretend this hasty wedding isn't happening. It's been all over the news."

"Your daughter is my choice of bride," Tarek said,

without comprehension. "She is about to become the Queen of Alzalam, the toast of the kingdom. Yet you speak of your convenience?"

The man bristled in obvious affront. Tarek did not reply in kind, an example of his benevolence he suspected was lost on this small and unpleasant man.

"Rescheduling is such a nightmare," the blonde on his arm breathed, her eyes on her husband.

"Excuse us." Tarek's tone was dark as he took Anya's arm. "Let us leave you to contemplate your calendar. We will continue with the celebration."

He steered Anya away from her scowling father, doing his best not to scowl himself, as that would only cause general agitation in the crowds all around.

"I cannot comprehend the fact I found you discussing your father's *inconvenience*," he said in a low voice. "As if he was not standing in the ancient palace of Alzalam's kings, in the presence of a daughter who will become Queen. He should have been stretched out at your feet, begging your favor."

And would have been even a generation ago, but the wider world tended to frown upon such things in these supposedly enlightened times.

Anya looked philosophical. Was Tarek the only one who could see the hurt beneath? And because he could see it, he could see nothing else.

"I suppose I should be grateful that no matter what he's doing, no matter where he finds himself or who he speaks to, my father is always…exactly the same," she said.

Tarek found himself even less philosophical as the night—and the week—wore on.

The kingdom overflowed with wedding guests and

those who merely wished to use their King's wedding as an opportunity to celebrate, now that the troubles of the past year were well and truly over. There were celebrations in and out of the palace, all over the capital city and in the farthest villages alike, as the people celebrated not just Tarek and the bride he was taking, but this new era of the kingdom.

Tarek was deeply conscious of this. He had promised them a new world, a bright future, and this was the first happy bit of proof that he planned to deliver. And in a far different way than any of his ancestors would have. His brother was in jail, the insurgents had been fought back, and Tarek had no fear of the world's condemnation or attention—or he would not have been marrying this woman.

Now was a time for hope. His new Queen was the beacon of that hope.

Love grows in the most unlikely of places… the more easily swayed papers sighed, from London to Sydney and back again.

From Convict to Queen! shouted the more salacious.

But either way, choosing this thoroughly American career woman—all previously considered epithets to his people—was having precisely the effect on Alzalam's image that Tarek had hoped it would. She was a success and their supposed love story even more so. All was going to plan, save his unfortunate obsession with the woman in question that he would far rather have coldly used as a pawn.

Yet no matter where he found himself in these endless parties, dinners, and the more traditional rituals prized by his people, and no matter the current state of his insatiable hunger for Anya herself, Tarek couldn't keep himself from noticing that Anya's father behaved more as if he was being tortured than welcomed into the royal, ruling family of an ancient kingdom.

"I told you," Anya said one night, looping her arms around his neck as he carried her from her terrace into her bedroom. He had not yet moved her things into the King's suite, in a gesture toward tradition—even if he did not intend to install her in the usual harem quarters. He wanted her much closer. "My father believes there is no greater more noble calling than his. What are kings and queens next to *the foremost neurosurgeon in all the land.*"

Tarek threw her on her bed and followed her down. "He acts as if it is an insult that he is here at all."

Anya had sighed as if it didn't matter to her, yet Tarek was sure he'd seen a shadow move over her face. He hated it. "He has always been easily insulted. The real truth, I think, is that he's used to being the center of attention. That's really all there is to it."

"At his own daughter's wedding?"

"In fairness, if I was marrying almost anyone else he really would be the center of attention. Because the father of the bride commands a different part of the wedding where we come from. At the very least he would have stacked the guest list with his friends and associates, all of whom would be far more impressed with him than a collection of royals."

"Anya," Tarek had said, not exactly softly. "Why do you feel the need to treat this man with fairness when he feels no compunction to extend the same to you?"

She had looked stricken, then kissed him instead of answering.

Tarek understood that was an answer all its own.

Today there had been a gathering earlier for a wide swathe of guests, but the night featured a dinner for family only. Given the size of Tarek's immediate family, this meant a formal meal in one of the larger dining rooms, with all of Tarek's half siblings, their mothers, and their spouses invited to make merry. Compared to the other celebrations that had occurred this week, it was an intimate gathering. Tarek should have enjoyed introducing his bride to all his sisters and brothers—save the one, who no one dared mention.

But it was Anya's father who once again had Tarek's attention.

"It is a delight to welcome your daughter to the family," said Tarek's oldest half sister, Nur, smiling at the sour-faced doctor. Tarek wasn't surprised that his sister admired his choice of bride. Nur had not taken the princess route as many of their other half sisters had. She had a postdoctoral degree at Cambridge, she had married a highly ranked Alzalamian aristocrat who also happened to be a scientist, and she had never been remotely interested in or impressed by poor Nabeeha, at large in Canada. "A real doctor in the palace at last. I fear I am merely a doctor of philosophy, myself."

Anya smiled. "You're very kind."

Beside her, her father snorted.

That was objectionable enough. But Tarek found himself watching Anya. At the way she lowered her gaze and threaded her fingers together in her lap, as if she was trying to calm herself down. Or as if her father had not merely made himself look foolish, but had hurt her in some way.

Unacceptable, Tarek thought.

"I wouldn't call Anya a real doctor," her father said

with a sniff. "There is such a thing as a waste of a medical degree. And for what? To wear pretty dresses and play Cinderella games? What a travesty."

Nur drew back, appalled. Anya's chin was set, her gaze still on her hands in her lap.

Tarek found he'd had enough.

"You forget yourself," he said softly from his place at the head of the table. Though he did not project his voice on the length of it, he knew that the rest of his family heard him.

A stillness fell over the room.

The doctor was staring at Tarek. "I beg your pardon?"

"It is denied," Tarek retorted. He leaned forward in his chair. "I do not know where it is you imagine you are, but let me enlighten you. This is the kingdom of Alzalam. *My* kingdom, which I have bled to defend." There was a chorus of cheers at that, startling the older man. "You are sitting at my table. The woman you insult will be my wife the day after tomorrow. Men have died for lesser insults."

There was more murmuring down the length of the table, rumbles of support from his family.

But Anya's father only blinked at him. "Anya would be the first to tell you that she hasn't quite lived up to expectations. She was raised to make a difference, not to…"

"Not to what?" Tarek asked.

Dangerously.

He shouldn't have been doing this, he knew. Not because there was any weakness in a man defending his woman—quite the opposite. A man who did not happily and thoroughly defend his woman, in Tarek's opinion, was no man at all. But because Anya would likely not thank him for complicating her family affairs.

But it was too late.

"Preston," said the man's wife, fluttering helplessly beside him. "You haven't even touched your food."

"Don't insert yourself into things you don't understand, Charisma," he replied in a cutting tone that made his wife—and daughter—flinch. "The adults are talking."

"Dad," Anya said then, in a fierce undertone. "This is not the time or the place."

"My daughter is a smart girl," the doctor said, glaring at Tarek. "I had high hopes that she might lead with her intellect. Make the right choices. But instead, this spectacle." He shook his head and looked at Anya. Pityingly, Tarek was astonished to note. "I told you what would happen if you joined that traveling aid organization. I even dared to hope that prison might get your head on straight for a change."

Anya shook her head at him. "You say that as if you were actually aware that I was in a dungeon all that time. I was under the impression you were maintaining plausible deniability so as not to make golf at the club too awkward."

"Of course I knew you were in prison, Anya," her father snapped at her. "I can hardly avoid camera crews on my front lawn. What I don't understand is how you could come out of an experience like that and decide to make your life even less intelligible. What do you intend to do? Sit on a throne as you while your days away? Useless in every regard?"

Tarek did not like the way that Anya flushed at that, flashing a look at her stepmother. He remembered what she'd told him. That her stepmothers were allowed to be pretty and useless while she was meant to be smart.

And it was clearly a downgrade to move from one column to the other.

"You will stop speaking, now," he decreed, and though the older man's eyes widened as if he planned to sputter out his indignation, he didn't make a sound. Like the coward he clearly was. "I will not bar you from your daughter's wedding, but one more word and I will have you deported."

Nur, sitting across from the Americans, did not applaud. Neither did her husband. But down the table, their other half siblings were not so circumspect.

"Tarek," Anya murmured. "Please."

Tarek kept his gaze trained on the man before him. The man who'd put shadows on his bride's face on what should have been a joyous occasion. More than once.

This was unforgivable as far as he was concerned.

"You and I know the truth, do we not?" Tarek did not look at Nur when she made a soft sound of agreement. Or at Anya, though he could sense her tension. "Your daughter is smart. Far smarter than you, evidently, which I imagine has scared you from the start. You wanted to control her, but you couldn't. And now look at you. A tiny little rooster of a man, prancing around a palace and acting as if it is his very own barnyard. It is not. I am a king. You are a doctor whose worth lies only in the steadiness of his hands. And your daughter has saved countless lives and will now save more in a different role, because that is real power. Not ego—"

The older man opened his mouth.

Tarek lifted a brow. "I do not make idle threats."

He waited as Anya's father turned an alarming shade of red. Tarek shot a look at Nur, who started up the conversation anew, and then Tarek sat back and stopped paying the older man the attention he did not deserve.

And it was only when the room filled with warmth and laughter again that Anya looked over at him and smiled.

Then mouthed her thanks.

Tarek had received gratitude before in the form of treaties. Surrenders. Invaluable gifts too innumerable to name, many of which were displayed with pride in this very palace.

But Anya's simple *thank you* lodged inside him like a heartbeat.

Until his chest felt filled with it—with her. Until it threatened to take his breath.

Until he wondered what he was going to do with this.

How was he going handle this woman he needed to be his Queen when she made him *feel*?

And not like the King he was—but like the regular man he could not permit himself to become.

Because Tarek knew well the cost of forgetting himself.

Rafiq had been the only person alive Tarek had felt he could truly be himself with. They had been so close. Tarek had depended on him. And Rafiq had used that affection to stab Tarek in the back.

Literally.

"*You cannot permit yourself the failings and petty feelings of common men*," his mother had told him time and time again. "*In a king these are fatal flaws, Tarek. Remember that.*"

He remembered her words too well.

What was he going to *do*?

CHAPTER NINE

THE DAY OF the wedding dawned at last.

Anya had been waiting for the sun to rise for hours, unable to sleep.

She had been ceremoniously escorted to her bedchamber the night before by Tarek's sisters and aunts. It was tradition for the groom's relatives to guard the bride and so they had, though the royal family's version of "guarding" had included more laughter and abundant food. They had told Anya involved tales about Tarek as a child, omitting any mention of his treacherous brother. They had painted her pictures of what he'd been like as an adolescent, too aware of the weight he would one day carry.

All with a kind of easy, warm familiarity that Anya had never experienced before. She hardly knew what to call it.

It wasn't until she'd gone and stretched out in her bed with only the moon for company that she realized it was…family. They were a family. More, they acted the way she had always imagined a family should. Teasing, laughing. Gestures of quiet support when more serious topics were addressed. The very fact they'd all gathered together to celebrate Anya when all they really knew about her was that she was Tarek's choice of bride.

But they loved him, so that was all they needed.

Anya had stared out at the moon and accepted a hard truth. She had long told herself that she didn't need the connections that other people took for granted. She had her chilly father, she'd told people when the subject came up, and that was more than enough family for her, thank you. She had friends, though she didn't see them often enough.

But Tarek's family wasn't the Turner version of family. It was the version she realized now that she'd always imagined in her head—but had assured herself didn't exist.

It left her something like shaken to discover that she was wrong.

More, it made her miss Tarek.

The solid weight of his stare. The sheer perfection of his body and the things he could do with it. The fire that burned so bright between them that she found she didn't want to live without it, not even for a night.

She suspected she knew what words she could use to describe all the things she felt about the man she was marrying, and none of them were *practical*. None of them were appropriate press releases.

But they were right there on her tongue. Dangerously close to spilling out at the slightest provocation.

"Until tomorrow," Tarek had murmured much earlier that night, out in the desert where they had taken part in rituals he told her his people had considered holy since the earth was young.

It had felt more than holy to Anya.

The sand and the sky. The stars.

The two of them in a circle of fire while the elders sang over them.

Anya sighed now, remembering the stark beauty all around them. The press of the songs and chants against her skin, winding all around their clasped hands.

"*If I hadn't ended up in your prison, I never would have known,*" she'd whispered to Tarek. "*How much beauty there is in the world. Particularly here.*"

Particularly you, she'd thought, perilously close to letting those words she shouldn't say spill out to join the rest of the night's magic.

"*Tomorrow, habibti,*" he'd said, his dark eyes gleaming.

Out on her favorite chaise, Anya waited as the sun rose. The city below her shook itself to life in preparation. Songs filled the air, alive with the sweetness of the coming day. She pulled her throw tighter around her, breathing in the desert air mixed with the palace's usual *bakhoor*, a smoky scent that would always be Tarek to her. She sighed as the first tendrils of light and color snuck across the sky while she watched. Yellows and oranges. A glorious purple.

As the sun climbed, the air warmed.

Anya did, too.

And the light danced all over her, reminding her that she was still free. That stone cells were a thing of the past. That what lay before her might not look like anything she'd thought she wanted—or should want—but made her feel, finally, that it might actually be possible to be happy.

A revolution, she thought.

Only then did she get up and head inside to begin the long process of getting ready for her wedding. Her royal wedding that would be broadcast around the world as part of the press release portion of the bargain she'd made with Tarek.

And in Alzalam, wedding preparations were a largely public affair. Her seamstresses swept in and out. All of Tarek's family returned, flooding in as if the dressing of the bride was a party they were throwing—more for themselves than her.

Once Anya was dressed in her finery and several thousand photographs had been taken, men were allowed in as well. Trays of food were brought in while the guests mingled all throughout the sprawling suite. Anya stood in one of the smaller salons, catching glimpses of herself in the enormous mirror propped against the wall while she thanked the guests for coming, one after the next, until it was all little more than a blur.

She looked like something out of a dream she hadn't known she'd had. Her dressmakers had truly outdone themselves, somehow managing to fuse both Tarek's world and hers into the sweep of the long white gown. She looked exactly as she should—like a beacon of a kind of hope.

Like the future she imagined here, bright beyond measure.

And then, perhaps inevitably, her father walked in.

She could tell by the way he marched into the salon, holding his body sharply and crisply, that he was still in high dudgeon from the other night. That he was *deeply offended* hung around him like a cloud, likely discernible even to those who hadn't spent a lifetime parsing his moods. The way he snapped the door shut behind him only underscored it.

That he wanted her to apologize to him—even though he'd had an entire day to get over what had happened at

that dinner, having not been part of yesterday's rituals—
was clear by the imperious way he glared at her as he
stood there, Charisma standing to one side and slightly
behind him, as if he didn't notice his only daughter on
a dais before him.

In a bridal gown, with jewels in her hair.

Tarek's sister Nur had teared up when she'd seen
Anya. "*You look like everything my brother deserves*,"
she'd said.

But her own father looked at her and saw only himself.

Anya kept herself from sighing, barely, because that
wasn't anything new, was it?

"It's so nice of you to come and wish me health and
happiness, Dad," she said, and she imagined she saw
Charisma wince a bit. "Thank you."

Dr. Preston Turner did not wince. He hardly reacted.

"This is a low, even for you," he told her, the force
of his outrage making his voice even crisper and more
precise than usual. "It's not enough that you should hu-
miliate yourself in this way and on such a grand scale
when you are clearly in no fit state to make decisions of
this magnitude. Look at the mess you've already made
of your life. But that you should sit silently by and allow
me to suffer such attacks…"

His voice trailed off. Anya mused, almost idly, that
she had never seen her father at a loss for words in all
her life. Not until now.

Point to Tarek, she couldn't help but think.

Sadly, he recovered. With a furious glare. "I thought
I couldn't be more disappointed in you, Anya. Trust you
to go ahead and prove me wrong yet again."

Anya looked at this man who she had tried and failed

to please for her entire life. This man whose expectations sat so heavily upon her that she had found a dungeon preferable to the weight of them.

She knew she favored her mother in looks, but she had always imagined that there were similarities between her and her father anyway. Not his famous hands, maybe. Not his drive. But certain expressions. The color of their eyes.

But today she looked at him and saw a stranger.

No, she corrected herself. *Not quite a stranger. Something worse than that.*

A father who had made himself a stranger to his only child. By choice.

"Your disappointment has nothing to do with me," she said, with a quiet force she knew her father did not miss. "I can't help you with it or save you from it."

Out of the corner of her eye, she could see her stepmother, fluttering as ever as she murmured something to Preston.

"For God's sake," her father snapped at her. "Just stand still, Charisma."

"She's not your lapdog, Dad." Anya shook her head at him. "I know you like to think she's stupid, but she's not. She knows exactly how to handle you, which is an art I certainly failed to master. You're lucky to have her."

"I'll thank you to keep your opinions about my marriage to yourself," her father barked.

Though next to him, Charisma blinked. Then smiled.

Anya smoothed her hands over the front of her dress, because it made her think of her wedding and the life she would live here, far away from her father's toxic disappointment. "I thought we were commenting on marriages today. Isn't that what you came to do? Tell me your opinions about the man I'm marrying in a few hours? Or did you miss that I'm standing here in a bridal gown?"

"I would advise you not to speak to me in such a disrespectful manner, Anya."

"Or what?" It was a genuine question. "I'm not a small child you can spank. Or one of your surgical residents or nurses you can bully. You're standing in a palace that is to be my home, in a kingdom I am to be Queen of in a few hours. Really, Dad. What do you plan to do to me if I don't obey you?"

"I'm your father," Preston thundered at her.

"And I'm your daughter." Anya felt the swell of something inside her, bigger than a wave. It crashed over her, into her, and she couldn't tell if it was drowning her or drawing her out to sea. But she found she didn't have it in her to care. "I'm your daughter and you treat me a lot worse than a lapdog. I've spent my whole life trying to make you proud of me, but I realize now that it's impossible. No one can make you happy, Dad. No one. You don't have it in you. And that has to do with you, not me. I can't make you a different man. What I can do is stop pretending that I'm someone I'm not when you don't even appreciate the effort."

She had been afraid of saying something like that her whole life. And now she had, and she didn't feel a burst of freedom and joy, the way she'd thought she would. Instead, she found she felt sad. Not for herself, but for him. For the relationship they'd never had.

"I have no idea what you mean," he was raging at her. "You had every opportunity to do the right thing and you squandered it, each and every time. That's on you, Anya."

And Anya was already swimming far from land. This

was already happening. Last night there had been too many stars to count, and here was her father, determined to ruin it.

She lifted her hands, then dropped them. Not a surrender, because it felt too…right.

Too long overdue.

"I don't want to be a doctor," she told him, the words she'd never dared say out loud falling from her lips as if it had always been easy to say them. As if she should have long ago. Because there was no sadness in this. There was only truth. "I never did."

Charisma actually gasped.

"Don't be ridiculous," her father snapped. "You have obviously let this awful place get to you. You need help, Anya. Psychological help. You've always been far too emotional and your ordeal has clearly put you over the edge."

What struck her then wasn't the dismissive tone her father used. Anya was used to that. It wasn't the contemptuous look on his face, because, of course, she was familiar with that, too.

But she wasn't the same woman she'd been the night she'd gotten arrested. Those eight months had changed her.

Yet she still paused for a moment, tried to look inside herself, to see if anything that he said had merit. After all, hadn't she wondered if she was suffering from some kind of psychiatric issue? Hadn't she made little jokes to herself—and her friends once she'd started using her mobile again—about Stockholm syndrome?

No, came a voice from inside her, deep and certain and undeniably her own. *That's your father talking. You know what you feel. You always have.*

"It doesn't matter what I want to do with my life," she said quietly. "In the end, it's really very simple. You either love me, Dad—or you don't."

And then she waited. She didn't look past him to the closed door with the palace staff waiting on the other side. Guests and soon-to-be in-laws celebrating as her own father couldn't. She didn't look at her stepmother, who was still standing at Preston's side. She didn't fidget. She didn't look away.

Anya trained her gaze on her father, direct and open. And watched as something impatient moved over his face. With possibly more than a little distaste, mixed right in.

"My God, Anya," he said. And when he spoke, that distaste was unmistakable. He didn't quite recoil, but managed to give the impression that he might at any moment. "You've become completely unglued." His gaze, so much like her own, sharpened in a way she hoped hers never had. She found she was bracing herself, though she couldn't have said why when she knew him. There was no point bracing for the inevitable, was there? "Unglued, emotional, and pitiful. Just like your mother."

He meant it like a bomb, and it exploded inside her like a blinding flash of light. She stared back at him, seeing nothing but his gaze like a machete, aimed right at her.

Aimed to hurt. To leave wounds.

On some level, Anya was aware that her father, brimming with triumph at the blow he'd landed, had turned and was marching for the door. She met her stepmother's gaze, bright blue and stricken, but all either one of them could do was stare. Then Charisma, too, scurried for the exit.

And once the door was open, the room filled up again. There was laughter again, sunlight and brightness and that glorious sense of expectation and hope that Anya herself had felt so keenly earlier.

She was aware of all of it. She smiled for her photographs. She shook hands, smiled wider, and did her job as the Queen she would shortly become.

Yet all the while, the bomb her father had lobbed at her kept blowing up inside her. Over and over again.

But not, she thought, in the way he'd intended it to.

Because all she could seem to concentrate on were memories of her mother she'd have sworn she didn't have.

She'd been seven when her mother died. Anya wasn't one of those who had memories dating back to the cradle, but she did have memories. That was the point. When all this time she'd convinced herself she didn't.

"*You are brave, Anya,*" her mother had used to whisper to her. She would gather Anya in her lap, tucked away in the corner of the house that was only theirs. Sometimes she would read books. Other times, she would have Anya tell stories about her day. About school, her friends, her teachers. Or perhaps her stuffed animals, if that was a mood Anya was in. "*You are brave and you are fierce. You can do anything you want to do, do you hear me?*"

"*I hear you, Mama,*" Anya would reply.

What she remembered now was that when she'd thought of all the things she could do, it had never been becoming a doctor. She had been far more interested in learning how to fly, with or without wings, much less a plane. And dancing, which she had loved more than anything back then, despite her distinct lack of talent or ability. And the masterpieces she'd created with her crayons, that she'd secretly believed were the sort of thing she ought to do forever, if only as a gift to the world.

Anya remembered walking in the backyard holding tight to her mother's hand, listening intently as Mama had pointed out a bird here, a bug there. She had repeated the names of flowers and plants, all the trees that towered over them, then made up stories to explain the tracks in the dirt.

She remembered her mother's laugh, her joyful smile, and if she focused as hard as she could, she was convinced that she could almost remember the particular smell of her mother's skin, right in the crook of her neck where Anya liked to rest her face when she was sleepy. Or sick.

Or just because.

Once one memory returned to her, all the rest followed suit. She was flooded with them. And it was clear to her, when it was finally time and she was led from her rooms, that somehow, this was her mother's way of being here today.

It was what her private moment with her father should have been, yet wasn't. All these memories dressed up more brightly now, and almost better for having been lost to her for so many years.

Because it felt like her mother was here. Right here. With her she walked through the palace halls, surrounded by Tarek's sisters and aunts. It was as if her mother was holding fast to her hand all over again, her simple presence making Anya feel safe. Happy.

And absolutely certain that there was nothing wrong

with her. No psychological damage from her time in jail. Just hope.

Anya knew, then, that every step she took was right and good, and better still, her mother was beside her for all of it.

She waited outside the great ballroom, open today to the even grander courtyard beyond, and she knew something else, too. As surely and as fully as if the words were printed deep into her own flesh. As if they were scars like Tarek's, angry and red at first, then fading into silver with the passage of time.

But scars all the same.

Because her heart was pounding at her. Her stomach was fluttery. But she knew that none of that was panic.

She thought of her long-lost mother and the things she'd said so long ago. That Anya was brave and fierce, capable of choosing any life she wanted. Anya had believed her.

Anya believed her so hard, so completely, that when she was gone it was as if she'd taken all of that with her.

Without her, Anya had never felt brave. Or anything like fierce. And she hadn't known what she wanted, except her mother back.

But that was never on offer.

And without her mother there, there was nothing to temper her father's coldness. Back then, he'd been a different man. She could remember him, too. Never as warm as her mother had been, but he'd smiled then. He'd laughed. He'd danced with her mother in the backyard on warm summer nights, and held Anya between them, her bare feet on his shoes. In every way that mattered, she'd lost both her parents when her mother died.

Anya almost felt sympathy for him, in retrospect.

But back then, as a little girl awash in grief, all she'd known was that she didn't want to cause her father more pain. She'd wanted him to love her. She'd wanted him to gather her up in his lap, tell her stories, and make her feel better. Dance with her in the yard while the summer night stretched out above them, warm and soft. But he didn't.

He never did.

So she'd made herself cold instead, to please him.

But she was not cold, no matter how hard she tried. And maybe, Anya thought, as she waited for a panic attack to hit her when surely it should—poised to walk down an aisle to marry a king in the full view of the better part of the planet—the panic attacks had been her actual, real feelings trying to get out all along.

The doors opened before her, then. And then it was happening.

She was walking toward Tarek. She could see him there, waiting for her at the end of the aisle, magnificent in every way.

But best of all, looking straight at her. Into her.

As if this thing between them was fate and they'd been meant for each other all along.

When she finally reached him, he took her hands and they began to speak old words. Ancient vows. Sharing who they were and becoming something else.

Husband and wife. King and Queen.

And so much more.

But inside, Anya made a different vow, there before the assembled throng. That she would not be cold another day in her life. That she would never again be buried in stone or locked away behind iron. That she would not allow herself to feel dead while she was alive.

Not with him. Not with this man who had freed her from a cell first, and then from the life she'd never really wanted.

So she married him, and then she lived.

She danced at the reception. She smiled until her cheeks hurt. And when Tarek finally stole her away, bundling her into a helicopter that raced across the desert, suspended between the shifting, undulating sands beneath and the heavens above, she loved him so much that she thought it might burst out of her like a comet. Another bomb, and a better one this time.

Anya didn't know how she kept it inside.

The helicopter dropped them in an oasis straight out of a fairy tale. The water in the many pools was an indigo silk, lapping gently against the sand as the breeze hit it. Palm trees rustled all around, while waterfalls tumbled over rocks like a song.

And a glorious, sprawling tent blazed with welcoming light, beckoning them in.

"Welcome, my Queen," Tarek said when the helicopter rose back into the air and the sound of its rotors faded away. He had led her into the vast living area of the tent, outfitted with a thousand pillows and low tables, like a desert fantasy. Now he smiled down at her. "This is the royal oasis. Some claim the water is sacred. Some believe it heals. We will have to test it, you and I."

Anya was sure that all the things she felt must be emblazoned on her face. But that wasn't enough. Nothing could be *enough*.

She reached up, placed her palms on either side of his beautiful face, and sighed a little as his strong arms came around her. She thought, *this is home*.

She was finally home.

"Tarek," she breathed, with her whole heart. With everything she had and everything she was. With all the bright hope inside her after this magical, beautiful day. "I love you."

And watched as his face turned to stone.

CHAPTER TEN

"YOU MUST BE TIRED," Tarek said, taking each of Anya's hands in his. He pulled them away from his face, as if that would erase the words she'd said.

The words that seemed to fill the tent and more, roll out over the desert like a storm, blanketing everything.

Burying him alive.

"Not particularly," she replied, that frown he liked too much appearing between her brows. "On the contrary, I've never felt more alive. And in love, Tarek."

In case he'd missed that the first time.

And there was that pressure in his chest. That pounding thing inside him that he thought was his heart, but it seemed too large. Too dangerous.

Too catastrophic.

"Come now, Doctor," he said, not sure he sounded like himself—but it was hard to know what it was he heard with that storm in him. "There are far more pleasurable things to do tonight than forget ourselves."

She was dressed in that gown that he had spent long hours today imagining taking off her, one centimeter at a time. Her hair was set with precious jewels, each representing a different facet of the kingdom. She was a vision, she was now his Queen, and the last thing in the world he wanted to talk about was love.

But Anya did not melt into him. She did not shake off the gathering storm. Instead, her hands found her hips.

"Forget ourselves?" she echoed.

This oasis was one of Tarek's favorite places in all the world, and yet he never came here enough. It had been years. There always seemed far too many things he needed to do in the city, far too many responsibilities in the palace alone. He had looked forward to the time he would spend here with Anya more than he should have.

It was his own fault. He accepted that. He'd allowed his obsession with her to get the better of him.

No wonder it had come to this.

"I take responsibility," he told her, as he had the day they'd met. When she had sat opposite him in her prison grays in a roomful of dizzy light.

When he had found himself stunned, the way he had been ever since.

His declaration did not have the effect on her that he'd been hoping it would. It was hard to say it had any effect at all. Anya only continued to stare up at him, still frowning, her hands still propped on her hips.

"I'm beginning to think that you say that as a way to deflect attention. It's nice that you want to take responsibility, Tarek. But no responsibility needs to be taken." She lifted her shoulders, then dropped them, a parody of a careless shrug when he could see the stubborn angle of her chin. "I'm in love with you."

"We are married," he ground out. "There is no need for…this."

"We can pretend that I married you because I was suddenly seized with the need for a throne." She actually rolled her eyes, something he would have taken exception to under any other circumstances. "But I think you and I both know that there are a great many more convenient ways to stop practicing medicine. I could have simply…stopped. People do that. Who knows? I could have moved to a quiet little town and opened a charming bookshop, if I liked. There are a thousand better solutions to a career that makes me unhappy than marrying a sheikh. A king. And everything that goes with that."

"We discussed what this marriage is and isn't," he managed to say, aware that his voice was little better than a growl. "Romantic fantasies were never a part of this."

"Oh, right." Another eye roll, that Tarek liked no better than the first. "I should have realized. This is the part where you attempt to convince me that I don't know my own feelings. This is where you tell me that I've somehow confused love with something else. A bit too much of the bubbly stuff, perhaps? I can see how a person might mistake the two."

"I think," Tarek said, carefully, though he was not doing a good job at keeping that seething, furious note out of his voice, "that it is easy to let the pageant of a wedding…become confusing."

Anya aimed that smirk of hers at him. "Are you confused?"

"I warned you, did I not?" And he was less careful, then. The storm was too intense, too rough and wild. "You can't help yourself. You're culturally predisposed to romanticize everything."

Any other woman of his acquaintance would have backed down in a hurry, but this was Anya.

"I wasn't sitting in my jail cell, rhapsodizing about the possibility of being swept off into the arms of a desert king, thank you very much," she hurled at him. "If I fantasized about you at all back then, it was to imagine your comeuppance. And I don't think that I've romanticized what happened since. We had an agreement, sure. But we also had everything else."

Tarek wanted to touch her. And knew that if he did, it would be betraying everything he stood for. Everything he was.

And still he had to draw his hands back as they moved toward her, seemingly of their own accord.

"I do not believe in love." He said it with brutal finality, but he felt no joy in it when she flinched. "I should have made that clear from the start. I rather thought I did. Love has no place in an arrangement like this. How could it? I am a king, Anya."

"You are," she agreed. She shook her head as if she didn't understand. Or as if she didn't think *he* understood. "But you're also a man. And that man—"

"There is no difference between the two," he said gruffly. "Don't flatter yourself, Anya. I married you because it was convenient. Marrying a Western woman, a doctor who the world decided was a prisoner of conscience, was a calculated political move. It suggests things about me that I would like the world to believe. That I am progressive. That I am capable of softer feelings and fairy tales. That my regime and my kingdom are soft and cuddly in some way, or that I have a more accessible side. When none of those things are true."

Her hands had moved from her hips and were hanging on her sides, curled into fists now. Another gesture of disrespect he would accept from no one else in his presence. She'd gone pale, but she was still holding his gaze, no matter that her eyes were far brighter than before.

What she did not do was back down.

"I understand the nature of a press release," she said, from between her teeth. "But that's not the only thing that's between us."

Tarek roamed away from her then. The tent was expansive, this room in particular, but it was still only a tent. There was only so much distance he could put between them.

He heard her follow him, her dress rustling in a way that set fire to parts of his imagination he wished he could cut out. Or dig out with his own fingers, whatever worked, just to be…*himself* again.

This was not how he had imagined this evening going.

When Tarek had looked up and seen her—there at the other end of the aisle that his staff had made through the center of the crowd, laden with flower petals to mark her way—he'd worried that he might truly have died where he stood.

Right there, in full view of the world.

He felt as if the skies had opened up and rain had poured down on this stretch of ancient desert that was lucky to see water from above perhaps twice in a decade. More, he was sure he'd been struck by lightning.

Repeatedly.

If possible, she was even more beautiful than she'd been only the night before, when he'd been bound to her in the desert, the fires all around them flickering over her and making her glow.

Tarek had wondered how it could be that every time he looked at her it was as if he'd never seen her before. He felt that stunning jolt of recognition. His heart beat at him, hard. He felt the punch of it in his gut. And always, that heavy fire in his sex that was only hers.

It was not Alzalamian tradition for a father to walk a bride to her husband. It was rare that a bride's family had even been present in weddings of old, when brides had been used to end wars and make allies of enemies. Tarek had never been gladder that he was made of this place, these sands and these proud tribes, because even the sight of her dour father would have marred the perfection he'd seen moving toward him on her own.

A vision in white. Petals at her feet and glittering jewels in her hair.

His Queen. His woman. His Anya.

Her gaze was fixed on him as if he was the sun. She was smiling, brighter than the desert sky far above them in the grand courtyard.

There was a part of him that knew news organizations from around the world, set up around the courtyard with their cameras, would capture that smile. That it would sell their story better than anything else could. Tarek was aware of it the way he was aware of the sky, the heat, the crowd. All the inevitabilities, but he didn't care about it the way he should have. He didn't feel as if it was a job well done, that smile of hers, or as if he ought to sit around patting himself on the back for the show.

All he could think was that her smile was his.

His.

For the first time in as long as he could remember, possibly ever, Tarek had resented the fact that he was the King. That he could not enjoy Anya's joyful smile privately. That he could not keep this perfect, exquisite vision of his Anya walking toward him to marry him to himself.

I do not wish to share her, he had thought.

And when she finally reached him, he'd gazed down at her in a kind of shock, torn between what he wanted and what was.

Duty and desire, as always.

But there was only one winner in that fight, and ever had been.

Tarek knew that. He had always known that. And yet here he stood, engaged in futile battles inside himself while she looked at him with eyes so soft it made him ache, speaking of *love.*

"You can't really mean to tell me that you think there isn't more between us than a bargain we made," Anya said from behind him.

He turned and braced himself, but she didn't look the way he expected her to look. Her arms were folded and she was glaring at him. She was not cringing. She was certainly not frail and fainting. If she was awash in whatever emotions he'd seen in her eyes outside, he could see no trace of it on her.

This is your American doctor, he reminded himself. *In case you have forgotten.*

Not the sweetly pliant woman who smiled at him like he was a sunrise and ran all over him like the heat of the day.

"You're talking about sex," he said, harshly. "I won't pretend I don't enjoy it. But it is only sex."

Tarek meant that to hurt. To cut her in half, or at least stop this conversation. And he did not admire that he had that in him. That urge to cause pain that did not speak well of him or his ability to control himself no matter the situation. How had he imagined he'd been tested before? He clearly had not been.

But he didn't take those words back, either.

He should have known better. This was Anya.

She laughed.

And by the time she stopped, he found his teeth were gritted. His jaw clenched so hard he was surprised he didn't hear something break.

"Oh, Tarek." There was still laughter in her voice, and she shook her head a little as she said his name. "You can't really think that I'll suddenly and magically believe that what happened between us is *just sex*, because you say so. It doesn't work that way."

"You are mistaken," he said, though his mouth was full of glass, he was sure of it.

"I was there." It was as if she hadn't heard him speak. Her gaze never wavered. "I know better."

And something inside him was shaking. Shaking, crumbling, turning to ash and that bitter glass even as he stood there. Suggesting that what he'd taken to be the solid iron foundation of who he was, who he needed to be, had only ever been wishful thinking after all.

"I understand what it is you want," he told her, trying to sound less like broken pieces and more like a king. "But you cannot have it. Royal marriages have always been thus. Each one of us has very specific duties, Anya. I must rule the kingdom. You must support the throne. There will be heirs and they must be raised to respect the country, its people, the traditions that make us who we are, and the future we must make happen if we are to thrive."

"That sounds like a civics lesson," she threw at him. "I'm talking about our marriage."

"Our marriage has even more rules," he retorted. "How could you think otherwise? This is not one of your romances. This is a union that must produce the next King. You and I do not belong to each other, Anya. We are not lovers. I belong to the kingdom. And you must know your place."

"My place." Her eyes glittered with temper and something else Tarek didn't think he wished to define. "Maybe you'd better tell me exactly what you think that is."

"I have been telling you." His voice was an iron bar and he wished he still was, deep within. He wished she hadn't made him doubt he ever could be again. "What do you imagine this last month has been?"

She did not laugh at that, as he half expected she would, this woman who sobbed out her pleasure as if she might never recover and then faced him down as no man alive would dare. He saw something in that gaze of hers falter as she searched his face. He told himself he did not wish to know what she looked for. "This last month?"

"Yes, Anya." He started toward her then, the lanterns flickering all around them. The tent was lush, done up in deep colors, soft rugs, and everything that might make the cold of a desert night more comfortable. But it might as well have been a stark, empty cell for all he noticed. "What did you think? I have been teaching you how to be the Queen I want."

"I didn't realize that class was in session." There was that brightness in her eyes again, but she didn't give in to it. She stood taller, lifted her chin the way he thought she always would, and as ever with this woman, met his gaze.

Defiantly, he thought.

But Tarek was an expert at putting down rebellions. And he knew that if he did not stop this one before it started, it would sweep them both up. He had seen it happen.

He had spent his childhood surrounded by his father's wives. Some of them loved his father. Others loved his power. But love was always at the heart of the jealous wars that swept through the harem, pitting wife against wife and even half siblings against each other sometimes. All for love.

Practical wives, like his mother, kept themselves above the fray.

"*A queen in love with the King is but a silly woman in love with an inconstant man,*" his mother had told him long ago, in the dialect that marked her as a member of the fiercest of all the Alzalam tribes. He knew his father had been forced to fight for her—literally, in a barefisted battle against her eldest brother. Only when he won did his mother's people, and his mother, consider his proposal. "*The world is filled with such women in love with lesser men. But there is only one King of Alzalam. And I choose to be his Queen first, last, and always.*"

He had to make Anya see.

"I have taught you well," he said as he drew close, impressed as ever that she did not back down. Even when he stood over her, perfectly placed to put his hands on her in temper. In passion. In any way he liked, but she looked unmoved by his proximity. "I taught you the kinds of meals that I prefer and how I like to eat them. I taught you how to give me your surrender when I wish it. Each and every kind of release I prefer. And how to please me with your compliance."

She shook her head. "Silly me. I thought *I* taught *you* that there's nothing wrong with taking out your frustrations on a willing participant."

"There's nothing I don't like about you, Doctor," Tarek gritted out, because that was no more than the truth. "I like your sharp tongue. I like your temper and your brain. And I think you know I like the pleasures of your flesh. But you must never mistake the matter. Those are part of the bargain we have made. Love does not enter into it."

"I think," she said softly, her eyes glittering, "that His Majesty protests too much."

"There it is again. That maudlin belief that all things end up tied in a bow while something sentimental plays in the distance. I understand that you can't help it. You can't change where you came from." He sighed. "But it's not real, Anya. It will never be real."

"I don't believe you."

"You don't have to believe me. It makes no difference. Not believing me won't make what I'm telling you any less true or real. It will only cause you heartache. Facts are facts whether you choose to believe them, or do not."

"Tarek," she began, a kind of storm in her eyes. "You must know that I can see—"

But he did not wish to know what she saw. He *could not* know what she saw.

He had only let his guard down once, and he bore the scars of that mistake.

He refused to do it again.

"Very well then," he bit off, wrapping his hands around her upper arms and jerking her toward him, as he should have done from the start. "Let me show you."

And he set his mouth to hers in a punishing kiss.

But as sensation stormed through him, lighting him up and making him yearn for things he knew better than to want, Tarek suspected that the real punishment was his, not hers.

CHAPTER ELEVEN

HIS KISS WAS ELECTRIC.

Anya could feel it in every single inch of her body, tearing her up. Making her wonder how a person could function when they were nothing but pieces, scattered and torn and tossed to the wind. Burned alive, yet wanting nothing more than to keep burning.

She had half a mind to pull away. Slap him, maybe, not that she wanted to cause him pain. But she wanted to *wake him up*.

To prove to him that he was wrong about this and she was right.

That not only did she love him, but he loved her, too.

But Tarek was kissing her, and it didn't take much for her to forget that there was anything in the world but that.

All the things she'd been thinking all day seemed to course through her then, its own kind of power source. Until everything was something far hotter and brighter than electricity, and she could feel it inside her, twisting all around and then sinking down deep.

To where she would always run hot and soft for him. All for him.

"This is what we are," he gritted out, in her ear. "This is what I want from you."

She wanted to protest. She wanted to beat him away with her fists. Or her mind did, anyway.

Because her body wanted nothing more than to be close to him. To be devoured by him and to devour him in turn. To be wrapped around him, and then, gloriously, lifted up into his arms once more.

Where I belong, she couldn't help but think.

No matter how many times he tried to tell her otherwise.

He carried her through the tent, one section after the next. She had the impression of salons made of tapestries, delicately carved furnishing, and wide wooden trunks. But she only knew they'd reached a bedroom when he laid her down on a wide, soft bed. Lanterns lit up the brightly patterned walls and made their own shapes out of shadows.

But all Anya could really focus on was Tarek.

His robes were ivory and gold again, but there was far more gold tonight. The light caught at it, making him gleam. He was resplendent and beautiful, powerful and pitiless, and she loved him so much and so hard it made her feel lightheaded.

That in no way made her *less* mad at him.

Anya was panting as much from the force of the things she wanted to say to him as his deep, drugging kisses, and she pushed herself up on her elbows so she could glare at him with the full force of her displeasure.

But all he did was follow her down to the bed, making them both groan as their bodies came together. He wasted no time in getting his hands on her, up beneath skirts and then streaking up to her knees. He found her upper thighs, and took a moment to trace the place where her stockings were attached with clips. Then he moved on, finding the white-hot, molten truth of her. Of this.

Of them.

Tarek stroked her then, intent and deep. She fell back down into the soft embrace of bed, piled high with silk and linen and surrounded by the scent that rolled over her the way this man—her *husband*, her King—did. She told herself to fight, but she was unable to do anything at all but lift her hips to take his clever fingers as they found their way into her slick, wet heat.

And she knew that she should be ashamed of this. That he could tell her there was nothing between them but sex, then prove it so easily. That she could claim she loved him and sex was the least of it, then succumb to his touch so wantonly.

But her hips lifted with abandon. Her back arched to give him better access. She was moaning out his name, even before he began to thrust his fingers deep inside her.

His other hand moved to her face, guiding her mouth to his all over again. Taking what he wanted. Showing her who she was.

Tarek kissed her, deep and hot, dark and demanding.

And when she broke apart, it was against his mouth. He groaned back as if he was consuming every last noise she made. As if she was his, and the sounds she made were his, and he was branding her mouth and sex alike.

But it was not love, he would claim. It was only sex, this mad possession.

Tarek moved over her and she could feel his hands working between them. A tug here, and adjustment there. Then the broad head of his hardness found her slick folds.

He waited.

Anya opened her eyes to meet his, stark and commanding.

"I love you," she whispered.

Tarek made a rough noise, then he was thrusting inside her, deep and hard. Reward or punishment, or both wrapped in the same shock of connection and belonging, hunger and dark delight—it was hard to tell.

She'd had him so many times by now. She knew his body so well. She knew his scent, his weight, the glory he could work with a twist of his hips or that merciless mouth of his.

She knew too much.

And this was different from what had come before. This was a storm all its own, a wildly different claiming.

It was raw, untamed, and just this side of *too much*.

It was like a fever. It was all those things she'd felt all day, whirling around and around, all of them a crisis.

And still he pounded into her, braced there above her, as he made her his in a new way to suit the new things they were to each other.

Husband and wife. King and Queen.

This.

He could call it what he liked. Anya knew better.

But still, when the explosion came rushing at her, she wasn't entirely sure she would survive it. Or even if she wished to.

Tarek let her fall apart first, but he kept going until she sobbed. His name, maybe. Or a cry for the mercy she both did and didn't want. Until her fingers dug so hard into the back of the robes he still wore that she felt a nail break.

Still he continued.

Proving a point, she was sure. Driving them both wild. Making her shake and shake, sensations roaring through her with such intensity it almost scared her.

"I love you," she cried out as she hurtled off a cliff she hadn't seen coming.

And only then did Tarek follow, with a roar she felt shake through her all over again, like a new kind of shattering.

And there was no drifting off into bliss. There was no oblivion.

Tarek lifted his head, shifting his weight to his elbows. Anya was too aware of how he was covering her then, that rangy body of his, heavy and muscled everywhere, pressing her down into the bed.

Another claim, she knew. Like the rings he'd put on her hand today. Like the title he'd bestowed upon her, the throne they now shared, the palace that was to be her home.

He had never looked more like a predator than he did then, the lanterns throwing odd shapes onto the walls of fabric all around them. He was stone and hawk, carved from granite and cast in metal.

And the way he looked at her broke her heart.

Tarek moved to wipe moisture from beneath her eyes. He used his thumbs, touching her carefully, but there was nothing gentle in the expression on his face.

Something inside her rolled over hard, then sank.

"That is a pleasurable duty," he said, horribly. Deliberately. "But it is a duty, Anya. Everything I do, everything I am, is that duty. Sex to me is about succession before it is anything else."

"Succession…" she repeated.

But she was winded. She could feel it as if he'd

reached in, scraped her raw, and then sucked everything she was out.

And in return, what was left was that familiar knot in her chest.

It swelled, then pulsed.

"You are a doctor," he said in the same darkly calm way. Still lodged deep inside her, his shoulders wide enough to block the light, as if he'd taken over the whole world. As if he *was* the whole world. "Surely you must have noticed that we have never used anything that might prevent nature from taking its course."

And Anya's brain…blanked out at that, more or less. Still, she heard him. She knew that he was talking about birth control and that she ought to have thought about it.

Why hadn't she thought about it?

Because she hadn't. It had been a month, she was indeed a doctor, and she had never even raised the subject in her own mind. No matter how many times they came together like this. No matter how many times she'd felt him flood her with his release.

Why haven't I thought about it? she demanded silently.

But no answers presented themselves.

There was a curious look on his hard face. "You look so shocked. I assumed it was what you wanted. You surely knew, and when you did not raise the topic, neither did I."

She couldn't quite catch her breath. Or move. "Why would you…?"

"I told you I wanted to marry you." He did something with his jaw that might as well have been a shrug, though there was nothing careless in it. "I am not a man of half measures. Of course if I wished to marry you, that would mean children to follow. You can tell me that you did not know this, if you like. But between you and me, *wife*, I don't believe it."

And there was a truth in his words that she didn't like. Especially not now, when she felt as if he had stripped her of everything, leaving her with nothing.

Nothing but that terrible knot that seemed to grow twice its size in a moment. Then three times its size in the next.

Worse, it hurt.

"You told me I could have whatever I wanted. You promised that no matter what it was, you would make it happen." She shook her head, horrified when she felt tears spill over, but completely unable to do anything but let them. "What do you call this?"

"Practicality," he said, there against her mouth, a bitter kiss. "We can none of us be anything but what we are, Anya. Remember that. It will save you pain."

Then he was moving. Anya struggled to sit up, some part of her thinking she ought to leap to her feet, chase after him, *do* something.

But she couldn't seem to move.

"What if I'm not practical?" she demanded of him as he stood there beside the bed. "Will you throw me back into your dungeon? It is called the Queen's Cell, after all."

"Now I know why," he threw back at her. "You decide if you want to be my Queen or you wish to be my curse, *habibti*. And I will respond in kind."

And then she watched, in shocked disbelief, as he left her.

On their wedding night.

When he had just finished telling her how little she truly meant to him.

She stayed where she was, trying to breathe. Trying to think of how best to keep fighting—

Until she heard the sound of a motor turning over outside, and she understood.

He wasn't simply leaving the room. He was leaving, full stop.

The message was clear. As long as she insisted on loving him, there could be no stopping him.

When the panic attack hit her that time, she honestly thought that it might kill her. Or maybe she wished it would, this time.

It came on all fronts, walloping her again and again.

She couldn't catch her breath. Her heart pounded so hard it frightened her. She was nauseated. Sweating. Hot, then cold. Then *this close* to bursting out of her skin—

And all the while the tent spun around and around and around, until she was so dizzy she was afraid she might fall down.

It took her a long while to realize that she was already lying flat.

Slowly, laboriously, she pulled herself up, but she couldn't stand. On and on it went, as if she was caught on some sort of horrid carnival ride. Eventually she made to the side of the wide bed, then to the floor, crawling on her hands and knees across priceless rugs, sure she would die there. Any moment.

There were too many things in her head. The certainty that this time, she really was going to die. That she'd minimized these attacks, called them *panic*, but this would be the end of her. Left behind in her wedding dress, on her hands and knees on the floor of a tent in a desert that even her emotionally vacant father had warned her she'd only chosen to stay in because something was terribly, terribly wrong with her.

She was sobbing or she was gagging, or it was both at once. But still, Anya crawled until she found the bathroom.

And then she celebrated her first night as Queen of Alzalam by curling up in a wretched ball next to yet another toilet, waiting for this violent death to claim her once and for all.

Which gave her ample time to think about all the things that Tarek had thrown at her tonight.

Her love. His horror that she would even use the word. His talk of duty, and her place.

She thought of the Queen's Cell and felt the panic rise all over again as she imagined him throwing her straight back in for another stint of cold stone walls and unyielding iron bars.

Not that it mattered, she thought miserably, there on the floor. Because wasn't this marriage just another kind of prison? Not the way she'd imagined it, but clearly the way Tarek intended.

A sick little repeat of her childhood and the life her mother had left her to, however unwillingly.

Anya already knew where that led.

To this, right here. To that throbbing, blaring knot in her chest and her in a ball on the floor, alone.

And then, through all of that noise and riot, nausea and anguish, she heard a voice as clearly as if someone stood over her.

She blinked, but she was still alone.

"*You are brave, Anya,*" said her mother in her head.

In her heart. *"You are fiercer than you know. And you can make your life whatever you want it to be."*

My life, she thought then. *And certainly my marriage.*

She pulled in a shaky breath, deep. Then let it out, and like magic, the panic disappeared with it.

As if it had never been.

Anya sat up carefully. Gingerly. Waiting for all of those terrible sensations to slam back into her and throw her straight back down into that miserable ball, writhing within reach of yet another toilet.

But it was still…gone.

"You are the bravest girl I know," her mother whispered, deep inside, where Anya understood, then, she always would.

She pressed her hand to that place in the center of her chest, the place where that knot had always blazed at her, and felt her eyes fill anew.

But for a different reason this time.

She'd thought it earlier today, hadn't she? That the panic was her feelings all along. That all those things she'd locked up in her attempt to please her father had only ever waited for her there.

Now she understood that it was more than that.

It had come out medically, because that was the only thing she allowed herself. It had burst forth in symptoms, so she could catalog them. List them. Pretend she could clinically examine her own breakdowns.

Because medicine was the only emotional language she'd ever allowed herself.

But now… Now she knew.

It had been her mother all along, talking to her. Telling her. Showing her by making her stop. By making her listen.

By coming to Anya in the only way she would hear.

She laughed a little bit, there on the floor of a desert tent, still wearing her wedding gown as she crouched there in yet another bathroom.

Because it had worked.

She'd had a panic attack before she chose her specialty in medical school, and knew she wasn't going to choose neurosurgery. She'd another panic attack, a terrible one, the night before she'd taken her medical boards. She'd had them with regularity as a resident. Then, for a time, she'd thought she'd gotten them under control.

Until that last one she'd had while she was still an ER doctor. The one that had made her realize that if she didn't change something, radically, she very well might die of that pressure in her chest.

"Thanks, Mama," she said now, out loud, though her voice was scratchy. "You were pushing me where I needed to go all along."

"Be brave, Anya," her mother had whispered the last time Anya had seen her alive. She'd held her tight, though she'd been so thin by then. So frail. *"I will be with you, always. You only have to look."*

Anya hadn't looked, but that was okay. Her mother had kept her promise just the same.

She wiped at her face. She took a breath.

And she knew, with a new sort of certainty that reached deep into every last part of her, that she was not going to have a panic attack again. Not ever again.

Because she'd finally cracked the code.

It was love. And who had ever said that love had to be all soft plush toys, big eyes and faint trembling? Anya loved a king who happened to also be a hard man, made of this desert in its formidable starkness.

Loving a man like Tarek was a challenge. Even a calling.

Her calling, she knew, without a shred of doubt.

And this time, Anya was choosing a calling because of love. Because her blood moved hot inside her and she had never felt so much all at once without it flattening her on cold, impersonal bathroom floors. Because she didn't fear him, she loved him, and that meant she could take whatever came. No matter what it was.

Even if what came for them was him.

She was not a soft and trembling thing herself, and that was why he'd chosen her. Tarek could say what he liked about practicality and duty and all the rest. But he'd chosen her all the same.

Just as Anya had chosen him. Because he was absolutely right. She hadn't spared a thought to the possibility they might make a child, and that was so unlike her it really should have been funny.

All along, no matter what they pretended—to themselves and each other—the two of them had been choosing each other.

Anya simply knew it. It was in her now, part of her DNA. And she could have stayed where she was, reveling in this new knowledge, but there was no time for that.

Because Tarek had given her golden opportunity to prove that she was truly his Queen. That she was deserving of the title, and that he might give her anything she wanted, but she would do better in return. She would give him what he needed.

If she had to walk all the way back to the palace, she would.

She staggered to her feet and wandered through

room after room of this marvelous, plush palace that was something far more than a *tent*. She found the entrance and pushed her way out, stopping outside when the beauty of the oasis hit her.

The canopy of stars. The soft lights that showed her date trees dancing in the breeze, and set to glowing all the glorious pools set into the sand.

But most beautiful by far was the figure she saw standing near the water, looking into the indigo depths as if tortured.

Anya glanced to the side and saw a jeep pulled up beneath the palms. When she had been so sure he'd driven it off. That he'd left her here.

Because that was something, she realized, her father would do without a second thought.

And she decided, then and there. This was not her childhood. She was not that daughter her father had ignored—and she was not her mother, either.

Tarek was her husband. This was her marriage.

And Anya was brave. She was fierce. She would make their lives exactly what she wanted.

All she had to do was be the Queen he had chosen her to be, at last.

CHAPTER TWELVE

TAREK STOOD BY the ancient pools, looking for wisdom in the water that men of his blood had long called holy, but seeing only himself.

And the monster he had become.

He despised weakness, and yet it had taken hold of him. It had eaten away at him, leaving nothing behind but the hunger he could no more control than he could feed enough to sate himself.

Making it impossible for him to leave tonight, when he knew that's what he should have done.

To prove to her that what he said was true.

That there was nothing between them but duty. Because that was all that *should* have been between them.

He heard the rustle of her dress first, sounding like the desert breeze. Like the date palms that danced overhead.

And then she was there beside him, reflecting back at him from the water's surface. Tarek turned to look at her, expecting to find her in pieces and already kicking himself for breaking her, no matter how necessary.

But his heart did the kicking, hard against his ribs, because this was Anya. She did not look broken in the least.

"I did not expect you to come after me," he said.

When he could.

"Why?" Her tone was arch, and she did nothing to conceal the evidence that she'd been crying from him. She stood beside him as if it was her place, her right, and made him wonder why he thought she should conceal anything. "Because women of your acquaintance are more likely to fling themselves on the mercy of foreign countries than confront you personally? I apologize. I never did learn how to cower."

He admired her, and that was only one of the problems. That was only one of the ways she was tearing him apart, and all she was doing was standing there, watching him calmly.

As if she could see straight through him.

And had every intention of doing it forever.

Something in Tarek...broke.

It was not the duties and responsibilities that marked his life. It had not been the losses he suffered. His mother when he was twelve. His father last year. Worse still, the brother he had loved unconditionally, until the night he'd come to kill Tarek. And had laughed while he'd tried, betraying not only Tarek in that moment, but all of Tarek's memories of their childhood.

As if Rafiq had died that night and killed Tarek, too. Yet both of them had to live with it.

He had survived all of those things, if perhaps more scarred and furious than the cheerful boy he'd been once. He'd had no choice but to survive.

But he didn't know how he was meant to survive this.

It was this. It was her.

It was this woman he never should have met in the first place.

And it was something about being here, far away from

the civilization of the city, the dampening influence of the palace, where he could never forget for a moment that he was the King. And what, therefore, he owed everyone around him, all the time.

But out here in the desert, he was only…a man.

With her he became the things he should not whether he wished it or did not.

With her he broke into pieces when he could not break. He tore open, when he needed to remain contained. Himself above all.

"*A broken man can rule, but only ever badly,*" his mother had always told him. Well did Tarek know it. The history of the world was littered with broken men who ruled their countries straight into the dark.

He had always intended to find the light. Always.

"You knew the rules going in," he heard himself say, louder than he could recall ever speaking before. As if he howled to the moon and stars above. "You knew what this was."

"But rules are not who we are," Anya replied, with that impenetrable calm he found a challenge. More than a challenge—it bordered on an assault.

"Rules are what separate us from the beasts," he thundered at her. "And emotions are what separate kings from mere men. I have a country I must think of, Anya. Do you not understand this? I cannot have *feelings*."

Because that was what this was. He understood that now.

He had become the thing he'd sworn he never would.

All because of her. The woman who stood beside him, when he had never wanted that. He thought of that soft, inconsequential girl he had been betrothed to and knew full well that none of this would have happened, had she done her duty. He would have felt nothing. He would have married her, even bedded her, with courtesy and distance. He would have treated her with respect.

He never would have felt a thing.

And now, instead, Tarek felt everything.

Every star in the sky above him was bright and hot and still dull compared to what shined in him now, all because of this woman.

Anya turned to him then, looking at him straight on the way she always did. Direct, to the point.

Honest, something in him whispered.

Neither hiding the emotion he could see on her face nor flinging it at him.

And a great deal as if she was daring him to do the same.

Daring *him*, when no one else would brave such an endeavor.

"I understand," she said, so evenly he had the mad urge to *force her* to sound as uneven as he felt. As messy. As ruined. "If it was easy to fall in love, Tarek, we wouldn't call it falling, would we? If it wasn't overwhelming, we might say we stepped into it. Or slid into it, maybe. But everyone knows falling can only end one of two ways. Either you stick the landing or you don't, and either way, it's probably going to hurt."

That word echoed in his chest. In his head. It beat in him like a pulse.

Like a drum.

"I have spent my life in service to this country," he threw at her. Then his hands were on her again, somehow, holding her close. The look in her eyes was killing him. *She* was killing him, as surely as if she wielded a sword or gun. When all she was doing was looking back at him as if she already knew all the noise and clamor inside of him. As if she heard that same drum. "My entire life, everything I have learned and everything I became, I've done so to better serve and rule this kingdom. And not merely rule from afar, as so many do. I put my body into the fires of war to protect my people. I always will. This is who I am."

"Of course it is," she said softly. "No one doubts you are a great king, Tarek. How could they?"

"What you're asking me to do is—"

But he couldn't finish.

And all the while the drums grew louder.

"I'm asking you to love me," Anya said, but she didn't sound anguished. She sounded resolute. "I'm asking you to let me love you. I'm asking you to let us build a family, but not because it's our duty. Not only because of that and not only because we intend to raise them in your family's tradition, but because we want them to really understand what a family is."

"Anya..." he gritted out.

"You're right that I never mentioned protection," she said, and to his astonishment, she smiled. How could she *smile* when he was being torn asunder where he stood? "I didn't even think of it and I used to give lectures on the topic. How could I possibly have failed to think about something so important?"

She shook her head, still smiling. Still wrecking him without even seeming to try.

Tarek tried to gather himself, but it was no use.

"I'll tell you why," Anya continued. "Despite some reports, I didn't lose my mind in that cell. If anything, it clarified my life for me. And then there you were, with your hand outstretched, and I knew."

He shook his head at that as if he could ward it off—push her away—but even as he did, he held her close.

"I couldn't admit it to myself," she told him. "I didn't have the words. But I knew, Tarek. And I think that every choice I made that day was in service to this. *Us.* To building the family we were always meant to be."

"Anya. *Habibti.*"

But she didn't stop. "I don't want a family like the one I already have, Tarek. I don't want the coldness, the contempt. I think it's possible that my father knew how to love a long time ago, but I don't think it's in him any longer. I don't ever want a child of mine to feel the way that I have, all these years. And I don't believe that the man you are—the King you are—would tolerate treating his own child the way you saw my father treat me. You leaped to my defense. How could you visit that upon your own?"

He didn't understand what was happening in him. The earthquake that was ripping him open when he could see that the palms behind her stood tall.

"My mother warned against this," he managed to get out. "She was never involved in the harem's squabbles, because she wasn't emotional. She thought that it made her a better queen that she did not love my father and I have always agreed. The less emotion, the better. But I neglected to guard against other kinds of love. I was reckless enough to love my brother so blindly I overlooked his flaws, and nearly died for that folly. I want no more emotion in my life, Anya. None."

"Your brother is a coward and a snake. He's precisely where he belongs, and you put him there. And loved him enough to let him live."

"It was an act of mercy, nothing more."

"Tarek. What is mercy if not love?"

He wanted to shout at her. He wanted to shout down the trees. He wanted to wrestle the stars, and beat them into darkness—but all he could do was stand there as this woman tore him apart.

"And maybe not loving her husband did make your mother a better queen." Anya held his gaze. "Maybe that was exactly what your father needed. But Tarek. Do you think I don't know who *you* are?"

And Tarek was a man who had always known who he was. From the day of his birth, his destiny was secure. He had never had a moment's doubt, never suffered from the trials of insecurity. How could he?

He knew who he was. What he was. What he would do, how he would do it, and how history would record him.

He had always known.

Now he gazed down at this woman, his wife and his Queen, who made his heart beat. Who made him want things he'd never considered possible or even desirable before.

And it suddenly became critical to him that he know who *she* thought he was.

"You don't need a cold queen, or a harem filled with women, none of whom love you so much as they love power," she told him when he didn't answer her question. Because he couldn't. "You need me and you know it."

And for perhaps the first time in his life, Tarek found himself appreciating the power of pure confidence in another. Because Anya wasn't asking him or begging him, she was telling him.

She kept going. "You would never have chosen a prisoner and elevated her as you did otherwise. You would never have defended me against my own father, in public. Or left me with your own family the way you did, with no worries whatever that I might embarrass you or act against you in some way. You need me, Tarek. The woman who loves you. The Queen who will defend you."

"Anya." And her name was that drumming thing, and that drumming was a song. He could hear it in the night all around them. In the wind and the sand. In him and between them. And, at last, Tarek stopped fighting it. "I fear…that want to though I might, I do not know how to love."

And her smile then was so bright it made the heavens dim.

"Then I will love you enough that you are forced to learn," she whispered.

This time, when Tarek broke, he understood it was nothing to fight. It was no surrender. It was no rebellion he needed to quell.

Unless he was very much mistaken…this was falling.

And she was right. It hurt.

But that hardly mattered. What was one more scar to add to his collection?

"And if I already love you," he managed to ask, though his heart ached. His temples were spikes of pain. He fell and he fell. "What then?"

Anya slid her arms around his waist, and tilted her head back to look him full in the face. "We will make our own rules, here and now. You and I. We can do as we like, Tarek. This is ours."

And he thought, then, of possibilities instead of problems. Of hope instead of tradition.

Of love—not instead of duty, but laced through it, making it glow.

He thought, *Have I loved her all along?*

And the thought itself seemed to fuse with that smile on her face, the stars all around them, and all the ways he fell. Until he was filled with a wild sense of wonder.

"I think I stuck the landing, *habibti*," he told her, and his reward was not only the way her smile widened and took the world with it. But the way it felt inside him, a wild rush that left him smiling, too.

"I love your scars, that you won in defending this kingdom even though it broke your heart," she said, moving her hands lightly over his chest, tracing one scar. Then the next. He felt it like light, though he still wore his robes. "I love your arrogance and your certainty, because it makes it so evident that you could never be anything but a king. I love my King, Tarek."

He wanted to speak, then, but he was filled with that wonder and a bright, almost painful *thing*—

It occurred to him, at last, that it had never been obsession.

This was so much more than that. *She* was.

"And you deserve to love me back, King and man alike," she whispered fiercely. "You deserve a place where you can hide, Tarek. Where you can be who you are. No thrones or kingdoms or worries. No people. Just you and me. Just this."

Tarek felt washed clean. Made new. He held her face between his hands again, but this time there was no darkness in it.

Because there was none left in him.

For she was a light far brighter than the desert sun, and he could feel her inside him like the brightest, hottest midday.

"Just as you deserve a place where you can shine,

Anya," he told her gruffly. "Queen always. *My* Queen, always. And whatever you want of me, you will have, as long as I draw breath."

"Tarek," Anya whispered. "I do love you. So much."

"I love you," he whispered back, because there was no other way to describe the tumult. The longing and the light. The fury and the fear. The endless need, the sharp joy.

Her. Anya.

It was falling and then falling more. It was a tumble from a height so high it made his whole body seize—

But the landing was worth the fall.

It was the way she smiled at him. It was the ferocity in her voice when she came to find him, wherever he'd gone. It was the way she'd knelt before him on a terrace long ago, taking him deep in her mouth and absolving him of the scars he wore, the wars he'd won.

It was the love in her eyes, then and now. Always.

"I love you," he said again, because it barely scratched the surface. It was too small a word, and yet it was everything.

"Tarek," she whispered. "I love you, too."

"Teach me how to love you," he demanded, urgently. "Teach me every day. And I promise you, Anya, I will give you the world."

She slid her hands up the length of his chest, then looped her arms around his neck. And then they were both falling, together, and that was no less overwhelming, but it was theirs.

This was all theirs.

And it was good. And Tarek intended to keep on falling, forever.

He was the King of Alzalam, and he would see to it personally.

"Don't you see?" Anya asked, breathlessly, still smiling as if she would never stop. "You already have."

And later, Tarek thought, he would think of that scene by the pools as the real moment they became husband and wife, man and woman.

Them.

Forever.

But here and now, he stopped wasting time, and kissed her.

CHAPTER THIRTEEN

TEN YEARS LATER, Anya waited for her husband near the pools at the oasis, on a night so like their wedding night that she found she couldn't stop smiling.

This time, she wore a shift dress and little else, sitting on a rock with her feet in the silky water. No bulky wedding gown that had required both of them to remove.

Eventually.

They had kept their promises to each other. There had been press releases and publicity tours, but that fell under the mantle of *duty*. They were both deeply dedicated to doing their duty.

But when they were alone, they were something more than a king and a queen, the embodiment of a kingdom's hopes and dreams.

They made their own hopes and dreams, together.

He told her stories of Rafiq and the childhood they'd shared, learning how to grieve what was lost without letting what had happened tarnish the good that had happened first. And because he'd trusted her with that, she told him about her panic attacks and her mother, and how she was reclaiming her own memories of the happy life she'd had when her mother was alive.

Because grief was love. And because they were together, there was no need to fear love, no matter how it presented itself.

Loving each other was the best antidote to fear that Anya could have imagined.

And it only grew with time.

Anya gave birth to Crown Prince Hakim before their first anniversary. She stood beside Tarek on the balcony called the King's Overlook where he'd taken her to announce their engagement, showing off the next generation to the crowds below.

"*You look so happy,*" she'd whispered, brought nearly to tears at the sight of this tiny creature they'd made tucked up safe and sound in his father's arms. And she didn't think it was entirely due to her new mother hormones, either.

It was him.

Tarek had turned to smile at her—the smile that was only for her, no matter where they happened to be.

"*I have long dreamed of this moment,*" he'd told her. "*But I find that now it is here, what I care about is you, by my side. My Queen outside these walls. My wife within. But most of all, mine.*"

"*Yours,*" she'd agreed. "*Always yours.*"

They'd made two more princes to keep Hakim company, then a brace of princesses. Each and every one of them a perfect bundle of dark eyes, dark hair, and a deep stubbornness they took pleasure in claiming came from the other.

"*Behold your work,*" Tarek had said one morning in the great courtyard, years back, shaking his head as his firstborn son and heir ran in circles. Naked. "*This is the future of my kingdom.*"

Anya had only laughed.

"*That sounds familiar, doesn't it?*" she'd asked him one afternoon, years later, when their tiny, perfect eldest daughter was found in one of the palace's public rooms.

And refused to leave.

"*No*," she kept saying. "*No*."

With all the consequence of a king.

Tarek had laughed too, but he'd also pulled Anya close and kissed her soundly.

They tended to their duties, they were deeply involved in the raising of their children, and at night they repaired to the King's royal suite and set themselves on fire.

Over and over and over again.

Year after year. Whether Anya was big with child or not. Whether they had fought for days or not.

They might not have always agreed with each other. They might have spent hours shouting. She was too direct and he was too arrogant and sometimes those things left bruises no matter how much they loved each other.

But they kissed each other's wounds, there in the dark of their big, wide bed. And when he moved inside her and she clung tight to him, they found their way back to each other. Sooner or later, they always found their way.

As the years passed, Tarek became a powerful new voice in the region. And Anya found ways to use the power he'd given her to truly do her best to make the world a better place. She and her sister-in-law Nur first became friends, then partners in a charitable initiative that promoted women's health and wellness.

"*Finally*," she told Tarek at the charity's inaugural ball. "*A use for all my medical knowledge.*"

"*You will always be my doctor, habibti,*" he'd told her, there in the center of the ballroom where his gaze told her what his hands and his mouth would, later. When they were alone and naked and making each other fall all over again.

Anya thought of her mother daily and never did have another panic attack, as she'd known she wouldn't. Instead, she pursued the dreams of that long-ago little girl. She danced often, because she was a queen and her husband was a king and there were an endless array of balls for them to attend. She had tried painting things as a hobby, but had found herself both terrible and bored.

Her true artistic genius was still in the medium of crayons, in her opinion—something she discovered by coloring things with her children and then festooning them about the bedroom for Tarek to find. Then find creative ways to both laugh at her and praise her at the same time.

Usually he chose to take her flying, without wings or a plane, as only he could.

The most surprising twist had happened back in Seattle. Charisma had left Alzalam a new woman. She had stopped fluttering and had laid down a series of ultimatums, the crux of which was that she no longer intended to be a lapdog of any kind.

Anya's father and his latest, youngest wife were still together, ten years later. With twins Preston doted on.

"Part of me wishes he could have been a better father to me," Anya had confessed to Tarek one night, after one of her father and Charisma's annual visits—something else her stepmother had insisted on. *"But if he had, would I be here now?"*

"That almost makes me like him," Tarek had growled.

She and her father were not close. He had never apologized and never would. She didn't understand him and never would. But they tried, in their way. And she and Charisma had become friends out of the bargain.

It was hard to imagine a better outcome.

And now a whole decade had passed, laced with its own share of disappointments, certainly. But brighter with hope, all the same. Stronger by far for the tests they'd faced along the way.

"Life is good, Mama," Anya whispered into the night. "Life is so good."

She heard Tarek come out of the tent, then. They liked to come here whenever they could, but that didn't mean he could always leave the palace behind. After their long, leisurely dinner in that bright and sprawling room where he'd once tried to put her in her place, he'd taken an urgent phone call.

Anya had checked in with the children and their nannies, had taken care of a pressing matter with her own doctor, and had come outside to wait for him.

She tilted her head, listening to the cadence of Tarek's voice and ready to be what he needed when he came to her. Sometimes he raged. Sometimes he grieved. Now and again he was lost.

He came to her as he was, however he was, and she held him. She challenged him. She was strong for her King and when he could be a man again, he was always hers.

Always and ever hers.

Tonight he sounded good. And then he ended the call and she heard him walk toward her.

And wasn't at all surprised when he simply lifted her up, turning her so he could hold her in his arms.

"Happy anniversary, my love," he said in a low voice, there against her mouth.

"Only a decade," Anya replied. "It seems like a week. And forever."

Tarek kissed her as he always did. As if it was the first time, desperate and needy.

And when she was panting against his mouth, he smiled. "Well?"

She laughed. "Why do you ask when you already know? You always know before I do."

Tarek moved back, then went to his knees before her. This big, strong man. This powerful King.

He slid his hands over her belly and kissed her there. Then grinned up at her.

"Every centimeter of you is precious, and mine," he said with all the dark arrogance she adored. "I know when something changes."

"Yes, I'm pregnant again," she said. "The doctor just confirmed it. But you knew that."

"I did." His grin faded, and something stark replaced it. Stark like the desert all around them, beautiful and vast. "You keep teaching me that no matter how much I love, there is always more. There is no end to it."

"There is never any end," she agreed, her eyes getting glassy. "Not as long as we're together."

Tarek stood them. He bent to scoop her into his arms and then he held her there, gazing down at her.

"Come, *habibti*," he said, the way he always did. The way he always would. "Let us fall the rest of the way together."

And then he carried her off into the night, falling sweetly into the rest of their beautiful lives.

* * * * *

WHAT THE GREEK'S WIFE NEEDS

DANI COLLINS

This book was written in early 2020
as the social distancing measures began to take place.
It's for you, Dear Reader. I wish we could all have
a sexy tycoon sweep in to release us from being
housebound and whisk us into a much more luxurious
world. At least I can give you one for a few hours.
Enjoy!

PROLOGUE

Five years ago

THIS WAS IT. Tanja Melha was a modern woman and she would go after what she wanted.

Which happened to be a man, leaving her to wonder exactly how modern she really was, but she was also human. Leon Petrakis was sexy and single, and she was headed back to university in a few weeks. This was her only shot at a summer fling that might cure her of a crush she couldn't seem to shake.

She sauntered down the ramp to the wharf, watching her step around the coiled ropes and other tripping hazards. The August evening was a few degrees cooler down here on the water, and laden with the scent of seaweed and tidal flats. *Home*, she thought, breathing it in.

Her childhood friends hadn't been able to leave the island fast enough, heading to Vancouver or Calgary or Toronto. Tanja went to the University of Victoria, and sometimes even that felt too far from Tofino, the small town on Vancouver Island's west coast where she'd grown up.

Which was another reason she had to *carpe* this man on this *diem*. Leon was Greek, but a citizen of the world, living off his sailboat. He was intending to stay the rest of the summer to help her brother expand her father's marina, but he was the type of rootless bachelor who could easily slip over the horizon at any moment.

As she came up to his slip, she saw him stowing something in the hold of the cockpit in the stern. He wore frayed denim cutoffs and nothing else but a tan.

Lord, he was perfectly made. She drank in his broad shoulders and the twist of his spine, the light layer of dark hair on his thighs, and the absent way he planted his feet and rode the movement of the boat when a rippling wave came in.

"Hey, sailor." It was supposed to be a casual greeting but came out throaty with the lust that was overtaking her.

He straightened and turned, unhurried and even more magnetically beautiful when his slow smile appeared.

"Hello, Books." She had a feeling he deliberately used her brother's nickname for her, trying to push her into the pigeonhole of "best friend's little sister." His black hair was long enough to show its natural curl, his eyes dark and brimming with masculine appreciation as he slid his gaze down her blue minidress with its spaghetti straps.

She did the same to him, noting the way the hair on his chest flowed out from his sternum to dance like flames toward the brown discs of his nipples. Another darker line drew her eye from his navel to the brass button that barely held his shorts on his hips.

"I'm all paid up on my moorage fees. To what do I owe the pleasure?"

She dragged her eyes back to his knowing grin. He'd seen where her attention had strayed and liked it, which made butterflies take flight inside her.

"I wondered if you wanted company for happy hour?" She held up the bottle of wine she'd brought. It was a crisp, dry white coated in condensation from the short walk from her car.

After the briefest of pauses, he tilted his head and said, "How could I say no? Come aboard." He took the bottle in one hand and held out his other to assist her.

He didn't move back to give her room. When she stepped down into the cockpit beside him, they were toe to toe, practically mashed up against each other. He kept her hand in his and looked down his nose at her.

"I'm too old for you, you know."

"At twenty-nine? Please. I'm twenty-two. I didn't come here to lose my virginity." But she *had* come here for love-making. She couldn't pretend otherwise. Not when her breath was hitching so unevenly that her breasts grazed his muscled chest.

The corners of his mouth slowly curled. "Should I open this now or later?"

Oh, he was smooth. She told herself that was why he appealed to her. She wanted to know what it was like to be with a man who knew his way around every piece of coastline on a woman's body.

"Later." The word was a husk in the back of her throat. She couldn't peel her eyes off his mouth.

"Come below," he invited.

She ought to be nervous. In some ways she was. She didn't do random hookups. She'd had a few boyfriends and had dated since being at university, but her two relationships that had been serious enough for lovemaking had been hard cases of puppy love, intense enough to dent her heart when they fell apart. Sex with the first had been many frustrating experiments in figuring things out, the second a much more successful and satisfying pairing, but they ultimately wanted different things.

The bottom line was, she was hardly an expert in the arts of seduction and eroticism.

"This is nice," she said of the interior. It was tidier than she'd expected, given how devil-may-care his personality seemed. The windows were surprisingly big and bright, showcasing the gleam of the polished wood and stainless steel. The upholstery was maroon, the curtains smoky gray, the accent cushions sage green and rusty orange.

"Thanks." He stowed the wine in the refrigerator and rinsed his hands, then dried them on a tea towel, hip leaned beside the sink. "I keep it this way. I wasn't expecting company."

"Weren't you?" She dipped her chin in a small challenge. She'd been flirting unabashedly since returning in June. He had finally, this morning, given her a low whistle and said, "Lookin' good, Books."

Now he didn't bother pretending to be sheepish. "I'm a sucker for a miniskirt. What can I say?" His gaze went down to her low-heeled sandals. "And long legs. Freckles." His gaze struck the ones on her chest, then her face. "Red hair."

"Why didn't you say? I'd have been here sooner."

"You know why." He opened his feet, slouching a little lower as he invited her with a roll of his wrist to come closer.

"I don't," she assured him, trying to act blasé as she moved into the space he'd made. "We're consenting adults."

A fine tremble of anticipation accosted her, belying the maturity she was claiming to possess. Her hands hesitated when she felt the heat off his skin hit her palms, then she gently let them rest on the firm muscles of his upper chest.

His wide hands came to her waist. He didn't kiss her. He looked deeply into her eyes.

"Mixing business with pleasure gets messy. As you see, I prefer tidy."

"Your business is with my brother."

"Mmm." His mouth pursed as though he wasn't convinced. His fingers dug a little more intently into her hips, as though he was undergoing some small struggle within himself. "And you're here for pleasure?" His gaze was incinerating her mouth.

"Hope springs eternal," she teased in a breathy voice, leaning a little closer. "So far it seems like you want to talk my ear off."

"That is not what I want to talk off you." He dipped his head, brushed her mouth once with his own as though testing whether she was sure, then he covered her lips in a long, unhurried kiss that sent an earthquake through her, unhinging her knees.

She had sensed that things would be different with him. Stronger. More exciting. She hadn't known he would fill her with the energy of a thousand storms.

She curled her arms around his naked shoulders, holding on and moaning at how vital and strong he was, enclosing her in hard arms, crushing her breasts to his chest. The scent of salt air and sunscreen clung to his taut, smooth skin. His light stubble abraded her chin and the faint taste of coffee lingered on his tongue when he swept it into her mouth.

He was only kissing her, and this was already miles beyond anything she'd experienced. All of her was flowering open. She was kissing him back with an abandon that wasn't like her at all, and she couldn't help it. The more deeply he kissed her, the more turned-on she was and the more she wanted to turn him on.

He made a deeply sexy noise in his throat, and his fingers dug through her skirt into the crease of her butt. He squeezed the underside of her cheek, pulling her hips into contact with his rippled fly and the hard shape behind it. They were fully plastered to one another, kissing like their lives depended on it. She began to think hers might.

Leon broke away to whisper in Greek. It might have been a curse.

"I really didn't expect this," he said in his sensual accent, nipping at her jaw and chin before burying his mouth in her neck. "Are you sure?"

His heart was pounding so hard she felt it against her breast. When he lifted his head, there was something sharp and bright in his gaze. A warning? A revelation that he was as startled by this as she was?

Whatever it was, it caused her belly to tighten and her bones to melt and her hips to press forward into firmer contact with his.

His breath rushed out in a jagged noise. With a lithe twist, he straightened and angled her backward toward a door, gaze locked with hers.

She would have stumbled if he hadn't steadied her, narrowing his eyes when she licked her lips. *Oh.* Her abdominals contracted again. She hadn't realized she had such power over him. She did it again, more deliberately, and color rose in his cheeks. His jaw tightened and his nostrils flared.

As they entered the captain's quarters, he flicked the curtains closed. She dropped the straps off her shoulders and shimmied the minidress to the floor, leaving herself in the pale blue thong she'd put on in hopes he'd see it. Like it.

He bit the edge of his lip as he looked her over, one hand touching the ceiling when the boat took a sudden rise and dip. His other hand released his button and fly. He dropped his shorts and he was naked. Naked and aroused. Really, really… Wow.

She swallowed, her own hand going to the edge of the nearby shelf to steady herself.

He slid onto the wide mattress that covered the entire space between the two sides of the hull. "Join me."

She did, flowing onto berth and man in one motion, fusing her mouth to his as she did.

He was so hot! His whole body burned her wherever they touched. The steely hardness of him was almost hurtful to lie against, yet so erotically good.

His fingers trailed down her back, both possessive and light, exploring with laconic purpose, mapping from nape to shoulders, splaying wide and tracing her spine. Gathering into her sides and shifting her against him as though celebrating everything she was.

She braced her hands by his shoulders and continued to move on him in a full body caress, moaning into his mouth at how good he felt beneath her. Rough and satiny smooth, hot and hard, vital and strong. His fingers tangled in the strap of her thong and his palms branded her butt as he guided her to straddle him and move higher on his body.

"I want your nipples," he said in a guttural voice that nearly undid her.

She shifted higher, sat across his waist, hand braced in the recessed storage space over his head so her breast dangled over his open mouth. He began to suckle at her and her whole body tightened. He wasn't shy about palming her butt and stroking her thighs and sweeping his touch beneath the damp placket of her thong.

She'd been thinking of this all day. For weeks. Months. Of course, she was slippery and wet. She moaned and squirmed as he teased and caressed, sucking strongly and seeking the bundle of nerves that were so swollen and aching she nearly went out of her mind. Within moments, a sharp climax struck, turning her into a quivering, shaking, panting mess.

He released her nipple and looked up at her with stunned delight and such carnality she felt a fresh rush of heat into her loins.

"I want to feel that when I'm inside you." His graveled voice made her skin tighten.

"So do I." Her voice was nothing but faint breath.

They shifted and she kicked away her thong while he quickly applied a condom. He settled on his back and invited her to be on top again. To take him in.

He was thick and hot and so hard he barely felt real, but there was no denying he was all man. His hands moved restlessly on her thighs as she settled into place. His teeth clenched and his throat strained with his effort to stay in control.

"You've been wanting this, too," she accused.

"I have."

"Then why—?"

"We're here now." His voice was guttural, his hips rising beneath her. "Tell me if that's too much."

"No, it's so good," she gasped. She pressed her hands to the low ceiling above her and began to undulate on him, moaning freely at how exquisite it felt to ride him in the same rhythm as the soft rock of the boat.

He ran his hands up her front, caressing and stroking, thumbing her nipples and plumping her breasts and letting his hands come back to steady her hips as he began to thrust with more power.

She had never felt like this. Like she was pure woman. Like her body had been made for exactly this purpose. For him. They were the only two beings in this world and they weren't *of* this world. They were something exalted. A god and goddess creating the universe with the charged union of their bodies.

When his touch strayed inward and his thumb lazily circled her swollen bud, she groaned in the sheer luxury of letting the tension build even more strongly, one glorious layer at a time.

"You're so beautiful." His voice was both faint and distant, yet reverberated in her consciousness. "Tell me when."

"Never," she said throatily. "Let's stay like this for— Oh." A tiny shift in the tide, a slap of a wave against the hull, caused a twitch in their rhythm that sent a shock wave through her.

He made a similar noise, one of gratification and delight. Anticipation. He steadied her and said, "Soon, lovely. Hang on a little longer. When I say." His thumb circled and circled, becoming her whole world. The point on which she existed while her inner muscles squeezed him and he continued those lovely, lazy thrusts.

It wasn't long before the noise she made became tortured. This lovemaking was becoming more than she could bear. She couldn't find words to express how good she felt. Couldn't say or do anything but push her hands against the ceiling and hold herself still for his upward thrust. For his caress. Waiting and waiting for his dark command.

"Now."

They shattered into a million pieces.

CHAPTER ONE

Present day...

WHEN THE HARD pounding on the door sounded as Tanja Melha was climbing into bed, her heart caved in. This was it. They had come for her. She was a foreigner and was being targeted for questioning. Perhaps worse.

Trembling, she dragged on her jeans. They nearly fell off her hips, but tucking in her T-shirt helped.

Everything in her urged her to run, but where? There was no way off Istuval, not since the tiny island off the coast of Tunisia had been taken over by rebels. They were holding the island—and thus her—hostage, all so some authoritarian in a far-off country could have a toehold on the Mediterranean's shipping lanes.

Tanja heard her friend and housemate, Kahina, call out that she was coming. Kahina's brother, Aksil, entered and said crisply, "Kahina. There are men here for Tanja."

Tanja's knees almost buckled, but she refused to endanger Kahina when Kahina had been so kind, harboring her through all of this. She would face whatever awaited her, but her hands were freezing and stiff, her whole body shaking.

Illi's little form felt snug and warm as Tanja touched her sleeping daughter. Her heart was sheared in two as she gave herself one last moment with her, biting her lip to prevent a scream of agony.

She didn't let herself give in to the hysteria. To think the what-ifs. There was no time. Heavy footsteps were scuffling into the bungalow. She touched her lips to the cheek of the four-month-old and deeply inhaled her sweet scent. Tears scorched her eyes, and her throat was so tight she could hardly breathe.

As she straightened, she felt as if her chest was crushed beneath a slab of concrete. Her feet pushed through quicksand as she made herself walk out of the bedroom to meet her fate.

Four men stood inside the door. Aksil must have run from his home across the street when he saw the soldiers arrive on the stoop. He wasn't wearing shoes and his head was uncovered. He hugged Kahina protectively into his side with a tense nod.

Two men wore olive-green uniforms and cradled automatic rifles in their arms.

The last man who appeared from behind them was as tall and wide and swarthy as the soldiers, but he wore a navy blue pullover atop black trousers and footwear that, in another life, she would have pegged as sailing shoes.

She brought her gaze back to his unshaven jaw, his ruffled dark hair and his fierce glower. The floor seemed to tip beneath her, causing her head to swim and her heart to swoop into her stomach. It soared, then hit the floor.

"Oh, my God!" She clapped her hand over her blasphemy—as if these mercenaries genuinely cared about religious observances. They imposed their restrictive laws for control, not true concern for modesty or faith.

But what on earth was her *husband* doing here? Could she even call Leon Petrakis that? They hadn't seen each other in five years. Not since he had abruptly left just days after their quiet wedding because his father had passed away without warning.

Do you want me to come with you?

No.

He had completely shut down from the charmingly seductive playboy she'd married. A week later, he had finally responded to one of her many texts asking when he would be coming back.

I'm not.

That had been that. He hadn't said much to her brother, Zachary, either. Leon had supposedly been waiting for the full release of his trust fund on his thirtieth birthday. He'd promised to inject capital into the marina when that happened, but he had ghosted the lot of them, destroying her brother's livelihood and their father's retirement in the process. Tanja had given up her school savings to help bail out Zach and still owed on the student loans she'd taken to finish her degree.

All of that meant she would rather kill and eat Leon Petrakis than be dragged out of bed to look at him, yet he opened his arms and spoke with what sounded like... tenderness?

"*Agape mou.* At last. I'm here to take you home."

He moved forward in long, confident strides, like the lion he was named for, snaring her with easy strength and pulling her into his tall, muscled frame.

Her heart lurched in alarm at the sheer size of him. She'd forgotten this dynamic energy of his, this magnetism and sex appeal. How he made her feel utterly cherished as he crushed her close.

It was a lie, of course. She felt his disingenuousness in the hardness of his muscles as he cradled her. She saw it in his features, distant and closed off. He wasn't so much older as altered. He was still beautiful, but now he was fierce. Hardened and serious. Everything about him was amplified. This was Leon two-point-O. Leaner and sharper and stronger.

The scent of salt breeze filled her nostrils along with damp cotton and faint notes of aftershave or some other manly, exclusive product. Underlying all of that was a scent that was masculine and familiar. Personal. *Him*. It was elemental power and a barbaric will that enveloped her the way his arms did, in a claim, like an animal leaving his scent on his mate.

Despite how false she knew this embrace to be, after so many weeks of worry, her body bought what he was selling. She gave an involuntary shudder and leaned into him, unconsciously latching onto him as a piece of her old life and the security and stability she yearned so badly to get back to.

She was losing her mind to fear, she realized, because some latent, ridiculous remnants of her crush on him pulsed heat through her. She hated him. She had decided that years ago, but instead of thrashing him with her fist and decrying him as the heartless profligate he was, she *relaxed*. Her most primitive self drew in his presence the way her lungs took in oxygen—as though it was something that could be absorbed and used to keep her alive.

Leon cupped her jaw to tilt her face up and stroked a thumb across her cheekbone. The men with guns disappeared, and tingles of pleasure raced across her skin as her husband bent his head and set his mouth warmly against her unsteady lips.

An unexpected spark leaped between them, bursting in her chest like fireworks, sending a singed line out to her fingertips, into her loins and down to her toes.

His flinty gaze flashed in surprise, as though he experienced something like it, as well.

They had only been lovers a few short weeks, but seeing that ember flare within him caused her own to intensify. Her mouth softened, and he deepened their kiss in a slow rock of his lips across hers.

She let her lashes flutter closed and leaned more completely into him. It was so intoxicating, so perfect and needed and right. She pressed into her toes, sealing their mouths. It was exactly as it had been five years ago. His kiss was hard and hot and held a hurricane of passion behind it that would have swept her into its eye if he hadn't tightened his hands on her and set her back on her flat feet.

She swayed, stunned to discover reality crowding in like dark shadows.

None of this made sense. Not his presence here or her pounding heart or the way her hands refused to unclench from his soft pullover.

Keeping his arm around her, he faced the soldiers, speaking French, which was more common than English here, after the local dialect.

"See? As I told you. She's my wife. She came to teach English, but when the changeover happened she was unable to leave without a male relative. I'll take her home now."

Changeover, she thought dimly. Such a well-scrubbed euphemism for *foreign military invasion*. She went with it, though. She slid her arm around his lower back and leaned into his side. Her other hand stayed on his chest, tensely crushing the soft knit as she gazed up at him, searching for clues as to how he'd known where to find her. Why had he come? She'd been sure he'd forgotten she existed.

The soldiers shifted restlessly, exchanging looks of

deep skepticism. "You live here? Without any male relative?" one asked her.

Aksil quickly spoke up. "My sister and Ms. Melha—"

"Mrs. Petrakis," Leon inserted.

"Yes, of course." Aksil nodded. "Mrs. Petrakis taught with my sister at the girls' school before it closed. I take my sister shopping when they need food, but Kahina will come stay with my family now." Aksil tightened his arm protectively around her.

Leon nodded as though it was all decided. He would have swept Tanja to the door, but she balked. The words *what about Illi?* formed on her tongue.

Even as his gaze flashed an urgent *don't test me* into hers, her daughter let out the beginning of a staccato cry, the irritable one that meant she wanted to sleep, but her tummy had decided she was hungry. Tanja suspected Illi was going through a growth spurt, and desperation was turning her inside out because they were so low on formula.

The sound of Illi's cry froze everyone into stillness.

Tanja looked to Kahina. Her friend would be welcomed at her brother's, but his house was already full of Kahina's nieces and nephews. Asking Kahina to take Illi would be more than an imposition. Illi would take food from the mouths of Aksil's children.

Illi might not have come from Tanja's body, but Tanja was her mother now. She wouldn't go anywhere without her daughter. That's how she had come to be trapped here.

There would be no taking back the way she played the next seconds, but there was only one way she *could* play it. This was her chance, her *one chance*, to take her baby home.

"Agape mou." She gazed imploringly up at Leon. "You must be so excited to meet your daughter."

As outrage flared in the depths of his eyes, Leon's expression hardened before cracking into a faint smile. "It's all I've thought about," he said in a distant voice.

"I'll get her." Kahina hurried into Tanja's bedroom.

Get in. Get out. Get a divorce. That had been Leon's straightforward plan when he had received the email from Tanja's brother, Zach.

Tanja is trapped on Istuval. She needs a male relative to take her out. My wife is due any day or I would go myself. Dad's on crutches and can't travel. Since you are technically still her husband...

Technically? He *was* her husband, despite the five years of estrangement. Dissolving his marriage hadn't been a priority while Leon had been rebuilding his father's empire. Divorce papers would have invited his wife to gouge him for a settlement, jeopardizing all he was trying to regain, so he'd let that task slide.

With this rescue, Leon had seen an opportunity to end things without her trying to soak him. He'd headed to Malta where he'd bought a racing trimaran, readied the vessel, set aside bribery cash in various currencies, and stocked up on diapers and formula.

Zach's email had said "they" were desperate for baby supplies. Leon had taken that to be a collective "they." That Zach was advising he bring infant goods to grease palms.

Leon hadn't been given a chance to mention the supplies or the money to his inquisitors. The moment he'd come near the harbor, he'd been boarded. He and the trimaran had been searched and the infant supplies moved onto the dock when he moored. He'd been roughed up, and accused of smuggling and trying to profiteer on the island's black market.

He had told the truth—he was here to collect his wife. He didn't have a marriage certificate on him, though, which had made the soldiers skeptical. The identification he did have could have got him detained for a ransom demand if they'd understood exactly who he was. He had a contingency plan in place for that, but thankfully it wasn't needed. Yet.

He'd been put in a vehicle and driven here to see his wife.

And his *baby*?

Given the supplies he'd brought, the existence of a baby was almost a blessing. *Almost*—because this was definitely not his baby appearing in the arms of the woman who lived with Tanja. He hadn't had any sort of contact with Tanja—intimate or otherwise—in five years.

"This is Illi." Tanja's voice was husky with deep, maternal love as she took the girl.

Something flickered in his mind's eye like a flashbulb taking a photo. He absorbed her tone and the tender way she cradled the baby so protectively. His memory took a snapshot to dwell on the fine details later because right now he had to stay anchored in the tension permeating the air around them.

The baby had neither Tanja's straight, red-gold hair, her pale complexion nor her hazel eyes. The infant's black curls and light brown skin could pass for mixed race if Tanja had slept with a man who looked like him, though. Which she must have done.

Why that dug such a deep thorn into him, Leon couldn't say. Their marriage had been a moment of temporary madness that he only recollected as a statement of fact. His father was dead. His age was thirty-five. His legal status was "married."

How Tanja had conducted her life these last years was none of his business.

But where *was* that other man? Surely he would be as affronted to have Leon named his baby's father as Leon was at having another man's baby passed off as his? Leon could hardly keep his dumbfounded fury off his face.

He manufactured a smile, though, hyperaware of the scrutiny they were under and that, regardless of who this baby's father was, the infant was completely helpless and innocent. If she was Tanja's, for the purposes of this rescue, she was his.

"She's beautiful." He tried to look smitten even though he'd never really looked at a baby before. This one was whimpering as she nuzzled her face into Tanja's chest.

"I'll make her a bottle." The other woman took the baby again and hurried away.

"I was upset that you and I were apart. My milk didn't come," Tanja said with an apologetic smile toward the soldiers for speaking of such things.

"See?" Leon leaped on her remark to prove his lie. "Her brother told me diapers and formula were difficult to find here. I brought them for my daughter."

One of the soldiers accepted that with a bored look toward his compatriot. He seemed ready to leave. His fellow soldier wore the look of a man with a hard-on for power. Leon hated men like that. He'd been raised by one and feared he had turned into one, which was why he was so filled with bitter self-loathing.

"Why were you here and not with your husband when you had the baby?" the antagonistic one asked Tanja.

"Things are different in Canada," she began while Leon spoke at the same time. "My father died—"

Leon bit back a curse and set his arm around her again, squeezing in a signal to let him do the talking.

She was nothing but skin and bones. That alarmed him, but he was more concerned with getting through the next few minutes without an arrest.

"We married in Canada, but I had to return to Greece when my father died." Ancient history, but true. "Tanja was already scheduled to come to work here. She didn't know she was pregnant or she wouldn't have traveled." He gave her a stern frown. Naughty wife.

He felt her stiffen, but she smiled apologetically at the men. "By the time I realized, I was too far along to go back. It's been difficult to make arrangements to leave."

Flights had to be chartered and women weren't allowed to leave the house, let alone the country, without a male relative.

The soldiers flicked their attention between him and Tanja, seemingly aware they were being strung along but unsure what the truth really was.

"My sister is a widow," the man from across the street piped up. "She let Mrs. Petrakis and the baby stay here as an act of charity. My uncle is a cleric." He mentioned the man's name, and presumably the uncle outranked these foot soldiers because they both stood straighter. "He's aware of all of this. Let me fetch him. He will determine if all is in order with her departure. Then we'll have no more inquiries from their governments."

The bored one nudged the grumpy one and gave a coaxing nod. The other sighed and jerked his head to send the brother out into the night.

From behind them, the baby's fussing abruptly ceased. Tanja broke away to say, "Why don't you feed Illi while I pack?"

Leon was starting to think they had a Broadway act in their future, if not a career in espionage. "I'd love to."

The little midge was placed in the crook of his arm. Milk leaked from the corners of her greedy mouth as she pulled at the nipple on the bottle. Sleepy brown eyes blinked open briefly. Her damp lashes were ridiculously long, her gaze trusting and oblivious of the thick undercurrents threatening to swamp and drown all of them. She let her eyelids grow heavy enough to close again, the simple action causing something to shift uncomfortably in his chest. Like the door on a stone vault was set ajar and a whistling breeze was stealing in. It ought to have been cold and uncomfortable, but it was warm and beckoning.

From the bedroom, he heard the swift thump of drawers and zippers being opened and shut. If the women communicated, they did it silently enough that the only other sound was the gulping from the baby.

Leon didn't bother contemplating how outrageous it was that he was pretending to be this baby's father. All he cared about was getting off this island with Tanja. Zach could have warned him she had a kid, but fine. Package deal. Whatever. His help with the baby should encourage Tanja toward an amicable dissolution of their marriage.

Tanja reappeared with a small case and an overstuffed bag that she pushed an empty baby bottle into. "Is she finished? I'll make another so it's ready while we travel."

She draped a cloth on his shoulder and guided him to hold the infant there.

The baby wobbled her head, then burped and let her head drop into the hollow of his shoulder. She was the tiniest creature he'd ever held and provoked a strange fire of protectiveness that stung his arteries. Her little noises of distress had him rubbing her back, silently conveying that she was safe, even though they were all balanced on a knife's edge.

Tanja rattled around in the kitchen. One of the soldiers checked his watch.

The door opened and the brother returned. "My uncle is on his way," he assured them, sounding as though he'd been running. "Five minutes."

Five minutes stretched to a tension-filled ten, then an excruciating fifteen. At least the baby fell asleep. Tanja held her and gently swayed, her movement hypnotic enough they all watched.

She looked like she hadn't eaten in a month, Leon noted. Her cheeks were hollow, her mouth tense, her eyes bruised with sleeplessness.

That fragility made the pit of his stomach feel loaded with gravel. His memory of her was one of athletic leanness with firm, subtle curves. She'd been quick with smiles and banter, and had possessed a core of surety that had made him think their affair would be a simple pleasure between unfettered adults.

Discovering the incredible sensuality beneath her veneer of sunny confidence had been as unexpected as it was dangerous. He'd had a brief surge of craving for her particular brand of heat and had wound up blinded by lust into marrying her.

He'd since told himself he'd imagined that depth of passion, but her siren-like allure was still going strong. It was stinging his lips after a kiss that was supposed to have been a one-act play. He'd had to press her back out of self-preservation or he might have let it engulf them both.

He steered his mind from further exploring that pointless fantasy. A car was approaching. An engine cut and footsteps arrived on the stoop. The door opened and an older man with a white beard and a black robe and cap entered.

Words were exchanged in the local dialect. Tanja offered their marriage certificate.

Leon had a fleeting thought at how strange it was that she had the document on her, but nodded verification that it was his name.

Passports were produced. Leon's came from the pocket of one of the soldiers. He'd had to keep his cool when that jackass had taken it at the marina. Thankfully, once the cleric recorded details from both, he handed everything back to Leon.

The cleric asked Tanja a few other things in the local dialect, recording her answers on a form. Leon wasn't sure what that was about. An exit permit, perhaps. There were so many threads of strain in the room, he couldn't tell which ones were being pulled. Was there some irregularity in her answers? Her allies, the woman who owned this house and the brother from across the street, seemed to be holding their breath and standing very still. Leon had the sense they expected this entire house to cave in on all of them at any second.

The cleric handed Tanja a piece of paper. She smiled politely, but her lips trembled. There was a sheen in her eyes. Her friends were glowing behind their stoic goodbyes.

Leon didn't waste time trying to interpret it.

"Everything is in order?" he confirmed, forcing the soldiers to look at him. "I'll take my wife and daughter to my boat, then."

CHAPTER TWO

"I'LL DRIVE YOU to the marina in my uncle's car," Aksil offered as the soldiers left. "His plates are known. We won't be bothered."

Tanja had one last chance to hug Kahina, who had become like a sister to her, then her friend hurried across to her brother's house.

Tanja cradled Illi against her shoulder as she climbed into the back of the sedan. Her bags were so meager Leon didn't bother putting them in the trunk, only set the small knapsack on the floor and the diaper bag on the seat beside her before taking the front passenger seat.

Now she felt as though she was running, not even worrying over the lack of a car seat. It was a short drive, and her muscles were tense and twitching, her skin coated in clammy perspiration while her lungs felt as though they couldn't sip enough oxygen. Escape loomed so close she could taste it. She only had to make it a little farther.

Tanja didn't fully understand who Kahina's uncle was, only that Kahina had appealed to him when the school had been shut down and all the female students forced into seclusion. The cleric and his wife had interviewed Tanja about how Illi had come to be in her care. After a few weeks of making inquiries, they had concluded she was telling the truth. Illi's parents were dead. Her only living relative, her adolescent brother, was impossible to locate. The cleric had decided Tanja could continue to mother the girl so long as she didn't draw negative attention to Kahina or the rest of their family.

Tanja had inadvertently broken that deal this evening. She had waited in terror for the cleric to denounce her to the soldiers, but he'd calmly forged a birth certificate and handed her the document before accompanying Kahina across the street to await the return of his car.

"I presume I owe your uncle a donation?" Leon asked as Aksil turned toward the marina. Leon stripped off his pullover so he was only in a body-hugging T-shirt, shoulders straining the light fabric. He unzipped a hidden pocket of the pullover. "This is euros. I had dinars, but they took it as a 'moorage fee.'" He pronounced that with disdain. "I also have American dollars and pound sterling on the boat."

"You hope," Aksil said dourly, pointing to the glove box.

"Not my first unfriendly port." Leon left the euros in the compartment. "They won't find all my stashes."

"We'll see." Aksil dropped his uncle's name when they arrived at the marina and escorted them down to the slip.

Despite the security the armed guards had supposedly offered, the trimaran had been relieved of nearly everything that wasn't nailed down. Some of the goods were piled on the dock beside the craft.

"At least they left the sail," Leon muttered.

"Do you think they siphoned the fuel?" Tanja asked in an undertone.

"Less ballast if I have to paddle," he retorted grimly, stepping aboard with her bags. "That's cargo I brought so take what you need from it." He nodded at the packs of disposable diapers and shrink-filmed cases of formula stacked on the dock.

The soldier who'd been guarding the stockpile shifted warningly. He knew as well as she did how much formula was worth here.

Tanja took what she needed for a few days of travel and, under the watchful eye of the nearby soldier, gave Aksil a last goodbye with Illi.

"We're going to miss you both," he said, touching the sleeping baby's cheek. "My children will be upset they couldn't say goodbye. Siman will cry."

"I wish you could all come," she whispered. The craft was so small it would barely carry the three of them, let alone a family of six plus Kahina, but she meant it.

"We have protection here," Aksil said with quiet confidence. "And this is our home. You want to go back to yours. But you'll bring our Illi back to visit someday."

"I will," she swore. "Tell your uncle *thank you*." There weren't words for what he'd done for them.

If only he could work a similar miracle with Brahim. She didn't let herself grow emotional over Illi's brother, though; otherwise, she'd be tempted to stay, and Brahim had made her promise to take Illi to Canada if she had the chance. Hopefully, once she was safely home, Tanja would be able to contact him and help him, too.

"The map you wanted…" Leon emerged from below to hand off what was no doubt another handful of notes to Aksil. "And some chocolate for your children."

One or the other would be a final bribe to the mercenaries circling like sharks. Whatever got them out of the port without being shot at, Tanja supposed.

Leon helped her aboard with Illi, then tried the engine while Aksil cast off. The motor turned over and so did her heart.

She ought to be urging Leon to wait until first light to set sail, but she was anxious enough to get off Istuval that she was willing to take her chances in the open waters of a dark Mediterranean. Leon was a very experienced sailor. She knew that much about him, even if he was a stranger in other ways.

Her marriage had become something of an urban legend among her friends, only mentioned if someone was persistent about asking her on a date or setting her up. Since the summer she'd married Leon, Tanja's life had been school and work, school and work. She hadn't had time for socializing, never mind a serious relationship. Perhaps if she had met someone who had really tempted her, she might have felt compelled to seek a divorce sooner, but she never had.

Nevertheless, when she had come to Istuval, it had been with the intention of going to Greece afterward, to properly end things with Leon.

Everything had gone sideways shortly after her arrival. Had she procrastinated contacting him? Absolutely. She'd been so hurt and angry after his initial betrayal, she had resolved to force *him* to come to *her* if he wanted a divorce. It was a juvenile attitude she had come to regret when five years passed without a word, but the longer their silence went on, the harder it became to be the one to break it.

So she'd put off reaching out to him until she reached Istuval. Then she had told herself she'd contact him once she was settled in her flat and job. She had pushed that until she had her class schedule and her lessons started. As soon as she felt comfortable teaching, she would definitely let him know she was in the "neighborhood."

By then she'd been so caught up in Brahim and Illi's

situation, chasing her absent husband for a divorce had ceased to be a priority.

Now here Leon was, arguably doing one of the most gallant, husbandly things a man could do. He had swooped in to rescue his wife *and* had shouldered responsibility for a child who wasn't his, without giving away the game.

Tears of gratitude arrived at the backs of her eyes like a battering ram. She could hardly see, but she braced her feet where she stood in the well of the outer deck, near where Leon took the wheel. With the baby clutched firmly to her chest, she waved at Aksil with her free hand.

Aksil waved once, but didn't linger. He exchanged something with the nearest soldier and made his way back to the car.

"PFDs were taken," Leon said tersely. "Go below so I don't have to worry about you falling overboard."

She didn't take offense at his abrupt order. She'd sailed with enough captains, her father and brother included, to know that even the best conditions required focus and potentially quick action. They weren't sailing into a storm, but it was dark and they would all be better off if she did as she was told and let him concentrate.

Even so, she was compelled to say, "Same." Turning any sailing vessel around to recover a man overboard was tricky. She didn't want to test whether she had the necessary skill. Not tonight. Not in the dark.

"Once we're under sail, I'll settle into the helm and won't leave it until daylight." He jerked his head to indicate he would be inside with her.

"Do you need help with the sails? I can put Illi down—"

"I can manage this alone. That's why I bought her. Go to bed." He might have glanced at her, but it was hard to tell in the dim glow of the running lights. "We'll fly once she gets going, but it'll be tomorrow afternoon before we reach Malta."

Was that where they were going? She probably should have asked. "You don't have to stay up all night. I can spell you off."

"I've raced," he reminded. "Sailed sleep-deprived many times. Go. You look like you haven't slept in weeks."

"Thanks," she muttered. Had he met *any* new mothers? "Wake me if—"

"I will. But I won't have to."

She ducked her head to go through the small door, shuffled hunched over through the tiny space that was the helm with its captain's chair and low-profile view over the bow, then negotiated the short, steep ladder into the cabin below. The saloon was a sleek, narrow space with a galley on one side and a bench settee with a long, narrow dining table on the other. An oblong door at the end led to the only quarters and was taken up by the V-shaped berth with storage space beneath and a skylight hatch above.

Everything was minimal and modest, not at all the opulent sailboat Leon had been swanning around in when they had met and married.

He had lost his father's fortune, she had read shortly after he left her in Canada. That's why he'd failed to invest in the marina her brother had taken over from their father. Recently, Leon had seemed to be coming back on top again—not that she made a habit of stalking him online. On the contrary, she purposely *didn't* check up on him.

Maybe he had lost everything again while she'd been cut off from the world on Istuval. Typical corporate raider, successively gambling away people's livelihoods.

She shouldn't be so cynical when he'd just saved her and her daughter. She knew that, but she had resented him for a long time, and her exhausted brain was having trouble bringing the two versions of Leon Petrakis together, especially because she was also trying to figure out where to put Illi down for the night.

Cats and trimarans didn't list as severely as sailboats, but Illi still might be sent rolling. She had mastered flipping onto her tummy and often woke up that way. The mattress was firm enough she should be fine sleeping next to Tanja, especially if she was tucked close to the bow. Tanja felt safe leaving her there with a pillow as a bolster while she brushed her teeth.

She didn't bother changing into her pajamas, just positioned herself as a second wall of defense to keep Illi safely on the bed, realizing as she lay down that she was actually exhausted. Despite the late hour and her weariness—Leon was right, she hadn't been sleeping enough—her busy mind fluttered like a trapped bird.

Obviously, her brother had asked Leon to come and get her, but why had Leon relented? What would happen next? Should she bring up divorce herself before she left for Canada? Why did the word *divorce* cut like a knife through the center of her chest? It was something she wanted. Needed. She couldn't live in this holding pattern forever.

Then what? How would she pay for her flight home? She would have to tell him—

The engine cut.

Either they were out of fuel, which was so disheartening a thought that she bit back a whimper of anguish, or...

A sail snapped. The boat wobbled and Leon's feet sounded on the deck above her. She watched for him through the hatch but could see only stars. After a moment, the constellations quit joggling and began to move in a steady path.

It shouldn't have felt like such a relief to be steering

into open water with wind their only propulsion. She had very limited supplies for her baby and suspected whatever groceries Leon had brought had been taken by the soldiers.

But when she heard him come inside and close the door, her entire being relaxed.

"Thank you, Leon," she whispered, and tumbled into heavy slumber.

Pink was staining the wispy clouds beyond the porthole when Illi began to whimper.

Tanja sat up, disoriented, murmuring, "I'm here, baby doll. Let's go find your bottle."

She had left the one she'd prepared in the tiny fridge, but when she went to the galley to retrieve it, she realized there was no microwave. Darn it, this might get loud.

"Everything okay?" Leon leaned down from the helm. He looked tired and scruffy, with a darker beard and weary circles around his eyes, but he was still sexy as hell.

Where the heck had *that* thought come from? The very last thing she wanted or needed was a recurrence of a case of the lusts.

She yanked her libido back under control and said, "She needs a bottle."

"Don't use the water in the tap unless you boil it first. I bought this from a fellow racer who had it stored on Malta. It's seaworthy, but the tanks are due for flushing. I didn't have time."

"Oh. Okay." She should have asked if the water was safe, but she'd been operating on autopilot last night when she had brushed her teeth. She had poured a glass of water, rinsed and spit, then drunk what remained in the glass out of habit. It had tasted stale and metallic, but she felt fine. Maybe a bit off, but that could be chronic hunger or mal de mer, likely both.

She only needed to warm Illi's bottle anyway so she set the filled kettle on the stove and started the flame. Then she swayed the unhappy Illi on her hip, keeping hold of a nearby ledge for balance.

"Soon, babykins. I promise."

Illi was sucking her fingers and pinching her arm, letting her know what a jerk she was for taking so long to give her the bottle she wanted.

"There's a hold they missed with emergency supplies." Leon directed her to lift the cushions on the saloon bench and open the narrow hatch beneath. "I had the chocolate in there with some extra bottles of water. I think there's a jar of instant coffee."

"And soup and porridge," she said as she exposed it and found the packets. It was all dry, hardly haute cuisine, but she was so thrilled she was giddy.

The kettle began to whistle. She found a coffee mug that would fit the bottle, then poured some of the hot water around it, lightly bouncing Illi while they waited for it to warm.

She made Leon a coffee in the meantime and passed it up to him. "I don't see any cream or sugar. I'd rather keep the formula for Illi."

"This is fine, thanks," he said drily.

She gave the bottle a shake and tried it on her wrist. It was tepid, but Illi greedily went after the nipple and drained the bottle in record time, eyelids growing heavy as she finished it.

They usually went back to bed after her early-morning bottle, but Tanja settled Illi on the berth with the pillow in place, then propped the door open so she could see and hear her. She came back to the galley to make a bowl of porridge that she took up to Leon.

"I can sit watch if you want to sleep," she offered.

He looked between her and the bowl and the coffee he'd set aside to cool, then to the various instruments. There was nothing in front of them except a light morning chop and a brightening sky.

"You're comfortable with all of this?"

"I couldn't navigate manually." She nodded at the rack of rolled paper charts, then clicked through the LCD screens on the hub mounted next to the wheel. "But it looks like we're a few degrees off the course you've plotted to avoid... That's a container ship?" She clicked to the Automatic Identification System screen to see the vessel's ID and call sign. Another screen told her, "The depth is good, but I'll keep an eye on it." She clicked to the radar screen. "And I'll watch for that little guy off our port bow."

"And the radio?"

"Hold that button and bust into any channel with noise."

"Good enough." He slid off the bench, crowding her in the tiny space, head and shoulders hunched because the ceiling was so low.

She was slouched with a forearm braced on the back of his chair. All she would have to do was tilt her head and lean. Their mouths would fit perfectly. She knew that because that's how it had been last night when he'd appeared out of thin air like the Greek god of rescues. He had kissed her like he'd meant it. She had kissed him back like she'd missed him.

As his flickering gaze went from her mouth to her eyes and noted where her attention strayed, her pulse began to flutter.

Something flared behind his eyes before he set his jaw.

"Give me twenty minutes, and I'll be primed for another twelve hours."

There was absolutely no reason she should hear that as bedroom talk, but she did. Which made her blush and shift out of his way in a small fluster, still clutching the bowl of porridge as she hitched herself into the pilot's seat.

He didn't bunk in with Illi, only went as far as the galley, where he settled on his back on the settee, knees bent because he was so tall. He crossed his arms and fell asleep in a blink.

She ate her cinnamon-flavored porridge slowly, wishing she could enjoy it more, but her stomach was really unsteady. Maybe it was the coffee. She hadn't had any in a while and it was pretty strong, but it was such a treat she refused to let the cup she'd made for Leon go to waste.

Maybe her tummy's protests were anxiety. Now that she was awake again, a tidal wave of apprehension was creeping up, threatening to drown her. Was there a Canadian consulate in Malta? She'd had three stopovers on her way to Istuval and doubted there were direct flights back. That meant she'd have to show a passport in Munich or Paris or some other country. Officials would want to be sure that Illi—who didn't look anything like her—was really hers.

Would her credit cards work? Tanja hadn't had internet access in ages and had failed to turn up for her first day of work at the accounting firm, even when they extended her job offer to accommodate her. Her last paycheck from her previous job had been twenty weeks ago and her sublet had only been confirmed for the three months she was supposed to be gone. That meant rent would have come out of what scarce savings she had left…

She sighed. Zach would scrape up what he could to get her home, but he wasn't flush with cash, given the new house and new wife and expected baby. Did she have a niece or nephew, she wondered? She would have to ask Leon if she could use his phone. Hers had been traded for food weeks ago. Which meant she would have to get a new phone and why did *that* feel like the most daunting task of all?

Then there was Leon. She glanced at his shins. How was he going to react when she asked for a divorce? When he realized what she'd done?

She had built him into such a sleazeball in her head. Too handsome. Smarmy. A horrible womanizer, a liar and an all-around reprehensible excuse for a human being.

Part of that had been defensive anger. She knew she was as much to blame for their rushed marriage. It hadn't felt like a hurry at the time, though. She had mooned after Leon for weeks as he came and went with Zach. Her brother had raced with Leon and had nothing but admiration for him, but when their father had decided to retire, Zach had come home to take over the marina. That's when Zach had cooked up a plan for Leon to invest in the expansion.

Leon had agreed to invest once he turned thirty and Zach had quickly been caught up in the excitement of purchasing more oceanfront property, chasing permits and rezoning bylaws, hiring engineers and architects. He'd borrowed heavily, expecting to pay it all down once Leon injected capital and the real work started.

Tanja had still been doing the books for the business. She'd tried to warn Zach against moving too fast, but she hadn't tried very hard. She'd been excited, too. In some ways more. Each time Leon came into the office, her entire being had sprung to life in the most mind-scattering way.

She had known it was only chemistry. Sexual attraction. Infatuation. She hadn't really known him as a person, but she had wanted to. When he finally flirted back, claiming to be too old for her even as he bent to kiss her, she had been over the moon.

Once they were intimate, her crush had bloomed into full-on enchantment. How could it not? Leon was gorgeous and led a glamorous life. For such an incredible man to look twice at her had been enormously flattering.

Then, a week into their affair, he'd proposed. *Of course* she had said a captivated and breathless yes. Their marrying would be perfect for *everyone*.

Given all the activity around the marina and Leon's travel schedule, they'd had a marriage commissioner come out on his yacht for an afternoon with just her father and brother in attendance. Leon hadn't wanted his parents to find out through online gossip so they'd kept the whole thing on the down low, tentatively planning a honeymoon in Greece to introduce her to them.

The honeymoon hadn't happened. Leon's father had died suddenly. Leon left and his promised investment money had never manifested. The marina her father had built had spiraled into bankruptcy. They had all felt duped.

Tanja hadn't wanted to admit she was married to the man who had ruined them. She'd gone back to school because she was enrolled, but she'd spent weeks hoping Leon would turn up and explain himself.

As the hurt of his abandonment solidified into anger, however, she had convinced herself that whatever she had felt for Leon had been for a man who didn't really exist. Had the sex even been as good as she remembered? Or was her memory of that as skewed as her vision of him had been?

Based on their kiss last night, he still had the same

physical effect on her. She cringed inwardly at suffering that soaring euphoria and wanton hunger again. It was so superficial! Great sex did not equal "great guy," as he had brutally demonstrated.

Yet here he was, upending her view of him again, sailing into genuinely treacherous waters to extricate her and her daughter from a dangerous situation.

That didn't exactly put her in a position to disdain him when she, a woman who prided herself on doing things by the book, had pulled a fast one to get what she wanted. Which was her *baby*. She would make no apologies for fighting dirty to keep Illi fed and safe and *with her*, but still.

Perhaps he sensed the waves of conflict and culpability rolling off her. Tanja heard him awaken with a long, indrawn breath. His legs disappeared from her periphery. It had been more like an hour than the twenty minutes he'd asked for. She heard him clatter around the galley, setting the kettle to boil before he appeared beside her.

"Stay there," he said when she started to shift off the captain's chair. "I'm going to adjust the sails. I'll clip on," he added in reassurance.

He clicked through the screens first, pausing to listen to a weather report in Italian, then went out on deck.

When he returned a few minutes later, the kettle was whistling. Tanja moved to make him porridge and coffee, then washed her bowl and sterilized Illi's bottle so it would be ready when she needed her next one.

She glanced in on Illi, who was fast asleep, then made herself a fresh cup of coffee and took it up to sit in the nook across from Leon where the sparkle off the water didn't blind her. No matter what happened from here on in, she had to say one thing.

"Thank you."

* * *

Tanja's voice was thick with such heartfelt gratitude it caused an itch in Leon's chest, one that made him think he should have known all along where his wife was, that she was in trouble. She shouldn't be sounding like he'd done her a huge favor when he'd only done what any decent man would do for his spouse.

Was he a decent man, though? The jury was definitely hung on that one.

He'd spent the night thinking about her, intensely aware of her in the berth below. His wife. A woman he'd married on impulse, mostly because her brother had learned they'd slept together. The expectation of Zach that Leon would propose had loomed like an aircraft carrier.

Which didn't explain why he had. Leon had never been one to buckle to peer pressure, but he'd liked Zach. They'd been embarking on a business venture together. And Leon had been a different man then. He'd been blinded by lust and living in the moment. *Carefree*, some would have called him. *Oblivious to consequences* was another way to put it. He hadn't expected their marriage would last, but that hadn't phased him. At the time, he'd seen marriage as something that served many purposes so he'd leaped in without regard.

Tanja had been different then, too. Inexperienced more than immature, but brimming with vibrant youth and promise. She'd had plans for her life, not big ones, but solid, sensible ones. She was always in steady pursuit of them, too. Always in motion, talking and laughing and bustling, not given to sitting still as a wraith, wearing dark shadows beneath her eyes, her profile difficult to read.

Motherhood had changed her, he supposed.

"Zach didn't tell me you had a baby. Where's the father?" He flicked his gaze to the horizon, ensuring they still had a clear course.

"Dead."

Before he could mutter *I'm sorry*, she continued.

"I didn't have Illi. Not in the pregnancy and delivery sense."

"But you told the soldiers your milk hadn't come in."

"It didn't," she said wryly. "Because I was never pregnant."

"You adopted her?" The unexpectedness of that news caused a bizarre shift inside him, like a seesaw that moved weight across his shoulders, lighter in some ways, heavier in others. It was disconcerting and left his ears ringing.

"Illi is the reason I didn't get on the flight when the other teachers were evacuated." She flicked him a glance. "I was fostering her. Zach put me in touch with officials in Canada to help with the adoption process, but internet was sketchy. Then I had to trade my phone for groceries and couldn't contact him at all. I warned him I would be off-grid, but I guess he panicked when he didn't hear from me and called in the reserves." She nodded to indicate Leon. "I should let him know you got me out."

"I only brought a burner phone and they took it. We'll have to wait until Malta. How did all of this come about? You being on Istuval?" Istuval was a popular destination for tourists, but usually travelers from Europe and Africa, not North America. Definitely not for anyone since the takeover.

"When I finished my degree and started—"

"You're an accountant?" He wasn't sure why that surprised him as much as the adoption. It was the career Tanja had been pursuing when she'd been at university. Once they married she had talked of putting off school to travel with him, though, leaving him with the impression she might have been after an MRS. degree instead of a real one.

"I'm unemployed at the moment, but yes. I'm a CPA. While I was articling, one of the firm's accountants returned from a stint on Istuval as part of a voluntourism program. It sounded interesting so I applied. I had to pay for my flight, but Kahina's school offered room and board for a nominal rate in exchange for tutoring women and girls in English. I also taught entrepreneurial skills. Basic accounting for small business, things like that. I signed up for twelve weeks, but it turned into six months."

"Is that how you met Illi's mother? She was a student?"

"I never met her. Both her parents are dead. I met her brother."

Leon let that roll around in his head. It just kept rolling, never coming to rest in a way that made sense.

"You're going to give me radiation burns, staring at me that hard." She sipped her coffee. "Brahim was fourteen. He showed up on my first day of class and said his mother was enrolled, but she was too sick to attend. He asked if I could give him a refund. I arranged it, but gave him some course material to give to her. He came back a few days later to ask me about it. He wanted to know how to start his own business so I invited him to join the class."

"That's shrewd business right there, getting his education for free."

"Don't be cynical. That's not how he was." She grew pensive. "Brahim is a very good person. He was trying so hard to support himself and his mother. His stepfather had recently died and he had a new baby sister. I presumed his mother was unable to work because of pregnancy and having a newborn, but she had refused cancer treatment because she was pregnant."

"Oh, hell." Leon winced.

"Yeah." She nodded and bit her lip. "That's how we lost Mom, so his situation hit me really hard. I wanted to do *anything* to help him. I offered to watch Illi if he needed to take his mother to treatment, things like that. His mother went back into the hospital and Brahim was staying with a neighbor, one who had other children including a baby. Brahim left Illi with her in the mornings so he could clean pools. That paid for the woman to watch and nurse Illi, but she couldn't keep it up. He washed dishes in the evening so he could buy formula, but he was so tired between that and looking after her, when he showed up for my class he fell asleep at his desk. I started taking Illi in the evenings and that turned into suggesting he sleep on my couch. We had a good little system for a few weeks."

"Why didn't you meet their mother?"

"I tried, but Brahim didn't want me to. He said the hospital thought Illi was with family. He was afraid if they knew he was relying on a foreigner, they would take her away from him. He loved Illi so much. I loved them both." She rubbed her breastbone. "When he told me his mother was terminal, I started looking into adopting them. It was going to be months of bureaucracy, but Kahina offered to extend my permit so I could stay and teach. It would have worked out eventually, but the café bombing happened. All the teachers packed up and left on any flight they could get. I couldn't leave Brahim and Illi. They were… I won't say they were *like* my kids. They *were* mine. In my heart, they're both mine."

She was pale as bone china. Her eyes glistened, and her voice was husky with an emotion that dug like nails into him. She was calm in her conviction, though, not trying to persuade him. These were the facts as she knew them. It was eerie, making his scalp prickle.

"Where's Brahim now?"

"I don't know." Her voice broke. She took a sip of coffee and her hand shook. "He disappeared a couple of times, came home with bruises. He didn't want to talk about it, then he got the news his mother had passed. He was devastated. She didn't even get a proper funeral because the military was cracking down. They closed the school. I kept thinking if I could just get them to Canada… But I couldn't even go shopping by myself. All the flights were canceled. Kahina took us in, but Brahim refused to come to her cottage. I realize now he was being pressured to enlist and was afraid to put us in their crosshairs because he knew they'd use us against him."

Leon swore and pinched the bridge of his nose. "He's a *soldier*?"

"The last time I texted with him, he begged me to take Illi to Canada. I said I wanted both of them to come, but he said he would be okay as long as he knew she was safe." Her breath hissed and she swiped at her cheek. "I saved those texts to my cloud account before I wiped my phone. As if anyone will give weight to a teenage boy's texts when deciding the custody of his little sister. I can't even prove she *was* his sister. Although they look alike. I have photos of him saved, too."

"How far have you gotten with the paperwork in Canada?"

"Not far enough," she said despairingly. "Kahina's uncle, the man who came last night? He and his wife pressured me to give Illi to an agency. Istuval is her home, I get that, but I couldn't—" Her voice broke again and she cleared her throat. "I kept asking him, 'Who will love her?' I really wanted an answer. Who would be her mother if her birth mother is dead? He tried to tell me she would be adopted, but we could hear gunshots the whole time we were talking. I finally said, 'If I have to stay on

Istuval to be her mother, then I'll stay.' He said I could continue to care for her as long as I didn't draw attention to the family, so I never left the house."

"You've been under house arrest?"

"Only for the last two months, but most women are living that way. Kahina has a garden and a few chickens. We grow lettuce and tomatoes and peppers. It's been okay, but formula has been a killer to find. Lately I've been giving my share of our eggs to the mother down the street. She's been nursing Illi a few times a day so I could conserve what formula Kahina managed to beg, borrow or steal."

"That's why you look like you haven't eaten in weeks? Because you *haven't*? Bloody hell, Tanja. You need to eat, too." His alarm came out as fury, making her flinch.

"So does a woman nursing two babies," she fired back. She added in a mutter, "And that's how I knew I was Illi's mother for real. I didn't care what I had to do or whether I ever ate again so long as she wasn't going hungry."

He didn't know whether to commend or berate her. He only knew it made him furious to think of her withering away even as he respected her level of devotion. The frustration of being sidelined and helpless to go back and fix any of that put an edge in his voice when he asked with exasperation, "Why didn't Zach tell me all this?"

"I don't know if he believed I was serious about adopting them until I refused to leave before it was finalized." She heaved a sigh. "He's had other worries. His wife was having complications with her pregnancy. He wasn't in the mood to indulge what sounded like bleeding-heart antics on his sister's part. The truth is, once the rebels took over, I was afraid to tell him how bad it really was. I didn't know how much they were monitoring, and I didn't want to stress him out any more than he was. We were as safe as we could be at Kahina's."

"He still could have told me." Leon had to wonder if Zach had feared Leon would refuse to help if he knew there was a baby involved, but he didn't want to believe he'd fallen that far in his old friend's estimation. "You have the paperwork now, though? The cleric approved the adoption or whatever?"

"In a way." She swallowed and something about her imploring gaze filled his gut with gravel. "He, um, issued a birth certificate for Illi."

"That says what?" Premonition danced across his shoulders and down his spine.

You must be so excited to meet your daughter.

"Tanja." He could hardly speak through a throat that was closing like a noose. "Do not tell me you have implicated me in the human trafficking of an infant."

CHAPTER THREE

"THAT'S A HARSH way to put it," Tanja protested, but couldn't help a wince of conscience. "The cleric is a recognized authority on the island," she defended. "He's like a government official. He's also a man with very traditional views. He was fine with me fostering Illi, but he was only willing to release her to my care because my husband was there. It's not just about propriety. He genuinely wanted assurance that Illi would have both a father and a mother to provide for her."

Leon glared at her as he snatched up the radio and sent out a broadcast seeking anyone within hailing distance of Malta.

"What are you doing?" Tanja clapped her feet to the deck, adrenaline spiking through her, but there was nowhere to run.

"I can't dock in Malta, can I? I was going to put you on a plane to Canada, but what if we're questioned? No. I will be in my own country, with my lawyer present, when *we* inform the authorities that she's not biologically ours."

"I'm not giving her up, Leon!"

"I didn't say you had to," he growled back. "But I'm not going to play ignorant to a blatant fraud. What are you trying to do? Send me to jail?"

"No!"

He glanced away. Someone was responding on the radio. He requested they relay a message to the *Poseidon's Crown* to intercept the trimaran. He added their course and instructions that the crew stock up on supplies for a baby before they left port.

"What's the *Poseidon's Crown*?" she asked as he ended his transmission.

"My yacht. I'll be on deck. I need to cool off."

"Clip on," she said to his back, but he was already slamming the door on her.

That went well.

She hissed out a breath and gathered their few dishes, taking them to the galley to wash them. As she did, she heard the radio crackle.

"*Poseidon's Crown* is leaving port within the hour," the other party said.

She radioed to thank them and signed off, then poked her head outside long enough to inform Leon. He nodded curtly.

"What, no makeup sex?" she muttered to herself as she closed the door and went below again.

Okay, she had known he wouldn't be pleased, but desperate times.

She went into the cabin to look at her daughter. Illi was sleeping so angelically that Tanja crawled in beside her and dozed off. Illi woke her an hour later. She was in a ridiculously good mood, wriggling and smiling and cooing and kicking. She really was the most adorable child ever created.

Tanja played with her on the wide berth, telling her about their change in plans. "I know I said you would meet your cousin soon, but the captain has changed course. It might take a little longer to get home."

Her stomach cramped with fresh anxiety as she wondered how long they would be stuck in Greece. She shouldn't be upset about going there. Flights out of Athens would likely be more direct. She had been planning to go to Greece anyway, to beard the Leon in his den and demand a divorce.

That still needed to be done, she realized, experiencing a fresh, stabbing pain in her middle.

"I just want to take you home," she told Illi, nuzzling the baby and growing teary with homesickness.

When Illi began to chew her fingers, Tanja rose to make her a bottle and nearly lost her balance as she stood.

"Whoa," she muttered, quickly setting the baby safely on the mattress while her equilibrium caught up to her head. Her stomach rolled with a harder pitch than could be blamed on the boat, and a cold flush of nausea washed over her.

"No," she moaned softly as she realized she was sick. She touched Illi, but she had no sign of fever. Her growing fussiness sounded like hunger and a wet diaper.

Tanja changed her and used a wet wipe to wash her hands, remembering the water in the tanks might not be potable. Was that what was causing these knifing pains that kept accosting her? They were a lot worse than monthly cramps, something she hadn't had in a while, probably due to worry and weight loss.

She had to leave Illi crying while she clattered around the galley, using bottled water to make the formula. The small task pretty much wiped her out. When she had the bottle ready, she made a herculean effort and brought Illi up to the seat across from the helm to feed her.

The door abruptly slid open and Leon halted as he saw them.

"I have to look at the horizon," she said with a lip-curl of self-deprecation.

"Seasick?"

"Yeah." That's what she was telling herself, even though hot and cold chills were rolling over her.

"Eat something." He moved to flick through the screens.

Her stomach had writhed with agony at the scent of the formula. She swallowed back a reflexive gag and said, "No, thanks."

"Take the wheel while I make a cup of soup?"

It was all she could do to hold on to the baby and move those few steps to slide into the pilot's seat. She concentrated on measured breaths, willing the growing nausea to subside.

As Illi was finishing her bottle, Leon brought two cups of soup and offered her one.

Tanja averted her face.

"I know you don't feel hungry, but it'll help." It was an order.

"I drank some of the tap water," she admitted.

"Why? I told you not to."

"You didn't tell me soon enough. I did it last night."

He sighed with impatience and set both cups into nearby holders. His hand suddenly loomed in front of her eyes, startling her into recoiling, but he was only wrapping his wide hand across her forehead. After a moment, he shifted the backs of his fingers to her cheek, his touch cool and incredibly soothing.

His tone, however, as he swore under his breath was less comforting. "You have a fever."

"It's a water bug. At least it's not contagious."

"We hope," he muttered.

"Move then. I'll get away from you."

He stepped back and she wriggled from the helm, juggling baby and empty bottle.

Her struggle must have looked pretty bad because Leon locked his arms around both her and the baby. He plucked the empty bottle from her hold and eased her into the nook seat, scowling at her with a disgruntled expression.

"Are you in pain? Maybe it's something more serious. Appendicitis?"

"Oh, that's very calming, thanks. It's not that bad," she insisted, even though she was so weak Illi felt as heavy as a bag of cement in her arms, one that wriggled and kicked with joy.

It was so nice to see her full and happy, Tanja couldn't begrudge her energy. She played a game of wiggling Illi's soggy hand against her soggy mouth, saying nonsense things. Illi released her infectious baby chortle, making Tanja chuckle in turn.

When she heard Leon snort, she glanced at him and caught him watching them with the strangest expression on his face. Amusement, but something intensely personal.

He quickly snapped his attention to the horizon, showing her only his stoic profile, but her heart took a stumble over what she had glimpsed. Envy? Longing? Tenderness?

"Oh," she groaned as a sudden stab went into her stomach, sharp enough to push the noise out of her. She swallowed, but didn't think the porridge was going to stay down. "Can you—" She stood and shoved the baby at him before hurrying to the head.

A few minutes later, feeling scraped hollow, she shakily returned to the helm.

"There are anti-nausea pills in my shaving kit." He had Illi clasped in one bent arm against his chest.

"They knock me out and I have to look after Little Miss."

"I can hold her. Go lie down."

"If I'm lying down, I might as well have her beside me." She moved down the ladder and held out her hands.

He hesitated, then crouched to transfer the baby. "Call me if you need help. It's only a few hours until we intersect with *Poseidon's Crown*. You might feel better once we're not rocking so much."

"I'm sure I will," she said, but already knew it was a lie.

When Leon made visual contact with his yacht, he slipped down to tell Tanja. She and the baby were fast asleep. Illi wore a healthy glow beneath her light tan skin. Tanja wore a frown on her brow and hectic patches of red on her pale cheeks.

"Tanja?" He touched her arm and she flinched. "We're moving to my yacht soon."

"'Kay," she murmured, not opening her eyes.

He touched her forehead. She was dry and disturbingly hot. He swore under his breath. "You're burning up. Did you take anything?"

"Your kit is gone. Pirates took it." The mercenaries on Istuval, he assumed she meant.

He checked for it anyway, but she was right. "Hang in there."

"I'm fine. Is Illi okay?"

"Sleeping. No fever," he assured her after setting the backs of two fingers against the baby's soft cheek.

Within the hour, he was close enough to *Poseidon's Crown* that he dropped the sails and bobbed in the water. The yacht was manned by a crew of a dozen. One would sail the trimaran back to Malta, so there were two men in the tender that came across.

Leon transferred their bags, then woke Tanja. She sat up and shuddered with cold, hugging herself and trying to drag the blanket back over her.

"Wear this." He removed his pullover and helped her into it. "I'll carry the baby."

"I can do it."

"You want to drop her? No. You're sick." He took the baby.

Illi didn't want to be disturbed. She began to cry when he gathered her, but a fussy baby was the least of his worries. Tanja nearly hit the deck when she tried to stand.

"Stay there," he ordered, pressing her back onto the berth. He carried the baby out and handed her across to the crewman piloting the tender.

When he returned, Tanja had stumbled into the galley, clinging to whatever was in reach. She looked like death and sounded panicked. "Where is she?"

"Waiting for us," he said evenly. "Let me help you."

Her weight loss hit him as she leaned into him. She was reedy and light as he boosted her up to the deck and lifted her from the trimaran into the tender. She folded into a seat and held out weak arms for the baby.

Leon exchanged a few brief words with the sailor taking control of the trimaran, warning him supplies were low and the water was boggy. When he sat down next to Tanja, he wrapped his arms around her, both to warm her and to help her hold the baby.

She snuggled into him with a grateful noise, head heavy as she nestled it onto his shoulder. Then she picked it up to ask with weak outrage, "What the hell is *that*?"

"What?"

Her gaze went up and up and up as they neared the yacht. "That's *Poseidon's Crown*? It's a cruise ship."

"It has staterooms for twelve, not twelve hundred," he dismissed, keeping to himself that *Poseidon's Crown* had been touted as the world's first "gigayacht" when his father had ordered it.

"I *saved up* so I could go to Istuval on a *working* holiday," Tanja said with indignation, eyes glassy with fever and fury. "I picked Istuval because it was close enough to Greece to make the side trip affordable. I was *dreading* asking you for a divorce because I thought I might get stuck paying legal fees and I don't have extra money for lawyers. Once I had Illi and Brahim in my life, I didn't know how I would pay for a divorce *and* adoption. And all the while you have *this*?"

A chill descended. It might have been caused by entering the shadow of the yacht's seven decks. *Poseidon's Crown* loomed like a skyscraper above them. But it might have been that word *divorce*. It might have been every word she'd just thrown at him like sharp icicles that still managed to penetrate his skin rather than shatter on impact.

"My father bought it," Leon said flatly. "It was tied up on lease to a sultan for its first three years. I couldn't sell it without taking a bath. Keeping it has allowed me to borrow—"

"*I don't care!* You've been sitting on this kind of money for years while I traded my smart phone for baby formula. You're the worst, Leon. You are the absolute worst."

The behemoth with its stair-step decks of sleek angles and spaceship aerodynamics looked as though it was made of quicksilver and glass. It was modern and visually beautiful, and Tanja knew it to be indisputably luxurious even before she boarded.

As they approached the stern, a wall of the hull opened, allowing them to step straight from the tender into the yacht's fitness club. Across from where they entered, a glass-walled weight room held treadmills and ellipticals pointed to enjoy the view off the port side.

A purser greeted them, introducing himself as Kyle. He sounded Australian.

"Toy room?" Tanja asked, reading the sign on a door in the stern wall.

"Jet Skis and kite-surfing gear, that sort of thing," Kyle said. "Forward of the gym is our sauna and spa, but the specialists can come to you for massage or nails."

Growing up at the marina, Tanja had seen some swanky vessels. Beasts like this tended to anchor offshore, though. She'd never been on one to see the extravagance within.

"You have an elevator," she noted with a scathing glance at Leon as they entered it.

"We have four," Kyle said helpfully.

"Oh? How many helipads?" She was being facetious.

"Two." Kyle was serious.

"Two," she repeated with a curl of her lip.

Her air of superiority died a quick death when the elevator stopped and she completely lost her balance.

Leon caught both her and Illi with a glower, then took Illi and kept his arm around Tanja as they stepped out. He was so *warm*. It took all her concentration to make her legs work. She wanted to melt right into his heat and strength, close her eyes and let him take complete control.

"Have the medic come to my apartment immediately," Leon ordered. "Tell the captain to keep us in heli distance to Malta in case we need to evacuate her to a hospital."

"Yes, sir." Kyle quickly set aside her bags and moved to pick up a white telephone mounted near the elevator.

"Helicopters do come in handy," Leon said pithily as he steered her along what would be called a gallery in a mansion.

They skirted an atrium that looked down to the main saloon—accessed by a glass elevator, she noted as they passed. There was a dome of colored glass above them, and now they were moving through double doors into, well, it was nothing less than a mini penthouse.

On one side there was a galley fronted by a wet bar with stools. On the other side stood a business area with a stately desk, a monitor on an articulated arm and a printer on a bookshelf that held a handful of novels.

They moved into a spacious and bright area for lounging and dining. Walls of windows on either side opened to the wide, surrounding deck. The windows continued wrapping forward past a partition wall that held a fireplace.

On the other side of the wall was a walk-through closet and a spacious head before she reached the massive bedroom with an equally massive bed. It was situated so the sleeper could sit up and take in a one-eighty view across the bow or walk out to the private forward deck and slip into a hot tub.

Her weak legs folded and she sat down on the foot of the bed. How did one process this much wealth and attention to comfort?

Leon hung back in the main living area to instruct Kyle to leave the luggage and find something for Illi to sleep in.

When he finally showed up in the bedroom, she asked, "Why did you bring us to your stateroom?"

"You need help with the baby." He was still holding Illi, who was making raspberry noises against her wet wrist. She smiled and held out her arm to Tanja.

"I can manage," Tanja insisted, lifting heavy hands to take her daughter.

"Can you?" Leon scoffed, offering her the baby, but holding on to her.

Good thing. Tanja's arms felt like wet spaghetti. She couldn't take Illi's weight and wound up dropping her arms empty to her sides, whimpering even as she glared resentfully when Leon's brows lifted in superiority.

The last thing she wanted to do was rely on him, but it was painfully obvious she would have to. For now.

The medic arrived with a message from the captain. "We were hailed by the *Pennyloafer* on our way to meet you. Dr. Kyrkos issued an invitation to meet them in Malta."

Kyrkos was a racing buddy from Leon's school days. He picked up the phone and told the captain, "Invite Kyrkos aboard if he's still in the area. Tell him it's a house call."

Leon then hovered, still holding the babbling baby, listening as the medic asked Tanja a few questions while taking her temperature.

"High, but not dangerously high," he pronounced. "My guess is that this will pass in a day or two, but I'd feel better if you had a doctor's opinion." He gave her something for fever and told her to rehydrate, promising as he left to order fruit juice spiked with electrolyte tablets.

"Can I shower while I wait for the juice?" Tanja asked.

"I don't know. Can you?" Leon made no effort to disguise his sarcasm.

"Ha-ha. Water was as precious as everything else at Kahina's. That's why I was in the habit of drinking whatever I'd poured." She grimaced. "And that's why I haven't showered in three days. Feeling grimy doesn't help me feel better at all."

"Go," he urged with a nod. "Don't lock the door. Call if you need help."

She sent him an *I'd rather die* stare over her shoulder.

He wanted to say something sharp about her taking advantage of the amenities on the yacht that so offended her, but he had a brief flash of how she'd almost collapsed on the trimaran. It had scared the hell out of him. She needed to conserve her strength, not pit what she had against him.

As for the vessel, he knew it was an obscene expense. He'd been considering unloading it, but it was damned convenient. It had brought him quickly and comfortably to Malta and was allowing him to take care of her and the baby with ease.

Her drink appeared as she emerged wearing his robe, still flushed and glassy-eyed, but with a healthier glow on her skin. He gave her a T-shirt to sleep in and she looked with worry at Illi, making no move to change.

He read the conflict in her. She was sick, but she still wanted to be the one to care for Illi. It was as clear as the maternal tenderness she kept showing the baby with such natural ease. It was a regard that was so foreign to him he couldn't help staring with fascination each time he noted it.

That's how I knew I was her mother, he heard her say again as he took in her sharp cheekbones and the way her collarbone stuck out. That evidence of deprivation stoked the frustrated helplessness in him again, the one that wanted to be angry with her for not looking after herself, but how could he fault her?

He couldn't. He could only order sternly, "Go to bed. I can hold her while I check emails. I'll let Zach know you're safe."

"Oh. Yes, please. Thank you," she said with subdued relief, and slipped back into the head to change.

Two hours later, Leon had watched a handful of videos on the basics of baby care. It turned out four-month-old babies didn't know how to sit up so he didn't need to be alarmed that Illi couldn't. For a few seconds, he'd been convinced he had broken her.

Which was all he needed on his conscience. *You're the worst, Leon.*

I know, he had wanted to shout. A weight greater than this tanker sat on him over some of his behavior in the past. Nothing criminally negligent, but not a lot that was particularly considerate of others. Then there were the things his father had done. At least he'd taken steps toward making reparation on those fronts.

Still, he'd been disturbed by Tanja's outburst over struggling financially. He hadn't sought a divorce because he'd been wary of what it would cost him, never dreaming she had thought he was so broke the legal fees would fall to her. Had she not seen a news report in the last few years? He'd been back on top for a while.

I traded my smart phone for baby formula.

That put a sick knot in his conscience. One that had him again thinking he should have made more of an effort to know where she was instead of trusting she'd moved on with her life and didn't miss him at all.

He realized the baby had fallen asleep in his arm. Her round face and dark lashes looked like an ad for life insurance or some other peace-of-mind product. Even his hardened heart lost some of its resistant tension as he gazed on her.

Don't get attached, he reminded himself, and gently set her in the cot Kyle had found, draping a light blanket over her.

He might have stood there and stared like a fool for hours, but a muted bell pinged. He picked up the phone and learned the doctor was boarding.

"Leon. It's good to see you," Kyrkos said a moment later as Leon stepped from the elevator into the main saloon where Kyrkos was waiting. Kyrkos never missed a chance to catch up if they happened to cross paths in their travels on the Med, so it hadn't surprised Leon that he'd hailed the yacht when he'd seen it. "I don't think you've met my wife, Cameron."

Not this one, no. Leon had been at the wedding when Kyrkos married his first wife, and had only heard through the grapevine that this youthful socialite had elevated herself from office assistant to mistress and recently to trophy wife.

"I made Kiki bring me, even though your captain said it's a medical call. I'm dying to see this yacht I've heard so much about. Do you mind?" Cameron asked with an appealing tilt of her head.

"Not at all." Lavish crafts like this existed to be shown off. "I'll have a steward give you a tour." Leon signaled to the crewman behind the bar.

"I thought I'd find you bleeding out," Kyrkos said. "Who needs attention? One of the crew?"

"No—" It hit Leon that he didn't have an explanation for who Tanja was. She was tucked in his bed so he couldn't dismiss her as merely a guest. If Kyrkos decided she needed urgent care, Leon would want to be identified as her closest relative to authorize medical care so he couldn't call her anything but what she was.

"I need you to check on my wife. Tanja."

"You're married? Oh, my God! Is she pregnant?" Cameron asked with hand-clasping glee.

"What? No," Leon said firmly, reconsidering honesty as the best policy. "Can you show our guest every courtesy while I take the doctor up?" he said to the hovering steward.

"Of course, sir." The crewman drew Cameron away while Leon took Kyrkos up the elevator.

"Wife?"

"Kiki?" Leon countered.

"I know," Kyrkos muttered. "But now you're married, you'll soon learn it's better to pick your battles than lose the war. When did you marry? How was I not invited to the wedding?"

"It's a long story," Leon dismissed, leading him toward his stateroom. "We were headed to Greece, but if Tanja needs a hospital, we'll go back to Malta."

The good doctor came up short at the sight of the baby cot.

"She is *not* pregnant, is she? What the hell, Leon? You have a *baby*?" He peered at the sleeping Illi. "How am I the last to hear? Cammy follows every gossip site in existence."

"It's not something we've advertised. My main concern right now is Tanja. We're assuming it's a stomach bug from drinking some stale water. She's been running a fever since this morning and she's nauseous."

Tanja blinked in disorientation when he gently woke her, but predictably asked, "Where's Illi?"

"Napping." He pointed toward the adjacent room. "This is Dr. Kyrkos."

"Hi." Since she'd gone to bed with her hair damp, Tanja's red-gold hair was bent in odd directions. Her face was pale, and his T-shirt hung off her bony shoulder when she sat up.

She answered his questions about her general health and the onset of symptoms, said "ah," and accepted a thermometer under her tongue.

Her fever had come down thanks to the pills the medic had given her.

"I agree with the medic's assessment. This will likely work itself out within a few days. Keep your fluids up, your fever down. If things worsen, definitely visit a doctor in Athens. I can take a sample to the lab in Malta as a precaution if you like, to be sure it isn't anything more serious. We're headed there."

Tanja held out her arm for a blood draw and then took a cup into the head.

"Is she a model?" Kyrkos asked while Tanja was absent. "She's very thin. Iron supplements and a multivitamin would be a good idea."

Leon texted that instruction to the purser.

As Tanja came out of the head, Illi began to cry in the other room. Tanja would have gone to her, but Leon stopped her.

"I'll look after her. Go back to bed."

"She hasn't eaten since we've been aboard, has she?"

"No, but I had all her bottles sent down to the chef so everything could be sterilized and ready when she needs it. I can handle it." He was speaking with more bravado than genuine confidence, but Tanja looked so weak and peaked.

She wore an indecisive look, but Kyrkos said, "It's a good idea to give her formula while you're under the weather. Keep your strength up."

"Oh, um—"

Leon could tell she was about to explain she hadn't given birth to Illi and therefore wasn't nursing. He signaled behind Kyrkos's back to keep that detail to herself for now.

"Okay," she murmured with a small frown of confusion. "Thanks for the checkup." She went back to bed, and Leon waved Kyrkos to lead him from the room.

Leon gathered Illi on his way out the door. She was looking very pitiful with her crinkled chin and teardrops on her cheeks. She rubbed her face into his shoulder when he held her against his chest, digging her way further under his skin with the small gesture.

"I know you're hungry," he said, unconsciously echoing what he'd heard Tanja saying to her when she'd been waiting for Illi's bottle to warm on the trimaran. "We're going to get you something right away." He picked up the phone by the elevator and asked the chef to prepare a bottle, requesting it be sent to the main saloon.

"I could have sworn we were kindred spirits when it came to kids, but look at you," Kyrkos snorted as they went down the elevator. "What's it like? Being a father?"

Leon wanted to choke out a laugh and say, *Ask me when I've been doing it longer than five minutes.* At the same time, he grew self-conscious with the knowledge he wasn't one. Not really. Which bothered him for some reason.

He couldn't explain that twinge any more than he could explain this well of concern for a baby he'd met barely twenty-four hours ago. He wasn't a sentimental person and certainly hadn't had much role modeling when it came to nurturing. Illi was very small and helpless, though. Everything Tanja had told him about her plight, losing the mother who had essentially sacrificed her own life to give her daughter hers, sat heavily on him, prompting an empathy at her loss despite the fact his own mother was alive and well.

Besides, who wouldn't want to calm an agitated baby? Any decent person would want to feed a helpless, hungry baby whether it was a kitten or puppy or infant. As far as magnanimity went, it wasn't a huge effort to pat her back and speak reassurances. It certainly didn't deserve all this cogitation and remarking upon.

"You didn't want kids?" he asked as a diversion from Kyrkos's question.

"It's the reason my first marriage fell apart. My time off is precious. When I get a break, I want to spend it on the water or the slopes, not... Well, I guess you're not inconvenienced, are you? Still enjoying life, sailing with a baby." Kyrkos flickered his gaze around the atrium as they came off the elevator. "If you call this 'sailing.'" The curl of his lip was a silent *must be nice.*

Thankfully, a steward forestalled further comments as he hurried toward them with the baby bottle on a tray as if he was serving a flute of champagne.

"The chef made it himself. He said the temperature should be perfect."

Leon shook a drop onto the inside of his wrist to be sure, then offered the bottle to Illi.

She took it greedily, smiling around it, which made his mouth twitch. Didn't take much to be a hero in her eyes, did it? He smiled back.

Kyrkos noticed the baby's effect on him. He snorted again, which made Leon defensive of his growing connection with Illi. Something aggressive rose in him, a protectiveness that bordered on irrational since he had a vision of throwing Kyrkos off his yacht.

Leon dragged his attention to the steward. "Where can we find the doctor's wife?"

"The pub, sir."

The bar in the stern was one deck down and meant for casual gatherings and cocktails before dinner. There was abundant seating and it offered potpies and burgers with its vast selection of beer. The three screens of satellite television were invariably tuned to sports.

"Oh. My. Gawd. You have a *baby*?" Cameron rushed toward them as they appeared. She quickly snapped a photo of Leon before he'd realized she was turning her phone on him.

"If you want to take my photo, *ask*," he said, barely keeping his temper.

"Cammy, don't post anything unless Leon says he doesn't mind," Kyrkos hurried to caution her.

"Oops." She winced a sorry-not-sorry. "I already posted, like, a million of the boat."

"The yacht is fine. Delete the one of me and Illi." Leon managed to keep a civil tone. Barely. Tanja hadn't approved such a thing, and he was genuinely incensed by the young woman's utter disregard of their privacy.

"Do I have to?" Cameron batted her lashes. "It's *really* cute."

"I was planning to thank your husband for the house call by arranging for you both to spend a week aboard *Poseidon's Crown* later this year." He let the threat of that rug being pulled hang in the balance.

"That's more than generous compensation for my time," Dr. Kyrkos said, giving his wife's phone a stern nod. "Delete the photo, Cammy."

"If you insist, Kiki." She pouted and tapped her phone. Thankfully, they departed moments later.

Tanja tried to go back to sleep, but when an hour had passed and Leon hadn't returned with Illi, she rose grumpily and put on a robe to go looking for them.

She got lost twice, mostly because there were two dining rooms and she confused them on the map. When she bumped into a steward, he made a call, then offered to make her a fruit smoothie before giving her directions up one deck and forward.

She sipped as she walked to the music salon, contemplating suitably cutting remarks about the yacht having a live concert stage for pop stars. She walked in to find Leon with Illi on his lap, sitting on the bench before the grand piano.

"You have to push harder," he coaxed. "Can you do

it?" He stuck his finger against the key she slapped, depressing it enough to make a soft *plink*. "Hear that? You try."

Both of Tanja's ovaries burst into song, throwing sunshine and confetti into the air while her bones softened in a giant, melting, *Awww*.

"They said you were giving her piano lessons." Her rueful voice wasn't quite as nonchalant as she was striving for. "I didn't believe it."

Leon glanced up, looking tired, but he'd cleaned up around his beard and wore a fresh shirt. "She was losing at roulette. I had to get her out of the casino."

"You do *not* have a casino." As she said it, she silently went all in that he did.

"I'd show you, but it's black-tie." He gave her robe a flickering once-over, gaze lingering an extra second on her bare ankles, just long enough to make her very aware that she wore only his T-shirt beneath the warm velour.

And that he'd always been a fan of her long legs.

Illi squawked with excitement at the sight of Tanja, little arms waving, making Tanja smile.

"That's quite a greeting." She set aside her smoothie and came forward to take her.

Her robe loosened and gaped. She fiddled with it before she gathered her daughter and nuzzled Illi's cheek, using the baby as a shield against whatever vibes Leon was throwing off that she was picking up so acutely.

Seriously, any virile man with a baby was going to be a straight shot of pair-bonding chemicals to a woman's inner cave girl. She shouldn't let this affect her so deeply.

"You're wearing fresh clothes," she noted of Illi's onesie. "Who changed you?" She glanced at Leon, expecting him to mention a maid or the doctor's wife.

"I did."

"Really? Why?"

"Her diaper blew out."

"You changed her *diaper*?"

"Why is that so astonishing?" He looked affronted.

"I didn't think you would know how."

"I called the chief engineer to walk me through it."

"Oh. Does she have kids?"

"I was being sarcastic," he said with exasperation. "He's an unmarried man who probably hasn't seen a kid since he was one. No, Tanja, I managed it all by myself. It's not rocket science. Take off the dirty one, swab the deck, put on a clean one. Her pajama thing was stained so I changed that, too. What did I miss?"

Diaper cream, but they'd run out ages ago. Thankfully, Illi's rash hadn't been too bad lately.

"I didn't expect you to be such a natural is all," Tanja said, mildly defensive since he was taking to caring for a baby like it was the easiest thing in the world. She and Brahim had had quite a few misadventures in the early days.

"It's all online," Leon muttered, then abruptly changed the subject with a nod toward her smoothie. "Were you hungry? You didn't have to leave the room. Dial zero for anything you need."

"When you didn't bring her back, I wanted to know where she was." She craned her neck to avoid Illi's grab for her nose.

He narrowed his eyes. "What did you think? That I gave her to the doctor to leave on a church doorstep or something? Didn't you trust me?"

She pinched her lips, wondering why *that* was so astonishing. "Can you blame me?"

She sank into a chair, still very weak, especially with Illi so energetic and wiggly. She was happily bouncing her legs in frog kicks while twisting and grabbing for anything she could touch.

"But I'm her *father*, Tanja." Leon's tone was so serrated, he could have sliced bread with it. "Surely you believe I could only have her best interests at heart?"

"So do I," she said, guilty of involving him without his consent, but he would wait the rest of his life for her to apologize for that. "You saw how difficult things have become on Istuval. Do you think I should have left her behind at an orphanage? Should I have asked Kahina to raise her when she can't work to support herself and will be living on her brother's generosity for the foreseeable future?"

He glanced away, grimly admitting, "No." He rose and brought her smoothie across, leaving it on a table within reach. "But you've put me in a difficult position."

"Have I? Gosh, that's a shame." She met his gaze. She could speak sarcasm, too.

Leon didn't move, only stood over her, hands pushed into the pockets of his jeans, not a whiff of humor about him.

She crossed her legs, reminded by his cold, steely stare that she wasn't wearing a stitch of her own clothing and was only off Istuval thanks to him. Her baby was dry and fed when she was in no shape to care for her. Illi was *hers*, also thanks to him.

"I'll quit taking cheap shots," she conceded begrudgingly. "But an explanation would be nice. You quit taking my calls. Did I do something to make you drop me cold like that?"

She subtly braced herself, having convinced herself long ago that his abandonment was somehow her fault and she was too dumb to see it.

"Are we doing this now? All right." He paced away

a few restless steps, hands still pushed into his pockets. "You must have seen the reports on how my father's empire collapsed when he did?"

"And that you had to restructure, yes. I understand you were busy, Leon. I'm talking about five minutes to write an email so I wasn't left wondering why you didn't want to come back." Or want to be married to her anymore. He hadn't wanted to even *talk* to her.

She had thought about climbing on a plane to confront him, but she'd been as broke as her brother and father. Leon clearly hadn't wanted to see her, so she had moved on with her life. More or less. She had focused on attaining her degree to avoid dwelling on the happily-ever-after dream she had lost. The money was one thing, the blow to her inner belief system and self-esteem quite another.

"The reports that were made public were the tip of the iceberg." His shoulders became a tense line. "I was doing everything I could to keep the worst of it out of the news. Things were happening very quickly and there was no bottom to the well. Each time I thought about calling you, my situation was worse than it had been an hour before. I couldn't risk revealing any of it and having it become public."

"And you have the nerve to question *my* lack of trust in *you*? I wouldn't have said a word if you'd asked me not to. What can you tell me now? Because silence leaves me making up stories and, believe me, you do not come off well in any of them."

"No?" he asked with derision, but his cheek ticked. "What terrible things have I done?"

"You bankrupted my father's marina."

"Your brother bankrupted it," he responded swiftly and firmly.

"You promised Zach you would invest with him."

"And then I told him I had no money and he should find someone else."

"No money?" she scoffed, looking wildly around at the polished brass and leather upholstery and *grand piano*. "Zach partnered with *you*, Leon. In good faith because he trusted you. And you completely screwed him over. *All of us*."

"I had every intention of working on the expansion when he proposed it. Once I realized how bad things were with Dad's finances, I had to stage a fire sale. That's business, Tanja. It wasn't personal and he knew that."

Tanja could only stare at him while Illi did squats in her lap, babbling against her fist.

"Zach took it personally," she finally managed to choke out. "We all did. *I* thought your defection was pretty personal, considering we were *married*. I was your *wife*, Leon."

"For a week," he scoffed. "Not even. And it wasn't a real marriage."

That hit her so hard she recoiled into the chair, quickly hugging the baby so she didn't let Illi slide right out of her arms since they seemed to have turned to rubber.

Leon flashed a scowl and moved toward her.

She looked away, blindly staring at the horizon of blue on blue through the huge picture windows. "Silly me, coming all this way to ask for a divorce when we only needed to clap three times and wish it away like a bad dream."

"The marriage was legal. Obviously," he said tersely. "And we are overdue to discuss divorce, I agree with you on that. But it's not as if we were in love, Tanja. We got married because your brother found out I'd slept with you. He said your father would expect it if I was buying into the marina."

"*That's* why you proposed?" Boy, he really knew how to kick someone when they were down.

"You knew that," he said with impatience. Then, after a beat, he added, "Didn't you?"

"Well, I thought you felt *something* for me." She swallowed, trying to clear the croak from her voice. "We were sleeping togeth— Oh, my God." She closed her eyes, hugging the baby and wishing she had the strength to rise and storm off. "You didn't even want to marry me. That's what you're saying, isn't it? I'm such an idiot. I mean, I kind of got that message after you didn't come back, but I thought I had done something to change your mind. Or that you realized you could have had anyone and decided I was too plebian and boring. When you proposed, we had already slept together. I thought that meant you cared about *me*, not just getting me into bed."

"*You* got *me* into bed. You showed up with wine. I wasn't your first lover. I didn't seduce you." He shot each word at her, blunt and fast, then paused, giving her space to correct him.

She couldn't. He was right, much to her chagrin.

"That doesn't explain why you bothered to propose," she choked.

"When big brother twisted my arm… Hell, I don't know why I gave in. I liked Zach." He shrugged. "We were going into business together. Marrying his sister seemed like a good way to secure my side of things. Honestly? Call me delusional, but I didn't think you would accept. I thought we were having a summer fling. You said you were going back to school."

"You bluffed and I called it? That's what you're saying?" she asked with disbelief.

"Pretty much. And there were things with my parents… My father wanted me to come and work for him. I thought a wife and my own business in Canada would get him off my back."

"So I was a bulletproof vest? Did your father know he was sick? And that things were falling apart? Is that why he wanted you there?" She frowned. "Did *you* know he was sick?"

"It was the sort of massive heart attack that was inevitable, given his lifestyle, but no, none of us knew he was on the verge of one. He hadn't seen a doctor in years. I thought he was being his overbearing self, demanding I come work for him so he could tell me I wasn't doing it right." His expression shuttered. "He'd done that twice before. I wasn't interested in going through it again."

"You must have had mixed feelings, though, after it happened. Must have wished you'd returned when he asked." Any child would. "Is that why you stayed once you got there?"

"I wouldn't have made a different choice if I had realized he was going to die," Leon said dispassionately. "I had made up my mind I wouldn't work for him. That I would start doing my own thing. He was the most entitled bastard you'd never want to meet."

It was such a harsh indictment she could only blink in shock.

She recalled Leon being oddly stoic when he'd taken his mother's call that his father had died. *She insists I come home. I'll be back soon.* It had been eerie, the way he'd taken the news without emotion and acted as though his mother wanting him home was an imposition. Everyone grieved differently, she had told herself, trying not to judge.

That had come later, when he'd ignored her calls and texts.

"I was a different man then." Leon scrubbed a hand

across his face. "Spoiled. As long as my credit cards worked, I didn't ask where the money came from. When I was forced to take over, I realized why he had micro-managed me in the past. He was hiding the fact his for-tune had been built on things like child labor, collusion, and skirting environmental rules."

"Are you serious?" She absently caught Illi's hand, keeping her fingers from trying to get into her mouth since her jaw was hanging open in shock.

"Completely," he said grimly. "That left me with two choices. I could walk away and lose absolutely every-thing, leave my mother destitute, and forever wonder if the industrial leaders who moved into our place took a more conscientious approach, or I could do things better myself. They weren't my crimes, but I had benefited from them. I had to clean it up. With great power comes great responsibility, but in order to take responsibility, I had to maintain the power. Understand? So I stayed and made the hard choices that kept us afloat—including backing out of my deal with your brother."

In a twisted way, she saw the logic, and something else. "You couldn't tell me that because you thought I'd go pub-lic with it? Spill the beans on your father's misdeeds?"

"We barely knew each other. Frankly, I expected you to come after me for a divorce settlement. The longer time went on and you didn't, the more I thought it was best to let sleeping dogs—"

She narrowed her eyes. He abandoned that metaphor.

"I figured you knew I was broke and chose to dis-tance yourself. Given the crimes my father had commit-ted, walking away from a wife who didn't want me and an investment opportunity I couldn't afford was nothing by comparison."

"It wasn't 'nothing' to us," she said in a raw voice.

"I didn't tell Zach to move as fast as he did," he defended sharply. "He got in way over his head without ensuring his financing was in place. I've had handshake deals fall into the toilet myself. That's business, Tanja."

"Yes, I can see how difficult things have been for you. It's not personal that you saved your own butt, not ours. Don't worry about it."

"Oh, climb off your high horse. If I was so terrible, why didn't you divorce me? Why did you even marry me? Love?" he taunted.

"At least that's what I thought it was!" A hot sting of embarrassment rushed across every inch of her skin. "I was young and romantic enough to think passion was a sign of something more enduring. It didn't hurt that my brother thought you were wonderful. Everyone wants their spouse to be friends with their sibling. Your investment would have given my dad a very comfortable retirement. My marrying you wrapped everything into a tidy bow of happily-ever-after, so of course I thought you were making all my dreams come true."

He snorted.

"I know that was immature and unrealistic! It still hurts that you didn't even feel that much toward me. Why did you bother coming to Istuval? You could have left me there to rot, never to darken your doorway again."

His expression hardened to granite. He was silent so long she feared she had overstepped in some way. Then he blinked and said, "I thought it would put me in the best position for negotiating our divorce."

That launched a fresh wave of outrage. "I don't want your stupid money, Leon. I just want to be free of you."

"Well, that's a little complicated now, isn't it?" He nodded at Illi, who was standing in her lap, singing in her ear.

"Not really," Tanja said stiffly. "I spent five years living my life without you despite your name being attached to mine on a piece of paper. It will be the same for Illi." She cradled the baby's warm hair and kissed her sweet-smelling cheek. "We don't need anything from you after this little pleasure cruise. I did bookkeeping on the side through school. Once I'm home, I'll hustle up some clients and support us fine. It's what I was going to do anyway."

"I'll give you a settlement," he growled.

A smart woman would snap that up. She had a child to feed. But she was too insulted.

"It wasn't a real marriage," she reminded with an over-bright smile. "Let's not turn it into a real divorce."

CHAPTER FOUR

IN ANOTHER LIFE, Leon would have seen Tanja's refusal of his money as a best outcome and moved on. Today, he was incensed.

Before he could open his mouth with a retort, however, the phone in his shirt pocket vibrated. He glanced down and tilted it to see the screen.

"Zach is texting. I'll see if he'll accept a video call." He withdrew the phone and tapped to place the call, then handed the phone to Tanja.

A smile of anticipation burst across her face, sunny with the stark love that she and her family seemed to express unreservedly toward one another. That affection was so constant and raw it was like a force of nature— the kind of thing Leon admired and respected, but didn't trust. Thunder and lightning were exciting to watch, but it would kill you if you were careless enough to be stuck in it unprotected.

"Oh, it's you." Zach's edgy voice eased into surprised relief. "I was worried when I saw Leon wanted a face call. I thought he might have bad news. It's so good to see you."

"Didn't you get the message that we're safe? Illi, look. Say hi to Uncle Zach." She shifted the baby into sitting on her lap to face the camera.

"Hey, sweetheart," Zach said warmly. "Good grief,

she's getting big. Well, I hurried out here to take this call, but since it's you…shh." His voice dropped to a whisper, raising hackles of suspicion across Leon's shoulders. "Shonda's sleeping, but look." After a pause, he whispered, "This is Bryant."

"Oh, Zach," Tanja gasped softly. "He's so beautiful."

Her gaze came up, so shiny with joy it shot an arrow straight into Leon's chest, leaving an ache that thrummed a vibration through him. She nodded an invitation for him to come see.

He didn't know why he went. He and Zach were barely speaking, but he moved to stand behind Tanja and saw a newborn swaddled in a yellow blanket and wearing a pale green hat.

"Congratulations," Leon said politely.

"Oh. You are there." Zach's tone went flat with dismay. The image jostled as he slipped from the hospital room out into the hall, then the screen flipped to show Zach's disheveled hair and weary face. "Thank you for getting Tanja off Istuval. Shonda was on bed rest and had an emergency C-section yesterday."

"Everything went okay?" Tanja asked anxiously.

"They're both doing really well."

"I can't wait to hold him," Tanja sighed.

"I thought you'd be on a plane." Zach frowned. "I was texting for a flight number. Where are you?"

"On Leon's yacht."

"Tanja isn't well enough to fly," Leon said.

"I can fly," she insisted, sending a disgruntled look over her shoulder at him.

"You can barely fight the baby for the phone." Illi was about to win in her quest to grab it so he plucked her from Tanja's lap, telling Zach, "Tanja and I have some legal things to sort out. We'll do that in Athens and let you know her plans from there."

"Finally getting a divorce? Good idea," Zach said in a cool voice that grew concerned as he asked Tanja. "What happened? How did you get sick?"

Leon moved across to a colorful abstract painting, giving Illi something to stare at while Tanja reassured her brother that she had seen a doctor and was already feeling better.

Leon was replaying her accusation that he had destroyed her brother financially. Was that how Zach viewed it?

It didn't hurt that my brother thought you were wonderful. Everyone wants their spouse to be friends with their sibling.

Leon hadn't worried too much about terminating their business deal. For starters, he hadn't had a choice, and as much as he'd liked Zach, he hadn't felt deep loyalty toward him. Growing up with seemingly unlimited wealth, toys, looks and freedom meant that Leon had always attracted a lot of friends, most of whom wanted to take advantage of their association with him.

Leon had met Zach when he'd hired him as a tactician after losing to a team Zach had navigated through the San Juans. Such a tight working relationship demanded a lot of communication and reliance so they'd come to know each other fairly well, but Leon had been stung by hangers-on in the past. He only opened up as much as was absolutely necessary.

Zach's pitch for a marina expansion had been nothing new. Leon had been drawn in because Zach had been dropping off the racing circuit to take over his father's business. It was the complete opposite of something Leon would allow himself to be pressured into. He'd been deeply selfish in those days. There'd been a part of him that had imagined if he helped Zach he'd have an angle to persuade him to keep racing. That's how Leon had been raised to view the world—favors begat favors. There was nothing money couldn't buy. Nothing was done out of genuine caring or friendship.

Learning Tanja blamed him for the loss of her father's business left a metallic taste of dishonor in his mouth. Especially when it had come about because he'd dumped Zach's deal to rescue his own father's business—a business built on lies and cheated negotiations.

Leon *hated* to see anything of his father in himself, but that tainted blood showed up at different times in ways that never ceased to make him loathe himself. Hell, he was so much like his old man that his wife felt scorned and tricked by him, the same way his mother had always felt about his father.

I thought you felt something for me. We were sleeping together.

Leon had felt toward Tanja what he had felt toward any attractive, available woman who reciprocated his interest—sexual desire. Granted, it had been an acute level of that sort of interest. Before meeting her, he'd had relationships of various lengths from one-night stands to yearlong affairs. All had been pleasant, and none had inspired more than basic levels of affection.

Tanja had been different. Obvious in her interest, which was always a kick for a man's ego, but mesmerizing in how she was both playful and earnest. Sincere.

Leon had known deep down that she took things more seriously than he did. The connection between her and Zach and their father was infinitely more complex and *real* than anything he could begin to comprehend. Being around them had been both fascinating and puzzling. Intimidating in some ways because it was one of the few things in life he knew he would never grasp or properly experience.

Leon had known in his gut that having an affair with Tanja would lead her on, which was probably why he'd wound up proposing. He'd been convinced they wouldn't last, that she would eventually figure out he wasn't capable of giving her the emotional depth she expected, but he'd wanted her anyway.

And she had been a grown woman capable of making her own decisions. That's how he'd rationalized it. In reality, he'd wanted to sleep with a woman who appealed to him. That's what kind of man he'd been—not devoid of conscience, but with a very superficial grasp of right and wrong. Not much sense of consequence, either. All that had mattered was getting what—or who—he wanted when he wanted them.

He'd grown up since then. Now he considered what was best for other people, not just himself.

Finally getting a divorce? Good idea, Zach had said a minute ago.

It was. But something in Leon balked. He was a champion at heart. That's why he'd won more races than he'd lost. That's how he'd pulled his father's company back from the brink. A stubborn refusal to fail wasn't much use when one party wanted to end things, though. He knew what it looked like when people who resented one another stayed married. He couldn't do that to himself, or Tanja, or the baby who rested her head on his shoulder.

He absently rubbed Illi's back, listening to Tanja wrap up with her brother.

"Let Dad know I'm fine. Tell him I'll call soon."

"I will. Love you, Books."

"Love you, too. All three of you." She ended with a

happy sigh and set aside the phone to hug herself. "I'm an auntie. How amazing is that?"

Technically, that made Leon an uncle, but he didn't allow that flitting thought to land and take root.

Tanja sipped her smoothie, then frowned.

"Not sitting well?"

"Just a lump of banana that surprised me." She took another sip and made a face. "I really am feeling a lot better. I think some of it was seasickness."

He came across to touch her forehead. She wasn't feverish.

Illi smiled and reached for her, making Tanja smile. "Hi, baby doll. Come here."

That brightness was back in her face. A woman in makeup and heels was undeniably attractive, but Tanja, fresh faced and wearing nothing but confidence and the sheen of unconditional love, was spellbinding.

He had an urge to cup her cheek and caress her soft skin with his thumb. He wanted her to look at *him* with that warm, unabashed smile.

Disturbed, he made himself give her the baby and picked up his phone.

"Don't try to rush your recovery. You've been through a lot." He had already relayed to staff that she needed supplements. He would ask them to add some rich desserts to the menu, too. She could stand to gain a few kilos.

"I don't want to rely on you any longer than necessary. Kahina was so generous and understanding, but you know what they say about houseguests."

He lifted his gaze.

"They're like fish. They start to stink after three days."

"Is that what they say?" He smirked as he went back to checking his emails. "Well, I've asked my lawyer to fly out to join u—" He swore as three different subject lines jumped out at him, all running a variation of *You're married?*

"What's wrong?"

"Secret is out on our marriage." He explained that Cameron had been posting photos of the yacht. "She must have said something about being aboard so her husband could check on my wife."

"So much for patient confidentiality. Why did you tell him we were married?"

"What else was I supposed to say?"

"I don't know." Her mouth pulled with uncertainty. "What does it mean? Will anyone care?"

"I am quoted and photographed from time to time," he said drily. More on the business side, not as much on his pursuit of pleasure since he'd given up chasing women and regatta trophies, but he was a rich and powerful man. Did she not realize that?

She was frowning with worry, smoothing her hand over Illi's hair.

"It's a scoop, not a scandal," he reassured her. "I'll talk to my PR team, release a statement." He shrugged it off. Even as he did, his phone pinged twice more. A fresh email from the head of a media conglomerate asked if he knew a photo of him with his baby was being shopped to news outlets.

Leon *really* swore.

"What?" Tanja asked, eyes popping with growing alarm.

"She didn't delete the photo with Illi." And this was why he hadn't seen the value in Zach's friendship when Zach had offered it. Leon had known Kyrkos most of his life, but the doctor was throwing away their lifelong relationship for what? Five minutes of fame for his status-seeking wife?

Tanja closed her arms around Illi. "But if it's reported that we have a baby, what if it comes out that our situation isn't entirely—"

"Legal?" he charged.

"By the book," she corrected. She bit her lip before closing her eyes and turning her nose into Illi's cheek. Her brow furrowed with deep anxiety. Fear of losing her baby.

That revelation of such deep vulnerability made the pit of his stomach churn with a primal compulsion to protect.

"My lawyer, Georgiou, is arriving tomorrow." His voice was a bass echo from deep in his chest. "I'll put him onto ensuring t's are crossed and i's dotted where Illi is concerned."

Tension lingered around her mouth, but she spoke decisively. "Take me to Malta. I want to fly home." Her voice caught on the word "home." "If I'm there—"

"You can't *get* home," he reminded her. "Illi doesn't have a passport. Customs agents will ask if you have permission from her father to take her overseas. They'll want to see her paperwork and it's not up to scrutiny."

"Write me a letter that says you give us permission," she demanded. "*I'll* write one."

"Another false document? Great idea. No, Tanja. I'm not like my father. I keep my nose clean, along with the rest of my life." He was terse now, annoyed that she was resisting his help. "Given the choice between throwing fuel on a messy story about abandoning my baby to my estranged wife or a very nice story about my wife and I starting a family, I'm going with the nice one."

"Oh, that lie is fine? She's not *yours*, Leon!"

"Check the paperwork *you* filed," he snapped.

She flinched with hurt and looked away, mouth trembling but jaw pugnacious.

He pushed his hand through his hair as he gathered his patience. "Look, I believe it's in Illi's best interest for her to be with you. I'm not going to let anyone take her from you. You have my word on that."

"Forgive me if I don't think your promises are reliable."

Maybe he deserved that, but it still cut like a whip.

"Like it or not, *you* made me responsible for her. I won't shirk that responsibility." He was *not* like his father, disregarding the needs of a child—his own son included—because it suited him. "You and I butting heads every minute won't help."

"I wish I'd never m—" She sealed her lips over whatever she'd been about to say.

"Met me? Married me? Then you wouldn't have Illi, would you?" he summed up brutally.

He took the baby from her, something she was too weak to prevent, and she could utter only a disgruntled sound.

"I'll keep her while you rest. Do you want to sleep here? On a lounger by the pool? I can help you back to the stateroom if you need it."

She looked between him and the baby, her body trembling with anger.

"I've spent a lot of time thinking you're a selfish jerk who is ruthless about getting what he wants. This doesn't change my opinion." She pushed to her feet and lost all her haughty air of superiority when she paled and had to hang on to the chair.

He steadied her, but she shook him off.

"Bring her up when she's ready for her nap."

"Of course," he said, because he might be selfish and ruthless, but he was also capable of magnanimity—once he got what he wanted.

Tanja woke with a sense she wouldn't fall back asleep. Not only had she been sleeping on and off for nearly twenty-four hours, but her mind leaped into a whirl of wondering what would happen now that her marriage was public. What would happen with her adoption of Illi? It was still so tentative.

She didn't want to rely on Leon and his lawyers to sort things, but what choice did she have? Her financial resources were depleted, and she couldn't work until she at least had a laptop and an internet connection. She couldn't buy anything until she had some income. It was a catch-22.

"Why are you sighing like that? Are you in pain?"

Leon's quiet voice beside her made her gasp and roll over, realizing as she did that he was lying on top of the covers beside her.

"What are you doing here?"

"Sleeping. Until you started huffing and puffing. Do you need a house blown down or something?"

"I'm just restless. Frustrated."

He left a nice round silence for her to hear the suggestiveness of her own words.

"By my situation," she clarified. "Jeez, seriously?"

"I didn't say a thing," he said mildly, but she had the sense he was laughing at her. He curled his arm beneath his pillow. He still wore the clothes he'd been wearing earlier, but she saw the pale glow of his bare feet in the dim light.

"You could have gone to bed properly. Somewhere else," she pointed out.

"This is *my* bed," he said drily. "The sofa is too short and I need to be able to hear Illi so you don't have to get up. You didn't even notice me here. Go back to sleep."

"She's in the lounge?" She lifted her head and cocked her ear, but their talking didn't seem to be disturbing her. "Thank you for helping me look after her."

"She said begrudgingly," he mocked, voice still low with sleepy amusement.

"I do resent needing your help," she admitted. "But you have to admit this is strange."

"That you've woken me to *talk*? Yes."

That caused such a stab of memory, of slithering against him in the night, naked skin brushing as their limbs twined, she made a noise of injury that she hoped he assumed was an impatient tsk.

"I forgot that you were up all last night. I'm sorry I woke you," she said stiffly, and rolled so her back was to him.

"I've been asleep since Illi went down at seven. It's fine." The humor was gone from his voice and now it was tinged with something more serious. Conciliatory, perhaps. "What do you think is strange? That we're five years fake married and now we're faking that we have a baby together? It wasn't on my bucket list, I'll say that."

She rolled back to face him even though she couldn't see him in the dark. "Haven't you wanted to…find someone else and get started on a family of your own?"

"No," he said, low and prompt and unequivocal. "I never wanted kids."

"Wow." And ouch. She hadn't expected such a strong response when he was actually very sweet with Illi. "I'm sorry we're imposing then."

"You're not. My childhood was lousy. That's all. I'm sure I told you that."

He had, but he had always deflected when she tried to pry anything more out of him.

"From the outside, it looks as though you had everything you wanted. I was always surprised to hear you call your childhood 'lousy.'"

"On the surface, I did have everything." He sounded resentful, but she didn't think it was directed at her. "The best food and clothes. Travel and education. It should have been ideal, but my parents' marriage was horrific. That skewed my view of family. I never wanted to subject a child to that tension and manipulation."

"I guess I should have asked if you wanted kids before we married. I always saw myself as getting married and having children. We really were doomed, weren't we?"

There was a profound silence before he said, quietly but powerfully, "I thought so."

That sent another knifing pain through her. "My God, Leon! Why did you even go through with it?"

"I told you. I wanted to get my father off my back."

"That's so *cold*."

"I'm being honest, Tanja. As honest as I should have been back then. Maybe if I had, you wouldn't have married me. Did you really believe we'd have the picket fence, two kids and a dog? End up in side-by-side rocking chairs on the porch?"

"First of all, we should be so lucky as to grow old at all." She bunched the edge of the blanket beneath her chin, thinking of her father losing her mother when they'd been so devoted to one another. "I didn't think marriage would be easy, but I thought we'd figure things out as we went along. Mom and Dad got married really fast and had challenges, but they found ways to get through them. They went into it intending to make their life together and made it seem doable, if not simple. That's what commitment is, right? Committing to figuring out how to stay together while working through stuff?"

"Why did they marry so quickly?" His head turned on the pillow. "Was she pregnant with Zach?"

"The opposite." She couldn't help the gossipy chuckle that came into her throat. "They both had really strict parents and were saving themselves for marriage, but couldn't wait so they had a short engagement. Isn't that cute?"

Leon didn't say anything.

"Do *not* say I should have done the same thing."

"I wasn't going to."

"What then?"

Nothing.

"Some things never change." She was hurt by his silence. She really should have seen how doomed they were from the way he had always shut her out like this. She had tried to give him space, thinking he would let down his guard eventually, but they hadn't had time and apparently he still didn't want to open up.

He suddenly came up on his elbow, looming over her. His imposing silhouette pressed her deep into the mattress. There was only a slanting glow from the other room, making it impossible to read his expression.

"I haven't been with anyone since you." He threw the words down like a gauntlet.

"Liar." It was too flabbergasting.

"Believe what you want." He sounded insulted. "It's the truth."

She wouldn't normally be so rude, but the man had been a sexual animal.

"Did something happen?" she asked with sudden concern. "Are you okay?"

"My mojo is *fine*, Tanja." Definitely insulted. "It was a *choice*."

"Really." She couldn't help that she was so skeptical. "Why would you do that? Or *not* do it."

The silhouette of his profile looked to whatever moonlight was sparkling on the distant ripples of the sea.

"I had already done enough things that made me like my father. He had committed so many atrocities… Infidelity felt like the last tawdry straw. If I could hang on to a shred of moral character, if I kept myself from doing that one thing, then for sure I was a step above the human garbage that he was."

His view of himself was so bleak it made her unutterably sad. "So celibacy was like…a form of self-flagellation?"

"Oh, yeah, I've done a lot of that," he assured her with a ripple of self-deprecating amusement in his tone.

She burst out laughing and shoved at his shoulder, not moving him an inch. "Is that what the kids are calling it these days?"

"I wouldn't know. No one admits to doing it." His teeth flashed.

This, she thought with a warm glow. This was the man who had so dazzled her that she had been unable to say anything but yes to his proposal. She'd been willing to do anything he suggested. The things they'd done on his sailboat? Whew.

She grew very aware of the rumpled blankets between them and the intimacy of the low light and the warmth off his body. His scent and solid strength. His weight tipping her toward him on the mattress.

Maybe that was simply his magnetism pulling at her.

He was looking at her. When he spoke, his tone was somber.

"It's fine that you've had lovers while we were still married." He smoothed a wrinkle from the blanket between them. "I didn't expect you to be faithful. That was my own baggage I was working through."

"I…" Was she really going to admit this? "What makes you think I've had lovers?"

A silence crashed over them, so loud it might have been a five-alarm fire bell.

"Why wouldn't you? You don't need punishing," he said evenly.

She folded her fingers over the edge of the blanket, loath to admit what a spell he'd cast, one so strong she was still under it.

"Tanja." He sounded so grave he made her heart shiver in her chest. When his finger looped to pick up a tendril of her hair, a tingling sensation swept down her nape into her breast. "Please don't tell me I hurt you so badly that you couldn't trust men. If you denied yourself the pleasure of sex because…" He swallowed. "It really would be too much for even my fairly impervious conscience to bear."

"It wasn't that." She licked her lips, hyperaware of his finger twirling that length of hair. "I mean, I was pretty disenchanted with men and the institution of marriage, but I had to work while I was in school. I didn't have time to do more than go for coffee. Anything more than that would have meant I'd have to free myself of you first and…"

This part was hard to admit because Leon had set a certain bar. No one had made her feel the way she was feeling right now, and he was only touching her hair. Since when were there electrical currents in strands of hair that ran straight to erogenous zones, lighting her up like a Christmas display?

"I never met anyone who—" *tempted me the way you did* "—seemed worth going to the trouble of filing the papers. You didn't break me, Leon."

"Good," he said after a pulse beat. "I don't want that kind of power."

"Too much responsibility?" she guessed in a voice that was strained by the reactions and emotions she was trying to stifle.

"Yes." He spoke frankly, but gently. His fist was resting on her shoulder and his fingertip extended to play with her ear. "You weren't even tempted to have a casual hookup, though? You're so passionate."

"Not really. Not if I can go five years without sex," she joked weakly.

"You're very passionate. That hasn't changed." His tickling touch dipped into the hollow beneath her ear, making her scalp tighten. "This may come as a surprise to you, but most people do whatever I tell them to do. You've always pushed back on me. It's frustrating, but I have to respect you for it."

"You must bring it out in me." She was trying to keep it light, even though his caress was making runnels of heat invade her limbs. If he knew what was happening beneath these blankets—the flush of sensual heat likely turning her skin pink, the peaked nipples that were stinging with anticipation, the flooding heat settling in an ache between her thighs—he would be on her like a wolf on a fawn.

"We do seem to play off one another, don't we? I haven't forgotten." It was a smoky warning that made her want to wriggle closer.

She pushed her palm against the weight of the blanket where his chest was radiating warmth into her side, resisting him as much as reminding herself that she ought to.

"Easy, sailor. After five years, I'm thinking a stiff breeze is all you need to get excited. Don't pretend your reaction has anything to do with me."

"See, that makes me think *you've* forgotten how good we are together."

He hadn't moved, and she was suddenly fixated on how close he was, willing him to close the distance between his mouth and hers.

She should have said something pithy, but wound up saying, "Perhaps I have."

And slowly, very, very slowly, the shadow of his shoulders shifted. His head lowered. The tip of his nose brushed hers and the heat of his lips settled feathery soft across hers. She let her mouth open slightly while he ever so gently deepened the contact, searching out the fit before he sealed them in a deep kiss and plunged them into a molten sea of passion.

She made a throaty noise of shock, expecting playful excitement, not this sharp jab of wanton hunger. Her breath dried up while her whole body flushed, accosted by lascivious longing.

He stilled as though their combined reaction startled him, too. Maybe he was weighing whether her noise had been a protest.

She brought her hand from beneath the covers to grab his wrist, silently conveying that she wanted him to keep kissing her.

He pressed into it, opening his mouth wider to ravage her unreservedly. His wrist twisted against her grip and his fingers slid between hers. He pressed her hand onto the pillow beside her head as he let his weight come over her and crush her into the mattress.

She was smothered by his weight, trapped by his bulk and the covers and the way he was making love to her mouth. It was magnificent. She moaned her encouragement, abandoning herself to the madness they conjured.

He made a ragged noise of suffering as he dragged

his mouth to nip at her jaw and skate down the side of her neck.

"It's better than I remembered," he said hotly. "You taste so damned good." His mouth came back to bite her earlobe, then suck, sending showering tingles through her. "Stop me."

She only turned her head to seek his mouth with hers. Damn these covers between them. She writhed, pushing her hip against the blunted shape of him. He closed his legs outside hers, trapping her into a tight line pinned beneath him.

She arched to feel more of him, moaning into his mouth as they played their tongues together. She wanted to touch him, *feel* him. Strip naked and take him inside her.

He leaned on one elbow and raked the blankets from between them, down to her waist. His free hand swept up to cup her breast, plumping it against the soft cotton of the T-shirt she wore.

"Seriously. Stop me or I'm going to keep going," he warned in a growl even as he dropped his head and opened his hot mouth over her nipple.

The muted sensation was strong enough she wanted to lift her knees and curl protectively. She couldn't. She was at his mercy.

The cotton quickly dampened as he lightly bit and sucked at her through the fabric, the attentions sending hot, stabbing sensations into her loins.

At least her arms were free. She roamed her hands greedily across his back, soaking up the heat of his shoulders and biceps through the fabric of his shirt, the hot skin of his neck beneath his collar. She filtered the coarse curls on his head through her fingers and opened her mouth against the soft-rough stubble on his chin.

She wanted to beg him to do filthy things with her. Her

body said it for her as she drew him back to kiss her and gave him her tongue.

He blatantly sucked and worked his own against hers, jabbing erotic thrills into her with the flagrant play, drawing more moans from her that echoed against his.

He shifted atop her, allowing her to open her legs beneath the blankets, welcoming his weight between her thighs. He rocked against her as he bit her bottom lip. She lifted her hips into his muted thrusts and clung weakly to him.

"Do you have a—"

Illi began to cry in the other room.

Condom was left unspoken. They were both frozen and pulsating.

Leon swore. He dropped his head into the pillow next to Tanja's ear, panting as though he'd been at the bottom of the sea and finally made it to the surface.

In the next second, he rolled off her, arm across his face to hide his chiseled features.

She weakly pushed her legs toward the edge of the mattress.

"I'll get her," he said in a strained voice. "Just give me a sec."

She was equally addled but desperate to flee. What had just happened? A cataclysm, obviously, but how? Why? What did it mean?

"I'll go." She kicked her way out of the tangled covers and snatched up the robe off the chair. "It's okay, baby doll," she murmured as she made her way through to the lounge. "Mommy's here."

She was still unsteady on her feet, but she didn't think it was remnants of her illness. She had nearly succumbed to Leon's lovemaking, and that was like a near-death experience.

She bent to collect Illi out of the cot and experienced a rush of light-headedness when she came back up.

"I had the chef make a bottle before I put her down for the night," Leon said from the shadows of the corridor, near the door to the head. "It's in the fridge behind the bar. If you can manage her by yourself, I'll shower."

"Of course. Thank you."

He walked into the head and firmly closed the door.

CHAPTER FIVE

Leon disappeared without a word after his shower.

Tanja put Illi back down and slept fitfully, waking alone in the stateroom when Illi did. She called down to order Illi's morning bottle, then sang to her as she changed her.

It was such a beautiful morning that Tanja opened one of the doors to the starboard deck, letting the fresh air stream in. They seemed to be at anchor, sheltered near a wall of stone with patches of greenery growing in the steps and crevices. It was stunning, the reflection nearly perfect in the calm blue water.

"Cythera Island," Kyle informed her when he delivered Illi's bottle. "Kýrios Petrakis asked me to relay that his team from Athens will arrive shortly—" He nodded toward the door she'd opened as the growing sound of a helicopter could be heard beyond. "Breakfast will be served on the lido deck if you feel up to joining them. If not, he'll check in with you later."

"That must have been an early start," she noted. "I'll come down as soon as I dress." She was actually starving and anxious to get a grip on how things would proceed.

Plus, she'd rather not face Leon alone. She'd rather not face him at all. Their make-out session had kept her tossing and turning with sexual frustration and mortification.

If Illi hadn't interrupted them, she would have made love with him. Tanja kept telling herself deprivation had caused her to react with such abandon, but Leon had lost none of his skill or appeal. One kiss and she'd been right back to the crush that had made her so reckless five years ago.

What he'd ever seen in her remained a mystery. Five years of forgoing carbs made stale bread look really appetizing, she supposed.

No matter why they'd succumbed to impulse, the fact was that the uneasy truce they'd established was impacted. Tanja's sense of who they were, individually and as a couple, had vanished. When she had been able to dismiss him as that jerk who had abandoned her, she had faced him without self-consciousness over whether he found her attractive or liked her. She'd been convinced he felt nothing toward her or he wouldn't have left her.

With the memory of his hands sweeping away the blankets and his mouth chasing across hers, however, she was plunged into overanalyzing and second-guessing. She eyed her crinkle cotton skirt and pale pink sleeveless T-shirt with a wish that she possessed something more flattering—or at least had her old curves to fill out what hung off her like wet laundry on a rack. She was still very pale, her lips almost white, her hair fine and flat.

Was this the real reason he'd forsaken her? Her lack of appeal and sophistication?

Who cared? She wanted him out of her life.

Didn't she?

Leon wasn't as feckless as she'd judged him. He was infuriating in his lack of remorse where Zach and the loss of her father's marina was concerned, but he'd explained enough that she understood better the pressures that had pushed him to act the way he had. The things he'd said about his father were particularly chilling. She was proud of him for trying to make reparations, but the experience had clearly left an indelible scar on him, one that would be with him always.

Her heartache on his behalf didn't change her desire to divest herself of a marriage that was nothing more than a piece of paper, though. She couldn't remain married in name only forever.

The problem was, his passionate kisses had reawakened a desire to have…something. With someone.

Not him, of course. He didn't believe in lifelong commitments and didn't want children.

Illi had finished her bottle and was rolling and squirming, ready to take on the world. Tanja could have stood there angsting over Leon and her appearance for the rest of the day, but she gathered her daughter and searched out the lido deck.

The dining area next to the main swimming pool was sometimes called the beach, Kyle had informed her.

Tanja emerged into the shadow of an awning, but the glare off the pool and the gleaming, polished deck made her squint. The view beyond was open to the stern. Rocky islands rose from an impossibly blue sea, reaching toward a cerulean sky. The salt-scented breeze caught her skirt, playing it against her shins in a tickling caress. Soft notes of a bouzouki came from hidden speakers while casual voices milled over a buffet spread.

"Tanja." Leon broke away to approach her. He wore crisp linen pants in a bone color and a collared T-shirt in rust red. He moved with his usual panther-like grace, stealing her breath. He'd tidied up around his stubble, but she couldn't read his expression, thanks to his mirrored sunglasses. "Good morning."

He casually claimed Illi and lowered his chin to say good morning to the baby in Greek, then caught Illi's hand when she tried to put a palm print on his sunglasses. His thumb tucked into her palm and she curled her tiny fingers over it.

That small gesture undid all the stern lectures Tanja had given herself five minutes ago.

"How are you feeling?" Leon asked her.

For one heart-stopping moment, Tanja thought he was asking about last night. In front of all these people. And everyone stopped what they were doing to look at her as though they were also curious to know how she felt after some heavy petting with her estranged husband.

As her stomach swooped and panged, however, she remembered she was sick.

"Feeling much better," she said in a strangled voice. "No fever. I'm actually quite hungry."

"Good. Let me introduce you." He drew her toward the half-dozen men and women in casual but crisp business wear. A few gave side-eyes at Leon's comfortable wrangling of Illi, but they offered Tanja warm smiles.

"Good morning," Tanja said shyly as she tried to memorize the names of two different lawyers, a PR manager, a photographer, Leon's PA, and a stylist who looked at her the way her brother looked at a salvaged boat—like scraping the seaweed and barnacles would be a ton of work but hopefully worth the effort.

"Help yourself," Leon said to Tanja, nodding at the heaping platters of brunch items.

He moved to where an infant swing had been suspended in the shade near the head of the table and secured Illi into it. He gave it a nudge, and they all laughed at the way Illi squealed and began to happily kick her legs.

Moments later, when Tanja came to the table with her filled plate, Leon loomed beside her, holding the chair closest to Illi, to the left of the head of the table.

His gallantry flustered her. Was he trying to show off? If he noticed her blush, he didn't let on.

"Kyrkos texted that you don't need antibiotics. Rest, fluids, and vitamins." He nodded at the pill bottle standing next to her water glass.

"Thanks. Did you ask what I should take for the rage blackout over having my child exploited?" she asked in an undertone.

"Ha." His barked laugh made everyone turn their heads, wanting in on the joke. "I already know what to take for that." The corner of his mouth curled with a lack of mercy. "The sweet serum of revenge. I've already ordered it."

She widened her eyes. "In the form of?"

"I've rescinded my offer to host him and his wife aboard this yacht. Presumably, whatever Cameron gets for the photo is sufficient compensation for his house call. The doctor's ex-wife and her new beau, however, have been invited to enjoy a month aboard *Poseidon's Crown* in the location of their choice."

"Oof." Tanja sat back against the cushions in her chair. "You're not a man to cross, are you?"

"I'm really not," he said with a flinty smile.

Tanja's heart went cold as she remembered *she* had crossed Leon.

"I've spoken to Georgiou about how things were left on Istuval." Leon nodded at the lawyer on his right. "We'll have several meetings through the rest of the day to address how we'll proceed. Eat up."

She looked at the scrumptious tropical fruits and flaky pastries before her, but her appetite was gone.

Leon had managed to keep his hands and lips off women for five years. There had been nights when he'd thought he would go around the bend with sexual frustration, but aside from ogling the occasional pair of legs or a really nice rack, he'd managed to keep his libido firmly leashed.

Until last night when he had completely lost his head.

Was that what celibacy did to a man? Because he shouldn't have gone from zero to a hundred in the space of a sigh. He'd still been catching up on sleep from pulling an all-nighter aboard the trimaran. And he'd been in a terrible mood, peeved about a lot of things, not least that one old friend had betrayed him while the other clearly couldn't stand him. His own hypocrisy annoyed him most of all. He was stung that Zach still resented him over their broken deal, but he had no intention of forgiving the opportunistic doctor for taking advantage of him. Yes, he was a blackened kettle calling out the pot.

When he'd settled on the bed next to Tanja, he had only wanted to turn off his brain and sleep. He hadn't even allowed himself to fall deeply asleep. He'd been listening for the baby so she wouldn't wake Tanja.

Tanja's restlessness had tripped something in him, though. He'd woken in a rush of sexual awareness that he might have ignored if their conversation hadn't turned so intimate.

Why had he felt compelled to tell her he'd been forgoing sex? It wasn't that he felt embarrassed or proud of it. He had never worn sexual conquests as a badge so a lack of them didn't prickle his ego.

But it had been a profoundly intimate thing to reveal. She had said that small thing about her parents and he'd had a flash of admiration for them. Of wishing he was a tiny bit like them instead of so much like his own father.

Then she had practically dared him to prove they still had chemistry, and the next thing he'd known he'd been trying to sate the most powerful sexual hunger he'd ever experienced. He'd been close to losing himself like an adolescent—and they'd had layers of clothing and blankets between them. What would have happened if they'd been naked?

He knew what would have happened. With a flood of heat straight to his groin, he vividly recalled Tanja's pale, lithe form straddling him the first time they'd made love. It was a favorite image in the highlight reel that he had replayed thousands of times since their very short marriage. He had believed it was nothing more than an embellished memory. They'd had fun for a few weeks, but sex with Tanja hadn't been any more profound than his other intimate experiences.

He had clung to that conviction until last night.

Now he was seeing his disinterest in other women in a different light. In the last five years, anytime he'd felt a glimmer of attraction toward someone new, he had reminded himself he was married. That he had scruples.

Did he, though? Or had his instinctual turning away gone deeper?

Those other women hadn't been Tanja. Their hair had been the wrong color. Their laughter too high-pitched or too husky, not the perfect balance of clear and throaty. They had talked about things that should have interested him, but failed to engage him intellectually. They'd projected small signals of receptivity, placing a hand on an arm or tilting a head with invitation, but he'd always been turned off, not on. He'd been aware of the opportunity, but something had stopped him from wanting to cross that line.

Maybe his faithfulness to his marriage vows wasn't about proving he was a better man than his father. Maybe he had imprinted on his wife like one of those animals that mated for life—like a wolf. Or a seahorse.

That scared the hell out of him.

Marriage was not a ticket to eternal happiness. He knew that. It was a shackle to another person's whims and hurtful behaviors.

Yes, he had let himself believe for five minutes that his own marriage could be different. Tanja had that effect on him. She made everything seem brighter and hotter and softer and sweeter. She was like a club drug—something he avoided because he didn't like the crash landing back into reality.

That's how he'd come down from his marriage, by returning to Greece and discovering that, even in death, his father caused both him and his mother untold anguish.

Leon had proceeded to do the same to his own wife. He'd failed to send the money, hurting Tanja and her whole family. He'd pulled back from her out of shame, grateful that she wasn't striking back. A cold war was better than an active one.

The minute he was back in her sphere, however, she had lobbed a grenade by naming him Illi's father.

Leon was still furious with her for putting his name on the paperwork without his consent. He'd been completely honest last night when he had told her he had never expected to be married with a baby. Family wasn't something he understood well enough to imagine he could do it successfully. He was bound to do more damage than good, and he hated failure.

On top of that, he was facing untold legal trouble and their clandestine, lusty, expiring marriage was tumbling into the public eye.

Behind him, Georgiou was trying to forestall the worst of what might come out. He was interviewing Tanja, making notes on all the people on Istuval who might help with changing Illi's paperwork and any who might threaten the process.

Yet, when Leon heard Tanja ask, "How will our divorce affect all this?" he spun from the ruminations he'd been directing out the window overlooking the view off the stern and came back to rejoin them at the small conference table in his office.

"We can't divorce," Leon said implacably, skin too tight because some force within him was pushing outward. "Not until Illi's adoption is finalized. No one will authorize an adoption to a couple in the middle of a breakup."

"But we don't know how long the adoption will take." Tanja looked to Georgiou for guidance. "Do we?"

Georgiou shook his head with regret. "A month? A year? We'll need patience and diplomacy so the authorities on Istuval don't make more of the irregularity than it deserves. Once they reissue the paperwork on their end, I imagine our government will be fairly accommodating."

"You mean mine." Tanja shot a panicked look from Georgiou to Leon. "I'm taking Illi to Canada." Her tone brooked no argument.

As much as Leon had never wanted to be a father, the responsibility Tanja had thrust on him wasn't one he took lightly. It was onerous, but not in the way he had always expected it to be, which confounded him. In fact, the idea of leaving the full weight of Illi's future on Tanja felt downright wrong.

"They won't adopt her only to you. You need my name on there. For God's sake, Tanja. Look what I can offer her. Take advantage," he insisted.

She might have balked, but Georgiou set aside his notepad and folded his hands on the table, drawing a breath as if he had something important to say.

Georgiou had extricated Leon from several of the tight positions his father had left him in and had listened to the situation with Illi with equanimity, but looked very serious now.

"I agree with Leon. My advice is that you take no steps toward divorce until the adoption is airtight. What we could do is negotiate a postnuptial agreement. It's not much different from a prenup. Details will be negotiated with regards to support, division of property, and custody. That way, when the time comes, you can part amicably without any loose threads."

"Custody isn't up for negotiation." Fear of betrayal was lurking in Tanja's eyes as she looked up at Leon. And something else. A mistrust that he had earned.

The strangest clench wrapped around his lungs and squeezed, but he gave only a terse nod of agreement toward Georgiou. "Send a template. We'll start working things out."

Tanja looked like she wanted to argue, but Georgiou rose and flexed his back.

"Excellent." Georgiou grimaced. "And please forgive me, Leon, but my wife will kill me if I don't try to sell you a couple of tickets to her fundraiser next week. It's an auction of modern art to benefit a children's center in Athens."

"Of course," Leon said. Buying a couple of plates for charity was expected whether he showed up to eat whatever was served upon it or not. "Will it help for Tanja and I to circulate in public? With Illi's situation, I mean."

"It couldn't hurt. The more happily married you appear, the better."

"Oh, but—" Tanja started to protest.

"We'll be there," Leon confirmed, speaking over her. "Black tie?"

"White." Georgiou took out his phone. "I'll have her send the details, and I'll fetch Ester so we can finalize the press release." He slipped out, closing the door behind him.

"Hi. Remember me? Your wife?" Tanja asked tartly, rising to shake off her own tension. "I know you're new to this parenting gig, but I'm guessing children aren't invited to his wife's bake sale. What do you suggest we do with Illi? Leave her in the coat check?"

"Right. We need a nanny." He texted that to his PA.

"Leon." He glanced up to find Tanja's hands closed into fists, arms straight, chin lifted to a stubborn angle. "Illi has lost her entire family. Now she's lost Kahina and the only other people who were familiar to her. She has *me*. I refuse to shuffle her onto a nanny."

"I don't expect you to." He bit back pointing out Illi had him, too. "The gala will be in a hotel. She'll be upstairs asleep, not even missing you. Or playing with someone who is doting on her, same as she is right now." The crew members were determined to spoil her silly. "Wouldn't you prefer to have someone consistent sit with her when we have social obligations? We'll have several."

"How many is 'several'?" Her voice rose with panic. "I packed light for Istuval and packed even lighter when we left."

"The stylist will ensure you have everything you need." He pointed to the door, reminding her of the woman who'd come aboard with garment bags and makeup cases.

"She brought a handful of outfits for the photo shoot." Tanja flung out a hand.

"She'll arrange more," he said with equal exasperation. "It's her job to source your wardrobe. I presumed you understood that."

"What will *that* cost? I don't have a job, Leon!"

"I don't expect you to pay for it." Seriously, how was she not getting this? "I will."

"No."

He threw his head back, insulted all over again. "Why not?"

"I'm an *accountant*." She was red faced and strident, hands cutting through the air with agitation. "All the debits and credits have to balance or I can't sleep. I already feel like I'm in your debt for whatever Georgiou does on Illi's behalf."

"Quantify it, then," he shot back, losing patience. "Give me a number for the damage I did to your family. Deduct the value of your freedom and Illi's future well-being. When you have all of that calculated on a spreadsheet, we'll sit down and decide whether or not you can accept a damned sundress."

"But it's not *just* a sundress, is it?" she cried, not cowed in the least.

"No. It isn't," he agreed just as forcefully. "It's couture gowns and designer shoes. Jewelry. Spa visits if you want your toenails painted and handbags that go for five figures and are only big enough to carry a lipstick. I'm not telling you what to wear, Tanja, but you're my wife. These aren't gifts or bribes. These are the things you'll need in the life we'll be living. If we were going to the jungle, I'd buy you a mosquito net hat."

"But I'm *not* your wife!" She hugged herself defensively. "That's what I'm saying."

Something fierce welled in him, something he couldn't interpret and didn't want to. It made him want to throw aside the long table between them and pull her close.

"You are," he asserted, speaking reflexively and straight from the center of himself. "Until it's safe for Illi that we divorce, you and I are married." He pointed at her. "And I'm going to do it right this time. I'll provide what you both need." That was not negotiable.

"So you expect me to just…" Her hand waved helplessly, and her brows came together with consternation. She bit her lip, tucking her hand under her elbow again, asking warily, "What *do* you expect?"

It struck him what she was asking and why she'd been so contrary for the last few minutes. It was a question that had been dancing around in his head while he avoided answering it himself. The way they were crossing swords right now told him the crackling heat between them wasn't going away. Hell, their midnight encounter had telegraphed that message loud and clear.

He drew a long drink of oxygen, trying to feed his lizard brain so it didn't take over and make him say or do something stupid. Somehow he had to remain civilized when what he wanted was purely instinctual.

"Given the way we both reacted last night," he said carefully, "I suggest we resume marital activities." His voice originated somewhere in the base of his chest, and heat detonated below his belt just thinking of what that might entail.

"Marital activities," she repeated in an astonished huff. A pink flush hit her cheeks, though. Pretty and shy and deeply aware.

Her flickering gaze was avoiding his, but he could see the latent sensations were teasing her, same as they were him. All he'd been thinking about since Illi interrupted them was that he wanted to crush Tanja close and celebrate her and *be inside* her.

"What do *you* expect?" he asked gruffly.

"I don't know what to expect from you!" Her anger resurfaced in a frustrated pang that caused a twist in his chest. "One minute you're so sweet with Illi and acting like a superhero, rescuing me and getting me a doctor. It makes me think I was right to be so enamored with you five years ago. Then you're ordering me to stay married and wear high heels to gala luncheons and resume having sex."

"I will *never* order you to have sex. Tell me you know that," he growled. "It's pretty damned insulting if you don't."

Her mouth quirked in concession. "I do, but you're still expecting a lot."

"Oh, like fatherhood?"

She stared flatly at him, refusing to engage on that one.

"Am I really expecting that much? It's dating, Tanja. Dinner and dancing and cocktail parties. Things we should have done rather than jump into marriage. What part of that bothers you? You've never been shy with strangers, so don't act like talking to people is a chore."

"I schmoozed my father's customers, asked them where they'd been and where they were going. That doesn't mean I know how to talk about history or modern art." She looked to her nails. "*You* didn't find me that interesting or you would have stuck around."

"Tanja."

"I don't want to be this insecure," she blurted, fist punching the air beside her thigh again. "I don't want to go back to thinking I'm less than you are."

He snapped his head back. "Why did you ever? *You're not.*"

"I don't have this, Leon!" She threw her arm out to encompass the yacht. "I didn't have anything you wanted enough to bring you back to resume our marriage. The only thing I can give you now is a divorce and I can't even give you that! So what do I have that you want? Except…" Her wary, limpid eyes sent a sabre straight into his heart.

"Be very careful what you say next." He flattened his hands on the table, more incensed than he'd ever thought someone could make him. "Because sex has never been a transaction for me. I will not turn it into one with my *wife*."

"What would it be then?" Her shoulders rose and fell, arms flailing helplessly. "Because we're only pretending we're married—"

"We *are* married."

"We're going to pretend that we're *staying* married and—"

"And act like any other couple who is married. Why not?"

"Because the only people I've ever slept with have been men I had feelings for. Men I thought had feelings for *me*." She jabbed a finger at him. "And you don't."

CHAPTER SIX

LEON DIDN'T GET a chance to respond to that. There was a knock and Georgiou let himself in with his PR manager, Ester. Their amiable smiles died as they hit the wall of tension between her and Leon.

"Should we come back?" Ester asked, looking between them.

"No. We have to get the press release hammered out," Leon said grimly.

Tanja sat back down, body buzzing with adrenaline. With the idea of having sex with him. Was it what she wanted? Yes. On a strictly physical basis, she absolutely did want to finish what they'd started last night.

Emotionally, she didn't know if she could withhold enough of herself to walk away unscathed afterward. They called it "making love" for a reason. She knew herself well enough to know she would fall in love with him. She'd done what she could to dismiss and deny how badly he'd hurt her when he left, but she'd been crushed.

"Tanja?"

She was yanked out of her reverie by Leon's voice. His expression was inscrutable.

"Do you agree?"

Ugh. She'd completely missed everything that had been said and had to beg Ester to repeat it. A few minutes later, they had settled on a statement that she and Leon had married years ago in Canada. They had separated when he returned to Greece and recently reconciled. They were on a second honeymoon, enjoying the family they had started together.

The truth of how their daughter had come into their lives wasn't addressed. The announcement was very short on details, very tall on fairy-tale ending.

Tanja was put in a pretty wrap dress with a tropical print. Her hair was left loose and windswept while subtle makeup enhanced her features. They were photographed in casual settings around the yacht, some with Illi, some with just her and Leon.

They were standing against the rail in the bow, the sun setting behind them, when he touched her chin. She lifted her gaze, and all her turmoil got tangled up with the inscrutable emotions in his eyes.

As she read lust and remorse and something bright and fierce and possessive, her heart juddered to a stop in her chest. His thumb grazed her lips once, twice. Then he dipped his head and pressed the most tender kiss imaginable onto her mouth.

Last night's passion flared anew, blue with confusion in its center, but twisting a coiled flame of wistful longing and sparkling with the embers of dreams she'd believed were nothing but smoke and ash.

She curled her hand around his hard, flat wrist, losing herself to the sensation of his lips traveling over hers, turning a simple kiss into an exploration. A journey from regret to reconciliation.

How could a man kiss like this and feel none of the things that were swelling within her to the point of causing a deep, anguished ache?

His hand slid down to her neck and he slowly withdrew.

Could he feel the way her pulse was pounding against the heel of his palm?

"That's beautiful," she heard from her right. She ducked her head. She'd forgotten they were under scrutiny and was mortified by all she must have let show nakedly on her face.

"That's enough," Leon said with an abrupt edge in his tone, cutting short the photography session with a jerk of his head.

When Tanja would have broken away from him, his arms hardened, keeping her in his embrace an extra second while he searched her expression. She set her hand on his chest and looked to the water, trying to compose herself.

But she felt his heart racing beneath the layers of muscle and bone, calling to her to stay close. Share in the tumult.

"Let's get them on their way," he said. "Then we can have a quiet dinner and talk."

It didn't work out that way. They had just said their goodbyes when Leon's mother texted. "I have to call her, prepare her for what to expect. You should touch base with your family. Let them know you'll be staying for the near future."

Before she could decide whether she wanted to protest his decree, Leon asked Kyle to fetch her a phone. Ten minutes later, she had unwrapped a brand-new smartphone, logged into her account and had her father on a video chat. It was so good to see him!

She didn't see Leon until she had put Illi down for the evening and was in the jet tub outside Leon's stateroom. He came out with a distracted, irritable look on his face.

"I hope you don't mind. Kyle found me a bathing suit." She self-consciously touched the halter strap of the neon pink bikini she wore, then pointed at the little device on the ledge. "And a baby monitor. He's like a genie. Why are you paying Georgiou to sort out our problems? Just ask Kyle to twitch his nose."

"Kyle's powers do not extend beyond the yacht." He began stripping down.

"What are you doing?" She snapped her head to the side, shielding her gaze.

"This tub is completely private. You don't need a suit. And it's been a long few days. I need to relax." His belt hit the deck with a faint, jangling thud. The rest of his clothes must have followed because he sank into the tub with a sigh of contentment. "Your Victorian aunt called. She wants her delicate sensibilities back."

"Ha-ha." Tanja couldn't tell if he was naked beneath the churning bubbles as she faced him across the small pool, but she would bet any money he was. The side of his foot grazed her thigh when he propped his heels next to her hip and splayed out his long arms.

"What did your mother say?" she asked, trying not to be a prude by shifting away. She was actually the opposite—some kind of libertine who reacted to the brush of a foot like it was the most erotically provoking caress imaginable.

"You know how to kill a buzz, don't you?" His face hardened and his shoulders regained all their tension.

"Is that what she said?" she joked lamely.

He snorted, but there was little humor in it. "She wants us to come to dinner when we get to Athens. What did your father say?"

"That he wants me home," she said with a wrench of homesickness she couldn't keep from her voice. "He understands, though. He's ridiculously proud to have two grandchildren." She smiled as she recalled her father's button-busting enthusiasm. He was also worried that Leon would hurt her or let her down again. So was she, but she kept that to herself.

"My mother didn't say any of that," Leon said flatly, cheekbones like calved glaciers they were so sharp and ghostly blue in the glow from beneath the surface of the water.

Tanja started to point out that Illi wasn't his so why would his mother welcome her as a grandchild, but the mood he was radiating didn't seem receptive to hearing excuses for his mother's behavior.

"When you said your parents' marriage was horrific, what did you mean?"

His breath left him in a disparaging exhale. "Name it. They both cheated. Used me against one another. Had ugly fights where they threw things and humiliated each other in public."

"That's awful. Were there drug or alcohol issues?"

"They didn't admit to it or seek help, so is that a valid excuse?" His arm bent and he used his thumbnail to scratch his eyebrow. "My father was a terrible person. Profoundly selfish and manipulative. My mother brought her own father's money into the marriage and would have divorced him if he would have given it back, but he refused. In fact, he hired a man to seduce her and take intimate photos, then held them as blackmail over her. I think I've got all the copies destroyed by now, but who knows? He could still haunt her with them."

"That's horrible!"

"It is. She was pretty horrible sometimes, too. I've had three DNA tests to prove I'm his. Frankly, I was hoping every time I wouldn't be. When I was eight, he sent me to boarding school purely to punish her. Sometimes I think I should have tried harder to refuse."

"You were eight. How much choice did you have?"

"None, but I knew she was upset. We had a decent relationship until then. It was damaged beyond repair after I left, and a lot of that is on me. She quit showing affection for me, though, so he wouldn't keep using me against her. It made it hard to tell if she wanted me to... I don't know. Fight to see her? I was just happy to be away from all of it so I took every excuse to avoid going home. That's how I got into racing. I crewed through school breaks and bought my first sailboat by saving up my allowance." His mouth twisted with self-mockery. He knew how spoon-fed that sounded.

"Did your mother know your father wasn't always operating within the law?"

"She had suspicions," he said with weariness. "She was afraid to ask too many questions." He was deep in thought, absently working his thumb against his bent finger. "When I came home for the funeral and we began to realize how bad things were, she cried for the first time I'd seen in years. She said, 'I hung on through all of that so you would inherit, and now there's nothing?' It was a kick in the gut to realize she thought she had been helping me by staying with him."

"So you rebuilt your father's fortune for *her*?"

His gaze flickered to hers, eyes flinty slits. "And the thousands of people around the globe who needed their jobs."

Right.

"Does she feel threatened by me? Not me specifically, but the fact you have a wife?"

He let his head drop back against the edge of the tub again. "She's angry I never told her I was married."

"Ever?"

"We aren't close," he said flatly.

Tanja slouched deeper into the water to absorb that,

absently bringing her feet up to the edge of the bench across from her. She jerked away when her foot touched Leon's firm thigh.

His hand slid beneath the surface and caught her ankle, bringing it back, holding her gaze as he set her foot in place on the bench next to his hip before his arm returned to the edge of the tub.

The heat and churn and burble of the water filled the air. It was a manifestation of the conflicting energy between them. Of the clear head she was trying to keep while, below the surface, her body was roiling with sensations. Her heart was doing somersaults, trying to take in how Leon's childhood had turned him into a man who had been charming, yet withdrawn. One who inspired confidence, then ultimately let her down.

"I wouldn't stay with a man who treated me like that," she told him quietly, meaning it, but also aware that his brief touch had left her simmering in more than the warmth of the water. Yearning was sitting in the pit of her stomach.

"Not even for Illi? Because you weren't *eating*, Tanja."

"I ate." Not enough, but she understood. "You're right, though. I don't know what lengths I would go to for my child, but I have the luxury of family and friends who I know would support me, which gives me options. Obviously, your mother didn't feel like she had any."

"I hate that I'm not on that list. That I had to hear through your brother that you needed help," he muttered. "I'm not proud of the way I left you. Or the circumstances I left you in. It's the kind of thing my father would have done. Waiting for you to come to me to resolve things was just like him, too. The fact you never did, that you had too much self-respect to make the first move…" His dark brows lowered with intensity. "Don't ever think you're less than me. You have far more integrity than I ever will. Than most people I know."

"That is an extremely generous thing to say, given the position I've put you in with Illi," she pointed out, both touched and contrite.

"You wouldn't have had to do that, wouldn't have gone to Istuval or wound up so broke you were going hungry, if I'd looked after you properly. I'm going to make that up to you with the postnuptial."

"I don't want your money, Leon."

"I know. But it's important to me that I do this right this time. My opening offer is a million euros per year of marriage."

"That's ridiculous! *No*," she insisted.

"And every time you say something like that—" he tipped his head back, speaking to the starry sky "—I'm going to double it."

She held back a reflexive protest, hesitated, then asked, "Don't you mean halve it?"

"No." His head came up. "Another woman might play those games, trying to up the amount, but you won't."

He said it confidently, as if he *knew* her. That seeming approval and admiration increased all the sweet tugs and pulls in her middle and provoked her into teasing him.

"What happens if I ask you to double it?"

"Done."

"Leon! Don't you dare."

"You understand that when it doubles again, we're going from two to four?" He tilted his face to the sky again, and she thought he might be laughing at her.

"Will you please be serious?" she asked, heart pounding with genuine alarm.

"I'm completely serious. I know you don't want my money." His humor was gone, his voice dispassionate.

"You've said it several times already. But I need the amount to be attractive enough that you'll leave if things get bad. *Before* they get bad. I need to know that I won't spend my entire life causing damage to another human being. That Illi won't be caught in the cross fire. I want us both to have a clean exit if things are unbearable."

"Would it be, though?"

He picked up his head.

"Do whatever you want with your money. I don't care, but—" She hesitated, then spoke her greatest fear aloud. "I'm afraid that if I sleep with you, I'll fall in love with you." Again. She didn't admit that last bit because she'd lost her ability to breathe. She felt as though her lungs were locked, no air getting into them.

"Have you been listening? I'm not worth your love." His jaw was clenched, his mouth tense, his biceps like smooth, tanned rocks.

"Your father was not a good person. It doesn't mean you aren't."

"I need you to stay realistic, Tanja." He spoke softly, but it didn't leech any of the power from his words. "I am capable of charm and consideration, but I'm not capable of love. Don't mistake my desire to be good to you for actual goodness within me. Don't mistake my desire for you as anything more than intense sexual attraction."

Her heart was being stretched in all directions by his words, until it was thin and threatening to unravel completely.

"But I do want you," he said thickly, making her heart lurch and stumble into a gallop. A tic appeared in his cheek. "Other women won't do. I want *you*. I want that fire we tasted last night. I made myself forget how uniquely well suited we are, but there's no denying it. And I can't *stand* the idea of not experiencing it again."

The backs of her eyes were hot. So was her throat. Her mind was reeling, trying to reason through all the warnings he'd just voiced that he couldn't be entrusted with her heart.

Ironically, his stark honesty made her trust him a little. Maybe she was only rationalizing what she really wanted, though. Because she wanted the fire, too. She couldn't imagine living her life alongside him, calling herself his wife, and not allowing their combined conflagration to engulf her.

Before she let herself think it through any further, she nodded. "Okay."

For two heartbeats, time stopped.

Then he moved like a shark. Like a sea monster. Like Poseidon himself as he scooped her up in the same motion of standing and rising from the tub. Water sluiced off them while she clung to him in shock.

He strode without ceremony into the bedroom and set her on the bed.

"We're wet—"

He was already coming down on top of her, naked and still dripping, body burning with heat from the water. Their skin was abraded with damp friction as he pushed a knee between hers and spread her legs so he could settle between them. His mouth came down over hers, smothering her. Ravaging her. Consuming her.

They were instantly in the center of the storm, where they'd been last night, but even deeper in the maelstrom. She jammed her fingers into his hair and angled her head so the seal of their mouths deepened. His tongue thrust in and she moaned as she greeted his intrusion.

His weight was a glorious pressure pinning her to the mattress while the steely length of his naked shaft sat firm and undeterred by the wet triangle of fabric between her thighs.

He lifted his head abruptly and drew the tied strap from behind her neck over her head, dragging it down to reveal her breasts, the pale orbs topped by nipples drawn tight as the warm night air hit them. One hot hand cupped her clammy breast, making her writhe at the conflicting sensations. His gaze dragged upward even as he toyed with the hard button.

"Your hair. Your skin," he said in a gritty voice, as though words were failing him. Or he wanted to use his mouth for too many things. His lips traversed from her cheek to her neck and back up to nip her jaw, then into her neck again, hot tongue sweeping into the hollow beneath her ear. "I want to lick every inch of you."

She wanted that, too. Everything. All of him. Fast. Her hands were moving over his flexing shoulders, the sweep of her touch drying him. Her legs climbed to hug his waist tight. As she lifted her hips into his erection, she breathed his name like a mantra. "Leon. Leon."

"Every inch, Tanja. Every damned inch," he muttered, trailing his kisses down her arm to the inside of her elbow before he crossed her arm over her chest, lifting and shifting as he rolled her onto her stomach beneath him.

He tugged at the tie on her top and yanked her bottoms down before his naked weight settled on her again. The steely heat of his shaft nestled in the crease of her damp buttocks and a cloud of humid, gratified breath touched the side of her face, telling her he needed this as badly as she did. She could feel his heart slamming into her back, could hear him swallow and pant another shaken breath against her shoulder.

Despite those signs of tenuous control, his fingers traced a deliberate, tickling line across the tops of her shoulders, skimming the wet tails of her hair away before he kissed the top of her spine.

She gasped, arching as his benediction sent a shiver to her lower back. He set about nuzzling her nape and the back of her shoulder, her ear and the back of her arm. He was braced on one elbow, using his free hand to caress from her waist to her ribs, causing her skin to tighten all over her body.

She was nearly helpless, dominated this way, but she lifted her backside to caress him, moaning to let him know how much she needed this—to be worshipped as he conquered her. Caressed and teased and adored.

His open mouth zigzagged across her back and he drew one of her knees up so she was exposed to his touch when his fingers sought the fine curls that protected her damp, intimate folds.

They both took shaken inhales as he found the honeyed sweetness there. He was barely touching her, but her flesh was so swollen and wanton, it only took the lightest of explorations to make her shiver and moan into the pillow.

"Good?"

"Yes. But I need more," she begged, barely able to speak. Her hands clawed into the blankets beneath her and she moved her hips, seeking his touch, rubbing her face into the pillow. "Touch inside me."

"Soon," he said in a rasp against her lower back. He set his teeth against one cheek in a playful bite, before he rose and rolled her onto her back again.

She was losing all inhibition. Her legs fell open so he had room between them, bikini bottoms dislodged so they sat across her mound. She stared boldly into his face as he loomed over her, waiting for his gaze to come back after he dragged her top free and threw it off the side of the bed. He ate up what he had exposed, his fierce expression terrifying in its intensity.

Yet she exalted in it. In being *his*.

Her breasts were swollen with anticipation. Her nipples drawn tight by the chill and arousal. With a growl, he dropped his head to close his searing mouth over her nipple and pulled so strongly, bright spears of sensation went straight into her loins.

"Leon," she cried, squirming at the intensity.

"Bear it," he commanded, and looped one arm behind her waist, arching her as he moved to the other breast to suck and tease.

She was losing her mind to pure carnality, ready to do anything at his command. She pulled at his hair, insisting, "Kiss me."

"I will," he said, prying her fingers from his thick curls and biting the heel of her hand before he slid down and rained kisses on her ribs, her stomach, her jutting hipbones.

She was trembling, shaking with anticipation. Weak.

He set the softest, sweetest kiss on her inner thigh. She nearly screamed.

"What's wrong, beautiful?" he teased. But as he looked up at her, the lust in his gaze hit her like a punch.

Her breath left her so quickly she was dizzy, and the heat flooding her loins redoubled. The ache there intensified as he took his sweet time playing his tongue into the crease of her knee and along her calf, biting her instep, making her wait and wait and wait.

When he caught his hands in her suit, dragging it off her hips and down her legs, she lifted to help.

Naked, she gave a slow thrash against the covers, all of her so completely afire by his hot gaze roaming over her, she barely felt the wet patches beneath her.

With one hand, he held his length in a restrictive fist. His other caressed her calf to her thigh to the crease of her hip, spreading her legs wider, gaze unabashedly drinking her in.

Her stomach quivered in nervous reaction. She glanced at the windows surrounding them, noted the doors to the deck and jet tub were still wide open.

"Someone might see us," she gasped.

"No one will come. Except you." He set a smile that turned into a kiss against her inner knee. "And me." He kissed his way up to her mound.

She spoke his name on a sob. A plea.

"I missed this." His touch parted her and his tongue swept through her folds, making her whole body jerk at the streak of lightning that shot through her. He made a reassuring noise and set a steadying hand on her stomach. "Tell me hard or soft," he murmured, curling his other arm around her thigh as he began to make love to her with his mouth.

She could only groan helplessly. Her hand tangled in his hair while wet heat built. Her thighs closed of their own accord, the ministrations of his mouth causing sensations so intense they were nearly unbearable.

She had missed this, too. So much. When he ignored her plea that he fill her, she abandoned herself to the pleasure he was determined to bestow. She gave in to the quivering tension building in her stomach. Abandoned herself to the growing waves of keening joy.

Suddenly a shuddering climax had her lifting her hips and muffling her cries with the back of her wrist. It was so good she could have wept.

Was he arrogant in his triumph when he rose over her? Hell, yes. He looked her over from hairline to the soles of her feet, missing none of the trembling, vanquished aftermath he had caused.

Did she care that he wore barbaric satisfaction like an aura? Not one iota. She was too sated. Yet empty. Yearning.

"Do I need a condom?" His voice was such a deep

growl it might have originated from the middle of the earth. Like an element. Iron. Or gold.

She nodded jerkily.

He sent her a look of amused mock terror as he reached into the nightstand. "There better be one in here."

There was. Seconds later, he settled over her and they both sighed at the press of their damp skin, like the sizzle on a hotplate.

And even though she was dying for him to thrust into her, he kissed her until she was lifting her hips against his hardness again. Inviting him.

He lightly bit her earlobe and said, "Tell me how much." The wide crest of his tip pressed against her sensitized flesh, stretching her with a pinch she hadn't realized she'd missed. It stung a little, but she arched to make it easy for him. He sank all the way in with one slow, inexorable thrust, until they were meshed to the depths of their flesh and she could feel his very heartbeat within her.

She could have died then, her sense of fulfilment was so complete.

They kissed, unmoving, his restraint making him shake as he passionately devoured her mouth. Sweet curls of renewed desire grew in coils of increasing tension, prompting her to wrap her arms and legs around him, wanting him deeper. Wanting to stay like this, linked and still. Indelible.

Eventually he shifted, and the small movement awakened her to the exquisite pleasures awaiting both of them.

"This," she groaned under his first lazy thrusts. She scraped her hands from his hair to his neck to his shoulders, down to his lower back and up again, trying to feel all of him at once.

His guttural noise agreed with her. He held himself on one elbow, his hand hooked beneath her shoulder so he could thrust with more power. He watched her with glittering eyes as she gloried in his lovemaking.

She welcomed each gentle slam of his hips, moaning with encouragement when he came back with more strength. She had forgotten this. Or hadn't let herself remember how utterly overwhelming their lovemaking was. Nothing existed but the sharp lines of his face, the pierce of pleasure that went through her with each stroke of his body into hers. Intense yearning held her still for each return, so the reverberations of pleasure spun out to sting her fingertips and toes.

They were both making animalistic noises, holding back nothing. Hiding nothing. That was the part that made their lovemaking so tremendous and devastating at once. They were watching the other, unable to hide their need, their craving, their rejoicing.

That honesty was too much. She knew her surrender would be written large, too. She couldn't bear it, yet she couldn't resist it. The tension between those imperatives couldn't be sustained.

Her nails dug into his shoulders. His fingertips bit into her hip. She clenched her teeth, trying to hold back, trying to maintain her slippery grip on this plateau of incredible connection. His face contorted with his struggle. He quickened his pace.

"Come," he commanded in a jagged voice. "Come with me. Do it now."

She gave in to the abyss. Pleasure detonated within her, sending her spinning in all directions while he slid his arms under her and bucked heavily into her. His head went back and his neck strained as he shouted his release.

CHAPTER SEVEN

How had he left that? That was Leon's first rational thought when he discarded the condom and flopped back onto the bed beside Tanja, completely spent.

His next thought was, *It's still too much*. He was so raw his chest felt torn open.

Yet, as the breeze danced across their cooling bodies, he couldn't make himself do anything but drag her close and tuck her head under his chin. The boneless lassitude in her heavy limbs and the satiated sigh that warmed his collarbone eased something in him.

"Did we wake Illi?" she asked with tremulous humor.

"She'd let us know if she was awake." The kid wasn't afraid to use the full capacity of her lungs if she decided to lodge a complaint. When he'd taken her out of the swing this morning, she'd publicly denounced him for human rights violations.

"That was really good." Tanja kissed his throat, skimming a light touch from his shoulder to his neck, but he felt the shaking that lingered in her. "Thank you."

That tiny betrayal of how deeply she'd been affected shook things loose inside him.

He wanted to pry at least a mental space between them since he couldn't make himself do it physically, but he had to say, "Thank *you*," because this had been better than good. It had been incredible.

He wished he could blame his powerful release on breaking his celibacy, but he knew it was more than that. He didn't understand how one woman could strip him down to such an elemental place. Tanja wasn't particularly unique. He'd met many women who were easy on the eye, smart and funny, tolerant yet assertive. Ones who liked sex as much as he did. Before he'd married, he'd made love with those other women and always enjoyed it, but he had never felt this same deconstruction of his inner self after the fact.

He'd like to think it was only happening because he had changed from the man he'd been, but if anything, he was more guarded, not less. And Tanja had affected him this way before he'd lost his father and left her. He remembered this same postcoital sensation of exposure that warned his defenses were down.

Was *this* why he'd left her and not looked back?

It was a disturbing thought. He didn't want to see himself as a child who ran away from something because it was uncomfortable, but that's exactly the coping strategy he'd employed for his early years. It had been disguised as school exams and regatta trials and whatever pursuits he could conjure as an excuse. It had been an avoidance tactic to escape his troubled home life and the toll it took upon him, plain and simple.

Since his father's death, he'd learned to face his problems head-on, though, and did.

But how could he face and resolve this? He could barely articulate the issue. Tanja wasn't purposely chipping away at his soul. He was opening up despite every instinct in him warning against it. It went far beyond physical. He had few inhibitions there, but he had revealed things to her about his father and his childhood, things he'd never told anyone. They were the sorts of things that could be used as weapons the way his parents had used their own weaknesses against each other.

He almost wished Tanja had told him to go to hell when he had made his case for them to resume having sex.

I'm afraid that if I sleep with you, I'll fall in love with you.

He was afraid she would, too. He couldn't lead her on again, but he couldn't dodge, run or otherwise distance himself. That would be cowardly.

The fact was that he wanted to be right where he was, able to put his hands on her as freely as he liked. Drinking in her scent and combing his fingers through the fine strands of her hair as she relaxed with a soft murmur against him.

With a sudden inhale of realization, she tilted her head back. "What if I never claim it?"

"What?"

"The settlement." A gotcha smile danced around her mouth. "If we never divorce, then I never have to accept your money. I've got you, haven't I?"

Whatever came into his features caused her expression to flinch and fall into stiff lines.

"It was a joke," she said with a note of hurt.

"I know. It's fine," he lied, tucking her face under his chin again, heart unsteady. He was barely able to pick apart the intense emotions that were throbbing like live nerve endings throughout his body. He had sudden visions of the arrows his parents had refused to cease aiming at one another, only this time they were aimed at Tanja.

No.

"I grew up with a brother," she was muttering. "I

learned to be competitive. I wanted to prove I could out-smart you, that's all." The trusting way she'd been relaxed against him had evaporated. She was nothing but bony, ropy tension now.

"I know," he assured her with a single sweep of his palm down her narrow back. But he'd heard more beneath her remark than excitement at finding a loophole. He might not know everything about his wife, but he knew she believed in people and futures and family. "But do you remember what I said about being realistic?" he asked gently.

She was silent for a long time, but the way she was holding her breath told him she was still awake. Hell, she wasn't fighting tears, was she? That would kill him.

When she spoke, her voice held the toughness he'd always admired in her. "I think you underestimate my desire to win," she said with quiet dignity.

And she was underestimating his willingness to lose, especially if it meant she and her child would be better off in the long run. He only kissed her forehead and said, "Let's just enjoy what we have right now."

Tanja woke in a lingering stupor from their lovemaking. Leon had risen in the night to close all the doors. Within moments of him returning to the bed, they'd been making love again with equally cataclysmic results.

That had been deeply reassuring, given how he'd reacted to her suggestion they stay married. She hadn't meant to sound so... Ugh. She threw her arm over her eyes, angry with herself over something that had been a stupid joke.

One that had brimmed with wistful yearning on her part, she had realized once he'd brutally shut down "forever" as an option. Recalling his "be realistic" warning—

twice—caused sharp cracks to fracture from the middle of her heart outward, making all her bones ache.

Tanja was a hopeful person by nature. She couldn't help thinking they had something, given that neither of them had slept with anyone else in five years. Their first time falling into bed again had probably registered on nearby seismographs.

But things were happening much as they had the last time. Leon turned her head. Of course he did. He was a man who had everything—looks and wit and smarts. Wealth and confidence and, as it turned out, a massive soft spot for a baby who wasn't even his.

Any woman in the world would find him irresistible and spin a few fantasies about hitching her future to his.

Tanja had opened her heart to him once already, though. And look what happened. He'd walked away and five years had passed without a word. He had only come to her in Istuval because he'd thought doing her a favor would make their divorce go more smoothly.

He *wanted* a divorce. She had to remember that. Leon might want her body, but he didn't want to make a life with her and her daughter. When all this was over, would he even keep up a relationship with Illi? If Tanja was being realistic, she had to go on the assumption she and Leon would part ways permanently this time.

Oh, that hurt. It felt like failure, which was silly. Her future would still hold Illi and, hopefully, Brahim. It would be a very rich life. She didn't need a man to complete it. She and Leon had never stood a real chance anyway. That's what she was learning.

Surely they could be friends, though? She "liked" the photos of her first love's baby and supported her high school boyfriend's music ambitions by downloading his songs. She and Leon were sharing intensely personal things, their bodies among them. Did all of that mean nothing to him? Would he really be able to walk away and forget her completely?

As she stared at the ceiling, heart aching, she had to reconcile herself to the fact she might, indeed, mean very little to him. He was a closed-off, compartmentalized type of man.

"Well, that's quite an opinion," she heard Leon say, which made a spike of awareness flash through her, as though he'd read her thoughts, but he was talking to Illi, quiet and indulgent. "I've had executives on my payroll who don't make as much sense as you do. Try to keep it down, though. Mommy is still sleeping."

Tanja realized the distant, garbled squawks she kept hearing weren't a seabird.

"I'm awake," she called.

A pause, then Leon brought Illi in. She was chewing her fist and wearing a fresh onesie.

Leon, the scoundrel, wore nothing but a pair of low-slung boxers and undiluted sex appeal. The sight of his strong arm curled so securely around her daughter lit up all of Tanja's biological buttons. *Love her. Love us both*, she wanted to beg him.

He set Illi on the rumpled blankets next to her. His expression was shuttered, but his lashes flickered as though his gaze saw through the covers and tracked restlessly over her naked skin.

"Her bottle is on the way. So is breakfast. I have to make some calls, but we'll take the helicopter to Athens as soon as we're ready."

"Oh." Reality. She was starting to hate it. Why couldn't they float along in this honeymoon-like bubble aboard the yacht?

His gaze finally hit hers, tangling up with the conflicted yearning twisting in her gut. His was mostly unreadable, but she saw the memories there of their torrid night, the flash of hunger in the way he stopped himself from swooping down over her like a hawk.

Before she realized what she was doing, she lifted her arm in invitation.

He dug his knee into the mattress and leaned across Illi's small, kicking body. The weight of his mouth pressed Tanja onto her back while she received the most tender ravishment imaginable.

She moaned in a mix of startled reaction and shaken nerves. She hadn't expected him to drag her so easily into the miasma of need for his mouth, his touch. She was distantly aware of Illi squirming beneath the bridge of his body, but each time he started to draw away, Tanja pressed her fingertips into the back of his neck and he came back. He delved and tasted, and left her hot and dazed and utterly breathless.

Finally, he disobeyed her urging and lifted away.

He remained braced over the two of them, his one hand on Tanja's far side, his gaze tracking over what had to be a very flushed and dazzled expression on her face.

"Temptress." It was more accusation than compliment, but his mouth twisted in self-deprecating humor. "Ogling me like I'm ice cream on a hot summer's day."

She folded her wet, swollen lips together and lifted the sheet enough to peek beneath, deliberately teasing him because, when they were like this, they were perfectly aligned.

"So I am." She sealed the edge across her breasts and pinned the sheet with her arm. "Too bad I can't show you. I'm definitely in the mood for ice cream. Not plain vanilla, either."

His gaze warmed with amusement and remained

locked with hers as he eased back. He touched Illi's fine hair on his way. As he straightened to stand beside the bed, he spoke in a voice that was more threat or command than the imparting of information.

"The nanny interviews start today."

Interlude of flirtation aside, Tanja climbed aboard the helicopter with reservations.

The romantic in her wanted to believe she was embarking on a chance to see if her marriage *could* work. She'd never been someone who did anything by half measures so she instinctually wanted to give their union a real chance, but beneath Leon's hot kiss and patience while she ran around looking for that one worn T-shirt she didn't need but didn't want to lose, she felt the inner walls he was erecting against her.

It hurt and made for a disheartening start to a difficult flight. Leon sat as copilot and Illi cried the whole way. Tanja was frazzled by the time they landed on Leon's rooftop penthouse in Athens. Leon's PA, Demitri, met them and showed Tanja to a spare bedroom that had quickly been converted into a nursery for Illi.

"Decorators will arrive today to take measurements and discuss color schemes, but I hope it suffices for the moment?" Demitri asked anxiously.

Illi had never had a real crib or change table, let alone a surplus of supplies, clothes and toys.

"It's perfect," Tanja assured him, relieved to have somewhere to safely put Illi down since she had worn herself out on the flight and her eyelids were already drooping.

Tanja tucked her in and carried the baby monitor as she explored the airy living space.

Much like the yacht, everything was modern and bright

and reflective of understated yet undeniable luxury. Beyond the wall of windows, Leon was sitting down with Georgiou at the courtyard dining table next to the infinity pool. Was that the Acropolis in the distance? It was so close it looked like she could swim to the edge of the water and reach out to touch it.

A middle-aged woman in the kitchen was making coffee and preparing platters filled with dips and bread sticks, olives and cheese, stuffed vine leaves and grilled octopus. She introduced herself as the housekeeper and chef, Valerie.

Huh. No wonder Leon had never felt a need for his wife to join him.

"I was hoping for a drink of water," Tanja said, glancing around for a glass.

"Sparkling or still?"

"Tap water is fine."

"I have this cucumber water to go with the meze?" Valerie brought a jug from the refrigerator.

"Um, sure. Thank you."

It was the same over-the-top level of service Tanja had experienced on the yacht, and it began to hit her that the yacht was not an exception. This was how Leon lived. He had lived like this all his life. It was disconcerting, making her feel as though she'd been transported into a movie or some other surreal world.

She would have loved a moment to catch her breath and process it, but she only had time to grab a bite with the men before a parade of appointments tied her up.

Her stylist from the yacht arrived and brought her into the other spare bedroom, now filled with racks of clothing. "We don't have to go through all of this right now, but I wanted to pick out a few key pieces so I can alter them if they need it."

Tanja was measured and pinned and soon turned out in a blue-and-white-striped sundress that she adored on sight—it buttoned down the front and had big patch pockets. But she had no time to browse the rest of the clothes. The health nurse arrived.

Tanja assured the woman she was recovering nicely but was given iron pills, and the chef was instructed on her nutritional needs.

The nurse left and Tanja was promptly served a protein smoothie and dense cookies filled with dates and nuts. Then the potential nanny arrived. Leon surprised her by joining her. He asked questions Tanja wouldn't have thought to ask, like how flexible the young woman was to travel and, "Can you start tonight?"

"I brought a bag in case you needed me right now," Britta said with a warm smile.

"Excellent." Leon looked to Tanja as she snapped a glare at him. "What? You'll be tied up getting ready."

"For what?" she asked with beleaguered panic.

"Dinner with my mother."

"That's *tonight*? I thought—" She didn't know what she had thought. She sagged into the sofa, stricken at how quickly things were spinning beyond her control.

"Will you take these to the kitchen, please?" Leon nodded at the empty dishes, dismissing the nanny. "Don't look so anxious," he chided Tanja. "Mother's apartment is two floors down."

"Then why don't we bring Illi? Doesn't she want to meet her?"

Something hardened in Leon's expression. "Let the nanny get her feet wet. This will ease you into trusting her, if you know you can come back up if it's not working."

True. She sighed her agreement, saying absently, "I

didn't realize your mother owns an apartment in this building, too." It seemed odd that she hadn't come up to greet them. Had Leon invited her?

"I own the building," he said very casually, as though it was a totally normal thing for a person to say. "My mother prefers the island and travels a lot, but she stays here when she's in Athens. Tell the stylist semiformal for dinner. I'll shower and change into a suit."

Tanja's heart lurched again as his outrageous level of wealth hit her. No wonder he had assumed she'd married him for his money. What a bumpkin he must have thought her with her sundress from the farmers market and her discount sandals.

She heard Illi on the monitor and fetched her to introduce her to Britta. They warmed to each other immediately, which was reassuring.

Tanja had to put her trust in the stylist as much as the nanny, accepting the silver-blue satin dress she picked out. It was deceptively simple with a deep V-neck and sleeves that went to her elbows. The bodice hugged her braless breasts and a wide band accentuated her narrow waist. The skirt was a voluminous A-line that ended midshin, perfectly showcasing a flashy shoe with crystal-encrusted heels. Thankfully, they were closed toe, because she was desperately in need of a pedicure.

"Tomorrow," her stylist promised her, sweeping Tanja's hair off one ear with a spangled clip.

Tanja nervously joined Leon in the lounge. It struck her that they'd never been on a proper date. They'd gone out on his yacht, and eaten barbecue with her family, picked up lunch for a hike, but they'd never put on their best clothes and gone out in public.

"I feel overdressed for dinner," she murmured to announce her presence.

He turned and stood arrested with a glass halfway to his mouth. After his gaze went to her ankles and came back, he finished his drink in one gulp.

"You look perfect. This is for you, too." He picked up a velvet ring box off a side table and brought it to her.

"That's not necessary. I have my wedding band," she stammered, glancing toward the bedrooms. "It's in my bag. I was going to trade it for groceries at one point, but—"

"You should have." His jaw hardened. "Why didn't you?"

"I wasn't sure of the protocol," she said with a humorless chuckle. "Like, I know you're supposed to return the engagement ring if you're the one who calls it off, but are you supposed to give back the wedding band if you ask for a divorce?"

"I don't know, but they're both gifts. Do what you like with them." He spoke firmly. "Sell this one tomorrow if you want to." He opened the box and her knees grew weak.

This was not the simple gold wedding band she had worn for a few months, then yanked off in a fit of pique. This was a platinum band with five emerald-cut diamonds set in a glittering row. It had to be worth five figures, maybe six.

"Leon," she said in a muted beg for understanding. "I can't."

"Can't what? Wear it or not. It's yours." He was speaking so abruptly, each word hit like little pebbles against her skin. "Or exchange it for something you like better."

"Of course, I *like* it. It's stunning. But…" She frowned with consternation, trying to make him see that wearing his ring *meant* something. Didn't it? "Is wearing it like wearing this?" She fluffed the fall of her skirt, and even that small action felt like blowing air against a scraped knee. "Part of the costume?"

His head jerked back.

"Because—" She was struggling to find words that wouldn't reveal how much she was tripping over her own insecurity and involuntary expectations. "I mean, I'll wear it if you want me to, so people don't ask awkward questions, but it's important to me that you know I don't expect any of this. I'm not here for dresses and jewelry." And all those other things he insisted he wanted to give her because she was his wife.

Was he compensating because he wasn't capable of offering himself? That struck her as heartbreakingly sad for both of them.

"I know why you're here." His voice held an edge. "If I could make Illi yours as easily as I can provide a dress or a ring, I would. For now, this is how we make that happen."

By playing the happy couple.

That's all this ring was. Window dressing. A means to an end.

With an ache behind her sternum, she put it on.

The ring looked a bit loose, but Tanja needed to gain a few pounds. It would fit perfectly in a few weeks. Would she still be here then?

Leon refused to think about that.

It bothered him that she'd been so reluctant to accept it even though he'd been perfectly honest in saying he didn't care what she did with it. Okay, that was a small lie. He damned well *expected* her to sell it for food or anything else she might need if she was ever in dire straits again— not that he intended to let that happen.

He'd given the ring to her for her future security and

because his mother would expect his wife to wear a ring of a certain quality. He told himself he wasn't attached to either ring or wife beyond recognizing they each held their own type of value and deserved his protection.

But he was inexplicably pleased to see the diamonds flash on her hand as they entered the elevator. He looked into the mirrored wall that reflected infinite versions of his pale gray suit and her silver-blue dress. Her fiery hair and cinnamon freckles stood out like sparking flames. A swell of pride filled him.

"You look stunning."

She relaxed into a natural smile for the first time since this morning and might have turned into his arms if the elevator hadn't stopped with a muted ping.

For half a moment, he'd forgotten where they were going. Now a clammy blanket descended on him. His mother. If he could have kept Tanja away from this, he would have. It was his greatest shame that he didn't come from a family like hers. If there was a silver lining to bringing her here now, it was that she would never have to meet his father—this would be excruciating enough. His mother would be...

Well, she would hurt Tanja without even trying. Because that's what she did.

Tanja's expression fell into the stoic one that had overtaken his own face. He clasped her hand and guided her down the hall to double doors that let into his mother's foyer.

His mother's living space was laid out much as his own, but there were two units on this floor, so hers was smaller with only two bedrooms and didn't have a pool. His mother had a more feminine decor and classic art pieces of fruit bowls and landscapes rather than the modern abstracts he preferred.

Truthfully, Leon gravitated to whatever was the opposite of what he'd grown up with.

"Leon." His mother guarded her appearance scrupulously. She was trim and should have developed more frown and worry lines, given how intimidated and angry she'd been for many of her sixty-two years. She wore a silk coat dress with a popped collar and broke from a small group of equally well-dressed guests to approach them.

Leon grimly surveyed the number of people she'd invited. He had thought they'd been invited for dinner, not a dinner *party*.

Tanja's hand tightened in his. Maybe she was reacting to his own firming grip. As his mother approached, his hackles rose out of instinctive protectiveness.

Tanja smiled with her natural appealing openness even as her gaze flickered to the crowd that was staring. Her smile barely faltered, though.

"Mother, my wife Tanja. Tanja, my mother, Ophelia."

"It's lovely to meet you." Tanja dropped his hand and automatically extended her arms for an embrace. Of course, she did. That's how she was with family, and his mother was now a member.

His stomach cramped as Ophelia neatly caught her hands and pressed them down into the space between them. She kept her arms straight and firm, holding Tanja off from closing the distance. Her smile tightened.

Tanja took it as the rebuff it was. Leon knew she did because he saw the flinch that she quickly stifled, reinvigorating her smile to hide it.

He mentally willed an invisible, bulletproof box to lower itself over her to keep her from the death by a thousand cuts that had shredded him his whole life.

"It's lovely to meet you, too, after all this time," his mother was saying, almost sounding sincere despite the way she had scorned Tanja's warmth. "Welcome to the family. Ah, Cornelius." She let go of Tanja and twined her hands around the arm of a heavyset older man Leon had met a few times. They exchanged nods. "Cornelius, this is my daughter-in-law, Tanja. Come. Let us introduce you to everyone."

They made the rounds. Leon stayed close, but Tanja quickly began to look less like herself. Her smiles became forced. Her cheeks grew pale, her responses careful. Was she feeling sick again? Or was she hating this as much as he was?

"Did I hear you're a model, Tanja?" someone asked.

"A CPA. In Canada, that stands for chartered professional accountant," she explained to all the faces that went blank. "I articled at a firm that serves hotels and other tourism-related businesses on Vancouver Island."

A man laughed, then abruptly sobered. "Oh, you're serious."

"Yes." She looked from face to face. "Why is that funny?"

"Well, it's just…" One of the women looked between them. "I mean, you work? *Why?*" She seemed genuinely perplexed. "You're married."

Leon drew a tested breath.

"She just had a daughter," his mother reminded. "Tanja isn't working right now."

"Oh, of course. Well done on getting your figure back."

His mother smoothly shifted them along to the next group, saving Leon from having to blister the ears of a stranger. He loosely encircled Tanja's wrist and felt the way her pulse was racing. Her gaze was darting like a mouse seeking a safe path through a roomful of cats. He wove their fingers together and tried to convey that he would keep her safe.

She brightened slightly as she was asked where she was from.

"Tofino," she replied with obvious fondness. "It's a small fishing and whale-watching town on the West Coast of Canada."

"Oh, yes. We stopped there once when we were sailing. A bohemian little place," one woman told the rest of the group. "Pretty enough to visit, but I can't imagine growing up there." She gave a small shudder.

"Greta," Leon warned the woman against being so rude.

"Many of my friends couldn't wait to get away," Tanja said with forced lightness. "It's a place you don't appreciate until you no longer have it. Will you excuse me a moment?" She extricated her fingers from his. "I want to call the nanny. Make sure everything is going well."

Tanja was so far out of her depth she was hyperventilating. Drowning.

Leaving.

"Tanja." Leon was right behind her as she reached the threshold.

"I can't do this," she said in subdued panic.

"It shouldn't have been this." He shot an impatient look back to the party. "But it's only a few hours."

"This." She waved between them. "I can't believe I thought I could even *pretend* to be your wife—"

He caught her hand as comprehension flared in his eyes. His mouth firmed and he pushed her into a powder room, closing the door on them.

Tanja had a brief impression of ivory wallpaper with silver stripes and roses, gold fixtures and burning candles that gave off a scent of bergamot and lavender, then

Leon was all that was in her senses. Tall and intimidating, broad and commanding.

"What happened? What did she say?" His tone nearly took out her knees.

"Nothing! It's all of this." She waved a hand toward the rooms they'd left and the one they were in. "I mean, I knew I wasn't in your league when we first got together. That's why I expected it to be an affair. And I get it now, why you left me, but I thought I could at least pretend we're happily married for Illi's sake. I just feel like such an *idiot*, though. Such a milkmaid to your—"

"Stop it." He caught her elbow, stilling her flailing gestures, not hurting but firm. Forcing her to look at him and pay attention.

He was the one who wasn't paying attention!

"I don't fit *in*, Leon." She tried to shake off his grip as though she could shake reality into him. "I'll do anything for Illi, but I can't act like I belong here." Hot tears of despair hit the backs of her eyes. "No one is going to believe you want *me*."

"I do want you. Exactly as you are." A fierce light flared to life behind his gaze as he drew her into him with a small crash of their bodies. *"You know that."*

"How?"

"It doesn't matter how. It just is. Feel it." His mouth burned across hers in one hot sweep, then another. "It's here. It's always been here," he muttered between kisses that tasted of anger, but not a kind that was directed at her. His hands were gentle but hard. Imperative. "It has to be you."

Her heart fell, and she tried to find emotional purchase on unsteady ground, but there was none. All of her felt unbalanced.

Helplessly, she clung to him. Slipped her arms beneath the open edges of his suit jacket, curling them around his waist while he pulled her in for a deeper, longer, harder kiss. One that took and gave and was so rife with layers of emotion, it softened her knees.

Amid the taste of anguish and desperation, yearning and his irrepressible will, physical craving crept in, making each kiss last longer. Flow deeper. Their hands roamed in anxious apology and hunger to connect, rebuilding the tenuous threads that bound them.

She slid her hand down to cup him through his trousers. He was hard and hissed under her exploring touch.

"Do you want me to…?" She glanced toward the door as her fingers sought the tab on his fly.

"I want *you*," he growled, reaching back to click the lock. "Isn't that obvious?" He reached into an inner pocket of his jacket and set a condom next to the sink.

She widened her eyes, unable to hold back a choking laugh. "You brought that to dinner with your *mother*?"

"If I learned nothing else in our marriage, it was to always carry one when I'm with you because we can't keep our hands off one another." He crowded her toward the sink.

Her heart was still fluttering, bubbles of laughter rising in her along with a deep craving for reassurance. She needed this. Needed to feel irresistible. Needed the reflection of hunger in him that matched her own urgent desire to break down their barriers and be completely intimate.

The vanity was too small to sit on. He turned her to face it. Her eyes widened in the mirror as he guided her hands to splay flat upon it. Then he ran his hands down her sides, shaping her hips and coming back up to fondle her breasts.

"Sometimes I think you have a very dirty mind," she

accused on a pleasured gasp, arching into his palms, pushing her backside into the hardness behind his fly. "That all you think about is sex and what we'll do next."

"Only sometimes?" His hands were slipping into her cleavage, warming and awakening her, making her breaths catch. "It's not sex I think about. It's *you*."

She shivered, possibly from his words, possibly from the way he teased her nipples before moving down her sides again, adjusting her, using his feet to nudge hers apart while his gaze stayed glued to hers, making sure she was with him for every breath and caress.

She was. It was blatant and lewd and they should have gone upstairs to the privacy of his penthouse, but the immediacy of their desire heartened her. It was as comforting as it was exciting. Part of her knew that it wasn't a strength to be this physically weak, but she drank in the fact he was as anxious to be joined with her as she was. It erased the deep sense of inequality that had been hitting her again and again all day.

His hands went farther down her hips to her thighs. Her dress came up with the next caress of his hands upward, smoothing over her thighs and hips and up to her waist.

"No, keep looking at me," he said in a jagged voice, forcing her to blink her heavy eyelids back open. "I like watching you lose focus."

She licked her lips, watching the heat gathering in his gaze as his caresses grew more flagrant, slipping down the front of her lace underwear and—

"Oh!"

"Eyes open, lovely," he commanded in a hypnotic tone. His free hand stole around to fondle her breast again. "Good?"

"You know it is," she panted. His touch was moving easily in the slick moisture he'd called forth.

"The only person you have to fit with is me. Understand? And we fit perfectly, Tanja. We always have. Yes?"

"Yes," she moaned, unable to resist rocking her hips to seek a firmer touch. Her eyelashes were fluttering as exquisite ripples of arousal rolled upward from his touch.

"Not pretending now, are you?"

"No," she said on a shaken laugh.

He released her, staying close enough behind her she felt the brush of his hand against her cheeks, the rough-soft wool of his trousers as he opened them. The hot weight of his naked erection rested against her cheek while he opened the condom. He applied it and she watched his gaze stay down, admiring her buttocks as he palmed her curves.

"This is terrible," she said, coming back to awareness of where they were. "We shouldn't be doing this here."

"Do you want to wait?" His eyes met hers and his wicked fingertip swept beneath her thong, teasing the swollen bundle of nerves at the top of her sex.

She shuddered in pleasure, her voice catching as she admitted, "No." She couldn't wait another second.

"Good." He moved the placket aside. "Eyes open," he reminded her huskily, then guided himself, seeking and pressing.

"Leon," she sighed as he began to breach her. He rocked lightly in small thrusts that took him a little deeper with each one.

"Battle conditions, lovely," he said as he coaxed inexorably for her to take all of him. "Fast and quiet." He held her gaze as he leaned forward to press his open mouth against her nape. His hand slipped in the front of her underwear again. "Can you do that?"

"No. Yes. Leon," she moaned softly.

He played with her, making pleasure spike upward.

Making her dance her hips back into his, urging him to move.

He did, and the friction was as inciting as it was rough.

She wanted to close her eyes so bad. This was too intimate, but she needed the visual connection as much as the physical. Needed to see him come undone even as her own vision blurred, eyes dampening as her arousal increased.

She bit back her most lurid noises, but couldn't help pushing her hips back into his, wanting the subdued slam that seemed to reverberate joyous sensations through her whole body. When they were like this, nothing else mattered. They were perfectly, utterly aligned.

"Tell me when," he said in a jagged voice.

"Now. I'm ready. I'm... *Now*," she gasped as her climax rose up to engulf her.

The heel of his palm stayed firm against her mound as his other hand took hold of her shoulder. He thrust hard and fast a few more times before he held himself deep inside her while his whole body shuddered.

He pulsed and throbbed within her, teeth clenched. His cheeks flushed dark, and his glittering gaze kept possession of her own.

CHAPTER EIGHT

"DON'T WE HAVE to go back?" Tanja asked when Leon drew her from the powder room and out his mother's doors toward the elevator.

"No." Leon knew he sounded like a Neanderthal, but his heart was still unsteady and, despite his powerful orgasm, his throat tight. He couldn't stop hearing Tanja's distressed *I can't do this.*

She had hurried to tidy her makeup, but she was pale beneath her flush of culmination. Her gaze on him as they entered the elevator was apprehensive.

He reassured her the only way he knew how, by dragging her close and kissing her until she melted. When he lifted his head, the wariness in her eyes was replaced with golden lights of yearning, the ones that urged him closer. Invited him to touch and hold her.

That's what he needed to ease this monster inside him. That quiet surrender of herself to him.

When they entered his penthouse, Valerie poked her head from the kitchen in surprise.

"Call my mother. Let her know Tanja is unwell," he said.

"Of course. May I get you anything?"

"I'm fine," Tanja murmured, sending him a doleful look for his lie.

"You've been unwell," he justified as he steered her down the hall. "And you weren't enjoying it."

"What exactly are you referring to?"

His mouth twitched and his tension eased. If she was making jokes, they were okay.

He had heard himself in her compulsion to flee, though. He had done the same thing for years, absenting himself from Greece however he had to. It had hit him hard that she wanted to flee *him* in that same way—as if he was causing her the emotional angst he had endured through his childhood.

They checked on a sleeping Illi and Tanja told the nanny she could leave for the evening. She brought the baby monitor into the master bedroom with them.

"I feel bad for ducking out on your mother," she said as they undressed. "Cowardly."

"Don't."

"Leon—"

"No, listen." He yanked his shirt from his trousers. "You should have had this life all along." He waved at the professionally decorated room with its satin drapes and silk area rug and bamboo sheets. "Get used to it because this is your life now, even after our divorce."

"But I don't *want*—"

"Tanja! *I* was pretending when we married. I pretended it didn't matter that I wasn't taking it seriously. That it was okay to leave you with nothing. Let me fix that much."

She was in bare feet, hair loose, hugging a silk kimono closed across her nudity.

"Maybe I even pretended…" He paced away, embarrassed to admit he'd wanted to be like her. Warm and sincere and surrounded by open affection. "It was never about *you* not being good enough for *me*."

There was a long, pensive silence before she said quietly, "I still can't help feeling I'm not—"

He pivoted to face her and cut her off. "You went to a foreign country to teach women how to be as financially independent as you are. You fostered a baby and now you're a mother. What makes you think you can't walk into a cocktail party of blowhards and hold your own? Win them over?"

"Fear," she admitted glumly.

"Well, stop it," he chided. "You're actually very brave and bright and likable. If anyone insults your hometown or tries to make you feel small again, say something about the yacht. That usually snaps people into their best behavior, in hopes of earning an invitation."

She snorted. "You do have a mean streak, don't you?"

"I come by it honestly." It should have been a lighthearted rejoinder, but it was too true. His father had held out carrots like that, playing with people's hopes, manipulating them with the promise of rewards that hadn't arrived.

When he looked at her again, her teasing smile had faded into a troubled frown.

"My biggest problem is figuring out what's real and what's pretend. Sometimes this feels very…"

He nodded, accepting that even as it caused a jolt of guilty conscience.

"I led you on the first time. I wish you could understand how angry I am with myself for that." The words came from the depth of his chest, scoring behind his breastbone like sandpaper and leaving a scrape in the back of his throat. "That's why I'm trying to be as truthful as possible now. I don't want to hurt you again."

"I know." She nodded jerkily, her lips clamped to withstand some inner agony. "But you will anyway."

That broadsword went through him so cleanly he could only hiss as it eviscerated him.

"I'm going to take off my makeup." She moved into the bathroom while he stood there frozen in torment. Absorbing the knowledge that she could—and would—hurt him, too.

"I've asked Demitri to reschedule all of your appointments today," Leon said over breakfast the next morning. "I heard what you said last night. This is a lot to adjust to. I'll go into the office and the staff will be out. Take the day to get your bearings."

Great. All the time in the world to dwell and brood and fret over the way they'd come together in a clash. She could pick apart the contradiction of a man who was capable of showing incredible care and concern, who delivered indescribable pleasure, offered remorse over the way they'd parted and said he wanted to make things up to her, but withheld himself.

Refused to open his heart.

She'd been up in the early hours to settle Illi. When she'd come back to bed, he'd spooned her into him, but that cuddle had turned into lazy, wordless lovemaking. He'd risen a few hours later when Illi stirred, leaving Tanja fast asleep and unaware he was even gone.

He could be so considerate and tender. It was no wonder she was beginning to tip into falling for him again, but even his offer to leave her at home alone felt like a withdrawal of sorts. A distance he was putting between them on purpose.

"No?" he prompted at her silence.

"No. I mean yes. Thank you." She smiled as a thought surfaced. "I could call Shonda."

"That reminds me." He rose and came back with a stack

of electronic devices. They were programmed with emails and numbers to reach him, his PA, and all his key staff.

She might have refused, but having a laptop would allow her to put out feelers for work. It felt a little defeatist to cold-bloodedly plan her life after her divorce, when they could be married for a year or more, but she accepted everything gracefully.

Once everyone was gone, she spoke to her family, then sent an email to Kahina that included a selfie with Illi. She asked after Kahina's family and let her friend know she and Illi were well and that Georgiou might be in touch as he worked on the legalities of Illi's adoption. Tanja also left messages on Brahim's stale social media accounts, urging him to get in touch when he could.

After that, she wallowed in the quiet of the penthouse, enjoying coffee outside before she sorted through some of the outfits in the spare bedroom and moved a few casual pieces into the section of the master bedroom closet that Leon had set aside for her. She had just fed Illi and was considering her options for lunch, Illi on her hip, when the landline rang.

"Hello?" she asked cautiously, belatedly realizing she should have said it in Greek.

"Tanja, it's Ophelia. I wondered if I might come up and meet the baby?"

"Um." *Don't be a coward.* "Of course. Um. We would love that. When were you thinking?"

"Would now be convenient?"

Tanja looked from Illi's soggy chin to her own comfortable but threadbare shorts and T-shirt. "Of course," she said with false brightness.

She had just enough time to wash her daughter's face and slip into a simple yet pretty summer dress, then pull her hair into a ponytail before there was a brief knock.

Tanja set Illi under her play set and hurried to let Ophelia in.

Ophelia looked as intimidatingly put together as she had last night, this time in a linen pantsuit with an emerald green blouse. Her hair was pinned in a smooth chignon, her makeup flawless.

"The housekeeper is out, I'm afraid, but I could make coffee and find some cookies?" Tanja offered as she led Ophelia into the lounge. "I should have called you myself this morning, to apologize for not staying last night. I, um, wasn't feeling well."

Ophelia gave her a steady look that was even more piercing and unreadable than her son's. "Leon has already explained that you weren't feeling welcome."

"That's not…quite true." Tanja flexed her linked fingers. "Out of my depth is a better way of putting it. This is all very overwhelming."

Ophelia halted to stare at Illi on the blanket on the floor.

"This is Illi." What had Leon told his mother about her parentage?

"She could be Leon's, couldn't she? With that coloring?" Ophelia's expression softened almost imperceptibly as she shifted to perch on the edge of a cushion, her attention remaining on the baby, while Illi batted at the toys dangling from the play set propped over her.

Tanja sank into the chair opposite, surprised and not sure how much she should reveal.

"Please don't be alarmed. Leon wouldn't have told me if he didn't trust me to keep the information to myself. We have our difficulties and I was shocked to learn he'd been married all this time, but he wouldn't lie to me about having a child."

"I very much appreciate the lengths he's been willing to go to help me keep her," Tanja said tentatively.

Ophelia studied her for a long moment, looking as though she wanted to say something. A small frown dented her expression.

"I disappointed him by inviting a crowd last night," she finally decided to say. "We have a relationship that is… I find it easier to have people around. A buffer." Her brief smile was deeply pained, then gone. "It's an old habit, but it wasn't fair to you. I apologize."

"That's not necessary, but thank you." Tanja's heart instinctively went out to her, reaching across the space that felt like a chasm because Ophelia was clearly clinging hard to her side, terrified to reach out.

Illi was kicking and grabbing at the toys, burbling away, easier to watch than looking at each other, so they did that for a few minutes.

Tanja snuck glances at Ophelia, though, and watched as her expression grew poignant. Her hand twitched and she leaned forward a little, almost as if she wanted to bend and reach out, catch at a flailing foot, but she seemed to think better of it and straightened again.

I think she quit showing affection for me so he wouldn't use me against her.

Tanja's heart clutched. "Would you like to hold her?"

"Best not to get attached," Ophelia said with a valiant smile. "Leon tells me this isn't a permanent arrangement." She met Tanja's gaze, and that suggestion of words wanting to be spoken was there again. This time she was a little braver, her voice holding a hint of emotion. "I take heart from the fact he's come this far. Until his call the other day, I was convinced he would never marry or have children. Even… Well, baby steps as they say."

"Wait until you see him with her," Tanja said with emotion-laden humor. "He's so sweet, you'll die."

"Oh, he won't let me see that," Ophelia assured her with another of those smiles that painted over what Tanja was beginning to realize was profound pain. "He was torn last night, afraid to hover over you too closely in case I guessed how much you mean to him. The lecture this morning was very telling, though." Her mouth twitched.

"What did he say?" Tanja asked with a rise and fall of hope and dread. "Whatever it was, I'm sorry. Honestly, I was overreacting. Suffering a case of imposter syndrome."

"Nonsense." Ophelia held up a hand. "You are not an imposter, and his anger isn't anything I don't deserve. I'm extremely sensitive to any sort of disapproval or criticism from him, though." She tucked her hands in her lap. "My first instinct is to protect myself proactively, thus the crowd. It always goes wrong, of course, but he does the same with me. The fact he kept his marriage from me for five years tells me how much you meant to him."

So many words of protest and correction jammed into Tanja's throat that she couldn't make any of them come out in a sensible way. They simply sat there with their sharp edges, suffocating her while Ophelia flicked a speck of lint from her sleeve.

"I had hoped after his father passed that Leon and I would develop a new understanding between us, but—" Her sigh was the epitome of despair. "Leon was faced with incredibly difficult challenges. I didn't help. I pushed him so hard to fight for what was rightfully his. If I'd known he had a wife to go back to… Well, I don't know what I would have done," she admitted heavily. "I can see now he was angry over what he was forced to give up in order to stay here. I won't say he blamed me," Ophelia continued in a tone of reflection. "But he must have seen me as part of the reason he was forced to stay here instead of returning to you. That's why we haven't been able to mend things."

"I'm so s—"

"Please." Ophelia forestalled her with a smooth show of her palm. "You are not the source of my troubles with my son. That lies entirely with me."

"I think you're being very hard on yourself," Tanja said tentatively. "Leon has only said a few things about his early years, but I get the sense there was quite a bit of tension. That your husband was a difficult person and bears much of the responsibility."

"You're very generous. I can see why Leon is so attracted to you. His father was a terrible bully, but I can't say I was at my best in the way I chose to fight him. I sank to his level far too often. When it comes to Leon, I'm reaping what was sown."

"Well, you can sow new things," Tanja said earnestly. "I hope you see me and Illi as a fresh field. You and I don't have to let any of those old weeds grow between us. We can define our relationship however it suits us."

Ophelia didn't say anything for a long minute, but a faint sheen of tears seemed to glimmer in her eyes. Her mouth might have trembled. It was hard to tell. She was very good at hiding her emotions.

"It would mean a lot to me if you and I were to become friends. It's difficult to feel close to my son."

You love him, Tanja wanted to say, but she had the feeling it was the sort of incantation that wasn't allowed to be spoken aloud in Leon's world for fear of breaking a spell. It explained so much about him.

"We are friends," Tanja assured her huskily. "Please join us anytime."

* * *

Leon was both pleased and disgruntled at his mother visiting, proclaiming, "She owed you an apology, but she had no right to invite herself into our home." Then he added gruffly, "How was it?"

"It was nice," Tanja said, privately breathless over him saying "our" home.

Everything seemed to be smoothed over two nights later when they invited Ophelia and Cornelius to dine with them. Cornelius was comfortable to be around, engaging and easygoing and smitten with Ophelia. She wasn't the most effusive person. Her tension around Leon seemed to feed his own so there was a constant static in the air, but she seemed sincere in her desire for Tanja to feel more comfortable in her world and offered gentle advice.

Ophelia's support bolstered Tanja's confidence when she and Leon attended Georgiou's wife's fund-raiser.

Tanja kept hoping she and Leon would find a comfortable set of boundaries, clear lines they couldn't cross, but they were blurry and forever shifting. They made love before they dressed and sent each other sly looks filled with sizzling memory, but she had to keep reminding herself this wasn't real. Tanja could put on a figure-hugging strapless gown in diaphanous pink with gorgeous beadwork in metallic silver and rose gold, but that didn't make her Leon's wife any more than it made her the movie star who ought to be wearing this for her own performance.

No one else seemed to notice she was a phony, though. She received dozens of compliments and was warmly welcomed by everyone they met.

It helped that Leon never left her side, ensuring any awkward questions were quickly fielded and the conversation steered into neutral topics. Overall, it was a pleasant evening, and she was even invited to join the board of directors for the foundation that Georgiou's wife ran.

"Do you want to do that sort of work?" Leon asked when she mentioned it the next day. "Because I have two corporate boards I could put you on immediately if you're interested. Paid, not volunteer."

"I don't want you to give me some placeholder job out of nepotism."

"Tanja." He clicked off his tablet. "You have a degree in accounting. You're not only qualified to provide knowledge and oversight, I *trust* you. One of the organizations I'm thinking of is run by a CEO who worked for my father. He wouldn't be with us if I had reason to distrust him, but extra reassurances are always appreciated. The other has a young woman at the helm who has star power, but she could use support while she finds her feet. Having another woman with solid business sense as a sounding board would set her up for success."

"You really trust me that much?" She was ridiculously flattered.

"Are there stages of trust? I thought it was one or the other and, yes, I trust you." He seemed to brace himself. "Don't you trust me?"

"Of course. I—" The words *I love you* caught in her throat, causing a full-body sting at holding back the enormous surge of emotion. Maybe she didn't entirely trust him. There *were* levels of trust. She knew she was physically safe with him. She would entrust her daughter's life, as well as her own, to him, but she wasn't sure how he would react if she made her declaration aloud.

Actually, maybe she knew him well enough—trusted him enough—to be confident he would withdraw from such a declaration and look pained at not being able to reciprocate.

"You what?" he prompted, touching her cheek to coax her face up so she couldn't avoid his searching gaze.

Her heart was right there, pounding in her throat.

"I do trust you. And the job sounds interesting, but what happens when…" She swallowed, voice fading to a husk. "When we're over?"

A flicker of something bleak flashed in his eyes before he dropped his hand and hooded his thoughts behind an impassive expression.

"That could be a year or two from now. You shouldn't put your career on hold if you want to pursue it. This would be valuable experience. If the postings interest you, take them."

He sent her the details a little while later. One was a solar power corporation, the other a fair trade importer. Both were different enough from anything she'd taken on before to be intriguing and challenging. Commitment-wise, the demands would be light enough to fit around Illi's needs and dovetail with her social obligations with Leon.

Things fell into place very quickly. Soon Tanja was dressing in a business suit once or twice a week to attend meetings. She spent another in jeans and a T-shirt, an-swering emails and reviewing reports, then put on cou-ture for evenings with Leon. When he had commitments in Rome, they took *Poseidon's Crown* since Illi's passport situation hadn't been sorted yet and anchored offshore.

When Leon had meetings in Singapore, he went alone. Tanja had feared she would feel like a guest if he wasn't here with them, but the penthouse was beginning to feel like her home. Like *their* home. Illi's room was a proper nursery with duckling wallpaper and an infant swing, a play saucer and every other toy Leon could find online.

Tanja had a desk of her own in Leon's office, and they often worked there very companionably.

She missed him intensely while he was gone, though, and had to fight saying so when he called her over the tablet. She missed him because she loved him. She couldn't deny it when it overwhelmed her in waves of euphoric angst. When her daughter tried to drop her face through the tablet screen to get to him and Tanja wanted to do the very same thing.

Perhaps he missed them, too. He walked in late on a Wednesday evening when she hadn't been expecting him until Thursday afternoon. He surprised her in her pj's watching an old rom-com, fighting her lonesomeness with a glass of wine and a bowl of popcorn.

He exhaled a huge sigh as he saw her. Before she could do more than set aside the bowl and rise to say, "You're home," he had planted a kiss on her that nearly made her faint.

Heart hammering, exchanging no other words, they peeked in on the sleeping Illi, then hurried to the master bedroom where they ravaged the hell out of each other. When he reached for the nightstand, she said, "It's okay. I saw the doctor. I have an IUD."

He fell on her and their naked joining took them to a new level of intimate pleasure, one that left her in a state of elation for days after.

Tanja began to believe he was coming to love her, too. Maybe, despite all the trials and tribulations and the five years of separation, she was married to her soul mate?

Leon sorted through the courier envelopes on his desk, separating out the ones addressed to him from the ones addressed to his wife.

He had half expected to feel bothered by sharing his

home. He'd never lived with anyone so closely and had always liked his space just so.

Tanja was fairly tidy by nature, but her cosmetics turned up on his side of the bathroom sink and her purse landed on his desk and sometimes the shirt he wanted was already on her back. As for Illi, she had a very attentive nanny, but still needed a lot of care and attention, often at the most inconvenient times, and for someone who had only mastered rolling, she was very good at scattering toys far and wide.

He had missed that small sense of disarray while he'd been away on his business trip. He should have embraced the time alone. He'd always preferred to answer to no one, but he'd been irritated that Tanja and Illi hadn't been able to come with him. He had felt as though he was holding his breath the whole time, annoyed at the way people rushed to do his bidding while each minute of the clock dragged.

The last thing he wanted was to become dependent, but he had rushed back early. Which disconcerted him. Tanja was the furthest thing from cruel, but she didn't have to be. She had the power to hurt him anyway, and that knowledge, that anticipation that she would, hung over him like a blade that could drop at any second.

It whistled down upon him when he opened the envelope from Georgiou.

"How would you feel if I invited my father to visit?" Tanja asked, coming in while he was still absorbing what his lawyer had sent.

Leon's blood was pounding so hard in his ears he barely heard her.

"What's wrong?" Her tone plummeted into something cold and filled with dread.

He gave himself a mental shake, wiping his face clean

of whatever was causing her cheeks to grow hollow and her eyes to widen with apprehension.

"Nothing," he stated. It felt like a lie. A grave one. "Georgiou's email the other day said things were going well with the officials in Istuval. He said we should have something soon. I thought this was the finalized postnuptial, but it's also Illi's adoption papers." He showed her the official certificates.

Tanja's eyes latched on to the Canadian passport and she snatched it up. "Oh, my God! When he asked me to get her photo taken for this, I thought it would take weeks."

She flipped it open, saw Illi's name and clasped the passport to her heart. Her eyes welled. "She's mine? Really? Oh, my God, Leon. Thank you. *Thank you.*"

She hurried around to throw herself against him in a shaking mass of every emotion—joy and relief and things he couldn't identify.

"It's okay." Leon reflexively closed his arms around her and ran soothing hands over her back. "Yes, she's yours now."

"I feel terrible for being this happy," she said through her sniffles. "I mean, her mother should have her, right? And Brahim is still out there—"

"You're still allowed to be happy, Tanja." He wondered sometimes how such a slender body could contain such a big heart. "You want her to be safe and loved, and she is."

"I just wish I could give him this, too. Bring him with us when we take Illi h-home."

He stiffened slightly.

She felt it and jerked her head up, fighting to get hold of her emotions. "We *are* taking her home, aren't we?"

He was tempted, so tempted to give in to what he wanted despite knowing it was the worst possible thing he could do to her. He refused to lead her on again, though.

No matter how much he wanted to let this play out until what could only be a bitter end.

"*You* are." His body was bracing so hard against the inevitable pain that was coming that he felt as though hairline fractures were creeping through his limbs and torso and neck.

"But—" Here came the hurt, the flash of betrayal that cut him in half, the profound anguish that filled him with guilt. "What do you mean? We're a family. Aren't we?"

His arms wanted to squeeze her in, but he made himself drop them away.

"You and Illi are. It's time you took her to meet the rest of yours."

"But—"

"This is what we knew would happen, Tanja." He spoke over her. "It happened sooner than later. That's good. I'm glad you didn't have to wait years to know she's indisputably your daughter. But this is what we agreed, that you would take her home when the time came."

"But I don't *have to*, Leon! I mean, I want to go home. I miss everyone and I want to meet my nephew and introduce Illi to everyone, but we could *all* go. And then—"

She stopped speaking, not saying aloud that they could come back here.

Because he was already dismissing the notion with a pained shake of his head.

"Think about this clearly, Tanja. This is the best outcome. It's not a fight. We're ending things on a civil note with a clean settlement already worked out." He waved at his desk where the postnuptial contract sat, thick and heavy and not nearly as satisfying as he had anticipated.

"So I'm supposed to just *leave*? With Illi? And we'll never talk to one another again? You don't even care that I'm taking her away from you?"

That was a knife to the vitals that gave such a hard wrench he could hardly breathe. He waved again at the document he had thought would make all of this easy, but it wasn't easy at all. He had to fight to hold on to a level tone.

"I have the right to expect regular updates. Photos and occasional visits." It wasn't enough. He already felt cheated. "We'll each provide for her in our own way, but we're both ensuring she has the best life we're capable of offering."

"And that's enough for you?" she cried with disbelief, backing off a few steps as though she could hardly take in all the ways he was disappointing her. "A couple of photos and the assurance that she'll have a good education is all you want from either of us? Don't you feel anything else? You acted like I was your salvation the other night!"

It had felt that way, and that was why he had to let her go before he couldn't.

"The goal was to end this on a civilized note," he reminded her, dredging up the cool ruthlessness he'd been raised on. "Can we?"

She flinched at his tone, making him feel like a bastard, but that was exactly why they had to end this. How did she not see that, eventually, this was what their marriage would devolve into, only so much worse?

Tanja stood before him with her hands in knotted fists, her body trembling with impotence, mouth working with hurt. Angry tears in her eyes.

"You have put me in an impossible position, Leon." Her voice was thick with outrage. "If I fight for you, for *us*, you'll see it as me trying to prolong this argument, which will only drive you away. So fine. I won't fight. If you want me to leave, I will. As soon as I can book a flight. But know this." She held up a trembling finger. "I am leaving *because*… I love you. I'm doing this *for* you, because I want to give you the thing you think will make you happy."

She started to walk out, paused at the door.

"But I won't wait five years again."

Leon spent the next weeks traveling. Each time he walked into his empty penthouse, he couldn't stand the silence, the lack of clutter or the profound absence. He found excuse after excuse to leave town, but only felt emptier and emptier as time wore on.

Tanja, damn her, had sent one text to say they'd landed safely and nothing else.

He hadn't reached out, either. They were back to the stalemate of their first five years of marriage.

Until she ended that, too.

When Georgiou sent him the notice that she'd finalized the papers and taken Leon's ten-million-euro settlement, Leon was knocked onto his ass. He sat down to get drunk and couldn't even do that. He just sat there with his bottle of ouzo on the coffee table, staring at the spot on the carpet where Illi had spit up and left a stain.

He should only feel satisfaction that she had taken the money. He wanted to provide for her and Illi, and some integral part of him was pleased he was able to do that much for them, but he genuinely hadn't expected her to take his money.

Even though she had told him she wouldn't wait for him, he hadn't expected her to end it. That was the stark truth. She had said she loved him, and some distant part of him had known in those seconds that he loved her, too. That the emotional connection between them would never die. It couldn't.

He had also known he didn't deserve her. *He* was the

one who'd been in the impossible position. If he gave in to longing and let their marriage go on, he would only be proving what a selfish self-serving ass he really was— exactly like his father.

Letting her go had been the only way to prove he was worthy of the love she'd offered him.

But she had gone through with the divorce. Why? To be free of him, as she'd once told him she wanted to be? Had her love died that quickly?

Unable to bear his own brooding, he abruptly had the helicopter take him to the island where he'd spent his earliest years. This was his mother's domain, where his father had mostly left her alone.

Leon's first thought on landing was to wonder what Tanja would think of it. Why hadn't he brought her here? It was pretty and quiet and might have quelled some of her homesickness, given its seaside location. The beach was beautiful. Once Illi was walking, they could have enjoyed it to no end.

If they'd been a family.

They weren't in his life anymore. It was such a punch in the chest each time he faced it that he could hardly stay on his feet. Illi wouldn't smile at him like he was a white night rescuing her from a tower when he walked in to collect her from her crib. Tanja wouldn't set him aflame with a sexy glance or make him laugh out of the blue or settle against him on the sofa and just make everything in his world…right.

"Leon." His mother gave him a frown that might have indicated concern if they were the type to express that sort of thing toward one another. "How was London?"

"Hmm? Oh. I don't know." He supposed that's where he'd been. It was all such a blur. "Cornelius here?" he asked politely.

"He's staking the tomatoes. You walked right by him, said hello and asked what kind they were. What's wrong?" Her dark brows drew together.

"Nothing," he insisted, trying to convince himself it was true. "Tanja and I are officially divorced. I thought I should tell you."

"I know. I'm so sorry."

That took him aback. "How do you know?" Was it on the gossip sites *already*? How humiliating.

"We video chat." His mother clasped her hands and pressed her lips into a self-conscious line. "Tanja said she wasn't certain you would tell me and thought I should know."

Leon swore and flung himself to face the window, then veered out the doors to the terrace, uncomfortable with his mother seeing how tortured he was by all of this. He braced his fists on the stone balustrade and stared at the green-blue sea, but he couldn't have picked out if there were boats upon it or giant squids. His entire body was aching. Writhing in agony.

"Are you angry I've kept contact with her?" his mother asked warily as she came to stand beside him. "It seemed rude to ignore her."

He choked at that, thinking his ignoring Tanja for five years was a lot worse than rude. It had been self-destructive madness.

Something in her hesitant tone plucked at an old, tight line of hurt inside him. She had never been able to make a right step around his father and neither had he. It was a reminder of exactly what he was trying to avoid.

"It's fine, Mother." He had to fight to keep the anger with himself out of his voice so she wouldn't think it was directed at her. "I'm glad that you're staying in touch.

How is she?" His ears were reaching for her words before she spoke.

"They seem well, but Tanja doesn't seem very happy."

I'm doing this for you.

Then why did it feel like she was doing it *to* him?

He hung his head. Some twisted voice inside him was convinced she was hurting him on purpose because that's what married people did to one another, didn't they? Tanja wouldn't, though. He knew that. In his heart of hearts, he knew she wasn't like that.

"I'm glad you're not angry." His mother's voice wasn't quite steady. "Because…" She sounded so fearful. "Well, I quite like her, Leon. It's nice to see the baby, too. I'm genuinely sorry things didn't work out." After another pause, she said quietly, "I blame myself."

"Don't." He didn't even know what he was trying to forestall with that blunt word. An apology? Being forced to acknowledge his own culpability in how they'd let his father damage them? He didn't want to examine their baggage. He never, ever wanted to have uncomfortable conversations about feelings, especially with her. There were too many. It would take too long and hurt too much.

"I thought I was standing up for myself with your father," she said, voice almost a plea.

She lightly touched his arm, but he didn't look at her. Couldn't. His heart was being crushed and squeezed and liable to burst under the pressure.

"I was young and felt responsible for keeping all of this for *you*. I didn't care that *I* was unhappy, but I see now that I caused you to think we're not the type of people who are allowed to be happy. That we're not lovable. We are, Leon." Her touch squeezed his forearm. "It's taken a lot of convincing, but Cornelius has made me believe that I'm worthy of being loved, and so are you."

"*You* are," he agreed stiffly. "But I was careless with her. I was filled with a sense of entitlement and threw her away like she didn't matter. I'm no better than he was—"

"You are a million times better than he was," his mother broke in vehemently. "I stand in awe of the man you've become *in spite* of the example that was set for you. My greatest regret is that I let him come between you and I, leaving you thinking a woman's love isn't steadfast. It is, Leon. I have always loved you. And so does Tanja."

But she divorced me.

I'm doing this for you.

His heart lurched. He couldn't bear this. Could she be right, though? Was there hope?

His mother's hand was clutched so tightly to his arm he was compelled to set his arm around her and draw her into his side. He held her as she began to weep into his shoulder.

"It's okay," he murmured, exactly as he would comfort Illi or Tanja or anyone else he loved. After a moment, he set his cheek on her hair. His misted gaze fell on the heavyset man propping up tomatoes in the garden.

Cornelius nodded approval.

Believing his ex-wife might still love him was one thing. Going to Canada to talk her into coming back into his life was quite another. Tanja was completely within her right to invite him to go to hell. He had pushed her out of his life twice. Why would she trust him a third time?

Nevertheless, Leon flew into Vancouver and chartered a seaplane from there. It landed at the marina he would have partially owned had his father not died when he had.

As he stepped onto the wharf and saw the fresh signage going up that read Melha Marina he stood there for a full minute, hands on his hips. The widest, most foolish grin split his face and refused to stop.

That's why she'd taken the settlement. Of course, she hadn't kept it. He couldn't be happier that she had divorced him if that was why she'd done it.

He walked up to a building that was in the process of being returned to its original blue and white. Inside, a man about his age stood with a baby strapped to his chest like the kid was a smoke jumper and Zach the parachute.

Zach pointed out something on a drawing and gave a woman in a yellow hardhat instructions on finding the property line. When he rolled the drawing and handed it to the woman, they both turned to the open door where Leon stood.

His old friend's surprised expression slammed shut. "Leon. What brings you here?"

Leon stepped aside to let the woman leave. "I'm looking for Tanja." Obviously.

Zach stiffened. "Is the money not coming through again?"

"It's *through*. Hers. Yours, I guess." Leon glanced around the interior of the office where he had first met "Books." Tanja had said something snappy to her brother, turning from a cabinet and going very coltish and still. The zing of attraction as she met Leon's eyes had been so undeniable and visceral, he was still trying to breathe through the power of it today.

"It's hers," Zach said. "She wanted it for Dad. I agreed to run it."

Leon dragged his attention back to Zach's hostile glare. "Look. I know I owe you an apology. I sincerely regret that our deal fell apart. I don't know if Tanja has explained—"

"What's to explain?" Zach shrugged it off. "You warned me to wait until the money was yours, but I didn't.

Dad told me I was moving too fast. Even Books had concerns about how much debt I was racking up. I didn't listen. I crashed and burned and it sucked, but live and learn, right?" He didn't sound particularly bitter, just fatalistic.

"If that's how you feel…" Leon grabbed the edge of the door. "Why do you hate my guts?"

"Because you broke my little sister's heart, jackass. *Twice*."

Tanja was half-heartedly reviewing three different job offers when there was a knock on her door at the bottom of the stairs.

She presumed it was Shonda, but her sister-in-law usually let herself in, calling hello as she came up. They were becoming like true sisters, confiding their new mother failures and triumphs, cuddling each other's infants as often as their own.

Tanja veered minute by minute between so much happiness she could hardly contain it, and such a profound sadness it was all she could do to breathe. She was exhausted and heartbroken and determined to pick up the pieces and move on anyway.

Shonda didn't appear, and another knock sounded.

Tanja rose and slipped down the stairs, glancing into Illi's crib on her way. She was fast asleep, taking to her new home the way she'd taken to all the other changes she'd been through in her short life. She was such a little trouper.

The entrance foyer was only big enough to hold a shoe shelf and a rack of coat hooks. Tanja unlocked the door and backed into the corner as she opened it.

"Sorry, I thought it was op…" She trailed off as she saw it wasn't Shonda on her stoop.

Her heart went into free fall.

How many times had she waited and yearned and willed for this to happen? Leon. Here. As recently as yesterday afternoon, when she'd left her divorce certificate in the fireproof cabinet at the marina, she had spared a moment to wish for him to appear and tell her this wasn't what he wanted.

And she had told herself *again* to quit being a fool. He wasn't coming. He was never coming.

But here he was, tall and lean, casually perfect in faded jeans and a light windbreaker. Fine sparkles of raindrops sat on his hair like glitter. His mirrored aviators accentuated his trimmed beard and stern mouth.

Her heart commenced hammering. Her whole being took the hit of being in his presence again. She wanted to throw herself into his arms and say, *Yes, I'm still yours.*

But he had never wanted her, not really. Not the way she needed to be wanted.

She thought about closing the door on him, she really did, but she could never shut out someone she loved no matter how badly they'd hurt her.

"Come out of the rain." She stepped back so he could wipe his feet and follow her up the narrow staircase to the one-bedroom apartment over her brother's detached garage.

"This is nice," he said of the space with slanted ceilings, gabled windows, moss-green walls, and hardwood floors. The kitchen was galley style in a nook off the living area. It had a peninsula counter that jutted out to provide an eating area. It currently held her laptop and the job offers she'd been scrutinizing.

"Zach and Shonda were planning to rent it by the week to tourists, but they're letting me use it until I find a job and figure out what I can afford."

"You were supposed to use your settlement to buy a house—" His breath sucked in as he caught sight of the crib tucked behind the pony wall at the top of the stairs.

He took off his sunglasses as he moved to look down on Illi. Her little arms were thrown up beside her curly hair, a corner of the knit blanket tangled in the fingers of one hand.

"She's growing," he said softly, moving her huggy bear into her side before he adjusted the blanket. His face spasmed with naked emotion as he looked down on her.

It was the most heartbreakingly beautiful thing Tanja had ever seen.

That's why he's here, she realized with a hard swallow. She wouldn't deny him time with Illi, either, even if it would cause her to feel jealous of her own daughter.

"Can I, um…" She had to clear her throat. "Can I make you some coffee?" She moved toward the kitchen.

"I miss you." He spoke so softly she was certain he was talking to the baby.

She turned to see it, to be included in some small way in his quiet admission to a sleeping baby. She told herself she only wanted to see him crack and reveal his love for her daughter, but he wasn't looking at Illi. He was looking at her.

The floor fell away and her entire being filled with helium. Not oxygen. No, there was not a bit of that in her right now.

"Both of you," he said with anguish creasing his features. "I hate going home. It's not a home anymore. But I don't know how to ask you to come back and make it into one. I don't know what I could say that would convince you."

"You do," she said faintly. The buoyant hope inside her butted up against the shadows of despair she'd had to make into friends. "You just don't want to say it. And I understand why, but—"

"No, I do," he said with a rasp in his voice and a jerky step forward. His gaze went to the window where the white curtains glowed with a sudden burst of sunshine on this changeable spring day. "I think I've wanted to say it for a long time. Maybe I thought it wouldn't matter. That it wouldn't change anything because it never had in the past."

Tanja set down the ceramic mug she had drawn from the cupboard, afraid her numb fingers would drop it to smash at her feet.

"I think I would have said it five years ago if I'd had time to understand what this feeling is." He clenched his fist in front of his heart. "It hurts. You know? Like a muscle that aches so bad after a run you never want to exercise again. I'd almost rather throw up than feel this much. It's too intense to bear."

"It is," she said, biting her lip. "It was how I felt when you left me." Her lips trembled as she added, "And when I left you."

"I'm mad at you for that," he admitted with a ragged laugh. His clenched fist lowered. "Hypocritical, I know. I'm angry you divorced me even though it's what I said I wanted and you used the money in the best possible way. But I'm angry because I want to be your husband, Tanja. I want to be Illi's father and the father of as many kids as you want in whatever way you want to bring them into our lives. I love you. And I want you to love me, but—"

"No buts." She rushed toward him and he caught her so tightly she couldn't breathe, but she didn't care.

"Say it again," he commanded.

"I love you. That's all it is and all it has to be, Leon. I love you. So much."

He drew one shaken breath, then his mouth found hers. Their lips fused with perfection the way they always did, but with a new sweetness. The kiss was frantic with reunion, yet tender and familiar and new. It was imbued with a love that she was realizing had always been there, deep and soft and unacknowledged beneath every kiss they had ever exchanged.

Now it was real. True. Celebrated.

"Will you marry me?" He broke away only as far as he needed to whisper the proposal against her lips. "Again? This time I mean it. No escape clauses. We commit to facing our challenges together. Figure out how to get through them together because I will *never* let you go again."

She showed him her hand where his diamond band sat securely on her finger, teasing her with flashes of hope and memories of passion and the symbol of an everlasting love she would feel forever, whether he did or not.

He captured her hand and kissed the inside of her wrist, clearly moved and not ashamed to let her see the sheen of emotion in his eyes. "You humble me."

"I don't think I could ever *not* feel married to you."

"Me, either," he said with bemusement. "I'm yours. I always will be."

Tanja had always had love in her life, but she had never known this kind. It filled her until she could hardly bear the breadth of it, but it was so good, she greedily let it grow bigger and bigger inside her.

They kissed and kissed, but it wasn't enough expression for the feelings that were surging between them, reacting and expanding. He lifted his head to glance toward the bedroom door. She drew him toward the tiny bedroom with its queen mattress in a wrought-iron frame. They sank onto the down-filled coverlet with mutual sighs.

The light shifted against the small window above the headboard, dimming. Rain began a homey patter against the roof as they tugged at each other's clothing, pressing kisses against each bit of skin they exposed.

"I want to spend all day touching and kissing and feeling you," he rasped. "I need every part of you." His heart was slamming so hard she felt it against her own. "But realistically…?" he asked ruefully.

"Thirty minutes," Tanja said on a soft laugh. "If we're lucky."

They got down to the serious business of reconciling. When he pressed inside her, their joining was deeply powerful, not simply because they'd been apart, but because their hearts were no longer shielded. Not one tiny bit.

"I love watching you come apart," he said as he moved within her, gaze tender as it was locked with hers. "I love knowing this is as good for you as it is for me."

"So good. Leon, I can't wait…" She speared her fingers into his hair and arched as climax gripped her.

He quickened his pace, taking her over the edge and tumbling with her into the joyous chasm of completion.

They cuddled under the blankets after, naked and glowing, caressing and murmuring lazily about how they might split their time between here and Greece.

"You would spend that much time here for me?" she asked. She'd seen his life in Greece. It was very demanding, not something he could drop on a whim.

"You are the breath in my sails," he said with a playful nibble of her chin. "I'll go wherever you take me. Isn't that obvious? Istuval. Parenthood…" He was teasing her, but that had been so poetic she teared up. *"Agape mou,"* he chided tenderly, kissing her better.

A questioning squawk of noise came from the other

room. It was Illi's usual noise that announced she'd awakened and wished to be noticed.

Leon and Tanja exchanged a look. Tanja's chest swelled with anticipation as Leon fairly leaped from the bed to slip on his underwear. She pulled on his shirt and followed as far as the bedroom door, biting her lip.

"Louloudi mou," he greeted as he approached the crib, calling her "flower" in the endearingly tender voice that undid everything inside Tanja. "How are you? I've missed you."

Illi let out a happy crow of excitement, one loud enough to cause ear damage, but it made them both laugh through their winces, especially because her little limbs went everywhere.

"I was afraid she'd forgotten me," he said with amused pleasure while Tanja clutched her heart and wondered how anyone could.

He cradled Illi into his shoulder and she curled herself into him, head on his shoulder while she bounced with delight.

Tanja was pretty sure her heart was going to bust right out of her chest.

Leon brought Illi to the bed and they played with her between them, exchanging light kisses over her excited squirms.

"Did I mention I want more kids?" He had hold of Illi's foot and was rubbing his closely trimmed beard against her sole. "Not right this second. I think we should at least get married again—"

"I'm sorry I divorced you," she said sheepishly.

"Don't do it again," he said lightly, but there was a flash of bleak pain in the dark depths of his eyes.

"Leon," she breathed with remorse, and reached for him.

"My fault." He caught her hand and kissed her palm.

He might have left it there, but he met her gaze and admitted, "But I felt like you'd cut us apart. Like I'd lost you forever. It hurt like hell. I won't pretend it didn't. That's how I know I won't let it happen again." He gently crushed her hand as though stamping the truth of his words into her skin and bones. "It didn't help one bit that I'd told you to do it. When I saw what you did with the money, though, I was glad you took it. Thank you for making that right." He kissed her fingertips, then his mouth twitched. "I saw your brother while I was there. He threatened to kill me," he said conversationally. "I pointed out that since you and Illi are my beneficiaries, that might look suspicious. I think we're good now."

"Leon, you didn't." She closed her eyes, never once having considered that she stood to inherit her husband's vast fortune.

"What? Who else am I going to leave it to? You're my *wife*. Do you want a big wedding this time?"

"No." She cupped his stubbled cheek. "I want you. Just you. That's all I've ever wanted."

"Same." He leaned across and they kissed. "You're all I will ever need. Well…" He sent a significant look to their daughter.

Tanja wrinkled her nose ruefully. "Same."

A week later, Leon bought a piece of property overlooking the ocean. When his mother and Cornelius arrived a few days after that, they all convened on the site of their future home. Leon and Tanja spoke their vows with their most cherished loved ones in attendance.

This time they meant it.

EPILOGUE

Five years later...

"BUT I'LL STILL live with you," Illi said anxiously, her legs tight around Leon's waist, her arm around his neck, her hand in his.

"You absolutely will," Leon told his daughter. "You will live with me forever." He briefly squished her tighter against him. "Even if you get married and have children and grandchildren. I love you too much to ever let you live with anyone else or go anywhere without me."

She giggled. "I have to go to school by myself. And you don't live with Yaya," she said, referring to his mother.

Smart as a whip, she was, and had a wonderful streak of independence he adored as much as every other part of her.

"How about this? You can always live with me if you want to. Will that work?"

"Yes." She nodded.

He kissed her forehead, not telling her he already resented having to share her with schoolteachers.

"Did it land?" Tanja asked as she returned with their son's hand clutched in her own.

"It did." He nodded at the flight board above where they stood.

Christo put his arms up, wanting Leon to hold him, too. He scooped up their toddler and asked him, "Did you go?"

Christo nodded.

"No. Just me," Tanja said ruefully. She was in the middle of carrying their next son or daughter, so a lot of Christo's potty training attempts were falling on her since she was always headed that direction anyway.

Leon loved seeing her pregnant, with her features round and sensual and rosy. Hell, he loved her when she was asleep or awake, sweaty from a workout or polished for an evening out. Grouchy from a bad night with a fussy baby or irreverently teasing him into laughter.

He loved her right now, trying to pretend she wasn't nervous as a mama duck and fierce as a mama bear beneath her glow of anticipation.

It had taken years to find Brahim and sort out his immigration. He wasn't a child any longer. He was nineteen and had wanted to come to Canada, even though things in Istuval had stabilized.

Leon had an office tower in Vancouver and Tanja would be off work with the new baby, so they had decided the city would become their base while Brahim settled in his new home. Illi was enrolled in a local school in the fall. They had a comfortable home on the north shore that would give Brahim an option between a guest house by the pool or a room inside the mansion with them.

First though, they would spend the summer at their home in Tofino, where the pace of life was slower and the rest of Tanja's family was looking forward to opening their arms and homes to their newest member.

"Thank you for this," Tanja said with a squeeze of Leon's arm when passengers began streaming from the secured area.

"Your children are my children. You know that."

She gave him a shaky, touched smile and a kiss, then turned to watch for Brahim.

Leon didn't have misgivings precisely, but he was fiercely protective of his family. Brahim had spent years as a drafted child soldier in a mercenary force. That sort of experience had to leave scars, so he was experiencing some apprehension even as he knew they would get through any bumps or nicks that might come about.

A few minutes later, a gasp was torn from Tanja's throat. She rushed toward a lanky young man, tall and dark wearing tattered jeans and an army green T-shirt.

He was looking up to read the unfamiliar signage and startled when Tanja was suddenly in front of him. He was disoriented and surprised, but his reaction was immediate. He dropped his duffel and hugged Tanja with such tangible relief it cracked Leon's heart clean down the middle.

"Is that him?" Illi slid down from Leon's secure hold.

He watched her walk forward, faltering slightly when Brahim released Tanja to look at her belly. His smile was exactly like his sister's, full of happy wonder as he said something that made her laugh.

He looked searchingly past her and froze as he saw Illi.

Leon held his breath, protectiveness surging anew in him.

"Illi." Brahim covered his mouth and sank to one knee. His eyes grew bright, and he blinked them fast and hard. He held out a hand. "Look at you. Our mother would be so proud if she could see you," he said in a choked voice.

Without any urging, she rushed in for a hug.

He clutched her tight, eyes closed, yet he showed such gentleness that Leon's throat tightened.

Tanja came back to him and buried her face in Leon's shoulder, trembling and clearly overcome. Hell, he could hardly withstand the intensity of this reunion.

"Mama?" Christo touched her hair.

"I'm okay, little man. Mommy's just really, really happy." She showed him her beaming smile and round cheeks tracked with tears. "Your brother is here."

Christo looked at her belly, making her laugh and stammer out, "The other one."

Brahim was asking Illi questions. Illi was nodding and wiping at her little cheeks, smiling as she shyly answered. When Brahim rose and shouldered his duffel, Illi took his hand, drawing forth a very naked look of love as he gazed down on her.

Illi seemed to have an instant case of the hero worships. She brought him to Leon. "This is my daddy and my brother, Christo. This is my brother, Brahim."

"Leon. Welcome." Leon released Tanja to offer his hand.

Brahim shook it, but his expression shuttered slightly, telling Leon the young man's trust wouldn't be won as easily by him as it had been by Tanja and Illi.

Christo dipped out of Leon's hold straight into Brahim's arms, though. Brahim caught the boy with surprise.

"You give hugs, too?" Brahim asked in accented English. "Thank you." He patted Christo's back with bemusement, making them all laugh.

"Christo always wants to do everything I do," Illi informed in the very important tone of a big sister.

"Well, he is obviously learning to be as loving as you are." He gave Christo back to Leon, but his defensiveness had receded a little.

Hours later, when they had made the final leg of travel home and everyone was abed under one roof, Leon said, "I told Brahim he could talk to me about his experiences if he's worried it might burden you. Or that we could find him a professional. He's liable to have PTSD or other lingering effects."

"Thank you for reaching out to him like that. I don't know that he's had any good male role models for a long time." She pinched his side, warning, "Don't say anything self-deprecating. You *are* a good role model."

"I'll defer to your better judgment," he said drily. "But I think we'll all be good for him." He cuddled his warm, supportive, incredibly generous wife into his side. "He's cautious, which is understandable, but the children will win him over. And you love so hard, you're impossible to resist."

"So do you. Is that news to you?"

He rolled and adjusted their positions so they were face-to-face. He smoothed a tendril of hair off her face.

"I didn't know I was capable of loving this much. I don't know that anyone else could have brought it out in me. And even though I don't know how all of this will work out, I know it will. That you and I will get through it, one way or another, together. Stronger."

"Leon." She cupped his jaw, and he drew her closer for a kiss.

She'd come to bed in a nightgown, already yawning, but desire sent his hands in search of skin. She made one of those receptive noises that turned him on, and they gravitated into each other.

"It's been a long day." He ran his mouth down her neck, inhaling her familiar scent. "I wasn't sure you'd want to."

"I always want to," she assured him, peeling her nightgown up. "I want *you*. I love you."

He set about demonstrating that his love and desire was as steadfast as hers.

* * * * *

MILLS & BOON

Coming next month

THE GREEK'S CONVENIENT CINDERELLA
Lynne Graham

'Mr Alexandris,' Tansy pronounced rather stiffly.

'Come and sit down,' he invited lazily. 'Tea or coffee?'

'Coffee please,' Tansy said, following him round a sectional room divider into a rather more intimate space furnished with sumptuous sofas and sinking down into the comfortable depths of one, her tense spine rigorously protesting that amount of relaxation.

She was fighting to get a grip on her composure again but nothing about Jude Alexandris in the flesh matched the formal online images she had viewed. He wasn't wearing a sharply cut business suit, he was wearing faded, ripped and worn jeans that outlined long powerful thighs, narrow hips and accentuated the prowling natural grace of his every movement. An equally casual dark grey cotton top complemented the jeans. One sleeve was partially pushed up to reveal a strong brown forearm and a small tattoo that appeared to be printed letters of some sort. His garb reminded her that although he might be older than her he was still only in his late twenties and that unlike her, he had felt no need to dress to impress.

Her pride stung at the knowledge that she was little more than a commodity on Alexandris's terms. Either he would choose her, or he wouldn't. She had put herself on the market to be bought though, she thought with sudden self-loathing. How could she blame Jude Alexandris for her stepfather's use of virtual blackmail to get her agreement? Everything she was doing was for Posy, she reminded herself squarely and the end would justify the means…*wouldn't it?*

'So…' Tansy remarked in a stilted tone because she was determined not to sit there acting like the powerless person she knew herself to be in his presence. 'You require a fake wife…'

Jude shifted a broad shoulder in a very slight shrug. 'Only we would know it was fake. It would have to seem real to everyone else from the start to the very end,' he advanced calmly. 'Everything between us would have to remain confidential.'

'I'm not a gossip, Mr Alexandris.' In fact Tansy almost laughed at the idea of even having anyone close enough to confide in because she had left her friends behind at university and certainly none of them had seemed to understand her decision to make herself responsible for her baby sister rather than returning to the freedom of student life.

'I trust no one,' Jude countered without apology. 'You would be legally required to sign a non-disclosure agreement before I married you.'

'Understood. My stepfather explained that to me,' Tansy acknowledged, her attention reluctantly drawn to his careless sprawl on the sofa opposite, the long muscular line of a masculine thigh straining against well washed denim. Her head tipped back, her colour rising as she made herself look at his face instead, encountering glittering dark eyes that made the breath hitch in her throat.

'I find you attractive too,' Jude Alexandris murmured as though she had spoken.

'I don't know what you're talking about,' Tansy protested, the faint pink in her cheeks heating exponentially as her tummy flipped while she wondered if she truly could be read that easily by a man.

'For this to work, we would need that physical attraction. Nobody is likely to be fooled by two strangers pretending what they don't feel, least of all my family, some of whom are shrewd judges of character.'

Tansy had paled. 'Why would we need attraction? I assumed this was to be a marriage on paper, nothing more.'

'Then you assumed wrong,' Jude told her without skipping a beat.

Continue reading
THE GREEK'S CONVENIENT CINDERELLA
Lynne Graham

Available next month
www.millsandboon.co.uk

COMING SOON!

We really hope you enjoyed reading this book.
If you're looking for more romance, be sure to
head to the shops when new books are
available on

Thursday 7th
January

LET'S TALK

Romance

For exclusive extracts, competitions
and special offers, find us online:

 facebook.com/millsandboon

🐦 @MillsandBoon

📷 @MillsandBoonUK

Get in touch on 01413 063232

MILLS & BOON

THE HEART OF ROMANCE

A ROMANCE FOR EVERY KIND OF READER

MODERN

Prepare to be swept off your feet by sophisticated, sexy and seductive heroes, in some of the world's most glamourous and romantic locations, where power and passion collide.
8 stories per month.

HISTORICAL

Escape with historical heroes from time gone by. Whether your passion is for wicked Regency Rakes, muscled Vikings or rugged Highlanders, awaken the romance of the past.
6 stories per month.

MEDICAL

Set your pulse racing with dedicated, delectable doctors in the high-pressure world of medicine, where emotions run high and passion, comfort and love are the best medicine.
6 stories per month.

True Love

Celebrate true love with tender stories of heartfelt romance, from the rush of falling in love to the joy a new baby can bring, and a focus on the emotional heart of a relationship.
8 stories per month.

Desire

Indulge in secrets and scandal, intense drama and plenty of sizzling hot action with powerful and passionate heroes who have it all: wealth, status, good looks…everything but the right woman.
6 stories per month.

HEROES

Experience all the excitement of a gripping thriller, with an intense romance at its heart. Resourceful, true-to-life women and strong, fearless men face danger and desire - a killer combination!
8 stories per month.

DARE

Sensual love stories featuring smart, sassy heroines you'd want as a best friend, and compelling intense heroes who are worthy of them.
4 stories per month.

To see which titles are coming soon, please visit
millsandboon.co.uk/nextmonth

JOIN US ON SOCIAL MEDIA!

Stay up to date with our latest releases, author news and gossip, special offers and discounts, and all the behind-the-scenes action from Mills & Boon...

 millsandboon

 millsandboonuk

 millsandboon

It might just be true love...

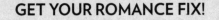

MILLS & BOON

HEROES

At Your Service

Experience all the excitement of a gripping thriller, with an intense romance at its heart. Resourceful, true-to-life women and strong, fearless men face danger and desire - a killer combination!

Sensual love stories featuring smart, sassy heroines you'd want as a best friend, and compelling intense heroes who are worthy of them.

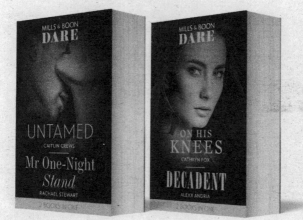